SCALESHIFTER:
THE GODS' GIFT

SHELBY HAILSTONE LAW

ACKNOWLEDGEMENTS

I couldn't have done any of this without my family behind me. 2020 and 2021 were rough years for everyone, but throw two toddlers in the mix, and it's been a total roller coaster. Thankfully, I have the best support system I could ever have asked for.

My husband in particular has been a stalwart support this last year. Not only has he helped me make time to write despite pandemic depression and busy kids but he has listened to me bounce ideas around until I knew how I wanted to lay out scenes and storylines. I can only write as much and as well as I can because of his support. Thank you, Matt. Love you.

Thank you also to my sister, Bethany, who has patiently read all of my stories and who helped me arrange all my thoughts so that I could be understood. Love you, sis. Thanks for being my editor and hype woman. I wouldn't be where I am without you.

And finally, thank you to my kids, Katherine and Rory. You make me want to be kinder, better, and braver every day.

TABLE OF CONTENTS

CHAPTER 1: A FRUITLESS QUEST

Caleb tugged at the collar of the soldier's uniform he was wearing. Ever since he had started changing back and forth from human to dragon, clothes sat differently on his body—and not just because he had more fat and muscle on him now than he ever had when he was a scared refugee boy running from dragon fire and war. The fabric was a constant, physical reminder of which body he was in, draping over his shoulders and back and brushing against his arms. He'd never been so aware of every stitch in the fabric of his clothes as he was now that he had dragon senses.

Each time he moved, he could hear the rustling sound of fabric and the slight metallic clink of the mesh armor underneath his tunic. And because he had never learned how to walk around with a sword without leaving bruises on his leg where the scabbard banged against his side, he kept his hand on the golden design above the hilt to steady it, drawing cold from the night air and heat from the lingering smoke and fire of war because of the metal's response to its surroundings. Even though the hilt didn't cool down enough to freeze his hands to it or heat up enough to burn him, he could feel the difference all the same. He was, underneath his human façade, a white dragon, and heat was his life blood. Even the warmth of clothing helped him build up his strength, and even the cool of night made him tired.

Or maybe he was hyper-aware of his clothes because he was wearing a Junnin uniform. The last time he'd been a soldier, he had worn the bright colors of the Hayna army. Now, he wore a dark blue tunic that looked like the sky at dusk, with a dragon symbol stitched in golden thread above his heart.

Still, his immediate thought upon donning the clothing hadn't been about the sides in a war that hardly mattered lately. Ever since he, as the dragon Kaal, had accidentally prompted the dragon council to attempt to raze humanity to ashes, the distinctions between kingdoms seemed so much less important than the distinctions between species. The council wouldn't care what colors the humans they slaughtered wore. They only cared about their long-held grudge against humanity, the last of the gods' creations.

Not that the rest of humanity understood yet that the stakes of the war had changed. They could see the warning signs but didn't recognize them for what they were. For example, Caleb and his friend, Ziya, had found a Junnin outpost in their search for their tormentor, Alan; Ziya had sent Caleb, in human form, to scout it out. In the few hours Caleb had spent exploring the ruins of the outer wall, he'd overheard Junnin soldiers talking about increased dragon sightings with no understanding of who they'd seen. They thought, because they had no reason to think that dragons were nothing but mindless beasts turned into weapons, that more dragons on the horizon meant an incoming Hayna attack. They thought, as Caleb once had, that wild dragons were extinct—or headed that way.

The outpost itself was a testament to the horrifying threat that a stronger-than-usual dragon attack would bring down on the soldiers stationed there. What had once been a proud fortress was now nothing but a tall mass of stones held up by sheer determination and likely a bit of magic. The inner structure of the fortress was still standing, with only scorch marks to tell the tale of its many battles, but the outer walls were crumbling. Each step Caleb took to reach the top of the wall threatened to plunge him down to the dry, dusty ground below.

And yet the Junnin had no reason to care about the state of their walls. Their enemies wouldn't come over land. The two kingdoms had long ago abandoned conventional warfare. Now, they sent dragons to do their fighting—and their killing. Soldiers in the age of dragon fire weren't sent to fight. They were sent to either fly or die with their arrows still pointed at the sky.

From the outpost, Caleb could see fires burning on both sides of the war. Night had fallen, making the flames easier to see, even without his dragon's eyesight. To the east, where the Hayna had once had a stronghold, the horizon was a deep red, and smoke hid the moon and the stars. But to the south, behind Junnin lines, the dragons from the council were actively attacking. Every once in a while, Caleb and the other humans could see a flash of yellow or orange—sometimes even blue—and the red glow in the dark of the horizon would flash brighter and spread wider.

The soldiers around Caleb watched the fires burning beyond their fortress with a mixture of fear and resignation. Some of them were skinny and young and still new enough to the army that every new flash of fire had them holding onto their weapons tighter. Others had scars and missing eyebrows and charred-black skin and watched the haze of smoke filling the horizon without moving a muscle. They knew what Caleb did: the humans on the ground, the ones who had nothing to do with dragons, had absolutely no control over what happened next. They could only seek shelter and, if they were excellent at aiming, try to bring down a dragon to lessen the severity of the attack. But in the meantime, they couldn't waste their energy with fear. If they did, they would never sleep.

As Caleb looked around the soldiers, searching for Alan's familiar, sharp features in the crowd, he heard footsteps behind him and heard a voice call out, "Maddening, isn't it?"

Caleb straightened up and turned toward the voice to see that one of the Junnin captains had come to stand close to him, his gaze on the fires burning beyond them. Ziya had killed a captain to find Caleb some clothes to wear, so Caleb was technically at liberty to speak freely to someone of similar rank. (He suspected that Ziya had targeted a higher-ranking soldier on purpose; the simple soldiers were young and scared and often hadn't asked to be there. She always thought ahead and made sure innocents were spared; he appreciated that about her.) But Caleb hadn't been around soldiers since he had helped Alan's prisoners escape; he still hesitated around them, the result of a lifetime spent trying not to be conscripted into the war.

Thankfully, he also had a lifetime of experience trying to blend in and become invisible. As soon as he realized his mistake in hesitating, he quickly covered for it with a heavy sigh and an open-handed gesture toward the glowing fires. "There's going to be nothing left at this rate," he said. He'd always thought the war would destroy the land until nothing was left to live on, but he'd kept his opinions to himself so he didn't draw attention. Now, posing as a Junnin captain, watching his worst fears happening, he had no reason to hold his tongue.

The other captain nodded, still watching the fires on the horizon. If they had been talking on a calmer night, Caleb would have had to rely on his keen dragon eyesight to see the details of his companion's face. On that night, the captain's ash-covered features were easy to see every time a flash of fire lit up the sky beyond them. The man looked like he was barely a few years older than Caleb's fifteen, but he *seemed* older, tired and worn down from the war. The simple fact that two teenagers were old enough to be captains, the simple fact that no one questioned their authority, was testament to how devastating the war had been to humanity. Practically no one else was left but orphans, widows, and former soldiers too injured to fight any longer.

The captain's expression as he watched his homeland being burned to nothing confirmed for Caleb what he had already told the dragon council: the humans, Junnin and Hayna alike, were tired of fighting. They wanted the war to end; they simply kept fighting because their leaders refused to surrender or negotiate.

"Where do you think *our* dragons are?" Caleb asked after a long period of silence. He had decided to investigate this outpost precisely because he and Ziya had seen dragons launching from this position and wondered if Alan had established himself there, where he could ingratiate himself into an already-existing program of training and using dragons as weapons. But since Caleb had arrived, he hadn't seen any dragons—and none had returned.

He had a sinking feeling that the true dragons had killed any human-made dragons they encountered, and he tried not to let that thought fester. Yes, many of the dragons who had once been human lost their minds to the process and became nothing but beasts, but Caleb had kept his mind. Ziya had kept her mind. Others had kept their minds. If the council had killed them, they would have died in fear and pain after living a life of slavery and humiliation.

No one deserved that.

"They're probably still fighting the invaders." The captain flicked a loose pebble off of the unsteady wall, and the two of them listened to the soft sound of its cascade until it hit the bottom of the rock pile. "I've never seen so many dragons at once."

"And I haven't seen any of our dragons return," Caleb said.

The captain nodded slowly, then let out a soft sound from the back of his throat and turned on his heel. "Don't let the men hear you saying things like that. If they think we're out of dragons, they'll lose hope entirely, and we can't afford to lose our defenses to fear."

Caleb frowned and nodded but didn't say anything as the other captain left. He'd come to the outpost to find more dragons or even more half-made dragons, but if the outpost simply didn't have any dragons left, if the captain was keeping up morale with a lie, Caleb doubted he would find Alan there.

By the time we find Alan, he'll have an army to use against us, Caleb thought, frowning as he walked the length of the outpost. He almost didn't notice that the other soldiers parted to make way for him, but when he did, he smirked. With the height and muscle he'd gained since transforming into a dragon, he looked the part of a captain on a mission, his gaze hard and his steps sure. When he was younger, he'd always tried to be invisible. Now, he drew the kind of attention that diverted gazes anyway. That was lucky.

Besides, he couldn't change his expression even now that he was aware of it. The longer Alan stayed hidden, the longer the council would have no reason to stop targeting humanity, the longer Caleb's people would bear the blame for Alan's sins.

Caleb liked to tell Ziya that the gods had asked dragons to look after the earth, and so, he was on a mission to remind the dragons of the gods' mandate by giving them the true source of the recent misery between their two peoples and taking away their excuse for violence. But Ziya insisted every time the topic came up in conversation that any answers Alan could give them were nothing next to the council's hatred of humanity. And Caleb was starting to agree with Ziya. Any council that could scorch the earth to kill a species couldn't be reasoned with, no matter what stories Alan told them.

But Caleb didn't know what else to do. Alan was the one who had organized a mass kidnapping on the shores beyond the council's island. Alan was the one who learned how to turn humans into dragons. Alan was the only white dragon other than himself Caleb had ever seen—and apparently, he was also the only white dragon others like Aonai, a council member himself, had seen. And Alan was the only other creature on this earth (that Caleb knew of) who could transform back and forth between human and dragon forms. If anyone deserved the ire of the council, it was Alan.

At times, Caleb felt like a child demanding *fairness*. He could almost hear his older brother, Tristan, chiding him for trying to use "He started it!" as an argument with centuries-old dragons. But he was barely fifteen. Yes, he had been conscripted into the army and forcibly turned into a dragon, but surely he could be allowed to hold onto a few childish things, like fairness.

Caleb could never gain back the innocence that the war and Alan had taken from him, but he had regained faith, something he had long ago given up. Faith in what, he wasn't sure. Faith in the gods, maybe. Faith in their plan for the earth they created. Faith in the people and dragons around him who believed in a better world than the one they were given. Faith in *fairness*.

Rikaa had once told him that he needed to be true to his name, because names held great power. His dragon name meant "clever," because Alan had liked to hear Caleb reason out his plans for him and gave him a name to match his favorite characteristic of Caleb's. The dragons Caleb had met liked that name, too, because they thought he spoke like a dragon. But his human name meant "faithful."

When Rikaa had told him to be true to his name, Caleb had argued that he had nothing left to be faithful to. He'd lost his family, his home, his humanity. What was left?

Maybe it was this. Maybe it was the idea that the gods wouldn't let the world burn, that the dragons could be better, that the world could be *fair*.

He passed through the soldiers, still wearing a thoughtful look, as he considered why he thought, despite the fires raging on both sides of the divided human lands, the world could be fair. He still didn't have a complete answer for his blind faith as he slipped past the outer defenses and made his way toward the nearby cliffs. Yes, he had felt more hopeful since becoming part of Rikaa's family, but since that time, the war had gotten worse, and he'd brought down the wrath of the dragon council on his own species. He had every reason to believe the gods the dragons believed in no longer cared about humanity. And yet, for some reason, he didn't.

Caleb sighed and pulled his cloak over his head, pressing on into the drifting remnants of fires that had long ago lost anything of substance to keep them burning. The fortress had been built alongside jagged cliffs that bordered a dried-up lake; what sparse plant life the fires had used for fuel was long gone now. And yet, despite his quiet seething when he saw how little regard the dragon council had for the state of the world they were meant to protect, he was glad for the smoke and ash raining down from the sky; it obscured him from view of the torches and lanterns the Junnin soldiers used to peer into the night and to try desperately to see their enemy before they could be attacked.

Besides, the smoke was excellent cover for Ziya, too.

Caleb smiled as he rounded the corner of a particularly long cliff face and saw Ziya exactly where he'd last seen her—poised to attack, her wings drawn back, her tail still behind her, her claws flared out, and her teeth bared. Underneath the smoke that had drifted toward the cliffs on the wind and gotten trapped against the rocky sides of old, craggy mountains, she was hardly visible except for her eyes and teeth. She was a black dragon, as dark as the deepest recesses of the ocean, designed by the gods to lie in wait and ambush her prey. The smoke might not have been water, but under the circumstances, it disguised her just as well.

Still, Caleb could see better than humans and not only saw his dragon friend but also noticed the scratches in the ground where Ziya had been sharpening her claws to alleviate her boredom.

"It's me," he said, holding up both hands in a gesture of peace and then raising them to the level of his head so he could lower his hood. "It's Caleb."

Ziya relaxed her stance but let out a growl all the same. "I heard footsteps," she explained.

"Sorry," he said. "I was lost in thought. I should have warned you I was coming."

Ziya bristled and let out a huff of smoke, her wings drawn back this time in a gesture of hurt instead of an offensive gesture. "It's hard to see little humans in the smoke, even with dragon eyes," she said, and Caleb nodded without saying a word.

THE GODS' GIFT

He didn't think Ziya was aware of how much Alan's torture and manipulations still affected her. Yes, she had told him about how she'd had to learn to let out her growls and to follow her instincts after spending so long under Alan's rules squashing even unconscious displays of independence. But she had only admitted to the most obvious conditioning. Caleb had a feeling she wasn't even aware of everything else Alan had done to her when she was so focused (rightfully) on the tortures she had endured on a larger scale.

She didn't seem to notice, for example, that she always waited for him to go to sleep before she fell asleep. When they'd first reunited, after she had been sent by Alan to drag him back to the army, she had slept out of exhaustion, not out of a natural pattern of day and night. Now that she wasn't going from one captor to another, now that she wasn't focused on the next fight, now that they were simply looking for trouble but not yet finding it, Ziya still acted like she expected to be attacked at any moment, even by Caleb. And while Caleb was also wary after a lifetime of going from one village to the next to keep himself alive, he still didn't think he was as suspicious and downright jumpy as Ziya was.

But the few times Caleb had mentioned that jumpiness to Ziya, she had reacted defensively, as if admitting that she was still living in fear was giving Alan more power over her than he already had. After a few failed attempts at trying to approach Ziya's distrust in conversation, Caleb was convinced she would never truly relax until they had dealt with Alan. So, in the meantime, he tried to smooth himself out for her. He didn't want to scare her.

That was what he'd always done, after all. He didn't want to draw attention or trouble.

"I'll whistle next time," he said. He sat down near her and took off his boots, letting his feet stretch out as claws flared from his toes. He shook out his torn boots in the red dust and then put them aside. Destroyed as they were, he never knew when he would find clothes again, so he had to keep some on hand at all times.

He was, actually, quite proud of himself for walking around the outpost and making the trek all the way back to Ziya's hiding place without anyone noticing the change in his gait because of the long claws trying to come out of his feet with every step. The constant smoke and the sound and sight of dragon attacks had him on edge, and he hadn't been fully able to maintain his human form. If he was nervous or in danger, he started to change into a dragon—and he still didn't have full control of those changes. He was simply lucky that he'd managed to keep the damage to a minimum. Even a captain didn't look out of place in worn-out boots in an underfed and overworked army. If Caleb's claws had lengthened or his feet and legs had bent to dragon-shaped bones, he would have been discovered. Fast.

Ziya shifted so that she could rest her head close to him on the ground, frowning as she watched him stretch his claws. "Did anyone see?" she asked.

He shook his head. "It was too dark to see anything that wasn't lit by fire and lanterns, and since you stole me a captain's uniform, most of them stayed out of my way anyway."

"Still, you're taking a risk in this state."

"Yeah," he replied and leaned against the cliff wall. He knew if he were discovered, he'd either be enslaved or killed outright. White dragon scales were rare, and no one knew the full extent of their powers. If anyone saw him with scales on his face, arms, or legs, he would be a target—and he knew it.

And yet the worst part wasn't that he feared the soldiers or desperate civilians. No, the worst part was that, when he considered what he'd do if someone tried to kill him for his scales, he knew the answer. He had killed soldiers before in self-defense, and he had even, recently, committed murder. He had killed a half-formed dragon in Alan's dungeons.

He knew all of the ethical arguments in favor of what he had done. The young man he killed in cold blood had been dying anyway. The fire Alan had poured into him to make him a dragon hadn't turned him into a magnificent creature of legend; it was burning him up from the inside. He would have died in agony, and he had *asked* Caleb to kill him.

And yet, Caleb could still see that young man's face when he closed his eyes at night. He could see the places where the stranger's skin was flaking, where scales should have been but where pale, white bone shone through. He could see tear stains where saltwater had made a path through the smoke and ash caking his face. He could, if he dwelt too long in the memory, hear the hiccoughs as that boy had sobbed with what little breath the fire left him and had begged Caleb to end it.

Once, Caleb had done everything in his power to avoid the army—because of what they had done to his older brother, yes, but also because he hadn't thought he was capable of killing anyone.

He'd been wrong.

Still, he couldn't dwell on the past for too long. He didn't like the dark place those thoughts took him to. Instead, he cleared his throat and tried to start a conversation with Ziya anew. "I really thought he'd be there," Caleb said as he tipped his head back against the rock wall, closing his eyes against the burning smoke. Even though he was part-dragon, his eyes were still human enough that the smoke and embers bothered him when they clouded his vision and stuck to his eyelashes, turning everything a soft brown color until he wiped the soot from his eyes. "They're desperate. It sounds like they're completely out of dragons. They need someone like Alan to give them more dragons to fight back."

"That might be *why* he isn't there," Ziya reasoned. "They're running out of resources, and his process takes time. The outpost will probably be destroyed in a few days, and Alan needs weeks to let his magic do its work."

"True," Caleb admitted in a sigh. "But if that's the case, I don't know that we'll find him in any outpost. He may have disappeared."

"That doesn't sound like him. He likes to be in power."

"No one has any power to give him right now." Caleb wiped his face, but his hands were coated in as much soot as his face was; the result was a smudge, not a clean brow. "*Everyone* is fleeing or facing fire. You can see the flames and the smoke for miles around from the stronghold. No one looking out at that destruction is going to give him the luxury of an experiment that takes weeks and doesn't always work." He paused. "And they won't let him be picky about his subjects, either."

Ziya was silent for a long time, staring at a point beyond him in the smoke and embers as she weighed out her response. "It doesn't matter," she said at last. "We have to keep looking."

"I know," he said, rubbing his eyes with his thumb and fore-finger, which helped lessen the sting of the smoke. "But maybe we should expand our search."

"You're the one doing the footwork. You can make that decision," Ziya said. Even though she had improved her ability to use human words, she still had an accent when she used certain phrases. Thankfully, Caleb understood what she meant; he'd had to learn to use the same hisses and sighs to force sounds he couldn't make on his own. He had even asked Rikaa to teach him the dragon language so he wouldn't have to awkwardly stumble through his words.

He missed Rikaa and his lessons and stories. He missed the family he'd built up for himself. He missed the feeling of home.

He frowned and shook his head. He didn't deserve to be selfish and think of home. If he and Ziya failed their mission, he would get his wish anyway—but at a price. If they couldn't get answers within a month, they would go back to Rikaa and regroup. Caleb didn't think Ziya would recover from a setback like that. She was determined to kill Alan to stop him from hurting anyone else, driven in a way Caleb only partially understood—but then, he hadn't been tortured as badly or for as long as Ziya had. If they had to go back home empty-handed, Ziya would lose faith. And having recently discovered his own faith, Caleb knew how vital it was that she hold onto it with both hands—or claws, in her case. Their people were dying; faith was all they had against the black cloud of smoke and despair settling over their lands.

"Let's try looking in a few villages far from the front lines," he suggested. "If he's hiding among humans, he might be somewhere he doesn't think the council will attack. Maybe he'll hole up with a small group of refugees or a town on the outskirts near the wilds."

Ziya nodded slowly. "It's worth trying," she admitted. She didn't sound as convinced as he did—which was saying something when he barely believed his own reasoning. They both knew Alan was too proud to cower with refugees, though he could easily charm a small village into helping him or at least hiding him. "But," she added slowly, "if we don't find him in the next three days, let's try searching the mountains again. He might still be a dragon, and he could use the cloud cover of the coming rainy season to hide from humans and dragons."

"Agreed," Caleb said, already promising himself that he would work even harder now that their deadline was so close. Ziya had fought with Aonai and Rikaa alike for their right to confront Alan

THE GODS' GIFT

on their own terms; he didn't want all her effort to be in vain. So, he closed his eyes, held his breath, and managed to desire humanity deeply enough that his claws retreated back into his toes.

There, he thought. *Now I'll be better able to blend in.* With that, he nodded to himself, pulled his boots back on, and looked up to meet Ziya's gaze. "Three days," he swore in what was as much a way to agree with her plan as a promise to himself that Alan's time roaming free was limited.

CHAPTER 2: MORNING ROUTINE

Before the land had been overrun by smoke, Caleb would have woken up with the sun. When he was younger, he used to sleep out in the fields after a long day of tending to the animals, and the sun would warm his face until his eyelids were too bright for him to pretend he didn't know the day had started. Now, when the sun rose, it turned the smoke an orange color, but it did little to light the sky until it had risen to its height at midday.

So, Caleb slept longer than usual, sprawled out across the rocky ground. And while he'd slept, he had acquired more dragon-like characteristics, like claws at the ends of his fingers.

That seemed to be the pattern: when he slept comfortably, in an environment that reminded him of home before the war had taken his family from him, he could stay human or even change back into a human from his dragon form. But in the smoke and rocks, he craved scales and fire.

He even stretched like a dragon as he woke up, on all fours, pushing his claws into the earth with the depth of the stretch, opening his mouth widely enough that he would have been showing off his fangs had he grown those in his sleep too. When he had first become a dragon, he had struggled with how often his human habits felt unnatural in his dragon form. Now, he had enough experience as a dragon that *those* habits followed him into his other form.

It was strange, Caleb reflected, to feel like he didn't belong in either body. Ziya said she was jealous of him, but he wondered if that would still be the case if she knew how *alone* he felt. He would never feel comfortable in skin or scales. And the only person who could possibly understand was *Alan*.

He scrubbed both hands over his face, frustrated but not surprised when he realized that his skin was once again coming off in flakes to make way for scales. He wouldn't be able to hide in the ranks of humans even under the cover of darkness when the scales became more visible. For now, his skin simply looked like it was recovering from a burn—an ailment everyone could sympathize with these days. But Caleb knew how quickly those flakes of skin could give way, and he couldn't chance being caught.

He sighed and pushed himself to his feet, then walked a small circle to stretch out his muscles. Once he felt more awake and alert, he checked to see if Ziya's breathing was still deep and even—which would indicate that she was still too asleep to approach—or if it was getting shallow. She was so much bigger than he was when he was human that he felt sometimes like he was walking up to a living mountain and hoping he wouldn't get crushed if she shifted her massive form in her sleep.

He didn't dare touch her when she wasn't fully conscious. If he had still been a dragon, he might have considered it, but as a human, he was too vulnerable. He knew from experience that Ziya didn't wake up peacefully if she startled from a dream or if she felt human hands on her. He dared not imagine what memories she might have been reliving in her sleep, but the pure panic that always filled her gaze when she woke up and lashed out at him told him more than enough.

So, he resolved not to scare her if he could help it. She had been tormented and terrorized enough; he didn't want to inadvertently make things worse for her.

And yet she seemed to wake more peacefully when he was a dragon. She still woke up in a panic if he interrupted a dream, yes, but she seemed to settle down much faster if she saw him as a dragon than if she saw him as a human.

He couldn't fathom why she felt safer in her barely-waking moments with a dragon than a human when she had made constantly clear to Caleb that she was jealous of his human skin and vastly preferred the company of humanity over that of dragons. She didn't trust dragons—beyond the few that had *earned* her trust by fighting alongside her—and she had told Caleb before they began their search for Alan that she planned to return to live with her mother once all of this was over.

He didn't have the heart to point out to her that she was a danger to her mother if she didn't learn how to wake up in the presence of a human without lashing out. He simply held his tongue and hoped that she would get used to him while they traveled together so that she would be used to Dahlia when the time came.

Caleb liked Dahlia. She had instantly started trying to take care of him when they met, and she had kissed his snout and made him promise to be careful before he and Ziya left. Yes, she'd also asked for his promise that he would look after her daughter, but the concern in her voice when she told him to look after himself as well couldn't be faked. Dahlia had a caring, gentle heart. And sometimes, when Ziya forgot to be angry, Caleb could see that same heart in his companion.

Caleb leaned against the wall of the cliff with his arms crossed as he watched Ziya. The first time he had seen her, when they had been rushing to escape, his first impression of her had been of how beautiful she was. Before he had known anything about other dragons, before he had come to know her as a person—or dragon—he had noticed the deep, mesmerizing black of her scales and the sleek, graceful form she had taken. At the time, he wouldn't have said she was attractive. He hadn't been a dragon long enough to think such things about the creatures he had once hated. But now that he had claws on his feet and smoke in his lungs, he was starting to entertain the notion that he *could* fall for another dragon.

Maybe.

He was too young to consider courtship, but he was old enough to appreciate beauty. And Ziya . . . he could appreciate Ziya. He liked the way her scales shimmered, and he liked the intricate way the scales near her eyes overlapped in a way that made her expression look perpetually fierce.

He had no idea what to do about any of those thoughts. He wasn't sure he *should* do anything about them. Ziya had been tortured in his name; she probably wouldn't react well to hearing that he thought she was pretty.

And what would Rikaa think?

THE GODS' GIFT

Rikaa had known before Caleb did that Caleb saw Ziya in a light he had yet to understand. Ever since Ziya had come back into Caleb's life, Rikaa had done nothing but tease Caleb about courtship and mating. Caleb knew Rikaa meant it in good fun, but when Caleb didn't fully understand what he felt, he didn't appreciate being goaded.

And he just knew that if Rikaa could have seen him in that moment, staring at Ziya with a smile tugging at the corner of his mouth and revealing teeth that were getting slightly more pointed with every second he thought of Ziya. . . . Well, Caleb would never hear the end of it.

So, he pushed himself off from the cliff and shook his head. He had better things to do with his time than stare at Ziya. Like finding himself some breakfast.

He pulled a knife from his stolen belt and ran his other hand along the wall, listening for the sounds of creatures hidden in the rocks. The farther he got from Ziya and the constant sound of her sleepy breathing, the more easily he could hear scratching and skittering. Most of the noises he heard were too small for him to bother following back to their source unless he had no choice but to make himself a dinner of small things; they were likely bugs or lizards. But after about fifteen minutes of quiet hunting, Caleb heard something different: the flapping of feathered wings.

Caleb smiled. If he could find that bird, if he could be quiet enough, he might even be lucky enough to have eggs for breakfast.

His mouth watered. *Eggs for breakfast.* He had grown up tending to the livestock for his small village. He used to have milk and eggs and plenty to eat close at hand. When he'd been young, when his stomach had been full, dragons had been faraway stories to scare him at night so that he'd have to crawl into his brother's blankets and demand softer, nicer stories to sleep by.

He smiled as he thought of home and then immediately winced when he stepped on a rock that suddenly felt sharper because he had bare human feet instead of claws.

Caleb swore as he massaged the bottom of his foot. He hated how unpredictable his changes were. Sometimes, he felt like he was starting to understand them and even to control them, and then something like that would happen.

At least I haven't lost my hearing, Caleb thought as he gingerly stepped around the rocks toward the sounds of fluttering wings. He never would have been able to find animals to hunt this easily before Alan turned him into a dragon—which was a shame, since he had been hungrier before he became a dragon, too.

Carefully, Caleb crept along the edge of the cliff until he found a tufty brown bird fussing over its nest. There were no eggs yet, so Caleb would have to forgo that luxury, but the bird was big enough to make a decent meal all the same.

With reflexes he had never had before his transformation, Caleb lashed out, felling the bird with a single strike. He scooped up its body and ran back to where Ziya was, stepping lightly so he didn't hurt his foot again. The last thing he needed was to face Alan with a limp.

Ziya was still asleep when he arrived, so he busied himself with making a small fire. Although he couldn't breathe fire as a human the way he would do as a dragon, he could sometimes create hot enough smoke to get a few embers. So, he crouched down next to his pile of sticks and blew smoke over them several times, watching carefully so he could fan any embers in the smoke into a fire.

The air was already thick with smoke, so Caleb kept blinking ash out of his eyes as he tried to start his cooking fire. Every once in a while, a hot breeze floated their way and pushed his own smoke back at him, and Caleb coughed a few times as he choked on the smoke of fires other than his own. But, at last, he managed to catch an ember on the firewood, and he quickly switched from blowing smoke to blowing air, trying to coax a fire into existence.

He thought he could hear Ziya stirring nearby, but he didn't look her way. He needed to focus on the task at hand; it had taken him too long to get an ember, and he didn't want to have to repeat the process. But just as the ember turned into a big enough flame that Caleb felt he could split his attention for a short time, Ziya let out a huge yawn and mumbled a quiet, "Good morning," that sounded garbled even without the usual impediment of a dragon accent.

Caleb smirked at his breakfast as he turned the bird on a long stick. "Good morning," he said. "I didn't want to wake you, so I found something to eat. Not enough to share, though. Sorry."

THE GODS' GIFT

Ziya picked herself up enough to rearrange her limbs and rest her head close to his fire. She let out a snort of a laugh when she saw the roasting bird. "Barely enough for you."

"I've survived on less."

"You were smaller then."

"True." Caleb looked down at himself. He was hardly the starving refugee he had been when Alan found him, but for some reason, he had to keep reminding himself of that fact when he was in human form. Maybe that was because he thought of his human self as the helpless, skinny young man who kept lying about his age in an increasingly hopeless bid to avoid being conscripted into the army. No matter how much healthier he was now, he would always remember the sting of hunger when he had a human stomach.

Ziya tipped her head to the side and let her eyes drift shut long enough that Caleb wondered if she had fallen back asleep. He pulled his bird off the fire, testing it to see if it was cooked all the way through before he dug in. He no longer had to worry about waiting for his food to cool down. When he had smoke in his throat, no other heat could compare.

"It smells nice," Ziya said, and Caleb startled.

"I thought you went back to sleep."

"I considered it," Ziya said, the corner of her mouth pulling back to show off her teeth. "But your breakfast smells so good."

"I'd share, but I doubt the portions would feel equal to either of us," he said.

Ziya chuckled. "No, they wouldn't."

Caleb smiled as he finished his breakfast and then stamped out the remnants of his fire. The smoke wouldn't give away their position when the air was rich with it.

In fact, it was getting thicker.

Caleb coughed into his hand and shook his head. Even with his own fire constantly filling his center, he wasn't immune to the haze. "I know we're trying to be careful, but can we get above this?" he asked her, gesturing around at the smoke.

Ziya groaned as she got to her feet and stretched her limbs, moving exactly the same way Caleb had moved when he woke up. "Are you sure?" she asked after she stretched—and then broke into a yawn that let her tongue dangle out of her mouth.

Caleb knew Ziya hadn't had enough time to recover from everything that had happened to her. She had gone from Alan's clutches to the council's to a battle to a hunt for Alan. She had to be exhausted. But she was the one who kept pointing out that they couldn't let Alan escape their grasp; she was the one pushing for speed. She likely wouldn't listen to him if he proposed a break.

He gave her a tired smile. "I might have dragon senses, but even I'm having a hard time seeing everything in this smoke. And the wind is against us—it's blowing the smoke our way. If we can get above it, we can find safer ground and look for Alan hiding away from the consequences of his own actions."

"And drag him into the war he tried to avoid," Ziya finished for him, her teeth flashing.

Caleb nodded but didn't join in her triumphant conjecture. He hated Alan; that much was still true. But he didn't have the same fire Ziya did. He would rather leave the problem at the council's feet and fade into the background. He didn't want the responsibility of an executioner.

Instead, he asked, "Are you ready?" and gestured to her back with one hand.

The first time he had ridden on her back, when they had first begun their search, he had wordlessly gestured to her in a tired question and climbed on without a word spoken between them. But she had been tense the whole time, her claws pushed out and her muscles stiff. Every time he shifted positions to get a better grip against the rough winds or to get more comfortable in peaceful gliding so he could fall asleep, she tensed up and woke him.

He hadn't immediately realized that his silence was disturbing her, but on the second night, he had been less exhausted and had talked to her while they flew. Then, he noticed how much more relaxed she was, even though they struggled to hear each other above the winds.

He had known that Ziya learned how to fly with a human trainer on her back, but he hadn't understood how traumatic the experience had been. He tried to ask her about it in quiet moments when they were both resting, but she would only tell him that her trainer, Jon, had been at the battle in which they had freed Alan's prisoners. And, on one night when his stomach was growling and she seemed to take pity on him, she had admitted that Jon preferred to teach with a spear.

She didn't need to give him more details than that.

So, Caleb tried to be the opposite of Jon. He let Ziya pick the locations of their searches. He talked to her like an equal. And he never, ever approached her without asking her permission for a ride.

He took those measures for more than just Ziya's comfort, too. Yes, he wanted her to avoid reliving the pain of her captivity and everything that had been done to her to turn her into a beast of burden and a weapon of war. But he had to admit that he had a second, more shamefully prideful reason: he didn't want to be compared to Alan and his men.

He already had enough comparisons to deal with. He was only too aware of the way humans and dragons alike looked at him when they realized that he was the only white dragon and the only creature able to change forms in the world—*aside from Alan*. He was good with words. He could lie easily. He was too much like Alan, and he hated it.

So, if he had the opportunity to distance himself from Alan's sycophants, he would do it.

He stood at a respectful distance until Ziya shifted her stance so her belly was flat on the ground and her legs were tucked in close. It was a stance Jon had taught her, one that allowed Caleb to climb on her back using her legs as footholds—and one that Caleb had never seen before he traveled with Ziya. Rikaa had allowed him to ride on his back, but he had made Caleb find his own climbing path.

It was just one more detail reminding Caleb that Ziya had been taught to be subservient.

Caleb didn't climb up immediately but went first to her head to rest his hand on top of her snout. She closed her eyes at his touch—not because she was wincing away but because she was leaning into him. A gentle touch on the face felt nice, no matter if it came from a dragon or a human. And he wanted to express his friendship before he used her for transportation.

Then, at last, he climbed up on her back and rubbed his hand over her scales. "Lead the way, Ziya."

CHAPTER 3: A FAMILIAR FACE

It was too easy to fall asleep on a dragon's back.

If Caleb had been traveling with Rikaa, he would have sung to pass the time and to remind his traveling companion that he was more than a beast of burden. He and Rikaa had traded songs and stories and traditions when they traveled. But with Ziya, Caleb wasn't yet comfortable enough to sing. Rikaa was safety, and Ziya was . . . a partner, he supposed. He didn't know what to call her.

Unfortunately, singing was the best way for Caleb to stay awake and the best way to reassure Ziya (or Rikaa) of his appreciation. Music could communicate in messages and emotions that could be heard above the winds. Simple words got lost in the air, leaving Caleb with nothing to offer but sound to show that he was more than a passenger.

So, he found himself falling asleep to the rhythm of Ziya's wings and the gentle heartbeat he could feel underneath him. The scales felt soft beneath his cheek, and he drew comfort from them, from the reminder of where he was and *who* he was. He was always taller when he slept on Ziya's back, because his body lengthened in response to his love of all things related to dragons—and his longer arms allowed him to hold on better, too.

He didn't know how long he had been asleep, but he jerked awake when Ziya flew through a cloud. She laughed when the cold water jolted him out of his dreams. He was *sure* Rikaa had told her that was a good way to wake a sleeping passenger, because Rikaa did the same thing to him when they traveled together.

THE GODS' GIFT

"Ziya!" he gasped, shaking water out of his dark hair and away from his face as best he could when he didn't dare let go of her this high above the ground.

She laughed again, a sound like a bubbling volcano. "Yes?"

He shook his head but didn't rise to her bait. He hadn't wanted to be asleep in the first place, no matter how much he loved the sun on his skin. White dragons craved warmth, but he preferred sunlight to the stifling sweat of ash; so, being close to its rays lulled him to sleep too easily despite his best attempts to share the burden of flight equally.

He looked around as Ziya flew above the clouds once more, trying to orient himself. They had traveled a good distance while he was asleep—he did feel bad about that—and were nearly on the other side of a mountain range. The mountain cast a shadow on a desert beyond them, but in between the snow-covered peaks, Caleb could see a small valley with a few houses dotting the land. Thick trees and sharp cliffs made approaching the village difficult but not impossible, and the simple fact that there was such lush greenery spoke to how well-protected the village was against dragons. Yes, Caleb could see patches of brown, scars on the mountainside where dragons had left marks, but it was a far cry from the barren wastes of other villages.

If Alan wanted to rest and recover, a quiet, hidden place like that would have been perfect.

Caleb smiled and rubbed his hand along the smooth, black scales at Ziya's neck. "Nice work," he called to her and smiled when she responded with a soft sound like a purr.

Ziya angled herself down so that she could land close enough to the village that Caleb wouldn't have to walk too far but far enough away that the villagers wouldn't think they were about to die in dragon fire. The closer they got to the village, the more they could see of their defenses. Tall towers hid among the trees, nearly invisible from the air; Caleb had only noticed them because a tower stood, half-burned, in the ruins of one of the patches of forest destroyed by fire. Seeing one tower, he had looked for others.

What's more, Caleb could feel something ringing through the air around the village, something powerful and magical. He was too young and inexperienced with magic to identify it, but it sent chills down his spine and forced a low growl past his lips, entirely on instinct.

So, they headed for the forest away from the towers and away from a rock-lined path that led up the mountain toward a larger cluster of homes ringed by brick and stone. They could take cover in the trees, and Caleb could follow that same path back once Ziya was safely hidden.

But just as Ziya ducked underneath the clouds, she and Caleb were greeted by a sharp snarl, and something rushed toward them from the mountainside. Ziya turned her body in a last-second attempt to shield Caleb from the attack, so all Caleb saw was a vibrant green color before their attacker collided with Ziya. The collision knocked him completely off of Ziya's back and sent him flying into the nearby cloud, soaking him through to the bone so that he was shivering as he fell to his death.

"Kaal!" Ziya roared out his dragon name, but he could barely hear her over his heartbeat rushing in his ears or over the sound of the wind as he fell.

The sky was far too big. He felt insignificant falling through the clouds, his arms and legs flailing as he tried to slow his descent. The ground below him seemed so far away, though the trees and plant life were getting bigger with every passing second.

Finally, after the initial shock of being thrown off of Ziya's back and then the sheer terror of a fatal drop had passed, Caleb put his arms out as if he were bracing himself. He closed his eyes so he couldn't see the ground getting closer and gritted his teeth, focusing on the single thought: *Change.*

For several agonizing seconds, Caleb could only feel the wind buffeting him like the last leaf of fall caught in a winter storm. But then, his spine caught fire, and he threw back his head in an agonizing scream that turned into a roar as a tail erupted from the base of his spine and wings shot out of his shoulders.

He was still screaming even though his wings had caught the breeze and suspended him in the air. He had the wherewithal to flap them a few times to gain altitude, but he could barely concentrate on those few motions and nothing else. He couldn't think long enough to stop himself from screaming and drawing more attention to himself —and therefore alerting whatever dragon had attacked him and Ziya

THE GODS' GIFT

to the transformation process. He couldn't think long enough to steer himself. He could only manage one instruction—*fly*—when everything else felt like fire and pain.

His arms and legs extended even more than they already had, and claws shot out of his feet and hands. Scales broke out across his skin. His ears extended into horns. His neck lengthened. And the only reason he was able to endure the torture of transformation *and* keep himself aloft was that this wasn't the first time he had felt his body tear itself apart in such a short amount of time.

Ziya often said that Caleb's ability to switch forms was a blessing, that he was lucky. But Caleb would have given anything to avoid the torture that always—*always*—seemed poised to drive him to insanity with each change. Others had lost their minds when they became dragons. Caleb lived with the ever-present worry that he would lose his grip on sanity when changing eventually became too much, when he had gone through it too many times for his body to take any more abuse.

When, at last, Caleb had completed his transformation from Caleb into Kaal, he gasped, finally stopping his scream. He opened his eyes and saw that he had drifted through the skies toward the village and was dangerously close to entering the range of the watchtowers and their defenders' arrows, and he quickly beat his wings to gain speed and direction away from them, scrambling with his legs before he remembered himself and tucked them in close to his belly in the proper form for flight.

His chest was still heaving, and he was blowing smoke with every exhale, but he couldn't relax until he knew what had happened to Ziya. He swiveled his head in every direction, trying to find the source of the attack, his claws pushed out, his teeth bared as he prepared for a fight. He saw Ziya rushing toward him, calling out his name, but their attacker wasn't chasing them . . . or doing much of anything, really. Instead, the green dragon who had seemingly come out of nowhere from her camouflaged perch in the mountain trees was simply hanging in the air, staring at Kaal.

He wasn't going to question their luck. If seeing him change from a human into a dragon left this dragon in a state of shock, Kaal would run with the opportunity to put distance between him and his attacker. "Let's go!" he hissed to Ziya as she caught up to him.

"Are you okay?" Ziya panted without slowing down her flight. She effortlessly course-corrected so that she glided beside him, and only then did she pause to catch her breath.

"Ask me again when we land," he told her, glancing over his shoulder to see that the green dragon had broken out of her shock and was headed their way. "Are *you* okay? She hit you, not me."

"Sore, but alive," Ziya said simply.

That was a fair assessment.

Kaal glanced toward their assailant once more and was surprised that the green dragon wasn't showing her teeth or claws. She was growling, yes, but she didn't show any immediate murderous intent.

And then, for some reason, the green dragon called out, "Kaal!"

Kaal stilled, his eyes wide. He couldn't quite place the voice, but he knew he recognized it. So, frowning, he turned toward the newcomer—though he kept his posture defensive. He heard Ziya growling beside him to let this green dragon know that she wouldn't let anything happen to Kaal because of his curiosity and was grateful for such a fierce friend. Ziya didn't trust dragons nearly as well as Kaal did, and Kaal knew that, sometimes, he *needed* someone on his side who would hold dragons to account. Someone who was prepared to strike should his trust leave him vulnerable.

"Kaal?" The green dragon pulled up short of Kaal and Ziya— and Kaal finally recognized her. He couldn't recall her name, but he remembered her as the green dragon who had taken her daughter to the council and had met him and Rikaa on the beach when he had gone to the council for help.

Kaal put himself between the green dragon and Ziya, since he and the green dragon hadn't parted ways on the best of terms. She had made it clear to him then that she didn't trust humans and that she would destroy him the second he turned on Rikaa. What's more, if he remembered right, she'd said that her husband would be bringing their hatchlings to the council after she brought her daughter; depending on how long her husband had waited before he approached the council, her family would have been on their way to the island or on their way from it around the time Ziya had accidentally led Alan's forces to ambush the dragons there. A few months was a short time to a dragon, and the hatchlings had still been young enough when Caleb had met this green dragon that not all of them had their names yet. If they had waited too long to determine fitting names for their children, if they had wandered and explored through the arduous journey to the island, if they had lingered on the council's island to talk to other dragons. . . . For all he knew, the younger hatchlings could have been caught up in Alan's schemes. Her husband could have been killed in the battle on the beach or the one outside of Alan's base. She could have every reason for revenge.

But she had called out to him, so he'd give her the courtesy of listening to her before he decided what to do.

"I remember you," he said cautiously, trying to be diplomatic to diffuse any tension preemptively. "I'm sorry; I don't remember your name."

"Lioia," she supplied for him, and he nodded.

"Right." He tipped his head toward Ziya but didn't relax his posture. "This is Ziya."

Lioia nodded sharply toward Ziya, and Ziya returned the gesture, but besides that brief moment, Lioia kept her gaze on Kaal. "Where is Rikaa?" she asked Kaal, her tone ringing with distrust—but again, she hadn't attacked him yet.

"With his family," Kaal said, "helping some friends of ours."

Lioia's expression betrayed her distaste. "Humans again? Or human-made dragons?"

"Yes," Kaal said without dropping her gaze as they glided toward the ground together. When her eyes narrowed and she let out a huff of smoke, he explained, "They needed the help."

"So you say," Lioia said.

Ziya let out an annoyed snort and repositioned herself so that Kaal was no longer flying between her and Lioia. "What do you want?" she asked. "You clearly don't like Kaal, but you haven't tried to kill us yet, so you must want something."

"Don't tempt me," Lioia shot back, baring her teeth and growling, much less at ease with Ziya than she had been with Kaal—and she hadn't been too comfortable around Kaal in the first place. She didn't trust easily, if at all.

Ziya replied with a growl of her own. "You don't scare me," she said. "I've dealt with far worse than you."

Kaal shook his head and once again got between them before things could escalate. "Stop it," he told Ziya—and before Ziya could argue, he turned to Lioia to say, "She's not wrong."

Lioia huffed her annoyance, but she stopped baring her teeth. Ziya had read the situation correctly; Lioia must have wanted something dearly to have dropped her defenses so quickly. "Let's leave the skies," she said at last, "so we can talk."

Ziya and Kaal shared a questioning look but couldn't see any reason not to agree, especially since Kaal was sore right down to his bones after transforming in mid-air. Still, they stuck close to one another, guarded and watching for any sign of betrayal as they followed Lioia down to the ground.

But no attack came, and they landed safely in the forest, fitting themselves between the dense trees that looked so green they were almost blue. Kaal could smell the dew on the trees and everything. Although most of the life in the forest scattered upon the approach of three dragons, Kaal could hear plenty of animals beyond the small clearing where they had landed. He was surprised by how much he missed that sound. The war had long ago chased life away from his village and every village around it. The forests were green but not dense; the animals were wary and scarce. Here, far from the front lines of the war, Kaal could almost remember life before he lost everything.

Lioia led the way as they walked until the trees blocked out the sky—and then, Lioia stopped, watching Ziya and Kaal, her tail moving slowly behind her and stirring the leaves, revealing rich mud beneath her.

"Tell me," she said at last, speaking as slowly and clearly as he had ever heard her speak, pronouncing each word carefully so that she couldn't be misunderstood, "what happened to the creature who created you. Tell me Alan is dead."

Once more, Ziya and Kaal shared a glance that carried with it an entire conversation. "Where did you hear that name?" Ziya asked.

"Answer me and I will answer you," Lioia replied, a growl weaving its way into her words the second Ziya spoke up with anything but Alan's location.

"We're hunting him now," Kaal said over the sound of Ziya's growl. "If you have any idea—if he's been through here—"

THE GODS' GIFT

Lioia shook her head, though she didn't say anything as she scratched her claws against the ground. "Why are you hunting him?" she asked at last.

Ziya spoke up first. "You didn't answer my question. Where did you hear Alan's name?"

Lioia huffed smoke through her nostrils, but this time, Kaal didn't try to put himself between her and Ziya—a silent display that he wouldn't try to take the neutral side again. Ziya was right; they had no reason to trust Lioia. The green dragon would have to participate in the give-and-take of information to keep things fair.

"He took my son," Lioia said at last, and Kaal felt his heart drop. Panicked, he wracked his brain, trying to remember the faces of the youngest dragons they had rescued. He had personally walked the halls of Alan's base to free the dragons, but he hadn't had *time* to memorize each face, especially when he had been trying to work as fast as he could. In an effort not to get caught—and not to get eaten or roasted by dragons who either thought he was an enemy or had lost their mind to Alan's tortures—he had sliced through any locks and ropes keeping dragons in place and then moved immediately on. Some of the dragons had stuck around to fight, but others had fled as soon as they were free—especially the youngest.

He sincerely hoped that Lioia's son was one of the dragons who broke for freedom as soon as his ropes were cut. A brand-new hatchling had no business in the middle of a battle, for one thing, but for another thing, Kaal selfishly knew that if Lioia's son had come back with news of Alan's transformation, Lioia would have even less reason to trust Kaal. All the other humans and dragons who realized that Kaal and Alan were the only ones able to shift their forms had immediately demanded answers of him; why should Lioia be any different? She had barely trusted him when he had Rikaa to vouch for him, and that was before Alan had sparked war with the dragon council.

"I'm so, so sorry," Ziya said, her own voice strained. In that simple statement, Kaal could hear exactly how much Ziya still carried her guilt over what had happened, what Alan had forced her to do for him.

Kaal had hoped that she would listen to *him*, at least, when he said he didn't blame her. He'd hoped that his opinion would have had more weight, since she had been sent to drag him back to Alan for torture and training. But she still blamed herself.

"We know what Alan does to the dragons he claims for himself," Kaal said before Lioia could draw conclusions about Ziya's guilty tone—especially because those conclusions would be too close to the truth for Ziya to defend herself against a wrathful mother dragon. "I'm sorry. Do you know what happened to him after Alan took him?"

"That," Lioia said, her tail still moving and her claws pushed out, "is the only reason I stopped my attack." She stopped to let a lizard cross her path; even as big as she was, she kept the forest animals from harm, as dragons were supposed to do. "I still don't trust you *or* your kind, Kaal. But my son came back to me and told me he escaped because you let him out." She watched him steadily. "I owe you his freedom, and I won't forget that. But I also won't forget that humans captured him in the first place."

"Don't hold us accountable for *his* crimes." Kaal's response was sharp enough that he had the opposite effect on the wildlife: several birds took off in panicked flight. He stopped and swallowed smoke in his throat. He believed in the dragons' mandate from the gods; he didn't want to hurt the earth and its inhabitants. So, he tempered his tone and tried again: "We're trying to stop him from hurting anyone else—human or dragon."

"Then you and I have a common enemy," Lioia said, her fire burning so hot in her throat that smoke was coming out of her nostrils and the sides of her mouth as she spoke. She was furious—and rightly so. "If not for how badly my family needs me. . . ."

Kaal shook his head, glad for the easy excuse to turn down her offer. He and Ziya needed allies if they wanted to face Alan with any hope of victory, but they needed *trusted* allies, not dragons who would likely attack them at the slightest provocation. "If your son was captured, he needs your comfort. We will find Alan and end this needless war, I promise you."

"He needs his father more than me right now," Lioia said in a sigh, the heat slowly leaving her as her anger gave way to the reality that she couldn't do anything to change what had happened. "My husband was badly injured in the battle at the beach. He's resting, but I think *all* of my children will sleep more easily when he is back on his feet." She paused, and Kaal met her gaze, already anticipating her next question but unwilling to rush her when he knew she didn't hold him in high enough regard to drop her pride.

And asking for help from a human was a huge blow to a dragon's pride.

"Tell me," Lioia said, speaking slowly and carefully without taking her gaze off of Kaal, "how well do you match the powers of the dragon you pretend to be?"

"That doesn't sound condescending at all," Ziya whispered under her breath to Kaal, and he let out a quiet laugh before he could remind himself that he was trying to be kind to Lioia's pride. Ziya had a way of cutting right to the heart of any situation and pointing out its absurdity.

Still, he schooled his expression and confined himself to the single huff of laughter. Lioia knew the forest better than they did. She could be a formidable opponent with both experience and environment to her advantage if she decided they weren't friendly enough for her liking. He had to tread carefully.

Dragons like Lioia occupied a space somewhere between Rikaa's family and the council. Rikaa and his family embraced humans and human-made dragons so long as they expressed a desire for peace and not war. The council painted all humans and the dragons who had once been humans to be enemies and savages. Lioia had the same opinion of humanity as the council did, but she was less willing to kill for her beliefs.

If Ziya and Kaal and others like them wanted to have any hope in their future, they needed peace with dragons like Lioia. The ones who could be convinced to dislike them without attacking them.

So, Kaal said, "I don't know what power white dragons have outside of the magic that made me, but I can heal, and my fire is hotter than that of other dragons." He paused. "If you're willing to trust me, I can help—whatever you need me to do."

"Kaal," Ziya started to say, but he shook his head minutely. If they wanted to get back to their search, they needed to make peace with the dragons who lived close to the village.

Lioia looked between the two of them and then sighed smoke. "I don't trust both of you in my home," she said. "You would have to leave your mate."

"That's not happening," Ziya said. She didn't correct Lioia on her assumption of their relationship—probably because it had happened often enough that, at some point, the two of them had decided without discussing their decision that it wasn't worth correcting everyone. "I don't trust you either."

"It's my home," Lioia shot back.

"And you're the one asking for a favor," Ziya replied evenly. "I'm coming."

"Ziya," Kaal started to say, but this time, she cut him off.

"No. I spend too much time waiting for you to return from danger. I'm tired of sitting outside of villages and outposts wondering if you're alive or not. Let me stand beside you." She drew herself up, her wings slightly unfurled as she made herself as big as possible and demanded, "Are we partners or not?"

Kaal sighed. He didn't like leaving Ziya behind either, especially since she was better equipped to deal with conflict than he was, but he hadn't realized she was so deeply bothered by his absence. Unable to answer her right away, when he turned his gaze from a defiant Ziya to Lioia, he was surprised to find Lioia smiling—even if the smile didn't last long. Still, it was an encouraging enough sign that Kaal felt confident in negotiating. "Ziya stays with me," he said, hoping that Lioia's moment of bemusement watching two adolescent, human-made dragons test out each other's boundaries would generate enough good will for Lioia to acquiesce to their request.

And, to his relief, it worked.

"Alright," Lioia said. "But if you harm my family—"

"I understand," Kaal said before she could complete the threat. He'd heard plenty in his lifetime. One more wouldn't bother him. "Please, lead the way."

Chapter 4: The Green Dragons' Forest

Kaal had expected Lioia's home to be like Rikaa's, part of the mountainside and carved out of rock. Instead, Lioia led Ziya and Kaal deeper into the forest until the undergrowth seemed too thick to proceed without cutting through the plant life. Lioia was adept at passing through the trees without disturbing too much, but Ziya and Kaal were, by comparison, clumsy and destructive and left a path of branches and trampled bushes. Then, when Ziya and Kaal both knew they could go no farther, Lioia cleared the path by putting her nose into a tangled mass of vines and bushes, moving them aside in one easy movement.

It was a *door*.

Kaal gaped, his mouth open just enough that his tongue escaped the confines of his mouth. The trees had grown together overhead so that no sunlight reached Lioia's hidden sanctuary—and as a white dragon who thrived on fire and sun, he sorely missed the light. A fire flickered at the center of the woods, with other, small flames contained in circles of stone scattered around the forest. There was enough light to see, but only just.

Ziya, on the other hand, seemed to feel right at home. She had once told him about how much she loved being on the ocean floor and watching the fish swim above her; Kaal wondered if the darkness reminded Ziya of the ocean that called her the way fire and volcanos called Kaal.

Unlike the rest of the forest, Lioia's home bore the marks of dragon involvement, the evidence that she and her family had shaped their environment to their liking. The trees in this section of the forest only had branches and leaves above the heads of the dragons that lived there. The lower branches looked to have been broken off with claws or teeth—and likely fed to the fires throughout the area. The dragons were hidden from view but were not hampered in their movements, especially with a forest so old that the canopy had grown into a patchwork blanket, no longer growing as individual trees but as one ceiling.

No wonder dragons survived so long even after humans started hunting them, Kaal thought.

Kaal heard the sound of hatchling voices in the trees but didn't see the small dragons until one climbed down from a tree nearly as thick around as a full-grown dragon's leg, using the hooked ends of his wings for purchase. Once the hatchling hit the ground, he bounded toward his mother, kicking up leaves and dirt and calling out to her in the dragon language. Kaal had lived with a dragon family long enough to recognize some of the words—the hatchling was saying hello and welcoming his mother home. After Lioi replied to her hatchling with instructions that sounded sharp but that Kaal didn't understand with his limited vocabulary, Kaal tried to ease the tension of the situation with a hello in the dragon language.

The deep green hatchling frowned as he looked between Kaal and Lioia, but he kept his distance all the same, watching Kaal and Ziya pass him by with his head tipped to the side and his tail swaying.

"You didn't know our language the last time I saw you," Lioia muttered to Kaal.

"I only know a little," he admitted. "I've been staying with Rikaa and his family, so I learned what I could when my time was not taken by Alan's machinations."

Lioia let out an interested noise but didn't say anything else until they reached a different area of her home. The light of several different fires burning close to a bed of leaves allowed Kaal and Ziya to clearly see a vibrantly green dragon lying prone, his breathing labored, one wing badly torn. His injuries were not life-threatening, but they hadn't become scars yet, either. Ziya and Kaal could see patterns of missing scales and light bleeding across this dragon's body, especially his legs and back.

Ziya let out a sympathetic hiss. "That looks bad."

THE GODS' GIFT

"He would have died if a bystander hadn't found him in the water before the sharks did," Lioia said, her gaze darkening. "His rescuer was only a young black dragon, barely past adolescence herself. She healed him from his near-drowning and halted some of the bleeding, but as you can see. . . ." She trailed off and then looked toward Kaal. "He will heal on his own, but it will take some time. I keep giving him what healing power I can without exhausting myself, but—"

"I understand," Kaal promised.

Lioia nodded once, sharply, and then lay down in front of her husband so that she could rest her head on top of his. He let out a soft purr and nuzzled his head underneath her chin, and the two of them spoke softly in the dragon language, their words so quiet that Kaal doubted he would have understood the conversation even if he were fluent in their language.

Then, Lioia got to her feet and stepped back. "Alright," she told Kaal, "he has agreed."

Kaal stepped forward, letting his gaze travel over the wounds this dragon had sustained. He heard the hatchlings hesitantly approaching, and he imagined how desperate their father must have felt during the battle on the beach. His son had been taken from him; he would have fought with everything he had.

Briefly, his thoughts drifted toward Alan, who must have known the deep parental instincts of older dragons and used it against them. He wondered if the soldiers had orders to target the youngest dragons and drag them back to the army base. Not only would the army benefit from young dragons who could more easily be terrified and traumatized into slavery but Alan would have a way to draw in older dragons.

He shook his head. Lately, whenever he thought of the effects of war on family, he found himself reliving the way Alan had tortured him in front of his dragon family—in addition to thinking of losing his brother and mother to war and grief. Although Ziya might have carried more obvious scars from her time with Alan, Kaal couldn't dispel Alan's influence in his mind either.

So, he thought of something else. If he was going to think about Alan, he would direct his thoughts to something more useful—the first time he had discovered his healing power. Back then,

34

Alan had ordered a thief killed in front of Kaal as punishment for his disobedience. Kaal had breathed an apology toward the young man, and his fatal wounds had closed.

At the time, Alan had seemed shocked. Now, Kaal knew Alan had only been surprised that he had finally found a human who could become a white dragon.

Kaal swallowed and focused on that feeling, that desperate wish to combat all the evil that Alan had left in his wake, and he held onto that wish as he breathed over Lioia's husband. He let his breath linger in the air before he let it wash over him again.

To his relief, Lioia's husband seemed to be improving after that second breath. The healing wasn't immediately obvious—possibly because internal injuries were more pressing and were likely mending themselves first—but when the dragon's breathing evened out and he stopped pressing his claws into the ground for comfort and stability against the pain, Kaal knew he'd made progress.

Lioia knew it, too, if the soft sound she let out was any indication. In a few quick steps, she skirted around Kaal to once more rest her head on top of her husband's, speaking to him in the dragon language in tones that had Kaal and Ziya exchanging looks and then looking at anything but each other, as any human teenagers would do in a setting of intimacy.

On the other hand, the rest of Lioia's family weren't put off by their parents' affection. Now that their father's wounds were starting to turn to scars at a much faster pace, the three hatchlings who had been in the periphery rushed toward their father, climbing onto his back and curling up on him with light purring sounds of their own. It had been weeks since Alan attacked the dragons. These poor little ones had been waiting in the trees for longer than hatchlings should ever have to wait to embrace their father and play with him.

Among the playing hatchlings, Kaal recognized Lioia's daughter. She was every bit as shy as he remembered her being, curled up on her father's other side so that she could peek out at the newcomers and hide behind her parents if she decided she didn't like the situation. But now that the hatchlings had come into the light, Kaal also recognized Lioia's second son, a little dragon with his father's vibrantly green hue and with short, white horns that curled slightly at the ends.

THE GODS' GIFT

When Caleb had freed Alan's captives, he hadn't had time to introduce himself to them all. But he had found a group of hatchlings and dragons young enough to be barely older than hatchlings and had freed them shortly before he'd been captured. He'd directed them to find Rikaa's grandsons and explain that Kaal had sent them, knowing Rikaa's family would bring them to safety.

That little green dragon had been part of the group.

Kaal was insanely lucky that the stars had aligned like that. In fact, he had to wonder if the gods weren't guiding his path with such coincidences laid out for him.

Not that he'd say as much out loud. Ziya seemed to think his newfound belief in the gods was a coping strategy. She might not have been wrong, to be fair, but he liked the way faith and hope felt in his chest, and he wasn't willing to throw them away after he had gone so long without them. If his faith in the gods' mandate of peace and protection was nothing more than blindness, he preferred blindness to anguish.

"*Aob*," Kaal said in the dragon greeting, smiling warmly.

Both of Lioia's sons watched Kaal with interest, but they didn't respond. Instead, Lioia gestured toward Kaal with her tail, speaking in the dragon language again. Kaal didn't recognize all the words, but he heard his own name and the word "*iloakaa*," the word for human. So, he dipped his head and kept his posture open so that the young dragons knew he was friendly.

Although the hatchlings kept a respectable distance from Kaal aside from whispered greetings, Lioia's husband blew a ring of smoke at Ziya and Kaal to catch their attention. "I owe you my thanks," he hissed, his accent heavy and not at all helped by his exhaustion and lingering hurt. "Thank you for my son and my health."

Kaal bowed his head low to the ground in a show of deference. "No," he said, keeping his head low. "I owe you an apology. I had the chance to kill the wizard who did this and didn't."

"Then do not miss next time." The dragon's words carried no accusation, but they carried no forgiveness, either. "I am Oad."

"Kaal."

"I heard." Oad shifted slightly so that he was more comfortable despite his children climbing all over him. "Lioia tells me you are hunting the wizard who attacked us."

Kaal nodded, though Ziya spoke for them. "We won't let him hurt anyone else if we can help it," she swore, her tone sharp and her eyes flashing. Although she liked to let Kaal talk to dragons—she didn't care for them or their customs—she also had a habit of speaking up whenever he became, in her opinion, too deferent to them. "He has a lot to answer for."

Oad nodded, his own expression sharp to match Ziya's. "He took our son. Do not hesitate this time."

"As soon as we find him, we will enact justice," Kaal promised. He didn't give details, and he didn't promise death. He still wasn't sure what he would do when he faced Alan again, and as determined as Ziya was, he had also seen her hesitate the last time they faced Alan. Both of them were terrified of Alan, yes, but more than that, Kaal didn't think he could murder anyone, even Alan, in cold blood. He could defend himself in battle, yes, and he had even learned that he was willing to kill another to end needless suffering; but he didn't think he could simply find Alan and kill him.

And Alan knew that. Alan had seen him refuse to kill a defenseless enemy soldier. He had used exactly that scenario to test Caleb, to see what kind of boy he was.

No, Kaal wouldn't promise anything. Nothing with Alan was ever guaranteed anyway.

"We were going to search the village near your home," Ziya explained. "The council has declared war on the humans, so we believe Alan could be hiding somewhere far from the armies that used to give him power and shelter."

Oad looked toward Lioia. "The council declared war?"

"I was going to tell you when you had your strength so that we could discuss what role to play in the conflict while we still have little ones at home," Lioia explained. "The attack you survived was the *humans'* declaration. The council acted to defend us."

"*Alan* attacked," Ziya corrected Lioia sharply, her claws leaving lines in the dirt as they extended. "He's the one who ordered dragons like your son captured. He's been killing and tormenting humans, too. The rest of us don't deserve to be killed because Alan courts death."

"No, I imagine you didn't want your commander to call down your utter destruction with his rash attack," Lioia said dryly.

THE GODS' GIFT

Ziya growled, but Kaal had already moved to step between her and Lioia. Both Ziya and Lioia had sharp tongues, and now, in the middle of a war, was not the time to make new enemies because of pride. "Ziya," Kaal growled her name to get her to stop, his eyes full of warning, and she shook her head at him, snorting out smoke in disbelief.

"You can't play peacemaker forever," she huffed, the words nearly lost in her accent and in her smoke, but he understood the message all the same.

He held her gaze a moment longer and then whirled to face Lioia, his teeth bared. "I told you when we met what happened to me. I told you the truth. It is not *my* fault you refuse to listen to me." When Lioia drew herself up in response, he held his head higher and matched her. "I came here to help. I did help. And yet you continue to act like I am the same as Alan. I'm not."

Lioia let out a growl that Kaal could feel underneath his scales, and all three of her hatchlings scattered for the trees. But with the three hatchlings no longer weighing him down, Oad could stand up and nudge Lioia in the side with his wing, drawing her attention.

"You are always looking for a fight, *nuur*," Oad said. Kaal didn't recognize the word he used, but from Oad's tone, Kaal could guess that it was a term of endearment.

"To protect my family? Yes," Lioia replied.

Oad shook his head. "That's not what I meant," he said. He kept his gaze on Lioia and kept his tone tender while he gestured toward Kaal and Ziya with his tail. "You want to kill the man who took our son? Go with them."

"Wait a minute," Ziya started to say.

"We don't need any help," Kaal said at the same time.

But Lioia wasn't listening to them. She had locked gazes with her husband, searching his expression for something neither of the two adolescent dragons nearby understood. Whatever she was looking for, she seemed to find it in his eyes, and so, she nodded and nuzzled her snout against Oad's, whispering something in the dragon language that Kaal couldn't understand even with context. He recognized "*naud*" for "little ones," but nothing else was familiar.

Ziya shot Kaal a quizzical look, but he shook his head. He couldn't translate for her. And he didn't know what he could say to

Lioia or Oad to turn down the offer of help without explaining why he couldn't possibly trust another dragon on this search. Lioia was already looking for reasons to justify her hatred of humanity and of Kaal. If she saw that Kaal and Alan were more alike than he cared to admit, he didn't trust her not to turn on him too.

In fact, he didn't trust her not to turn on them as soon as Alan was dead regardless of what she saw. This wasn't an equitable arrangement.

"I can search the area around the village for any travelers," Lioia said, turning to Kaal and Ziya, her tone perfectly prim, as if they had always planned to ask her for help.

"Wait," Ziya said, shaking her head. "We didn't actually ask you to come."

"And I didn't ask your permission," Lioia replied. "You said yourselves you didn't kill this monster when you had the chance. You need someone with you who won't hesitate."

"I *won't* hesitate," Ziya said, her tone one of cold confidence that belied the fact that Kaal had seen her waver under Alan's gaze too many times to believe her.

"Then you will not turn down help," Lioia said. "I know these woods better than you do."

"And you don't understand Alan like we do," Kaal said, trying to sound reasonable. "He's no ordinary human. He knows magic beyond what even the dragon council understands."

Lioia snorted in annoyance. "And what makes you think we cannot benefit from each other's knowledge? You two are lost, and Kaal can barely keep his form. You're as likely to get yourselves killed as you are to stop Alan." When neither Ziya nor Kaal looked convinced, Lioia shook out her whole body from her head down to her wings down to her tail. Then, she strode past them. "I'm going. You don't even know your way out of these woods. If you want to leave, follow me."

Ziya and Kaal glanced at each other, and Kaal saw his same frustration mirrored in Ziya's expression. But Lioia was already leaving; they had no choice but to follow her. "Wait," Kaal called out, taking a few running steps to catch up with Lioia, who didn't even pause or look over her shoulder.

"Coming, then?" Lioia asked.

THE GODS' GIFT

Kaal let loose a frustrated growl. Ziya did the same, but hers was more muted. "Wait," he said again. "If you go after Alan, you won't find him if he's—if you don't know what he looks like."

"Kaal," Ziya growled her warning.

"Would you rather she find out when she blunders into his path later and blames us for keeping secrets?" Kaal shot back without looking toward Ziya. When Lioia finally stopped, obviously intrigued, Kaal sighed and dropped his shoulders. "Alan is the reason I can change forms. He can too."

Lioia's eyes narrowed, and her claws flared out defensively, but she didn't otherwise make a threatening move. "Can all human-made dragons do that?"

Kaal shook his head. "Not all," he said simply. "Don't ask me any more questions; I don't know anything. I only know that Alan turned me into what I am, and I saw him in his dragon form." He paused. "That's how he was able to escape us. We didn't know he could do that."

For a long time, Lioia scratched her claws against the ground, gradually pulled her lips back from her teeth until they were entirely exposed. "Then," she said at last, "I will need to show you how to hunt a dragon."

CHAPTER 5: FOR WANT OF CLOTHES

Z iya, Kaal, and Lioia landed not far from the human village, in a spot that Lioia promised was hidden from view of the village defenders. There, the mountains on either side of the valley were full of tall, thick trees, disguising all sorts of caves and cliffs. One particular grove jutted out from the mountain, and behind that cliff, the dragons could perch on craggy boulders. The grove of trees blocked them from human eyes, but if they came right to the edge, they could look down on the village.

The humans likely knew about this weakness in their defenses. Kaal could see several archers' towers near the wall of the village that faced the cliffside grove. But unless Kaal and his allies flew out of their hiding place, the humans could only watch and listen—not attack.

Still, Kaal found himself wary as he watched the far-off flickers of movement in those towers. Soldiers had always made him nervous, but now, as a dragon, he found himself warring with the instinct to consider those archers mortal enemies. Yes, they would kill him without a second thought, but they didn't know he had been born human. They didn't know he was their ally. And so, he dreaded the thought of fighting them.

"So," Lioia said as she perched on the mountain and looked at the village below them, her expression as close to a sneer as any Kaal had seen on a dragon's face before, "what now?"

"Now, he tries to turn back into a human so he can look around," Ziya said, her voice lower than usual. She hadn't been able to stop growling since Lioia joined them, and Kaal didn't think she would. He wasn't so sure leaving the two of them alone together was a good idea, not when Lioia made no effort to hide her contempt for humans and Ziya made even less effort to pretend she didn't blame dragons for letting the world fall apart and then claiming moral superiority.

"Maybe we could camp for a while before I try to sneak in," he offered, though neither Ziya nor Lioia seemed to listen to what he had to say.

"I thought you had no control over the changes," Lioia said, her eyes narrowed Kaal's way, ignoring his offer entirely.

"I'm learning," Kaal said carefully, though he could feel his claws stretching into the dirt beneath his feet. He didn't want a fight. "I know now that if I want to find my human form, I need to feel safe, and I need to feel like the human I was before all this happened. So, yes, I can change when I mean to. Sometimes."

Lioia huffed. "This search is entirely unreliable. How you've come as far as you have relying entirely on *feelings* is beyond me."

"Do you know anyone else who can search through human villages for a wizard who can become a dragon at will?" Ziya challenged Lioia. She looked even more prepared for a fight than Kaal did, not only with her claws pushed out but with her wings slicked back and her tail still behind her.

"I could always set fire to every human I found," Lioia said, her eyes glittering.

"That makes you no better than the council, who have betrayed everything they say they stand for in order to punish humanity for what its corrupt leaders and dangerous wizards have done," Kaal said, growling despite his best attempts to swallow back the sound. "Dragons are supposed to defend this world and those who live in it. Killing innocents is *not* what the gods intended."

"Oh? You speak for the gods now?" Lioia stalked toward him until they were standing nearly nose-to-nose. "You, a terrible creation of magic? You who betray the gods' intentions by your very existence?"

"I am only telling you what I learned about your role as they intended," Kaal said, struggling to maintain his even tone of voice. Rikaa had once told him that his ability to change forms was a gift from the gods, but Lioia seemed to be of the same mind of Ziya, viewing his gifted dragon form as a curse and an abomination. "Take that as you will."

Lioia huffed out smoke but didn't say anything else, turning away from Kaal and Ziya. Kaal hoped that meant she could see the wisdom of his argument and was too prideful to admit it. Every dragon he'd met so far, even the ones he liked, couldn't see past their own self-importance at times. They didn't admit to being wrong often, and they especially wouldn't admit to agreeing with a human.

"Now," Ziya said, her smile evident in her tone even before Lioia turned to see it, "I know it's going to be hard for you, but try to stop growling and picking fights. Kaal needs to feel safe to change into a human, and you keep acting like a threat."

The sound Lioia let out perfectly communicated her annoyance at being dictated to, but at the same time, she bit back any caustic remark she might have made. She had, after all, seen Kaal transform on the beach. She had even been the one to suggest that his changes were based on a measure of defensiveness.

Maybe the gods knew what they were doing when they led her to us. She might hate me and everyone like me, but she understands my gift better than anyone outside of Rikaa's family, Kaal thought. *The gods must have senses of humor, too.*

As Kaal settled down on the rocks with his legs tucked beneath him, Ziya sat down beside him, taking up nearly the same position. "Just think," she said in a teasing whisper. "Imagine what Tristan would have said if he could see our alliance now."

Kaal barked out a laugh. He had told Ziya once that her way of finding humor in any situation reminded him of his lost brother, and he appreciated that she had remembered all he told her about him. Tris had been Caleb's hero; he always felt more like himself when he thought of how much he wanted to be like him.

"There would be *no* arguing. Tris could stop a fight before it even started to brew," Kaal said, closing his eyes. It had been so long since he'd seen his brother that he was starting to forget the sound of his voice, but when he concentrated, he could hear Tristan's laugh or his off-key singing or picture the way he swung his legs on the fence surrounding the sheep. His caterwauling would always, without fail, scare the sheep if he sang loudly enough—and so Tris did.

THE GODS' GIFT

And then, Caleb had to chase the sheep, red-faced and yelling back at Tris to stop making so much noise.

Those were the only arguments he could remember having with his brother—the ones that stemmed from teasing taken slightly too far. They had never truly *fought*, not even when Tris left to join the army. Caleb had been young enough then to believe all the war stories and the songs of glory and honor. He'd seen Tris off with a wide grin and told everyone that his brother was going to win the war, that the world would write songs about Tris and that Caleb would make everyone learn those songs.

He missed his brother, even now. He'd thought that time would make the ache in his chest easier to deal with, but it hadn't. When he thought of Tris, he still remembered feeling like his world had ended when a soldier told him and his mother Tris had died. Not even a new body and a new purpose from the gods could take that away from him.

He heard Lioia gasp as his wings folded into his shoulders, and he tried hard to ignore her reaction as he focused on the ache in his chest that was Tristan. He thought of the way Tris had pretended to be a dragon when Caleb was so young he still needed corralling. When their mother would call them in for meals, Tristan would growl and hold his hands out like claws, chasing Caleb all the way inside.

He smiled as he thought of what Tristan would say if he could see Kaal now: *You had to outdo me, didn't you?*

By that point, Kaal could actually feel the changes taking place. For some reason, when he changed from a dragon into a human, the transformation didn't hurt nearly as much as the change from human to dragon. He didn't feel his spine compressing and didn't feel any sharpness as skin grew over scales. He supposed that was a good thing, since he didn't think he could keep his mind intact if *every* little change hurt, but he did wonder why only one change felt like torment. Perhaps his dragon form would always pain him because it wasn't his natural one. Or maybe shrinking hurt less than explosive growth no matter what.

Another question to ask Alan, I suppose, he thought—and then immediately pushed that stray thought aside before it could take hold. If he thought of Alan, if he thought of how afraid he was to

44

face the man who had humiliated him and treated him like a pet, he might not change into a vulnerable human form.

Holding his breath, he peeked one eye open and was relieved to find that he hadn't sabotaged his transformation too badly. He still had enough height that he could be mistaken for a tall, broad adult, not the long-limbed teenager he was when he reverted fully. And he could still feel the nubs of wings on his shoulder blades and a slight tail. Both of those things could be hidden with clothes, though, and since he didn't see any scales spreading over his skin, he decided he'd gotten close enough to human that he could work with his current form.

He didn't stand up, too aware that Ziya was already averting her gaze, but sat back and pulled his knees up to his chin. Because he was taller than usual, he felt awkward, like he was trying to fit too much of himself into too small a space. "Clothes?" he asked, glancing up at Ziya.

Ziya didn't look his way, but she did shift her wings so that Caleb could reach a small pack that he had tied to her back leg before they left on their hunt for Alan. At the time, they had gathered what few clothes they could from the humans who had followed them to Iuan's home, knowing even a cloak would be helpful against the elements when Kaal changed to Caleb and lost his scales.

Every once in a while, Ziya still had to look for clothes that fit the situation, like the Junnin soldier's uniform he'd lost when he fell off of her back. But, thankfully, Ziya didn't have to hunt down clothes for him too often. Neither of them was entirely comfortable with taking clothes from dead men.

Caleb slipped on a hooded cloak and tied a makeshift tunic around his waist. Before they left, Ziya's mother, Dahlia, had tied aprons together, gathered from a few young girls who had been forced to work in the army's kitchens. She'd said at the time that she wanted him to have as many clothes as he needed; now, her foresight meant Caleb still had barely enough to maintain his modesty.

Unfortunately, the pack was nearly empty. He had a few extra bits of armor and a pair of gloves, but other than the aprons, he was out of clothes.

Caleb sighed and adjusted the way the cloak sat on his shoulders, pulling it around himself with one eye closed in a grimace. "I'm going to see if I can trade some work for clothes. This far from the worst of the fighting, they should have enough to spare for someone in dire need." He gestured down at himself to emphasize his point.

Ziya finally turned his way, a smile pulling at the corner of her mouth once she saw him. "You look ridiculous."

"Thanks, Ziya. You always know how to fill me with confidence before I go out into the world."

Ziya chuckled. "You'll be fine. Use that talented tongue of yours and get some sympathy."

"And what do you expect us to do in the meantime?" Lioia asked, breaking into their camaraderie and nearly startling Caleb. He had fallen into such easy teasing with Ziya that he had honestly forgotten she was there. "Don't tell me you have been wasting your time waiting for him."

Ziya's chest expanded, betraying her embarrassment like a blush would betray a human. "Not always," she said.

Lioia huffed. "Hatchlings."

"Technically, we are," Caleb pointed out. He looked down at himself, grimaced, and then looked back up. "I know I don't look it right now because I couldn't get any smaller, but I'm fifteen, and Ziya is almost sixteen. That's young for a dragon and adolescent for a human."

"And you are the ones entrusted with tracking down the evil human responsible for this war." Lioia barked out a laugh. "I told Rikaa he was foolish. I didn't realize how much so. Your strategy is based entirely on your ability to intuit your way through changes you don't understand, and Ziya watches for trouble neither of you wants to confront. Is it any wonder you haven't found Alan yet?"

"Ziya is the only reason I'm still alive, so mind what you say," Caleb said, speaking more sharply than he meant to. He felt his face flushing red, and he wasn't entirely convinced it was due to anger.

Lioia flicked a rock with her claws. "Infatuation."

"No, I simply know who to trust," Caleb shot back. "I barely trust you—and only to side with us against the man who took your son. But Ziya has my full trust. She has kept us from human soldiers and dragon scouts and rescued me from Alan himself. What have you done except berate her?" By the time he finished, he had drawn himself up to his full height, his gaze brimming with fire.

"He's exaggerating," Ziya started to say, but Caleb gestured impatiently. She didn't let him talk poorly of himself; he wouldn't let her do so either.

"And she still believes all the terrible things Alan told her to break her will," Caleb said. "Besides that, she's still healing from the *months* Alan had her in his grasp. He made her pay for our escape by punishing her twice over." He turned his attention back to Lioia. "She's more than earned the right to play lookout. *You* haven't done anything but point the way to a hiding spot and complain about the way we work together."

Lioia frowned between the two of them, but when she saw how both Caleb and Ziya had drawn themselves up to their full heights, united against her despite how small Caleb was in relation to the two dragons, she gestured sharply with her tail. "I was only trying to understand why you seem to lack any urgency if this man is as evil as you say he is."

"He is," Ziya said without hesitation.

"But that doesn't mean we push ourselves beyond what we can do," Caleb said. "Ziya has been flying all day. A search tainted by exhaustion won't yield results."

"True," Lioia said, though she sounded like the admission itself annoyed her.

Caleb sighed and then turned his back on Lioia to reach for Ziya, resting his hand on the side of her mouth and then touching his forehead to the front of her snout. "Try not to kill her while I'm gone," he teased.

"You should be the one staying behind," Ziya teased right back. "You have more patience than I do."

"She *can* help us. She knows this area, and if the council comes, they won't attack her," Caleb said. "We need every ally we can get, even the ones that join us out of hate."

"I know. You like to turn every disadvantage to an advantage. I should have known you'd find the good in this." Ziya nudged her snout against his hand, and he rubbed her scales. "Try to be quick."

"Don't worry. I know you don't want to be trapped with our new partner too long," he promised. He stepped back, smiled at her, and then waved at Lioia before he began the long trek down to the village.

THE GODS' GIFT

He placed his footsteps deliberately so that he didn't cut himself on any rocks, trying to find the easiest and gentlest slopes down the mountain. The trees jutted over the mountainside in odd places, and he used the roots to steady himself where he could find them. In some places, the climb would have been purely vertical had he been a human from the village trying to find hidden dragons; he was lucky he was going down the mountain and not up. And he was lucky not to be fully human. At least he knew that if he fell the long distance to the ground, he had wings to catch himself.

Caleb slid a few times on loose dirt, missing the signs of precarious footing thanks to the darkness settling over the valley as the sun set. *Stay human. Don't change*, he kept chanting in his mind, focusing on those words and on each step. For some reason, reminding himself of which form he wanted to take made a difference in his transformations, and he would use every tool he accidentally discovered to master the otherwise unpredictable power Alan had given him. He didn't want to spend the rest of his life looking for old clothes or hiding from cold weather.

Finally, he got to the bottom of the mountain and headed for the lantern lights that he could see farther down the valley. A few of those lights made a path not far from his position; he assumed that was the same road he and Ziya had seen before.

Sure enough, as he got closer to the line of lanterns, his feet found a smoothed-out road, and he followed that until he saw the first villager.

It was strange, he thought, to see other humans in a setting that had nothing to do with war. He had been forced out of homes and villages just like that one so many times that he'd given up on living a normal life—but that was exactly what those people had. The only sign that the war had touched them was the towers from which their archers protected the village from dragon attacks. Otherwise, they looked . . . peaceful.

He could see a few toys lazily discarded outside of mud-brick houses. The kids inside weren't worried that someone would take them. He could see laundry left out to dry. He could see empty tables that would, in the morning, be filled with food and other items to trade. He breathed in the smoke coming from someone's house and recognized the taste of a stew.

It feels like home, he realized, coming to a stop not far from the entrance to the village, his breath caught in his chest from the weight of *loss*. This place . . . this place felt like home, but it wasn't home. He'd lost his home long ago. And this little village was like stepping into a memory.

He realized he was shrinking only when the tied aprons stopped fitting him properly, and he hurriedly re-tied them onto the body that now looked much more like a teenage boy. Since becoming a dragon, he no longer looked thin and ragged and starved enough to pass for younger than he actually was—and he had gained enough weight and muscle that he could even pass as an army captain when he wasn't wearing a cloak and some aprons. But he was still a boy, still thin and gangly and growing into his body.

Now, he looked either like a runaway from the army or a refugee from a dragon attack, with nothing to his name but enough strength to get to the nearby village.

So, that was what he would tell people.

He found the only inn in the small village—a cozy-looking place with smoke coming from its chimney and wooden balconies where guests could overlook the village—and knocked on the door, waiting in the lantern light for whoever was inside to answer. He couldn't hear a bustle of activity inside; this village was so tucked away in the mountains that it had escaped both the war and the flood of refugees the war had brought with it.

Finally, a girl about Caleb's age answered the door. She was wiping her hands on a towel and had something smudged on her arms that she hadn't yet reached, but when she looked up and realized a stranger was on her doorstep, she froze, blinked, and then called out, "Dad!"

Caleb kept his cloak pulled closed in front of him with one hand, unconsciously trying to draw less attention to himself now that he was around other humans again. He still couldn't quite break out of that habit. Until he had become a dragon, strangers were potential trouble. They could steal from him or hurt him. And so, he automatically tried to look smaller, hiding his bare chest and pulling his shoulders in.

Eventually, the girl's father—a silver-haired man who used a walking stick to lean on because his left leg wasn't as easy to use as his right—came out of the door beyond the main entrance and immediately took a tighter grip on his walking stick, holding it up in front of himself rather than leaning on it.

"What do you want?" the man demanded. His gaze was steady, and Caleb could see danger behind his eyes. No matter how much age had weathered him, this man was still a threat.

Caleb quickly held up his free hand in a gesture of peace. "I'm looking for a place to stay," he said. "I can work in exchange for food and clothes—"

"We've stayed out of the war this long. We don't want it coming to our door," the man said, still holding Caleb's gaze with steel in his eyes. "And you are a soldier."

Caleb shook his head. "I swear, I'm not."

"Don't *lie* to me," the man said, taking a step forward, his walking stick still raised and pointed at Caleb. "I was a warrior once. I know how you all are. Even a disgraced soldier like you still carries himself like he's unafraid of attack."

Caleb's lips parted slightly, and he found himself at a complete loss for words. He couldn't begin to explain to this man how wrong he was, how he had lived every second of his life before he met Alan waiting for fire to consume him the way it had his big brother, how he had lived after Alan's potion like a hunted creature, unwanted by humans or dragons. He expected attack at any moment; of *course* he lived in fear of it.

And yet. . . .

Caleb frowned as he considered everything he had been through, everything he had become. He felt more like a dragon than a human lately, and with that identity came a confidence he hadn't had since he was small. He also trusted in his dragon form, so he didn't fear death as much as he used to—especially not when he was Kaal. And his sharper senses alerted him to danger sooner than Caleb's would have before he met Alan.

So, yes, he supposed he carried himself with dragon-like pride, the very thing he and Ziya teased their dragon friends about.

With that realization in mind, then, he dropped his shoulders and sighed. "I won't stay long," he said. "At least let me help you clean or chop wood, whatever you need, so I can trade you for something to wear." He gestured down at his bare feet. "Please."

"Dad," the girl said softly, catching both of their attention, "it's night. We can't turn him away now."

"I told you a thousand times, Mira," her father replied. "We don't take in soldiers."

"I can sleep outside," Caleb offered.

Mira turned to her father with her eyebrows raised and one hand thrown out toward Caleb. "See? It's a fair trade, Dad. He doesn't even have shoes. What threat can he be?"

Her father shook his head. "You've gotten reckless, Mira."

"No, you've gotten obstinate," Mira replied. Then, she turned toward Caleb and gestured for him to come inside. "Besides, your timing is perfect. I was just cleaning up for the night. I'll see if I can find you something to wear, and then I'll show you what still needs doing."

Caleb bowed deeply. "Thank you."

Mira smiled at him, her light brown eyes twinkling. "Don't thank me until you're done working," she replied, already pulling her curly, black hair away from her face. "There's a lot to do in this old inn."

Caleb nodded, taking a seat at one of the tables where, no doubt, the inn's guests would eat when the sun came up. The tables were thick and hardy, likely carved out of wood from the forest around them, and he could see the scuffs and marks of years of guests eating on them. They looked old, but so did everything else in the inn. Old but well-cared-for.

Caleb kept his silence until Mira was gone, but then, he looked toward her father and tried to explain himself. "I was conscripted and ran away; I don't even know how to use a sword. I can promise you I'm not a soldier in any way that matters."

"Do you think I haven't heard stories like that before?" the man asked. He finally stopped pointing the walking stick at Caleb and made his way to a seat at a different table, still glaring his suspicion Caleb's way. "Not many people can find our home, but those that do are always the same. We try to help those who can't help themselves, but the men and women who kill each other and then try to find peace bring nothing but trouble."

"I don't like soldiers much either," Caleb said, trying to defuse the situation with a small smile. When that didn't work, though, he tried again. "My brother died in the war. I swore I'd never fight for the same army that killed him. That's why I ran away as soon as I could. Please don't hold it against me that I didn't escape without being changed."

The man snorted. "You're smarter than the other soldiers we've had. They ran to the edges of the kingdom and expected to be welcomed despite their violence."

"Thanks," Caleb said.

"That doesn't mean you can stay."

Caleb absently traced the pattern of the wood on the table in front of him. "Like I said, I can sleep outside if you'd prefer. But I don't want to travel at night." When the man didn't respond, Caleb shifted and pulled his cloak slightly tighter around himself. "Is this how you treat everyone who comes through?"

"Only the soldiers."

Caleb nodded, a thought nagging at the corner of his mouth until it became words. "You probably haven't seen him if you turn away soldiers, but I have to ask. . . . My former commander ran away from a defeat. I'll be honest—I hope he hasn't come here if you've managed to avoid the war so far. He has a habit of bringing down the worst kinds of trouble and not caring what happens to the men under his command. I doubt he'd care what happened to your village if he decided to hide out here."

The man got to his feet and made his way over to slam his hands down on Caleb's table. "I knew it," he said, his voice a dangerous whisper. "I knew you weren't just passing through."

"I—"

"Go look for trouble somewhere else."

Caleb held the man's gaze and then got to his feet. "Thank you for your hospitality," he said through his teeth. "I'm going to stay the night. If my former commander isn't here, I'll leave. You have my word."

"I don't trust your word, boy," the man spat out. "You can't get by on trust you don't have."

"Fair enough," Caleb said. "But I'll keep my word anyway. It's all I have to my name."

That much was true. Yes, he lied and stretched the truth to keep himself out of trouble all the time, but his promises, his word, were still true. He didn't want to give up entirely on the good person Tris had taught him to be—or what was the point? If he couldn't cling to any part of what made him human, the war had won.

But he couldn't explain that to this man, not when they barely knew each other. So, he simply stayed where he was and waited for Mira to return.

CHAPTER 6: MIRA'S SPELL

As promised, Mira had come back with clothes for Caleb to wear as well as a list of chores for him to do around the inn. And despite what her father had said, she even offered him a bed for the night—because, she said, he looked so worn and weary she couldn't in good conscience turn him out.

The whole thing felt strangely . . . normal.

When Caleb had been growing up, he'd worked with animals. After he'd lost his home, he had done odd jobs wherever he could find someone willing to part with food or shelter. Now, sleeping in an actual bed after a hard day's work that had absolutely nothing to do with dragons, he felt more like Caleb than he'd felt in a long time.

It felt so *wrong*.

He didn't understand it. He should have been thrilled. If he wanted to, when the war was over, he could return to exactly this kind of life. This was a taste of what humanity could give him if he chose to stay in the skin he was born with.

But this life didn't have Rikaa in it. This life didn't have the feeling of wind underneath his wings. It didn't have the peaceful bliss of sunlight on his scales. No matter how soft his pillow was, no matter how calm the night sky was with no dragons on the horizon, a life in his human body felt empty.

He'd tried to explain that feeling to Ziya before, but she hadn't understood. She wanted nothing more than to be human again and to have a life *just like this* with her mother. And Caleb would gladly have traded places with her. He'd told her that he didn't like being a human, that he didn't want to go back to being a starving refugee.

Now, after spending time in his human form and realizing that he had more power than he'd ever had before in his old skin, that he didn't have to be that scared little boy anymore, he *still* preferred his dragon form. It felt right in a way he couldn't explain.

He felt ungrateful. The gods had given him his humanity back after Alan took it from him. And then, they'd led him to the village near Lioia's home and shown what peace could look like.

Caleb frowned and readjusted his pillow. *Maybe I should stop trying to figure out what the gods are up to. They told dragons to worry about the fate of the world; I should live up to that instead of waiting for their help.*

With that, he closed his eyes, trying to sleep—though sleep didn't come, despite his exhaustion, until he blew smoke over his pillow and finally drifted off with the light scent of dragon fire in his nose.

After so much journeying and so much work at the inn, Caleb slept hard and didn't wake up until the sun was high in the sky. He groaned and shifted, stretching and then catching himself as he let out a yawn that sounded like the rumble of a sleeping dragon. He held his breath and waited for someone to come rushing to investigate, but to his relief, no one seemed to have noticed.

He ran a hand through his hair so that he looked less like he'd slept in as late as he had and then made his way to the main area, pointedly ignoring Mira's father and his deep glare to look around the inn and see what kind of visitors had made their way to that remote village.

Instantly, he was reminded of the refugee camps that had been his home for so long. The people who had run away to this place were the ones the army hadn't managed to track down and force into work. At the farthest table, Caleb saw a young mother trying to wrangle three small children, her expression one of both exhaustion and grief. She hadn't yet developed the stony look of other widows, so her loss must have been recent. At another table, Caleb saw an old woman eating soup, her hands shaking as she tried to steady her spoon. And at another, a young boy with no family around, skinny and nervous.

Caleb stared at the boy for longer than he meant to. *Is that how I looked to the others?* he wondered, frowning. This boy looked so *vulnerable*, so small and lonely. He moved with a panicked energy, as if he were waiting for someone to carry him off to the war at any second. Caleb understood those furtive glances only too well.

He thought briefly about sitting by that boy but then decided against it. When he'd been that scared, he would have bolted at any sign of attention from someone like Caleb, someone who looked like he could have been a soldier.

In fact, Caleb was suddenly and acutely aware of the attention he was getting from the few wayfarers in the inn. The mother was keeping her children close, and even the old woman was watching him, looking between Caleb and the young boy with the kind of protective glare Caleb was familiar with from his brief interactions with Ziya's mother.

This is probably why they don't let soldiers stay here, Caleb thought, keeping to himself as he sat down at the table farthest from the others. *Everyone here is trying to escape horror, and I'm a reminder and a threat.* He sighed. If he hadn't been on a mission to find Alan, he would have left that very second. The last thing he wanted to do was cause fear and misery for those who had managed to escape it.

"You're welcome to a late breakfast if you're willing to wash up," Mira said, breaking into Caleb's thoughts as she came out of the back room, somehow still as busy and good-natured as she had been the night before, despite how little sleep Caleb imagined she'd gotten after showing him the ropes and then getting up early for the guests. "There's some bread and cheese left."

"Thank you," Caleb said and got to his feet, glad for the excuse to leave the main area and the prying eyes of the village's guests. With his dragon's hearing, he could tell that the guests relaxed once he was gone; he could hear the children playing more freely and could hear a conversation striking up now that he was out of sight.

He didn't say much as he washed the dishes alongside Mira, and she didn't press him for conversation. Instead, she busied herself with other chores, starting a few things for lunch and sweeping the crumbs off the floor. He thought he could see some magic at work, too, helping her complete her duties faster than Caleb could keep up.

Had Mira grown up outside the village, talent like hers would have been seized the second anyone connected to the army realized her power. Watching her do something as mundane as cleaning with her magic was so jarring that Caleb nearly dropped a plate when he saw a brush zoom past him. Open magic, peaceful quiet . . . this place was like no other he'd ever been.

Still, he didn't ask her about her magic. He didn't ask about her father. He didn't want to rouse suspicion, so he waited until he was seated in a chair in the kitchen gratefully breaking off small pieces of bread to pop in his mouth before he asked, "Is that everyone who's escaped to your village?"

Mira might have been more good-natured than her father, but that didn't mean she was naïve enough not to be suspicious of his question. She narrowed her eyes and stopped short of handing him the bit of cheese she'd promised. "No one is allowed to come here to cause trouble. Don't make me regret arguing with my father. He'll never let me forget that he was right and I was wrong."

Caleb held up the hand that wasn't holding bread. "I swear I don't want to disturb the peace that you've set up for yourselves. Really. But like I told your father last night, my commander went missing recently, and if he's here, you've already got trouble in store; you just don't know it yet."

Mira shook her head. "You've seen how my father reacts to soldiers. Everyone else in this village would do the same. That's the rule: soldiers can't stay here. We won't turn away anyone in real need—like you and your lack of clothes—but according to our rules, you'll have to leave before sunset tonight. If your commander was here, he was turned away."

"He was injured," Caleb said softly. "He ran away after losing a battle."

Mira hesitated just long enough for Caleb to realize that, in the silence, he could hear her breathing becoming shallower.

"Mira, he tortured me and several others. He chained me down on my hands and knees and treated me like an animal," Caleb said. His tone was gentle, but his words were sharp and urgent. "If he's here—"

"No," Mira said, shaking her head, though she was still visibly nervous. "We had an injured soldier ask for food and shelter, but he's not anything like that. He stays in his room because he can't move well, but he. . . ." She pushed the cheese into his chest with more force than necessary. "No. He's been nothing but kind to me and my father. He's even helped me perfect a few spells to help with the chores—to earn his keep."

"What kind of spells?" Caleb asked in a bare whisper that carried some smoke with it. He hoped, belatedly, that she hadn't noticed.

"Nothing elaborate. I already knew some household magic; he helped me learn to do multiple spells at once. I'd been having a hard time learning from the other wizards here, and he showed me a few tricks I've never tried that work wonders for concentration." She seemed to realize in the short silence after her explanation that her concentration had, in fact, been disrupted and that her sweeping spells were no longer active. She swore, waved and hand, and got the brushes moving again. "Why do you care?"

"My commander was a wizard," Caleb explained, putting in real effort to keep his tone even and his fear and anger in check so that he wouldn't let out any more smoke. "Part of the way he tortured me was forcing me to drink a potion. This injured man hasn't given you anything to drink, has he?"

Mira shook her head, her eyes wide. "No, nothing like that. Like I said, he's been helping me do my chores."

Caleb relaxed slightly, but he knew he wouldn't be able to leave until he found out for sure who that wizard was. "Did he give you a name?"

"Des," Mira replied.

Caleb turned the bread over in his hands a few times, thinking over his argument carefully. The people in this village wouldn't trust him easily, but he wouldn't be able to live with himself if Alan brought down fire and torment on those who had managed to avoid that very thing for so long. "I'd like to see him," he said at last.

"No."

"I know how it sounds," Caleb said, pressing ahead, having expected that reaction. "And I swear to you that I won't do anything if he's not who I think he is. I don't care which colors he wore in the war. I don't care what he's running from. But if he's my commander, I have to take him with me. He *can't* stay in this village. He's dangerous."

"He's injured, and besides that, he's already agreed to leave as soon as he's recovered."

"Please," Caleb said, gesturing with both hands, the bread and cheese long forgotten. "Please. You don't know what he's capable of." When Mira kept frowning, her arms crossed, holding onto her elbows, he sighed. "If you're not careful, he'll do this to you," he said, allowing *some* of his power to show. With a harsh snort, he sent smoke out of his nose, enough to be visible long after the initial breath.

It was a gamble, he knew. After all that effort hiding what he was, he could have brought down the very fight both he and the villagers were trying to avoid. But so far, Mira hadn't given him a reason not to trust her, and he hoped that she would be shocked enough to listen.

As soon as she saw the smoke, Mira took a step back and grabbed the nearest knife from its cutting board, holding it in front of her with a shaking hand—but in a grip that told Caleb she wasn't nearly as inexperienced with a knife as he had once been with a sword. "What are you?" she demanded.

"I'm what my commander, Alan, decided to make me," Caleb said, holding his hands out in front of him. Yes, he'd taken a risk showing her his power, but he wasn't going to be *reckless* and look like a bigger threat. "He poured dragon fire into my body to create a weapon of war." He paused and saw a look of dawning horror creep over Mira's expression to overtake her suspicion and her fear. "And it *hurt*."

"I . . . it . . . he. . . ." Mira struggled a few more times to form a response, though she never lowered the knife. "How do I know you won't burn down our village?"

"If I were going to do that, don't you think I'd have done it by now?" Caleb didn't drop her gaze. "Please, I'm just asking to *see* this guest of yours. If he's who he says he is, no one has anything to fear. I'll leave immediately. I can survive on my own for a while."

"I'll bet you can," Mira muttered under her breath.

Caleb smirked. "I hate what he did to me, and I'll never forgive him for what he put me through, but it does have its advantages," he admitted. "So please, let me see him. And then I'll leave and never look back, I swear."

Mira watched Caleb for a long time—longer than he'd thought she would take to answer and long enough that he started to feel uncomfortable under her gaze, wondering what she was looking for. He hadn't lied to her, and he could use that knowledge to meet her gaze steadily, without blinking. But she seemed to be searching him for something *more*.

Finally, she nodded once, sharply. She didn't lower her knife. "I will take you to see him," she said, slowly and carefully. "But on my terms."

"Of course," he said, relieved she'd agreed to that much and hadn't yet run off to tell her father and the other villagers about the monster in their midst.

"First of all," she said, enunciating every syllable through her teeth, "I don't care if he is the man you're looking for. You will not attack him in my inn. If he's who you say he is, I can get my father and some of the others, and we'll escort you *both* out so you can work out your grudge away from our village. But you will *not* bring your fight to our homes."

"Agreed." He'd expected a demand like that, given how jealously the villagers guarded their safe haven. And even if she hadn't asked it of him, he would have tried to keep her village from harm anyway. He had never seen any place like this; he'd never seen a village untouched by war. He'd never seen magic in the open or refugees being fed without begging. This place was all the good in humanity the dragons wanted to deny; he couldn't possibly wreck their hard-earned peace and quiet.

"Second of all," Mira said, barely acknowledging that he'd accepted her first terms, "I will be right beside you, and I'm taking this with me." She moved the point of the knife up with a flick of her wrist. "If you go back on your word, I'll do what I have to do to keep my home safe."

For one, brief moment, Caleb thought he might call her bluff. He knew intimately how hard it could be to take a life, how that choice lingered, how even the excuse of self-defense did nothing to dull the ache in his chest when he thought of the lives he'd extinguished, how he could *still* see the face of the half-dragon he'd killed by his own request.

But on the other hand, peace in the middle of war could only be maintained with sharp defenses. He'd seen the archers on the outskirts of the village. Mira might have hesitated to kill a human, but she might well have dealt with her share of dragons, especially if she had any magical skill to speak of. If she knew how to do more than clean with her spells, the knife was the least of his worries. The threat of death from someone who had already sullied their soul with the violence of war was too credible to ignore.

So, he simply nodded. "Agreed," he said. "Now, please, take me to see Des. I think you'll sleep better if we act fast, so I can leave your village behind as quickly as possible."

"Fine." She gestured for him to get to his feet, still holding her knife up. "Just so you know, I still don't trust you."

"You trusted me more before you saw what my commander did to me."

"I saw a boy about my age with no clothes and nowhere else to go."

"But now that I'm a threat, you don't see that boy anymore?" Caleb got to his feet slowly. "I didn't do this to myself, you know."

"No, but you admitted that you're willing to use it. You aren't hiding away and trying to start a new life. You're using what he gave you and making yourself a weapon just like he wanted you to be," Mira replied coldly. "You're hunting him down. Tell me that isn't exactly the kind of thing a commander would want someone like you to do."

Caleb stopped short, losing all of the color to his face. "I—I'm not like him," he stammered, though the words sounded hollow to his own ears. He'd said them so many times—how many times? How often did he have to repeat the lie to make himself believe it, to erase from his memory all the times Alan had pointed out their similarities and even *praised* him for them?

What made him so convinced he was different from Alan, anyway? He had been willing to kill soldiers to get his own freedom. He'd killed more when he had stormed Alan's base to rescue dragons. Once, when he was young and had no power to speak of, he had said that he would never fight in a war; now, he stood before an innkeeper bargaining for the chance to capture a war criminal.

Only the smallest of differences remained: Caleb refused to torment and humiliate those he defeated. He was willing to fight and willing to lie and willing to join a quest for revenge, but he had never stooped to torture. He had never been *cruel*.

THE GODS' GIFT

He hoped that crucial detail was enough to matter in the grand scheme of things. *He* thought it did, but the more people compared him to Alan, the more he wondered if that was true.

Caleb forced himself to swallow his shock and hurt, closed his eyes, settled the knot in his stomach, pushed it down so he could ignore it the way he used to ignore hunger and humiliation when he was a refugee, and then looked Mira's way again. "I promised myself—and I promised others—that I wouldn't let Alan do this to anyone else," he said, feeling steadier as he reminded himself that he was acting on behalf of others, not himself, unlike Alan. "If that makes me the weapon he wanted me to be, so be it. But I can't let him go on torturing people when I have the power to stop him."

"Noble words. We'll see how true they are," Mira said. The bright-eyed girl that had greeted him at the door the previous night was completely gone; she couldn't afford to trust him, and he understood that. She gestured for him to walk ahead of her and finally lowered the knife—if only so she wouldn't draw suspicion from anyone they might pass on their way to see this mysterious guest. She still kept her grip on it, so Caleb kept his distance, wordlessly following her directions to the correct room.

Once they arrived, Mira stopped and pointed at him with the hand that wasn't holding a knife. "Remember your promise. And if you scare him and he's not who you think he is, you *will* apologize. We promised him this would be a safe haven while he healed."

Caleb put his hand over his heart. "I promise."

Mira let out a huff of a sound that didn't indicate one way or the other whether she believed him. Then, she knocked on the door and opened it slightly so she could peek in. "Des? Are you awake?" she called out.

"Come in," the guest replied, and Caleb froze, holding his breath. This close to seeing Alan again, Caleb suddenly realized that he didn't *want* to confront Alan. He knew he had agreed to find him, and he knew it was the right thing to do, but he suddenly couldn't get his feet to cooperate with him and take the few steps forward to enter the room. He suddenly didn't want to confirm who was inside.

Stop being such a child, Caleb chided himself. *Ziya and Lioia are waiting for you; what are you going to tell them when you go back, that you let him get away because you couldn't face your fears?* With that, he nodded, trying to convince himself with his actions before his mind caught up to his body's decision. He strode past the door—and once again froze when he saw Alan lying in the bed, propped up against an old, wooden headboard, a tray of food remnants on the three-legged table at his side.

Alan looked more *vulnerable* than Caleb had ever seen him look before. Apparently, his fight with Rikaa and Aonai had been more damaging than he'd let on, and Caleb took no small measure of glee in that, considering how badly hurt Rikaa and Aonai had both been after fighting Alan. Alan had bandages across his arms, and judging by the way his clothes hung loosely at his chest, Caleb had to guess that he was wrapped around the middle as well. He looked pale—likely from blood loss—despite the wicked gleam in his eye when he saw Caleb.

"Hello, Caleb," Alan said, his mouth pulled back in a cruel smile that carried echoes of his power despite his injuries. "You've come a long way just to find me."

Caleb forced himself to meet Alan's gaze and ignored the way his stomach twisted until he was convinced he would never want to eat again, not when he felt so sick. "I came all this way to stop you."

Alan chuckled and pushed himself up so that he wasn't lying back in the pillows anymore. He didn't stand—Caleb wasn't sure if he could or if he was playing up his injuries to take advantage of Mira's kind heart. "That doesn't sound like you, Caleb. That sounds like Ziya." When Caleb bared his teeth, Alan chuckled again. "Where is she, then? Waiting outside the village like a good pet?"

"Leave her alone, Alan," Caleb replied, every word dripping in a growl that made Mira take several steps away from him and draw up her knife again.

"Who's Ziya?" Mira demanded.

Alan laughed. "I see. You thought he was a lost waif, didn't you?" he told Mira. "He's always been good at drumming up sympathy, coming up with the right stories." His eyes sparkled with malice. "Caleb lied his way through life until he was caught lying about his age. I plucked him out of the rank and file and offered him a chance to be something better, and he's upset with me because it *hurt*." He let out a moan as he shifted. Caleb didn't believe that moan. "Ziya is a dragon, Mira. She probably brought him here to drag me out to her so she can kill me herself. She hates me, and she's convinced Caleb to hate me as well."

"Ziya was turned into a dragon *against her will*, just like Alan tried to turn me into a weapon," Caleb shot back, still growling. "Don't lie, Alan."

"I didn't lie, Caleb," Alan said calmly. "Before you met Ziya, you were afraid of me. You never would have sought me out. She's turned you into a weapon right alongside her." He smiled cruelly. "I'm almost proud. I asked her to bring you back to me so I could put you both on the right path, and she's already done so much of my work for me."

Caleb felt his teeth elongating as he snarled, "Leave her out of this. I won't ask you again."

Alan didn't look the least bit intimidated. If anything, he laughed more when he saw Caleb's display. "And now what are you going to do, hmm?" He gestured at himself. "I'm injured and unarmed. Are you going to murder me in cold blood? I doubt you have that in you, no matter what Ziya has charmed you into thinking about your revenge quest." He laughed again. "You've fallen for her, haven't you? I thought you abhorred violence, but in pursuit of a beautiful dragon—"

The growl Caleb let out reverberated through the room so that everyone present could feel it in every inch of their bodies. He could feel himself getting taller and could feel his claws itching at the tips of his fingers, ready to burst out so he could use them, so he could kill Alan.

Except. . . .

He saw, out of the corner of his eye, that Mira had her knife raised as she looked between the two of them. Caleb *had* promised her that he wouldn't fight Alan in the middle of her inn. He *had* promised that he wouldn't put any more innocent lives in danger.

So, he tried to swallow down his growl. "You're coming with me," he said through his teeth. "And if you try to hurt me or anyone else, I will do what I have to do."

"Attack me?" Alan gestured outward with both hands. "Really? If you're looking for a fight, I'm happy to give you one, but you should know that I will burn this place to the ground the second you move."

Caleb froze, and in the silence, he heard Mira bite out a choice swear word.

Alan laughed again. "I'm sorry, Mira. I don't want to see your inn burned down any more than you do, but Caleb is being unreasonable. I'm not going to let him drag me away; I have to fight back. You understand that, don't you?"

"I heard what you said," Mira said through her teeth without agreeing with either one of them—which was a relief for Caleb to hear. He'd honestly been worried that she had studied for too long underneath him and that she would stand by him because of his lessons . . . and the fact that, at the moment, he looked more human than Caleb did. He hadn't growled or let smoke out of his nose, after all. He was, in the eyes of anyone who didn't know him, a defenseless, weak, injured man.

"Then you wouldn't mind escorting Caleb out of here, would you?" Alan flashed her a smile that would have been warmer if it met his eyes. "He's threatening me."

"He is." Mira turned toward Caleb, and he took an instinctive step back, nervous for the first time about someone other than Alan. He didn't fear her knife, but he did fear what spells Alan might have taught her, not the mention any spells she might have known by virtue of growing up in a village besieged by dragons long before the current war took root.

"Mira," Caleb started to say, but she shook her head at him, and something in her expression convinced him to close his mouth and wait.

"Thank you, Mira," Alan said, leaning back into his pillows. "Don't you worry. I'll teach you magic that will keep him from bringing any dragons here for his revenge."

"I wasn't worried," Mira said—and turned so quickly that neither Caleb nor Alan had enough time to stop her. In a flash, she got to Alan's bedside to grab his staff and point it at him.

Once she had the staff in her hands, she wasn't, however, fast enough to cast her spell in enough time to prevent the two men in the room from reacting. As soon as she grabbed the staff, three things happened in quick succession: Alan snarled his displeasure with enough smoke dripping out of his mouth that Caleb knew he had a raging fire in his throat; Caleb threw himself forward to try to

THE GODS' GIFT

put his body between Alan's fire and Mira; and Mira issued a freezing spell from her staff.

Caleb was caught between the fire and ice, but with his back to the fire, the ice was the bigger problem, especially for a white dragon.

His blood ran cold, his lips turned blue, and he passed out.

CHAPTER 7: A FROZEN DRAGON

Caleb's return to consciousness came in the form of a boot in his side.

Someone kicked him hard enough to jolt him awake and leave a quickly-forming bruise near his ribs, and he gasped, instinctively curling in a smaller ball, surprised that he hadn't changed into a dragon. But then, as soon as he was awake, he realized he was shivering. He was coated in a light frost, the remnants of Mira's freezing spell, and he could hardly move or think clearly because he was so cold.

It took him, for example, far too long to realize that someone was shouting at him, even longer to recognize the voice as belonging to Mira's father, and longer still to figure out what the words were:

"What did you do? What happened to Mira?"

Caleb fought against the pull of his eyelids, though his body wanted desperately to slip back into unconsciousness. White dragons lived for fire, especially the heat inside active volcanoes, so ice could do more damage to Caleb than any swords or arrows could have hoped to do. He'd almost frozen to death once before, and now, he felt just as tired and weak as he had then.

"Answer me!" Mira's father demanded, and Caleb realized his eyes had drifted shut only when he opened them to look up at him. The man looming over Caleb looked more scared than angry, desperate for answers, desperate for his daughter.

Slowly, Caleb blinked around the room. Alan was gone, and so was Mira. There were scorch marks in the floor around Caleb, but the fire, thankfully, hadn't spread—possibly because of Mira's spell. She'd been smart to use ice against Alan when she knew that Alan had been pouring fire into people. If Caleb hadn't gotten in the way, Alan would have been gravely injured, possibly dead or dying.

But then Mira would also have been dead. White dragon fire was hotter than any other kind of fire, and Caleb didn't think her ice spell would have stood up against Alan's fire breath.

Caleb could still hear Mira's father barking questions at him, so he forced his mind back to the present, with real difficulty. He was freezing, and he realized, belatedly, that his shirt had been burned clean off where it touched his back, exposing his bare skin to the cool air. His shirt was sticking to him around his chest, though, because Mira's spell had frozen everything in place.

Mira's father kicked Caleb in the side again, and he winced, sure that another kick like that would break something. He couldn't transform into a white dragon when he was this cold; he'd die in that form. But that left him too vulnerable to blows from an angry father.

"Stop," he whispered, the single word hanging over his mouth in cold droplets.

To his surprise, Mira's father did stop, apparently satisfied that Caleb was now awake enough to answer his demands for answers. He crouched down, glaring at Caleb, one finger in his face. "I knew I shouldn't have let you in," he practically snarled at Caleb.

"I know." Caleb groaned and tried to sit up, surprised but grateful when Mira's father helped him do that much. The man might have been furious and terrified of losing his daughter, but he could plainly see that Caleb needed help too. "C-cold," he stuttered, and Mira's father sighed.

"Don't die," he said. It sounded more like an order than like concern.

Caleb closed his eyes all the same, unable to resist the pull of unconsciousness. He woke up again, quickly, when Mira's father knelt down beside him and shook him hard. While he'd been unconscious, Mira's father had moved him to Alan's bed and propped him up so that he could take the hot broth being pressed into his hands.

As soon as the warm bowl touched his hands, Caleb could feel his body reaching out to the heat. He gulped the broth down gratefully, relishing the warm feeling as it ran down his throat and heated his insides. Already, the blankets were taking away the sting of the frost still clinging to him, and the broth did the rest of the work so that Caleb at least felt like he was ready to rejoin the land of the living.

He gulped down the contents of the bowl and then set it aside, clenching his hands in the fabric of the blankets clinging to him to try to get them to stop shaking. "I'm s-sorry," he stammered, unable to keep his teeth from chattering no matter how warm the broth was. He brought his hands up to his face and breathed hard, and the barest line of smoke reached his palms. He sighed and rubbed his hands over his arms, trying to generate heat that way. He needed to warm up faster, or he'd be no help to Mira—or to Lioia and Ziya, for that matter.

"I don't want apologies," Mira's father snapped. "That girl is my world, and you got her taken from me. Where is she?"

"I d-don't know," Caleb said. He rubbed the spot on his chest where the ice spell had hit him squarely in the center of his body. Any higher and it would have hit his heart. He didn't think he would have survived that.

"You're going to have to do better than that, or I'll turn you out right now," Mira's father said.

Caleb nodded, his eyes screwed shut, though even his thoughts were slow to change in the cold. "He was my c-commander," he stuttered. "A magician. A t-torturer. I d-don't know if he was as injured as he p-pretended to be. I can't guess how f-far he's gotten."

Mira's father letting out a frustrated sound and then paced a small circle that took him away from Caleb. Then, he came back around and put his finger in Caleb's face. "This is your fault."

"It's his," Caleb replied. Yes, he had been the one to seek out a confrontation, and he would absolutely have taken the blame if Mira and her father had been housing any other soldier and that person had attacked Caleb for being from Hayna. But Alan manipulated people and circumstances to get his way; he had to have been planning possible exits for some time. He would likely have taken Mira with him regardless of whether or not Caleb had found him. And Caleb was done taking the blame for *Alan's* actions. "I'm s-sorry he reacted to my presence, b-but he was training Mira. He invested too much in her to leave her behind."

THE GODS' GIFT

Mira's father slammed his fist against the wall. "This is why we don't take in soldiers."

Caleb nodded, still rubbing his arms. He felt like he was getting the feeling back in his extremities, at least. "How long has it been since they left?"

"I don't know," Mira's father replied. "Usually, Mira handles Des herself. I only came here because she hadn't gotten the meals ready, and I was starting to wonder about his intentions." He scoffed. "I was right, but I wish I'd been right about what I thought he wanted from her. At least she knows what to do with men like that." He gestured to Caleb's bedridden form. "Thought that might have been what happened to you, to be honest, until I realized Des was gone too."

Caleb frowned, not at all liking the implication. "I wouldn't—"

"That's not the most important argument right now, soldier." Mira's father turned sharply on his heel. "I'll be right back. Don't lose consciousness again. I can't promise I won't break something if I have to hit you again to wake you up."

"Got it," Caleb promised, though he doubted his voice carried enough to reach Mira's father when he was already in the hall.

But that left Caleb in the cold, clutching blankets tightly to his body as he shook feeling back into his fingers and blew as much smoke over himself as he could manage. The warmer he felt, the more smoke he was able to generate, so the process sped up the longer he kept at it. But it was exhausting work, drawing the last of his energy when the cold kept inviting him back to sleep.

More than that, it was exhausting to keep his mind and body working on a task as trivial as staying warm when he knew Alan was out there with an innocent young woman. And Alan, Caleb knew, wouldn't hesitate to use her as a shield.

As much as he hated to admit it to himself, Caleb wasn't sure how effective that shield would be. Ziya had been careful to warn the dragons about the innocents among Alan's soldiers, so Caleb trusted *her* not to attack Mira, but Lioia was another matter entirely. And even Ziya might make the wrong move if Alan told her that Mira was his latest apprentice. If Caleb couldn't get out of that bed, if he couldn't get to Alan and Mira in time, he couldn't warn his allies on both sides not to be tricked into turning against each other.

He had to get up. *Now.*

By the time Mira's father came back, Caleb had forced himself into feeling well enough to at least attempt to chase Alan down. He didn't think he could risk transforming even after he left the village —because he still felt shaky and slow and didn't think his dragon body could handle that—but he no longer felt like he was on the verge of death.

Rikaa had warned him that charging after Alan was a foolhardy move, but Caleb had assumed his friend simply meant that he and Ziya were letting their hearts lead without a real strategy for killing the man who had tormented them for so long. Now, Caleb realized that, in his wisdom, Rikaa had meant to warn him that he and Ziya hadn't looked far enough ahead to understand who *else* might be affected by their stumbling attempts at justice. And Mira was now paying the price. He had to get to her, or he would have her fate on his conscience.

So, Caleb pushed against the bed, straining to get to his feet, but he gasped and slumped back. He was feeling warmer, but now, his ribs protested each movement. But Caleb didn't say *why* he couldn't get up; he doubted Mira's father would give him any sympathy when he had been the one to inflict those wounds in the first place.

Wordlessly, Mira's father handed him another bowl of broth, and Caleb drank it down as quickly and hungrily as he had the first one. Only once Caleb set aside the bowl did Mira's father speak up again. "Tell me about your commander," he said. "Tell me what spells can stop him."

"We need to find Mira before we can worry about that kind of thing," Caleb pointed out. Then, when her father glared at him, Caleb winced and amended his statement. "She was right to try a freezing spell, though. He likes spells that have fire, and he's even poured dragon fire into people to get what he wants." He didn't dare elaborate with any personal details. He had *barely* trusted Mira with part of his secret; he didn't trust her father with even a hint of it in himself. "I saw it in person. I saw people burning up from the inside. But when it worked, it was deadly."

"Do you think that's what he wanted from my daughter?"

Caleb shook his head quickly. "No, I asked her if he'd tried to get her to take a potion. His process would require her to drink the

fire into her body. I think he was looking for another apprentice."
He stretched his legs experimentally over the side of the bed. He felt
strong enough to try walking. "His last apprentice died in the battle
that left him with those wounds."

"You sound like you were there."

"I was."

"And you let him get away?"

"I didn't mean to," Caleb said. "He caught me when I was trying to save the people he had captured. The only reason I escaped
was luck and good friends."

Mira's father narrowed his eyes, his gaze focused away from
Caleb. "I see."

Caleb didn't respond when he knew that no words could comfort a worried father. Instead, he pushed himself to his feet, finding his balance slowly. For one worrying moment, he saw the world
through a tunnel, but then, his vision cleared, and he nodded to
himself as if that would keep him upright. "She'll be alright as long
as she doesn't take that potion. Anything else can be undone."

"Good," Mira's father said, holding onto his walking stick
tighter, something powerful flashing behind his eyes. It wasn't the
same kind of power that Caleb had seen in the gazes of dragons like
Rikaa and Aonai, but it had the same spark.

Magic.

Caleb almost laughed. He should have realized that walking stick was more than that, the way Mira's father gripped it like
a weapon. "How many wizards does this village have, exactly?"

Mira's father responded with a grim smirk. "Everyone here
learns basic magic as soon as they're old enough to bear the responsibility. We live on the edge of ancient dragon territory—or did you
forget about *that* enemy because human armies managed to find and
tame a few?"

Caleb reached for the bedside table to steady himself but managed to stay upright without needing the crutch. "I grew up thinking
there weren't any wild dragons left," he said. "Where I'm from, the
dragon wars are legends."

"You believe that because you only think about what affects
you." Mira's father shook his head. "You're young."

"I can't help that."

"No, you can't." Mira's father set his shoulders and gave Caleb an appraising look, still gripping his walking stick tightly. "Do you think you can make it? If I must, I can go without you, but you're the one who knows what your commander and his dragon curses can do."

"I can make it," Caleb said—with far more confidence than his body had in the promise of his words.

Mira's father gave him a look that said exactly what he thought of Caleb's lie but didn't speak, instead offering Caleb his shoulder to lean on. Caleb stumbled a few steps and winced when he realized that Mira's father had to throw his hand out against the wall to keep them both upright. But the more steps he took, the more confident he felt in his body.

Finally, at the bottom of the stairs that led into the entrance and dining area, Caleb paused, gasping in air as if he'd run all the way down the stairs. He could feel Mira's father watching him but didn't look at him, keeping his gaze to his feet to force himself the rest of the way out of the inn and into the fresh air.

The sun was low in the sky, and Caleb's heart sank. He hadn't realized how long he'd been unconscious. Alan could have been *any-where* by then, disappearing into the wilds beyond the village, flying off into the cloud cover, or finding a place among the cliffs to hide.

No, if he flew off, Lioia and Ziya would have seen him, Caleb corrected himself, though that didn't make him feel any better about Mira's fate.

But the thought reminded him—"I have a favor to ask," Caleb said, leaning less on Mira's father the longer he was in the sunlight. Even though the light was fading, he had been so close to death that the small amount of heat it still gave off was a balm to him.

"You aren't in a position to ask any favors right now."

"Yes, but I'm going to ask one anyway."

Mira's father narrowed his eyes and came to a stop. "Is that what they teach you in the army?" he asked. "Empty confidence and demands?"

"No," Caleb said. "The army didn't teach me anything except cruelty, and I'm doing everything I can to ignore that lesson."

"Was that a threat?"

"No."

THE GODS' GIFT

"Good."

Caleb sighed, swallowing down his irritation in favor of necessity. "My commander used to force dragons under his command. He even recently stole away a few hatchlings. If you see dragons coming after him, don't stop them unless they threaten Mira. The dragons may do our job for us."

"You want me to trust those arrogant beasts with my daughter's life? They'd just as soon kill a human as look at one," Mira's father spit out.

Now, that was an assessment Caleb couldn't ignore. "What do you know about dragons?" he asked as they walked out of the village together.

"A great deal more than you, soldier," he replied gruffly. "My clan and I have sat on the edge of this kingdom since before this was a kingdom. Everyone else might be focused on the war between the Junnin and Hayna, but those of us that live here remember who the *true* enemy is." With every word that Mira's father spoke, his gaze hardened—and Caleb's stomach twisted.

Caleb had spent so long promising Rikaa and every other dragon he'd met that humans weren't the bloodthirsty warmongers dragons remembered from the war between their two species, and here was an entire village full of people ready to prove him wrong. If the council knew about this village—and Caleb was sure they did, considering how close Lioia lived to them—then that would at least partially explain why they hated humans as much as they did. And it only made Caleb's task of convincing them not to rekindle a broader war with humanity that much harder when some humans had never stopped fighting that very war.

"I've worked with dragons before," Caleb said, "in the army."

"That's different," Mira's father said, waving him off. "Those were creatures cowed into servitude. Wild dragons are different matters entirely."

Well, he's not wrong, Caleb thought dryly. "Still," he said, "some of the dragons he captured escaped, and I've seen them searching the skies and the ground. If they found him, I think their revenge would be worth leaving them be for a little while, don't you?"

"I think you're horribly naïve for a soldier who claims to have seen what dragons can do," Mira's father replied shortly. "I'll do whatever is necessary to keep my daughter safe. I won't let a dragon anywhere near her. Do you understand me?"

Caleb let out all his breath. "Yes," he said, his thoughts drifting toward Ziya and Lioia. He doubted Lioia would hold back if she were attacked, and he was already dreading the fight he knew he couldn't avoid if they met up.

He wondered if he'd been right to think that the gods had set out a path for him when, so far, the so-called allies he and Ziya had made had only served to make things worse. Lioia was probably antagonizing Ziya, and Mira's father was rushing into a confrontation that would be that much worse because he was (rightfully) protective of and worried about his daughter.

This had been so much easier when it was just him and Ziya.

ZIYA

CHAPTER 8: HUNTING LESSONS

Ziya had known Lioia for barely more than a day, and she was already coming up with excuses she could give to Caleb when they reunited for why she'd attacked Lioia or left her behind for the humans to shoot down. Not that she'd actually act on any of those fantasies after she'd met Lioia's *hatchlings*—she couldn't possibly bring herself to take a mother away from her children—but the mental exercise kept Ziya from hurting her.

She missed Caleb.

It was funny, actually, how well she and Caleb worked together. They had been a good team on accident when they had tried to escape together, but Ziya had once believed she wouldn't be able to rekindle that when she saw him again purely because Alan had conditioned her to hate Kaal. When they'd met up again, she had been pleasantly surprised by how well they *still* worked together.

She didn't think their alliance was helped by fate or the gods or anything that Kaal had come to believe in, though. As far as she was aware, she and Caleb worked so well together simply because they understood each other in ways no one else possibly could. Very few creatures in the world could say that they had both human and dragon perspectives, and even fewer had kept their minds because of it. Add in the fact that they had been in the same refugee group and were transformed by the same cruel wizard, and they spoke the same language of trauma.

Lioia, on the other hand, seemed to speak only in threats and brash declarations.

Ziya had always believed the dragons were proud to a fault, but Lioia went beyond even Ziya's estimation of dragon haughtiness. She refused to listen to a single good word about humans, and she acted like Ziya was practically a hatchling herself, as if Ziya had nothing to add to their temporary partnership other than information about Alan.

At least the other dragons Ziya had met—like Iuan and Aonai—were willing to let Ziya and Kaal try their hands at leadership, to take back some of the control they'd lost over their own lives. Lioia was trying to position herself as the leader of a mission she had joined the previous evening, and Ziya chafed against another taskmaster.

She missed Caleb. He went out of his way to make sure she never felt like a servant, to make her feel like an equal, even if sometimes she still wound up feeling like a pack animal. And then, when he caught her looking frustrated or upset about her role, he always tried to reassure her.

Ziya often wished that she could transform into a human like Caleb could, but lately, she found herself wishing as much for a different reason. If she could have gone with Caleb, they wouldn't have had to split up. She wouldn't have been stuck with Lioia. She'd get to stick with a partner she actually got along with.

Still, Ziya didn't actually give voice to any of her frustrations. She'd gotten very good during her time with Alan at hiding what she was feeling and at biting back growls and caustic remarks. Even though she'd promised herself that she would stop holding back her thoughts now that she had escaped from Alan's grasp, she found herself relying on those old skills in an attempt to keep the peace. She and Caleb didn't need any more enemies than they already had.

But in biting back her anger, Ziya had nothing to contribute to a conversation, so a pregnant silence stretched on between the two dragons as they scoured the mountainside looking for any hint of another dragon.

Well, silence except for Lioia's occasional orders.

"You're wasting your time," Lioia said in a bored drawl, already flying away from the rock formation that Ziya had thought looked quite promising. It was wide enough that she could slip into it, so it could have been a good hiding place. The moon was full, and since neither Ziya nor Lioia had been able to sleep comfortably in each other's presence, they intended to use the bright night to search for their shared enemy—and bring their uncomfortable alliance to an end quickly.

"He's not looking for a home as big as yours; he's looking for a place to lick his wounds," Ziya shot back, landing on the surface of the rocks near the opening to stick her head in and look around.

To her dismay, she immediately realized Lioia was right: the opening didn't go far enough into the rock to allow a dragon to hide inside, even if it was wide enough at the surface to look like it might. The trees that Ziya had thought would make for good shade and a good hiding place were actually a further detriment to the cave, pushing thick roots through the opening to make it even less inhabitable.

Lioia landed not far from Ziya and looked over the edge of the opening, making a sound from the back of her throat. "What did I say?"

"How was I supposed to know it wasn't that deep?" Ziya challenged her.

"Did you listen to it?"

"*Listen* to it?" Ziya flared her wings out without meaning to. "What's that supposed to mean—listen to it? It's a crack in the rocks!"

Lioia let out a snort that carried embers in its fire. Then, she picked up her wings and flapped them without leaving the ground, letting the sound catch in the grooves of the rock. She resettled her wings and then tipped her head pointedly toward Ziya. "You can hear the wind as your wings force it toward the ground. Listen to your surroundings. Deep cracks invite the wind inside, but shallow cracks stop it short." And if Lioia had simply given Ziya her explanation, Ziya might even have thanked her. She had appreciated all the help Aonai gave her as he taught her more about the ways of dragons than Alan ever had; she had thanked *him*. But unlike Aonai, Lioia wasn't a gracious teacher, and she couldn't resist snapping at Ziya: "Don't you know anything?"

Ziya could feel the tips of her wings pushing out even farther than they already had. "I have only been a dragon for a few months," she pointed out through her bared teeth. "I spent most of that time being tortured. You can't expect me to know anything but how to fight."

"I would have thought they'd teach you how to look for a renegade dragon, in case one slipped away like you and Kaal claim to have done."

"Claim?" Ziya repeated, her fire hot in the back of her throat, waiting to be used. She wasn't going to let that word choice slip; she was tired of being questioned on every front. The council had accused her of treachery; Alan had accused her of being utterly unremarkable, and Lioia now accused her of being a liar. No one cared about her unless they could tear her down—no one but Caleb and his newfound family of dragons, anyway. And Aonai, but he cared out of misplaced guilt.

Lioia matched Ziya's defensive posture with her own flared wings and bared teeth. "I already said I don't trust you," she snarled. "I believe you want to kill the wizard, or I wouldn't have gone with you. But I don't believe every word of your stories. I know you're hiding something from me. And when you do as humans always do and turn on the dragons you claim to ally yourself with, I will strike you down."

"Or maybe we haven't told you every detail of our lives because we don't want to relive our abuse each time someone demands answers from us," Ziya growled. "You're looking for excuses. You've already decided to hate me and Kaal."

"You're human," Lioia replied. "Our two species might not be at total war, but in the places where humans and dragons meet, there is always a fight." She gestured with her tail toward the village where Caleb was searching for Alan. "That settlement alone has caused more issues for my clan that anything or anyone else until this Alan creature came along. Those humans never agreed to the truce with the dragons. They still hone their magic to kill us." She let out a haughty snort. "They may stay away from your war, but that does not mean they are peaceful."

"And yet, not every settlement does that," Ziya shot back. But when Lioia glared and flared her claws, Ziya realized they were veering dangerously close to a physical confrontation instead of a mere war of words. And so, rather than fight a dragon she knew she couldn't beat, she forced herself to relax her posture and to look

THE GODS' GIFT

more submissive—another skill that she'd once sworn she would never use after escaping Alan. Caleb thought that the dragons were wonderful protectors, but Ziya had to react to them the same way she reacted to her tormentors' in captivity. They were nothing but bullies, to her mind. "I'm tired of this argument," Ziya said, her tone purposefully soft, even if she couldn't quite pull her claws all the way back. "I'm tired of listening to dragons blame me and Kaal for every wrong humans have ever done. *You* wanted to come with us, and *you* invited yourself along, but all you want to do is blame me for things that happened before I was born. Either stop holding me accountable for wars I was too young to know about and for the horrors inflicted on me by exactly the kinds of humans you claim to hate or stop pretending to be my ally, even temporarily." She lifted her chin to meet Lioia's gaze. Even though she no longer looked like she was poised for a physical fight, she didn't hold back the fire in her eyes. "I spent too long under Alan's thumb being told that I was nothing but a weapon. I won't listen to anyone else who says the same things he does."

Lioia looked stunned, her mouth open enough that Ziya could see the light of the fire in the back of her throat cooling off. And yet, after a few sputtered attempts to refute Ziya's accusations, Lioia simply gave up.

In tense silence, then, they scoured the cliffs and forests, keeping within eyesight of each other but maintaining more distance than they had before. And without the distraction of conversation, Ziya could better recall the advice Lioia had given her, even if it had been couched in an insult.

She glanced over her shoulder to check that Lioia wasn't watching before she positioned herself so that her body was flush with the rocks and flapped her wings mightily. In response, the wind underneath her wings rushed at the rocks and then back to her, carrying with it the sound of the cliff—but not in a way that Ziya could immediately parse.

Ziya frowned, still hovering close to that section of the cliff. She could see several openings crisscrossing the red-brown mountainside, but checking each of them could take some time. Lioia would be able to search an entire mountain with her wind trick in the time it took Ziya to check that section of cave-like pockmarks.

Besides, Ziya did actually want to learn how to use her body to her own advantage. She might not have asked to be a dragon, but she had long ago accepted that she could be a weapon of war if she *chose* to be, that she could bring an end to monsters like Alan if she sharpened her claws and her teeth and learned more than what little Alan had allowed her to know. So, she tried again, straining to hear what the wind brought back to her when she beat her wings—just once—close to the scattered fissures.

This time, she thought she could hear a slight difference in the way the sound returned to her. Curious, she approached the gaps, landing near one that looked deep. When she peered inside, she saw that it went on for some time, so she blew fire into it. The flames caught in the dry roots of dead plants, but even with the added light, Ziya could see nothing but rocks and a now-dead snake, its skin charred black from her fire.

Ziya moved on to another crack in the rocks, this one too shallow to hide anything more than a couple lizards and an old bird's nest. Nodding to herself, Ziya pushed off from the cliffside and then stayed in the air close to the caves she had explored. She couldn't understand what the sounds coming from the cliff meant without context. Now that she knew where she could listen to the sounds of one deep and one shallow opening, she could learn to identify depth—and could use that knowledge to search the rest of the cliffside.

At first, Ziya still couldn't tell the difference in sound between the two caves. Both of them sounded like the rush of air and the beat of leathery wings that she had learned at a young age to identify as an oncoming dragon and a portend of death and fire. Hearing her own winds amplified back to her reminded her yet again how much she hated her new body. Even the sound of her own flight brought to mind all that the war had taken from her.

Still, she tried several more times, beating her wings close to the rocks and straining to hear what Lioia could hear. After half a dozen attempts, Ziya finally heard the slight difference: the deeper opening had a lower pitch and a richer sound than the shallow one, which dispersed the wind and had no echo.

Satisfied, Ziya flew away from the openings she had already explored and tried the same experiment in a few other places. An opening that looked long and narrow sounded deeper toward the middle, so she landed to explore it. To her delight, she had been correct in her assessment form the air: the fissure deepened not far from where she had landed, and a family of goats had made their home there.

She could hear terrified bleating the moment she landed, and she very nearly felt bad for the poor animals. She wasn't hungry, so they had no reason to fear her—but they didn't know that. So, she took off from the cliffside once again, now much more confident in her ability to search from the sky as Lioia did. She wasn't as confident in her search as Lioia was, and she still had to land more often to check cracks in the rock that didn't quite sound deep *or* shallow, but she made better time than she ever would have done on her own.

This is why Kaal didn't completely chase her off from our alliance, Ziya thought. *I'll have to thank him later. His level head is going to keep us alive.*

By the time the first streaks of pink and purple colored the sky, she was in a much better mood than she had been when Caleb left. And the distance seemed to have done Lioia some good as well; the green dragon didn't go out of her way to avoid Ziya when they both came back to the outcropping they had chosen as their hiding spot. As the sky shifted from purple to blue, both Ziya and Lioia knelt down in the loose dirt, resting their wings after a long hunt. Now that dawn had arrived, they might sleep to avoid the keen eyes of the humans on the watchtowers—if they could relax.

And yet, neither Ziya nor Lioia went to sleep. Ziya stretched her muscles and watched the sunrise, while Lioia watched every motion Ziya made with an intensity that made Ziya uncomfortable. At first, Ziya thought Lioia might simply have been wary or distrustful, but the longer Lioia stared at her, the less patience Ziya had for her presence. She'd been studied before; she didn't like it.

"What?" Ziya asked, unable to stand the silence any longer.

"I'm considering our options," Lioia said.

"We should be resting."

"We can do more than rest," Lioia argued, turning away from Ziya to look toward the human village as a low hum of noise signaled the start of the daily bustle of human activity. Soon, the whole village would sound like mixed conversations, and the scents of dozens of different breakfasts being made would waft toward the hiding dragons. "You said yourself you don't know anything about your new body except how to hurt humans. I don't know if you can do what I'd like to suggest."

At least she'd being honest with me. And she didn't insult me this time, Ziya reminded herself in the interest of maintaining the peace between her and Lioia. She sighed, shook her head, and pointed out, "I won't know unless you tell me and I try it for myself."

"That's what concerns me," Lioia said. "This technique is hard to master in ideal circumstances, and you're practically a hatchling."

"Try me."

Lioia let out a sigh of smoke. "Alright," she said. She let her tail still behind her and stretched so that she was seated comfortably. "There's a way to look for Alan if he is in his dragon form. I don't know if it will work if he is still human, but that's why Kaal is in that village; he's searching for the human, while we search for the dragon."

"Depending on the technique, it might work if he's human," Ziya mused quietly. "Kaal keeps a lot of dragon traits when he changes."

Lioia flicked the end of her tail against the trunk of a tree; Ziya didn't think she'd meant to do it. Dragon tails seemed to have minds of their own when their owners were lost in thought. "Maybe," Lioia said slowly. She watched Ziya for a few seconds longer and then nodded to herself, making her decision physical. "You'd need to find the power within you that the gods gave all dragons. I don't know if you have it, since you weren't made a dragon by the gods but by a wizard trying to emulate the gods. But if you do, you can use it to search for a connection to another such power."

Ziya narrowed her eyes. "I'm not sure I understand."

"Of course not," Lioia said dismissively. "You said yourself you don't know how to be a dragon. What do you know of the gods' gifts?"

"Kaal believes in those stories," Ziya said, automatically defensive even though Lioia was right and she didn't know much about dragon lore and culture. She simply didn't like being talked down to. "He told me what Rikaa taught him while we were traveling together. I know some of the legends; they're nice to listen to after a long day of flying."

The Gods' Gift

"They're more than stories," Lioia said.

"I'm waiting for you to explain how to use this gift of the gods," Ziya said before Lioia could get offended yet again for Ziya's ignorance. For one strange moment, Lioia's sharpness reminded Ziya of Kaal, of the way he got so passionate about his newfound belief in a mission granted by the gods.

Kaal really was better at being a dragon than she was.

Lioia cut through the root of a nearby tree, smoothing out the area around her. "I *did* explain it," she said. "You search for the power inside you and then listen through that power for any others like it."

Ziya let out a soft hiss. "That doesn't clear things up. At all."

"That's not my fault. I didn't raise you."

Ziya's hiss deepened into a growl.

Lioia matched the growl with one of her own. "I'm trying to *aid* you, Ziya. You act like every piece of advice or direction is an insult and then accuse *me* of pride!" She growled again. "You humans are all the same. Warlike."

"And you dragons choke on your haughty morals and don't bother to live up to them," Ziya snapped back. "And your advice comes with insults."

Lioia brought her wings in close to her body, streamlining herself in a position that would allow her to attack if Ziya kept pressing her luck, though she did manage to keep her words civil: "Be that as it may, *I'm* going to look for Alan. You can search for your inner power, if you wish. Or you can sleep. You've had a long journey."

With that, Lioia laid her head on her front legs and closed her eyes, ending the argument with no other fanfare. She wasn't asleep, but she would seem that way to any humans who stumbled upon their hiding place. But Ziya could see that Lioia's breaths weren't deep enough for dreams, and Lioia's body held enough tension in it that she could spring into action as soon as she found the connection she was looking for. She had done as she said she would: she was looking for Alan, and she didn't care what Ziya did while she worked.

That left Ziya sitting in the trees, blinking in silence. She could hear the faint sounds of villagers calling out greetings, but other than that, only the breeze moved the leaves of the trees. As several minutes passed and Lioia remained in the same position, Ziya heard a mouse skitter across the ground, and she heard a bird perch nearby. And still, Lioia didn't move.

I could try looking, she thought, though the very idea left her feeling nauseous. *Or I could stand guard. Lioia can't possibly pay much attention to her surroundings in this state.*

She glanced toward the village and saw a flicker of movement in the archers' towers. The changing of the guard. Yes, she could stand watch for the far-off humans, but then what? She and Lioia hadn't even moved and were hidden well enough in green and black that even a human passing their way on the mountain itself might not notice them while they were both still and quiet.

Stop kidding yourself, Ziya. That's not why you want to stand guard, Ziya chided herself. No, Ziya had to admit that she didn't want to search for the power Lioia mentioned, because she didn't know if she'd find it.

She might have ridiculed Kaal for his sudden conversion to the dragons' beliefs about their place with the gods, but she *had* listened to his stories. And she liked the idea of being part of a species designed to help others, of having a purpose greater than war. But if she looked inside herself and found only a bitter human personality that had been hidden inside a dragon body, she was afraid she'd prove every dragon who railed against her and Kaal right. Everyone kept telling her and Kaal that they weren't real dragons, that they would never be worthy of the mantle dragons wore.

And so, if Ziya looked inside her heart and found no gift from the gods, no power meant for the care of the earth, then she would be what she had long considered herself to be since becoming a dragon: a beast with just enough humanity left within her to fight for justice but who was otherwise nothing but a poor echo of a dragon or a human.

You're letting Alan get to you again. She shook her head and forced herself to focus. Even if she didn't find power when she looked within herself, she would make do. She didn't need the gods to give her added power when she had learned strength from everything else that had happened to her.

She closed her eyes, looking for the same *something* she had once reached for in order to heal Aonai, the same thing she had reached for to save Caleb. Her healing power came from the strength she had as a dragon, and it *had* to be a gift from the gods; what else would the gods gift the creatures tasked with watching over all life but the power to keep life from being lost?

When she reached for that *something*, she could only find the warmth that she felt for Aonai and for Kaal, the love she felt for her mother, and the determination she felt to keep them all alive. It hadn't been dragon emotions that helped her find her healing. In fact, she'd felt more like Neva, her human self, when she thought of her healing and her friendships than she had felt since she'd been changed.

So, no, she didn't feel any power. And she tried to hide her disappointment as she laid her head down on her front legs, glaring into the trees and convincing herself that she was standing watch for Lioia, not pouting.

In the silence, with nothing to do but watch the far-away movements of a bustling village and dream of what she would do if she had human skin again, Ziya could feel her eyelids drooping. She and Lioia were far enough away from the village that, Ziya reasoned, it would be safe to close her eyes, and she gave in to the temptation to nap in the warm sun a few times, drifting in and out of sleep. Each time she woke, she would check her surroundings, make sure Lioia was still breathing despite the fact that she hadn't moved an inch, and then go back to her dreams.

Besides, she never drifted off into such a deep sleep that she wouldn't be able to spring into action. Neva and her mother had been forced to sleep on the road before, and they'd learned how to give their bodies rest while never fully giving in to exhaustion. Ziya was still aware of the sounds around her, and she woke a few times at the snap of a twig or the patter of footfalls. Each time, the interloper turned out to be nothing more dangerous than a small animal, but Ziya wasn't willing to shrug off even the possibility of something worth her attention.

The morning had given way fully to afternoon and was even starting to flirt with evening when Lioia finally took in a deep breath and stretched her legs and wings, pushing her claws all the way into the ground with her stretch. She'd been in one position for so long that Ziya wasn't surprised she felt cramped.

"Well?" Ziya asked, though she didn't expect good news. Lioia had been searching for too long and hadn't jumped into action and anger when she opened her eyes again. If Lioia *had* found Alan, she would have rushed to confront him.

Sure enough, Lioia let out a long, tired-sounding sigh. "The only dragons I could find were you and me," she admitted. "I know there are others beyond the area surrounding this settlement; if we went back the way we came, I'd be able to find my hatchlings and husband. But I can't even find Kaal, and I know he's close by."

Ziya frowned. "Do you think something happened to him?" she asked, not immediately processing her relief at hearing that she did, in fact, have a dragon's power capable of being detected by Lioia's magic when Caleb's fate was more pressing. "If you can't find him. . . ."

Lioia narrowed her eyes. "Maybe," she conceded. "It could also be that I can't hear him when he's in human form."

"He gets into so much trouble, I'm shocked he's still alive," Ziya said. The words constituted a tease, but her tone couldn't quite match up with the words, not when she felt a familiar panic creeping into her throat. This had happened before, when she and several other dragons had sent Caleb into Alan's army base to free Alan's captive dragons. Ziya had been forced to wait outside with her worries and guilt, and when she'd seen him again, he had been writhing at Alan's feet.

She sincerely hoped the sinking feeling in the pit of her stomach was wrong and that she wasn't about to relive another version of that scenario.

Lioia looked toward the village. "Maybe," she said slowly, "we should patrol the outskirts of that settlement."

Ziya didn't hesitate to agree, already stretching out her wings. "Yes. Let's."

CHAPTER 9: A POSSIBLE ASSISTANT

It was nearly sundown when Ziya spotted Alan, walking leisurely out of the village with a young woman by his side.

If Alan had been alone, Ziya wouldn't have hesitated to kill him. She would have waited for Alan to leave the circle of the village's defenses and then snatched him in her jaws before he could transform. She had seen Caleb turn into Kaal a few times now and knew the change wasn't instant. She could take advantage of the gap between forms; Alan would be much easier to kill as a human than as a dragon. And she had spent so long plotting and planning his death that she felt nearly relieved to see him; her long quest to make him pay for all he'd done to her and to Caleb was almost over.

But Alan wasn't alone. Instead, he was leaning on a young woman for support, obviously injured. The sight of him limping gave Ziya a perverse sort of pleasure. He had alienated everyone he forced into his circle of influence; he had no one left willing to heal him of his battle wounds. And remembering how injured Rikaa and Aonai had been after tangling with him, she was glad to see he hadn't gotten away without lasting damage.

And yet the very fact of his injury meant he had the perfect excuse for a human shield when he left the safety of the village.

Ziya huffed out smoke. She *tried* to talk herself into attacking Alan despite the girl's presence by reminding herself that Elena had been human too and that Alan had used her up as readily as he used up the dragons he made. But this girl helping Alan out of the village didn't seem to be an assistant, not when she kept glaring at Alan and

90

seemed to have found a way to give him her support while making as little contact with him as possible.

Curious, Ziya landed in the trees and then did her best to be silent as she crept as close as she dared to the entrance to the village. In the densest parts of the forests, she could still hide in the shadows, but much of the land around the village's outer wall had been cleared away—likely to prevent dragons from sneaking up on them using exactly the same methods Ziya was using. In fact, Ziya could see a few humans walking the length of the wall and knew that she wouldn't have dared to get as close as she was for anything but the sight of Alan *without Caleb nearby*. Had she seen Caleb following him out of the village, she would have waited and trusted her ally.

Now, she could only think of the last time Caleb had gone into a stronghold where Alan resided. If he'd been as badly hurt as he had been in Alan's cavernous army base, Ziya would be inclined to never let Caleb out of her sight again. He seemed to stumble into the worst kinds of trouble the minute she took her eyes off him.

She didn't tell Lioia what she was up to, but she heard the green dragon land not far from her position and whispered a nearly silent, "Don't do anything yet. I need to see something."

"What?" Lioia asked, steadily moving closer, her footfalls silent in the woods that she knew far better than Ziya did.

"I need to know who that girl is," Ziya whispered. "Shh."

Lioia drew her wings up the way a bird would ruffle its feathers, obviously insulted by being shushed, but to Ziya's relief, she didn't argue. Slowly, Lioia stalked toward Alan and the new girl, moving more softly than Ziya could and therefore getting close enough to pounce if they heard something amiss.

Ziya held her breath as she watched Lioia move. Unlike Iuan, Lioia had no qualms about fighting human bystanders. So, Ziya wasn't exactly comfortable with how much closer Lioia was to Alan than she was. If things got complicated, Lioia would just as soon burn up the young woman Alan had with him in order to kill Alan as she would listen to Ziya.

When Ziya and Lioia had landed, they were far enough away from Alan and the girl that they wouldn't be heard even with Alan's dragon hearing, but as they crept closer, and as the two humans walked away from the safety of the village, they could hear arguing:

THE GODS' GIFT

"It's your own fault, really. I thought your people were renowned for your suspicion, but you took his side in a heartbeat, didn't you?" Alan sneered at the girl, sounding as self-assured and sadistic as usual.

"Actually, I was ready to throw you *both* out, but you were the one who threatened my home," the girl replied heatedly.

"You overreacted," Alan said, as if he was chiding a child. "I was baiting him."

"Baiting him into a fight that would have wrecked the inn my family and I have watched over for generations." The girl shrugged her shoulder underneath the hand he kept on her to maintain his balance, shying away from his touch without actually stepping away from him. "If he hadn't gotten in the way—"

"Don't delude yourself, *girl*," Alan replied, losing his patronizing tone in a heartbeat, as he often did when those he was talking down to talked back to him and he wasn't looking for any reaction but cowardice. "If Caleb hadn't stepped between us, you would be dead now."

"So would you," the girl replied without missing a beat.

I like her, Ziya said, though she couldn't quite smile when she was now even more worried about Caleb's fate than she had been when she landed. *This is just like what happened with that little girl on the mountain,* Ziya thought, remembering how she and Caleb had been chosen out of a group of refugees and marched up a mountain. Caleb had drawn down trouble carrying a girl on his shoulders when that girl had stumbled, and from what Ziya had seen and what she had been told by both Elena and the dragons Kaal had befriended, that wasn't an isolated incident. He had a habit of acting without thought to protect others.

Caleb, what have you gotten yourself into now? Ziya wondered, keeping her head low to the ground as she watched Alan and the girl.

To Ziya's relief, Lioia didn't make a move toward the two humans despite hearing Caleb's name come up in conversation—obvious evidence of Alan's identity. Ziya didn't know if she could say that Lioia trusted her enough to wait for her signal, but she guessed that, if nothing else, Lioia wanted more information. The girl walking with Alan had admitted to trying to kill him; perhaps that simple admission had convinced Lioia not to kill her. For now.

Whatever the case, Ziya found herself trying to be as still as possible as Alan and the girl got closer and closer to her hiding place, still meandering away from the village as if nothing was the matter outside of their argument. Alan didn't even look like he was wary of his environment.

Ziya didn't trust him.

Alan and the girl were nearly to the first light curve in the path down the mountain when Alan came to a stop, pulling the girl with him so that she nearly stumbled a step to match him. He ignored her glare and looked around the trees with eyes that Ziya knew could see better than the average human because of his dragon-like traits. Even before she had known he could turn into a dragon, she had felt when she was his captive that Alan could see straight through her.

As Ziya watched, a slow smile spread over Alan's face, and he called out, "I know you're out there."

Ziya froze and looked toward Lioia, who was similarly still and watching Ziya, her gaze silently searching for an answer Ziya didn't have to give. She didn't *think* they'd been spotted, but she couldn't be sure.

"Come now, Ziya," Alan said in the condescending tone he always took with her, the one that made her blood boil. "Caleb told me you two were traveling together. He has such a bad habit of finding weaker creatures to slow him down, doesn't he?" As he spoke, he leaned heavily on the girl, so that she couldn't avoid having to use her free hand to hold him up unless she wanted him to fall.

Ziya wondered what threats or promises Alan had made to get that girl to agree to help him at all.

"Ziya, you're not fooling anyone, my dear," he continued. "Come out or the girl dies." With that, Alan shifted, suddenly able to stand of his own accord. The girl had been so focused on and furious about holding him up that she was thrown off-balance when his weight suddenly lifted, and that gave Alan the opening he needed to put his hand around her neck. He accentuated the threat by changing forms slightly so that he had not fingers but claws underneath the girl's chin, even drawing blood that ran in a thin line until it dripped over her shoulder.

The girl froze, her chest heaving but every other muscle still as she tried not to cut herself any further on the sharp points of Alan's

THE GODS' GIFT

claws. And in the silence that followed Alan's threat, Ziya could hear the girl calling Alan every foul name under the sun.

This was exactly what Ziya had hoped to *avoid*.

Ziya caught Lioia's gaze and saw that the green dragon was shaking her head, slowly and carefully so as not to make a sound. Just as Ziya had suspected, Lioia wasn't as concerned about human casualties as Ziya was.

But Ziya had decided not to be the monster Alan made her. She'd decided she wouldn't be like the soldiers in the army who turned their backs on all the people who starved and suffered while they had food and shelter and uniforms to keep them warm. She'd *insisted* that the dragons she allied with value human lives. And so, she stepped forward and out of the forest—but only far enough that Alan could see she was there. She kept her wings slightly away from her body and her claws pushed out. If she had to fight, she would, but she would rather flee; Alan had too much of an advantage as the situation currently stood.

When Alan saw her, his smile spread slowly until it overtook his face. "There you are," he said, sounding perfectly delighted, even though the girl he was with let out a noise of alarm, and all the blood drained out of her face when she saw Ziya. A dragon so close to her home couldn't have been a welcome sight at the best of times, let alone when she was Alan's captive.

"Let her go," Ziya said, letting out one of the lowest growls she had yet managed since becoming a dragon. The depth of her growls seemed to match the depth of her anger.

Alan pulled the captive girl's chin closer to him so that he could play at having a private conversation with her. "Can you believe this dragon?" he laughed. "She's young. She doesn't know anything about the wizards who live here. She doesn't know you could kill her in a heartbeat. She only knows I have you, so she wants you alive. You have to admire that kind of hatred, really."

"Don't listen to him," Ziya snarled. "He lies with each breath." She realized, belatedly, that her dragon accent gave her insults less punch, but she wouldn't let him define her, even to a stranger. "I don't want innocents hurt."

"Innocents?" Alan repeated and laughed. "Please. This whole village is full of killers. Ask any dragon."

"She's not part of my quarrel with you," Ziya shot back, her low growl still lacing every word and, unfortunately, making her accent harder to understand. But since she had promised herself she wouldn't bite back any growls she wanted to give Alan, she didn't try to stop it, either.

"Ah, so noble." Alan's sneer revealed pointed teeth. "What Caleb sees in you escapes me. You can't be bothered with broader fights than the one in front of your nose."

"I don't care about any fight bigger than me. The ones who like wars don't have to die in them," she replied. "Now let her go."

"No."

Ziya let out a frustrated snarl that made the girl flinch. She would have felt worse about it if she weren't trying to save her life. "What do you want, Alan?"

"A guarantee of safety—and healing."

Ziya's growl was so deep that it drowned out her response, and she had to repeat herself when she realized Alan was still waiting for her to give voice to her anger. "No," she snapped, her eyes flashing. "What makes you think I'd *help* you?"

"You care about Caleb," he said, infuriatingly calm. "You want him safe. So, you'll do as I say, or my new assistant will take me back to her inn, and I'll finish what she started."

Ziya's growl died in her throat as she looked between Alan and the girl glaring at him in pure distaste. She could absolutely believe that this girl was his new assistant, because she remembered vividly how Elena had admitted to knowing Alan would throw her away. The fact that this girl had tried to kill Alan wasn't necessarily proof positive that she *wasn't* his assistant—just that she didn't want him to use her up like he had Elena.

"I'm not your new anything," the girl insisted, stomping on Alan's foot hard enough that smoke came out of his mouth as he bared his teeth at her.

"You are what I say you are," Alan hissed at her, the points of his claws trailing blood at her neck once more.

"I've heard enough," Lioia said, suddenly announcing her presence, stepping out of the shadows in such a swift motion that Alan and the girl with him couldn't react quickly enough. She lashed out with her foot and bashed into the girl, knocking both Alan and the girl off their feet. When the two humans hit the ground, Lioia flicked the girl away from her captor with her tail, and the girl hit a tree and lay stunned on the grass.

"Lioia, stop!" Ziya bounded toward the injured girl, only to come up short when Alan got in her path, already growling and growing, breathing fire between himself and the two other dragons. His goal was not to hurt them—since dragon fire didn't hurt dragons unless it had a spell attached to it or was white-hot—but to distract them and make it difficult to find him while his body rushed through the changes necessary to become a dragon.

Lioia did stop, though Ziya doubted it was because of her directive. Instead, she looked toward the village, snarling at the sound of humans raising the alarm. The village defenders had seen the dragons and were likely preparing to kill them.

That meant that they didn't have time to waste if they wanted to kill Alan. So, Ziya turned her attention from the injured human girl toward Alan. She rushed through the fire without seeing Alan clearly; she only had an idea of where he had been when he started to transform. She wasn't rewarded with the feeling of flesh or scales underneath her claws, but she did hear him growling practically right beside her, the kind of growl that she was far too familiar with, a growl that couldn't be stopped and was the result of sheer agony. He might have hidden from her sight, but he couldn't hide from the torment of his body tearing itself apart to make room for his new, larger form.

Ziya nearly smiled. Alan might have pretended he was better than Ziya and Kaal, but he wasn't unbeatable. He could be hurt. He could be killed.

As soon as she realized where he was, she lashed out to her left, with teeth and claws, until she connected. She thought she could feel something soft between her teeth, but as she bit down, she found leather instead, until she had a piece of wing in her teeth. It wasn't the devastating blow she wanted to land, but she bit down harder all the same and then shook her head, tearing open his wing so that he couldn't easily fly away.

She reveled in his roar of pain and in her blood rushing in her ears. *This* was what she'd wanted to do for so long. She had fought him before, in defense of Kaal, but she'd had to leave the battle between Alan, Aonai, and Rikaa to free Alan's other captives. Now, she could feel herself smiling as she snapped at him again, *enjoying* the thrill of tearing into him, especially now that he was injured; she could better keep up with him.

He finally finished his transformation—she could no longer hear him growling—and lashed out at her in return, barely missing with his claws. He snapped at her as well, but she all but leaped out of the way, remembering too well what his venom felt like in her veins. She didn't want to suffer through that again.

By that point, Lioia had rushed to join the fight as well, though Ziya didn't see her ally because she was so focused on trying to tear Alan down, her thoughts on all of the terror and torture he had put her through and on how *good* it would feel to get her revenge after all that time. So, she didn't know Lioia had arrived until Alan cried out in pain despite the fact that Ziya had failed to get her teeth around his neck like she wanted to.

Alan snarled as he whirled on Lioia, who had torn open a hole in one of the soft spots where his legs met the rest of his body. In his blind rage, he missed her with his teeth but managed to hit her with his tail in a two-pronged attack. Lioia stumbled toward the trees, her claws barely missing a figure lying prone.

All at once, Ziya realized with horror that the fight had drifted close to Alan's possible assistant. The girl was still unconscious—but breathing—but Ziya doubted she would survive if one of the battling dragons stepped on her. Ziya glanced between the fallen girl and the dragon fight and let out a frustrated snarl. Once again, she had to choose between Alan and innocents—and this time, she didn't know for sure that the girl was an innocent.

But even if the girl had been Alan's new assistant, she was the only one besides Alan who knew what had happened to Caleb.

No, this girl couldn't die. But only because Ziya couldn't stand to lose Caleb. He was, somehow, her best friend in the world and one of the only beings who understood all she'd been through. He reminded her of her humanity while also giving her hope for what she could do as a dragon. She *needed* him.

So, Ziya lunged toward Alan, but not to fight him. Instead of attacking his wings, neck, or belly, she went *past* him to sink her teeth into his tail and yank, startling him and pulling him backward enough that Lioia was able to take advantage of his surprise. Heaving herself forward, Lioia bashed into him and sent him sprawling—away from the unconscious human girl.

It wasn't the most elegant of solutions, but it worked.

Ziya glanced toward Lioia and Alan and was relieved to see that Lioia had the battle well in hand. Alan had stumbled badly when Lioia bashed into him, and he had one leg pinned underneath him as Lioia tore at the softer places in his scales. He couldn't get back up with both of her front legs on his side, her talons sinking deeper under his scales with every passing second. The only reason Lioia hadn't killed Alan yet was that Alan kept biting at Lioia, getting uncomfortably close several times. And Lioia, knowing what Ziya and Kaal had told her about Alan's venom, had to keep ducking his teeth while keeping Alan pinned down.

Still, Ziya didn't want to leave another battle up to chance, so she had to move the girl quickly so she could return to help Lioia. She skidded to a stop next to the human girl, leaving long trails of claw marks in the dirt behind her, and lowered her head as close to the girl as she dared, watching the rise and fall of her chest. Gently, she nudged the girl, and when that didn't work, she tried growling right next to her ear, hoping to scare her awake.

No luck.

Ziya swore as she tried to concentrate not on the battle nearby but on reaching for the power she knew she had, the strength she had given Aonai and Kaal in order to heal them. She had to *want* to heal someone in order to do it, so she couldn't be distracted by Lioia's snarls or Alan's pained growls or the fact that this girl might wake up and attack them all under Alan's orders. She couldn't think about how badly she wanted revenge; she couldn't think about how unfair it was that she'd yet again been drawn away from the fight she so badly wanted. No, she had to focus.

Surprisingly, she found the power beneath her skin relatively easily. She wondered, briefly, if the simple fact that Lioia had confirmed for her that she could feel a dragon's power from Ziya had given her more confidence in her dragon abilities, but she could think about that later. She might even ask Caleb about it once they found him again; he had a knack for explaining dragon sensations in human terms.

Once she found her power, she breathed out a gentle sigh that carried with it her hopes not necessarily for this little human but for what her health meant for Caleb. Thankfully, that seemed to be good enough. With a soft groan, the girl stirred awake. Ziya could tell by the way she carried herself and the way the girl's eyelids fluttered several times that the simple healing Ziya had given her hadn't done more than give the girl the tools to return to consciousness, but that was still better than lying on the ground waiting to be trampled by dragons in the throes of battle.

Finally, the girl got herself upright long enough to take in her surroundings, and she blinked at Ziya as if she were trying to place her face. "Alan," the girl slurred out—which had Ziya pulling her wings tight to her body in a defensive move, not at all trusting anyone who woke up with Alan's name on her lips. "Des. Whatever his name is. Did you kill him?"

Ziya gestured with her front claws and then remembered she was a dragon and gestured with her tail toward Lioia and Alan. "Working on it."

"Do it faster," the girl said through her teeth as she tried and then failed to get to her feet. Ziya lowered her head so the girl could use it as leverage to stand but then backed away when, with a sharp gesture, the girl waved her off. The girl used a tree to keep herself upright, obviously wary of any offer of help from a dragon. "I tried to kill him," the girl said once she caught her breath from the small exertion, "and he threatened my home and everyone in my care."

"He does that."

"I noticed." The girl took a deep breath and then straightened up. "Do you know if his staff transformed with him? Is it part of the spell?" she asked, already searching the ground with her gaze. "If I can get my hands on it, I can stop him permanently."

"You can hardly stand," Ziya pointed out, though she looked around as well. Getting Alan's staff, even if this girl was too weak to use it, could definitely keep Alan out of trouble if he somehow managed to get the upper hand on Lioia. And as she knew from watching Caleb transform, clothes and other human objects didn't stay with those that changed their forms once they became dragons.

"I'll be fine," the girl replied, though she swayed where she stood, and Ziya automatically moved toward her to steady her.

THE GODS' GIFT

So, of course, that was when someone new entered the scene with a strangled cry of, "Stay away from my daughter!" The next thing Ziya knew, an all-too-familiar spell moved through her body, the kind of spell Alan had used when he was tormenting her for her attempted escape with Kaal, the kind that left her seeing white and screaming in agony.

CHAPTER 10: SECRET IDENTITY

Ziya swore liberally, cursing whoever had stepped into the fight. Alan had been *losing* to Lioia, and now, someone had disrupted the balance of power. She could hear both of the other dragons snarling in pain and knew that this newcomer had hit all three of them with the same spell; that meant that Lioia wouldn't be able to finish what she'd sworn to do. Alan was still alive, and some moron was tormenting the two dragons who had pinned him down to kill him.

Somehow, the simple knowledge that Lioia hadn't yet killed Alan was enough to override the pain of the spell moving underneath her scales, and Ziya growled in frustration, struggling to her feet and stumbling toward Alan. She'd finish what Lioia started no matter how badly she was hurt; she couldn't bear the thought of hunting him down again.

"Stop!"

The only reason Ziya lurched to a stop was that she recognized Caleb's voice, and she was too relieved to hear him to think at first about the fact that he wanted Alan alive, that he wanted answers—and so he was just as likely to keep her from her goal as whoever had stepped in.

Wait. She shook her head as she realized the tenor of her thoughts. She *had* agreed, before she and Kaal left, that Kaal deserved answers from Alan. She had never pledged to take Alan to the council to give them his answers, but she had agreed with Kaal that they would decide *together* what to do with Alan when they found

101

him. And she'd nearly forgotten that pledge because she had been so lost in the thrill of near-victory, intoxicated with the thought of long-delayed revenge.

The thought hurt nearly as much as the sharp spell. She was *trying* to overcome the way Alan had molded her into a weapon, the way he had taken away her humanity and turned her into nothing but anger and grief and hatred and fear. But she had slipped yet again into those patterns without even a second thought.

This was why she needed Caleb around. She needed the reminder of what she was trying to be.

And there he was, pale and drawn and sick-looking as he slid down the forested path toward her. His hair was wet, for some reason, and he moved stiffly, but he didn't seem to be dying, so she could help him heal from whatever else ailed him.

What's more, she wasn't surprised at all to find that the painful spell cast by a strange wizard let up as soon as she saw Caleb. He had a knack for convincing others to his cause. She'd once compared him to Alan, and he'd taken offense, but she'd meant it as a compliment. He was as talented as Alan could be but wasn't corrupted by that talent; that was a good thing. She knew too well how easily those that Alan turned could fail to live up to their moral beliefs; Caleb's gift was in turning people *toward* their consciences.

The spell let up, but it left exhaustion in its wake, and Ziya collapsed not far from Alan and Lioia. *At least Alan can't get away*, she thought when she saw that both of the other dragons were in heaps and unable to move.

"You'd better start explaining yourself, boy." A gruff voice echoed through the trees, followed by a relieved and delighted sound from Alan's hostage, who rushed toward an older man who stood several paces behind Caleb on the path. The man had a walking stick but held it aloft like a magical staff; he must have been the wizard who broke up the dragon fight.

Caleb didn't look back at the reunion between the girl and the wizard, instead crossing the distance between him and Ziya to run his hand over her snout. She leaned into the touch automatically. She really had missed him. She hadn't realized how much she relied on him to be her moral compass until she was without him. And now that she could see him up close, she could smell fire on him, the tangy scent of burnt hair and flesh juxtaposed strangely with his soaking wet hair.

He got into the worst situations without her; she would have to ask him what happened when she healed him later—after they dealt with Alan.

"Are you alright?" Caleb asked in a whisper meant solely for her, searching her with his gaze as thoroughly as she had been searching him.

"I am, but Alan was nearly dead before you showed up," she hissed back, pointing with her tail toward the other two dragons— and drawing the attention of the humans.

"Make another move, dragon, and I'll kill you," the old man said in as close to a snarl as humans were capable of, breaking away from hugging Alan's hostage to point his walking stick at Ziya.

"Dad, wait," the girl said, one hand on her father's arm and the other around his back, supporting him after his display of magic and his trek out of the village despite his limp. In that simple gesture, Ziya understood how protective the two of them were of each other. The girl was still badly hurt despite Ziya's meager healing, but her focus was on her father. No wonder the man had attacked them without a second thought. "She protected me."

Her father narrowed his eyes. "Mira, dear, you have a horrible habit of befriending the worst kinds of trouble. What in the gods' names have you gotten yourself into now?"

"It's not her fault," Caleb started to say, but Mira's father gestured sharply, and Caleb quickly closed his mouth.

"I don't want to hear what you have to say for yourself and your friends," the man snapped. "The simple fact that you've allied with dragons is bad enough, but you got my daughter kidnapped, and you threatened the peace in my home on top of that. I have half a mind to kill you with your scaly friends."

Ziya growled a warning, but that wasn't nearly as effective as Mira hitting her father's chest lightly with the back of her hand. "Dad," Mira said, the single word carrying with it both affection and warning. Ziya had done the same thing with her own mother when she felt Dahlia was getting overprotective.

"Let me explain myself before you pass judgement," Caleb said. "That is what you wanted me to do, isn't it?" When Mira's father nodded his grudging agreement, Caleb gestured with one hand toward Alan, keeping his other hand on Ziya's snout in a display both of protection and of trust. "That white dragon is the man you know as Des, though I know him as Alan."

"That's ridiculous," Mira's father scoffed, but Mira tightened her grip on her father's arm.

"It's not," she said softly. "I saw him transform." She bit her lip and turned toward Caleb. "And he's not the only one."

Ziya couldn't turn toward Caleb to show her surprise, and she didn't have eyebrows to raise—or she would have done either of those things. Caleb's ability to transform was their closest-held secret. They had gone to great lengths to hide him. And yet, Mira knew Caleb's secret despite the fact that he didn't have even a hint of scales on his skin or claws on his hands.

She didn't know what had possessed Caleb to take leave of his sense, but if they lived through this and escaped together, she'd give him the tongue lashing he so richly deserved. She'd never known him to be *reckless* before. And Mira wasn't worth the risk. She came from a village full of humans who knew how best to kill dragons— what made Caleb think he could trust her?

Boys, she thought, barely resisting the urge to roll her eyes. Once, she and her mother had made fun of soldiers who lost their heads over the women in their ranks or the girls in their towns. Somehow, she'd assumed Caleb hadn't grown into that particular defect—maybe because he'd kept telling everyone he was younger than he was and kept to himself so successfully. But then, all that time with Rikaa had aged him—in a good way. Maybe he'd come into adolescence on dragon's wings.

Ziya, on the other hand, had *firmly* informed her mother that, no, she wasn't interested in courtship or even jokes about courtship—not until the war was over and the dragon council stopped trying to capture or kill her. Nothing had changed from when she was a refugee and the war had kept her from concerning herself with boys; the only difference was her outer trappings.

Boys, she thought again and let out a smoky huff that drew a quizzical look from Caleb. She didn't feel like explaining herself.

Besides, they had more important matters to attend to—like Mira's father pointing his walking stick at Caleb like a weapon. His eyes flashed with power Ziya instinctively backed away from as he demanded, "Talk. Fast."

"Alan—or Des or whatever his real name is—took starving refugees and turned them into dragons," Caleb said. He kept both hands raised and never dropped Mira's father's gaze, speaking calmly and clearly so he wouldn't be misunderstood. "He poured a dragon's magic into them—into us—and then waited to see what happened." When Mira's father's response was to hold his walking stick somehow closer to Caleb, Caleb gestured toward Ziya. "This is a friend of mine. She was human before Alan took her and locked her up. He put me in chains. He put her through worse. We're only here because he escaped from us when we freed his prisoners. All we want to do is get answers about what he did to us—and then make sure he never does it again." At that last promise, Caleb finally looked toward Ziya again, so that she could see the hesitation in his gaze. He wanted answers more than he wanted revenge—but then, he had always been more of a pacifist than she was.

With his walking stick still pointed at Caleb's head, Mira's father nodded toward Mira. "And you believe him?"

"I believe my own eyes," Mira replied. Instead of standing around and posturing like her father was doing, she had turned her attention to more important things, like trying to find Alan's staff, shuffling through the trampled bushes and felled trees left in the wake of a dragon's battle. Finding a staff, even an ornate one like the one Alan owned, in the middle of so much fallen foliage would be a difficult task at the best of times, let alone when Mira was still hurt. And yet, the air was so charged with the threat of another fight that no one could do anything else, either.

Alan, for his part, seemed wary of moving, probably because he was so badly injured that the ground beneath him was dark and wet but also likely because of the threat Mira's father posed. Still, Alan kept his gaze on Mira, not on the conversation between Caleb and Mira's father, treating Mira as the bigger threat.

Ziya didn't understand why everyone *but* Caleb could see that Mira couldn't be trusted.

"What he says is true," Alan said, suddenly, surprising everyone there in the broken trees and twisted undergrowth. He even caught Mira's attention away from peering around the roots of an uprooted tree, though she returned to her search with a snort of annoyance at being interrupted. Alan's eyes flashed at being ignored, but he looked toward Mira's father, the easier target for manipulation, and continued, "I found magic that would help win wars. Of course I used it. But they're lying about the rest. I don't *force* anyone to drink the magic."

"Don't hide behind half-truths," Caleb snarled, his hands in fists. He didn't lose his temper often, and when he did, he always surprised Ziya. As much as he hated being compared to Alan, she had to admit that he had the same way of changing his moods without warning. She suspected that the truth was that he kept so much to himself that the slight things that set off his temper were simply one step too far for him to ignore. But even knowing him as she did, he scared her sometimes.

Caleb's outburst hung in the air heavily as the only sound other than Mira's footsteps as she searched for Alan's staff. And then, Alan chuckled. "Really, Kaal," he said, in the infuriating tone he often took with Ziya, too—the one that sounded like a disappointed parent.

"You're the one hiding behind the idea that offering nothing but a potion to a dying, starving child is the same as asking for volunteers," Caleb shot back, speaking through teeth that had become suddenly sharper in his mouth. Ziya wondered if he was aware of the change—and wondered if anyone else had noticed it. "Everywhere I go, I have to fight to get anyone to believe me when I say I didn't *want* this magic. Don't make this harder."

"You wanted an escape from starvation without dying a foot soldier's death. I told you already that beggars don't get to dictate their salvation," Alan said coldly, then turned his attention back to Mira's father. "You said you wanted to stay out of our war. Stay out of it. Kaal and I can sort out our difference of opinion between us."

"As much as I'm tempted to do that—and believe me, I'd love nothing more than to let you two try to kill each other somewhere else—I'm afraid I can't let you leave, Des," Mira's father replied, his eyes narrowed.

Ziya and Caleb shared a glance but didn't dare say anything. Mira's father had specifically told *Alan*—or Des, as the villagers knew him—that he couldn't leave. He hadn't made a sweeping demand of all of them. This complicated matters—even if it was a relief not

106

to have to fight the villagers. If Caleb wanted answers from Alan, he had to stick close to him, but that could only mean staying in a village that distrusted him already.

Alan growled at Mira's father. "You only think you have power here, Alwar. You cannot give me *orders*."

"No, but *I* can," Mira said, standing up straight with Alan's staff clutched in her hands. Now that Ziya was focused on the staff itself, she saw that it was much more battered than it had been when she last faced Alan, at his cavernous base. Now, the staff was charred in places and had long gauges in its sides, defensive wounds that showed how close Ziya and the other dragons had come to taking him down. She imagined that when Alan had first arrived in a village that hated dragons, the dragon-inflicted scars on his body and staff had helped him secure their trust.

Mira knew how to handle herself with a magical staff, too. Once she had it in her hands, she widened her stance, bracing herself for the power of whatever spell she might use if Alan moved against her or her father. Her eyes flashed, and once again, Ziya saw power there that she usually saw in dragons.

Ziya wasn't entirely sure that she believed the gods had much of a hand in her life, but she'd spent enough time around dragons who believed in the gods with everything they had that her immediate thought was that the gods didn't reserve their power solely for dragons. People like Mira had the same fire in their hearts; their power simply didn't come from *real* fire.

And she wondered, briefly, if the power Lioia had been able to feel when she searched for Alan was power that Ziya had when she was Neva, if that power had been transformed like the rest of her body into a dragon form.

Alan turned toward Mira with a heavy sigh and with much effort. "Dear girl," he said, and Ziya started to growl simply because his condescending nicknames always riled her after he had used them so often on her. "If you and your father insist on enacting revenge, I'll renounce my offer to teach you. You can run along and leave me be. I'll deal with Kaal myself."

"You'll answer to the lord of the village," Mira replied evenly, her staff leveled at Alan. "I don't care what you and Caleb are arguing about. I'm glad to see him alive after you tried to kill me, but this

THE GODS' GIFT

is more than personal." She tipped her head to indicate the path to the village but didn't otherwise shift her stance. "No dragons are allowed in Ytona Village. Any that enter are not allowed to leave alive." She narrowed her eyes. "Lord Teyo might grant you a small reprieve because you came to us as a human. You might be imprisoned here rather than executed. We'll see how lenient he feels when I tell him of your threats."

Alan laughed. "If you intend to take me, you must take Caleb. You said yourself you saw what he can do."

Ziya growled, already stepping in front of Caleb, ready to fight back. Once, she had wanted nothing more than for Caleb—or Kaal—to live out the rest of his life in shackles, in captivity, suffering the way she had suffered. But away from Alan's influence, she had found nothing but friendship with Caleb. He had already been through enough; she wouldn't allow him to endure anything more.

But to Ziya's surprise, Caleb put a hand on her snout, pushing her back enough that she could see that he was *smiling*. He wasn't simply trying to step around her because he didn't want her protection; he had a plan.

Caleb approached Mira, his hands spread in a gesture of peace. "I already admitted he poured a dragon's power into me, but you can see for yourself that I'm still human."

Alan scoffed. "You've survived for so long on your lies, and that's all you can say? I changed in front of Mira; your excuses are nothing."

Caleb kept smiling. "You can try to take me down with you, but it won't work, Alan." He turned toward Mira's father, who had shifted to point his walking stick at Caleb while Mira had the staff pointed at Alan. Ziya knew neither of them would hesitate to cast a spell if either Caleb or Alan made a move they didn't like, so she hoped Caleb knew what he was doing. "Alwar, right?" he asked Mira's father, who nodded but didn't stop glaring. "You saw me after Alan burned me and Mira put a spell on me. If I were a dragon, don't you think you'd see scales? Something more than sharp teeth and smoke?" He spread his hands out even wider. "I've got a dragon's power, not a dragon's body. The potion didn't do the same thing to me that it did to Ziya, and Ziya hasn't set foot in your village. My friends and I haven't broken any of your laws."

Ziya wasn't good enough at schooling her expression as a dragon to hide the look of disbelief she was giving Caleb. She'd learned how to hide anger and bite back growls, but that was an entirely different matter from hiding the rest of her emotions. And so, she could only stare at Caleb—and hope that he knew what he was doing. He was good with words, and she'd told him as much, but he wasn't *that* good of a liar. She still remembered how he'd tried to convince the other refugees at the base of the mountain that he was twelve.

And by the looks of things, Caleb wasn't nearly as convincing as he thought he was. Alwar's eyes were mere slits, and he stepped forward with his walking stick leading the way toward an attack—but Mira spoke up before he could. "He did save my life," she reminded her father gently.

"Fine," Alwar spit out through the corner of his mouth, still prepared to attack Caleb anyway. "But he'll have to answer to Lord Teyo just like the other dragon."

"I'll speak to whoever you want me to speak to," Caleb promised, his hands open, palms out. "I will only request that you don't give me the same punishment as the man who *forced* dragon power into me."

Alwar shook his head slowly. "I can't promise anything. I'm not the lord."

"The only promise I'm asking of you is that you don't hold anything Alan did against me, especially when I'm trying to make him pay for every torture and every threat. I'll talk to the lord myself; I already said I would. Just, please, don't treat me like an enemy."

"Keep talking like that and Lord Teyo might turn him over to you for your claim to justice," Mira said, her eyes shining with anger and laughter at the same time, apparently teasing Caleb even in a tense standoff.

For just a moment, Ziya felt a keen pang of jealousy in the center of her chest—not because of Mira's quickly-formed soft spot for Caleb, obviously, but because Mira could so easily tease and joke around. When Ziya had been human, when she'd been Neva, her sense of humor and her tongue were both sharp. She was known for a quick wit and for finding the right words to cut down anyone who wronged her, no matter their status or stature. She was still trying to find her way to being some balance of Neva and Ziya, to finding who she was after all that Alan had done, and Mira's casual joke reminded her that her wit had been robbed from her. Once she acquired a dragon's tongue and a dragon's accent, her insults were harder to understand, and she was forced to think over each word before she spoke.

Funny how it's always the little things that I miss, she thought.

"I'll plead my case then," Caleb said, smiling Mira's way and bringing Ziya out of her thoughts. "But what about my friends? They don't deserve your wrath."

Mira and Alwar shared a loaded look. "As much as it pains me to let any dragon go free," Alwar said, bitterness ringing in his tone, "you're right. They didn't come directly into our village." He pointed at Caleb, who kept his posture as nonthreatening as possible. "But if I find out that you're lying, or if they come any closer—"

"Thank you," Caleb said before Alwar could complete his threat.

"You can't be serious," Alan hissed. At first, both Alwar and Mira turned toward him ready to argue, but Alan had his gaze locked onto Caleb, not the villagers. "You can't trust *them*. What in the gods' names have you been up to that you trust *anyone?*"

"That's enough," Mira snapped, shooting some kind of light out of Alan's staff that moved through Alan so deeply that his scales looked blue rather than white where the magic touched him. Ziya could literally see the way the spell followed the path of Alan's body until it reached his eyes and forced them shut, putting Alan to sleep despite the words she could hear him whispering in the dragon language. His counterspells allowed him to keep his eyes open long enough to growl and breathe fire toward Mira, but Lioia stepped into the path of that fire, and Alan succumbed to sleep before he could try again.

It happened so quickly that Ziya did a double-take, her eyes wide as she stared at Lioia, wondering if the green dragon realized that she had openly defended a human. And not just any human but one whose entire village dedicated themselves to fighting against dragons.

Maybe Caleb was onto something letting her come along, Ziya thought. She nearly smirked. *Exposure does wonders for perception. I wouldn't have defended dragons before I became one of them. And I doubt she would have protected Mira if she hadn't spent so much time with us.*

Mira looked as surprised by Lioia's move as Lioia herself did, though Mira couldn't see Lioia's expression. Instead, Mira cleared her throat softly, and Lioia moved aside without saying a word. Ziya doubted that Lioia knew what to say after such a display. And apparently, Mira didn't either. That was likely why, rather than thanking Lioia, she turned toward Alan and let her pretty features twist into a glare. "And to think I believed him when he promised he could teach me. He seemed so . . ."

"Don't feel bad," Caleb told her. "He's a master manipulator. I think he uses words like a game; he used to tell me and Ziya half-truths and then wait to see if we could tell reality apart from his manipulations." He walked slowly toward Alan, each step crunching on fallen leaves and other dying vegetation. "That's why I need to talk to him. That's why I need answers. I need to know what was a lie and what wasn't. I need to know what he turned me into."

"I'm interested in answers myself," Alwar said, finally lowering his walking stick and using it as it was designed to be used, leaning his weight on it as he turned back toward the path that led out from the village. "We'll need help getting him contained. I'll be back with others. Mira, I trust you can handle yourself?"

Mira smiled as tightly as she was gripping Alan's staff. "I'll be fine," she promised.

"Good. Don't let any of them out of your sight—and don't let Des or Caleb leave."

"Yes, sir."

As Alwar hobbled up the stony path, Ziya leaned toward Caleb to nudge him with the end of her nose. "I hope you know what you're doing, Kaal" she said in a soft whisper. "If they find out the truth. . . ."

Caleb reached out to run both of his hands over her snout and then touched his forehead where his hands stopped. "I know," he whispered. "But I need answers, Ziya. If they kill him before I know what I am, that's going to haunt me for the rest of my life."

Ziya sighed, and her breath moved his dark hair away from his face. "Be careful," she said urgently. "Your life isn't worth those answers."

THE GODS' GIFT

Caleb smiled and brushed his hair back into place. "I've survived this long, haven't I?" He started to walk backward away from her, his hands out and his palms turned toward her. "I'll see you soon, Ziya. I promise."

CALEB

CHAPTER II: THE DRAGON SWORD

Even though Caleb had agreed to come back to the village, even though he was walking in on his own, even though he had *wanted* to come back so that he could interrogate Alan himself, he still had to work to quell the growl in the back of his throat and the sensation of claws pushing at the edges of his fingers and trying to break through. The village felt more like a threat than it had since he had arrived there, and he was all too aware of his dragon-like traits, the ones that might get him locked up *again*.

He knew Ziya didn't understand the risk he was willing to take to get answers. Ziya saw Alan only as the enemy, and that was fair. Understandable, even. Caleb hadn't lost sight of everything Alan had done. But for the first time, he had a shot at approaching Alan when *Alan* was at a disadvantage, when *Alan* was captive. And Alan had always been more willing to part with information when he wanted something. Putting him at the mercy of these villagers might make him more talkative.

Then again, forcing him into captivity could make him recalcitrant and reactive. For all Caleb knew, he had just ensured that he would never find answers, because Alan would hold his curiosity over his head as punishment for his role in his humiliation. Ziya might have believed that Caleb understood Alan, but that wasn't the case. Caleb was as uneasy as Ziya was about this plan; he just didn't show it.

He glanced toward Mira, who had agreed to show him the way to the lord of her village after several large men had carted off

Alan's sleeping form. She kept watching him steadily, her body language anything but calm. The simple fact that she was prepared to act against him if he showed any sign of malice or of turning into a dragon kept him from relaxing—and put him in even more danger.

Nothing about his situation in that village was tenable; he simply had to hope he could get his answers and leave. And quickly. Otherwise, he might have escaped Alan's clutches only to become a prisoner of another war, this one much older and with higher stakes.

Caleb sighed and stretched his fingers out to their full length. The motion wasn't nearly as satisfying as it might have been had he been a dragon stretching out his claws or sharpening them against the ground, but it gave him something to do with his hands when they were practically crying out to him with the need to form claws. Maybe a dragon-like habit would be enough to sate the instincts that had so easily overtaken any sense of his human self.

At times, Caleb felt guilty. He had so completely abandoned himself to being a dragon that he knew Ziya was right to criticize him. He thought of himself as Kaal more than Caleb lately, as evidenced by his habits, which were more and more dragon-like. Even human, he stretched and fidgeted exactly the way a dragon would. Even human, he expressed himself in growls and smoke. He'd embraced Alan's changes so completely that he felt like a traitor to his own people.

But he didn't let that unease show. Not if he could help it. Ziya seemed to think he had his identity figured out, and the confidence she saw in him had gotten him through arguments with dragons much older and smarter than he was. He'd made his way through life pretending to know more than he did, pretending to be what he wasn't, pretending he believed his own lies. This was no different.

Stretching his fingers didn't help him as much as he'd hoped it would, so he found himself taking long, even breaths, watching the air in front of him for any sign of smoke. He thought he saw an ember once—which in itself was a bad sign, as it meant he was suppressing flames hot enough to catch fire in his throat—but otherwise, he showed the world around him the lie he wanted them to see. He was human. He wasn't a dragon like Alan. He was safe in this village.

THE GODS' GIFT

He felt like he was a teenage refugee too close to the army for comfort. Again. The slightest sign of deception could turn his life around.

And if Caleb was honest with himself, he didn't know if he could endure captivity again, even if he suspected Mira and her people would be kinder captors than Alan had been. Yes, they hated dragons, but they had met him as a human. That might garner him enough good will to avoid the misery and near-starvation as well as the humiliation Alan had put him through. The rest—the bars, the cells, the darkness, the isolation—would be standard fare, he told himself.

He knew the risks of going back to the village. He could have tried to run away with Ziya and Lioia; he chose instead to run after answers he might never receive. And yet he felt like a coward. He was nothing compared to Ziya, who had been tortured endlessly by Alan with Kaal's name on his lips. Ziya had endured all that and still managed to give him her friendship, even if she was loath to use the word. She still kept her compassion and her wit. Alan might have left scars on her body and mind, but she was ready to lead the battle against Alan and do what was necessary to stop him.

Caleb, on the other hand, could hardly breathe when he thought of returning to another cell. He hadn't been through nearly what Ziya had, and yet he felt cold and clammy at the thought of being in chains again.

Ziya had talked about how Alan compared her to Kaal and how Alan always decided that Kaal was the better of the two of them. Caleb wasn't so sure. If the tables had been reversed and Ziya had escaped, leaving Caleb as Alan's captive, he would have succumbed to Alan entirely. That was what he always did; he surrendered himself to whatever lie he needed to live to stay alive. And if Ziya had been able to change forms, she wouldn't fear the retribution of the villagers. She would demand answers from Alan, kill him, and leave with the blessing of the villagers and their gratitude for stopping Alan's evil from spreading.

As happened so often lately, Caleb found himself thinking of the gods, wondering what they saw in him to give him the form he had now. The only advantage he had over Ziya was his tongue. She had wit and bravery and sharp determination; he had a talent for diplomacy and lies. The one explanation he could see for his gifts was his potential to make Alan answer for his actions. But if the gods wanted a leader or a hero, he felt woefully inadequate.

I don't know what you want me to do, he thought, wondering if the gods could hear him—or if they were even paying attention. Maybe he was being egocentric, thinking that the gods cared what he was doing when they had bigger matters to concern themselves with. Maybe he had more confidence they'd pay him any attention because he was a dragon now and had taken up the dragon's appointed mission of protection. Maybe that made him even more of an egoist.

At any rate, it didn't matter what the gods thought of him or what they wanted for him—not if he couldn't keep his wits when he spoke to Lord Teyo.

He knew instantly which house was the lord's. The stone-paved pathway that cut through the center of the village turned after a neat row of houses and led to a clearing just before an imposing cliff jutting out of the mountain. The lord's house seemed to be built into the mountain, made out of stone and other fireproof materials. Even the roof looked like it was covered in well-baked mud. What's more, the house looked older than everything else around it, as if it had aged with the mountain. Caleb imagined the home had probably belonged to the village founder, likely a wizard who built himself a fortress and stood against the dragons when humans and dragons were more openly at war.

It must have taken a lifetime to perfect.

Walking up to the lord's house felt much like sneaking into the Junnin base had felt. He was painfully aware that these people would turn on him as soon as they realized he was their enemy. But while he had lived close enough to Junnin land when he was young that he could approximate their way of speaking, he couldn't lie his way through a transformation if he were found out here. A tail was much harder to hide than an accent.

The door to Lord Teyo's home opened with an echoing sound that filled the huge entryway. The interior of the home would have felt like a cave if not for the human touches—the drapery, the paintings, the furniture, the long, red carpet showing the path that visitors should take to approach the head of the village. And yet, those things felt too small compared to the size of the mountain.

THE GODS' GIFT

Or maybe he was simply used to dragon lodgings in mountain settings.

Caleb and Mira weren't the first visitors to Lord Teyo's home. In the halls, even soft conversations seemed to echo, though the words lost their meaning when the tapestries absorbed their sound. For the human residents of the village, that meant no one could truly eavesdrop on the lord. But Caleb, with his dragon senses, could hear enough of the conversations to make out the words before they echoed.

". . . a guard at all times," someone was saying. Caleb didn't recognize the speaker. "The volunteers have been made aware. . . ." At that point, the echoes of the man's words blended too much with the rest of his sentence for Caleb to parse what he'd said until he paused for breath again. "And, if what he's saying about the other soldier is true. . . ."

Caleb felt the blood drain out of his face. He didn't have much hope of convincing the lord he wasn't a threat if arrangements were already being made for his own imprisonment. The thought of living the rest of his life locked away under guard had his heart racing, and he stopped in his tracks.

Don't change now. Don't change now, he repeated in his mind, over and over again, trying to remind himself that he was in no danger— at least no danger that would not become instantly worse if he *did* change forms.

Mira stopped with him and put a hand on his arm, misreading his hesitation entirely. "For what it's worth," she said, "I don't think you have any reason to be nervous. You weren't born a dragon, and you didn't ask for these powers. That counts for something in my eyes. I believe Lord Teyo will agree."

"We'll see," Caleb said. He caught himself flexing his hands and crossed his arms. Some irrational part of his mind was convinced that these people, with all the methods they had perfected to find and kill dragons, might recognize his dragon-like tics when they questioned him.

The conversation in the other room drifted off; Caleb couldn't hear them anymore. Still, he tried not to look too much like he'd been expecting the door to open—once more trying to hide his gifts. He purposefully paused when he saw that several men in lightweight armor stood inside the main hall. He might have known that they were already making plans for his capture, but he needed his surprise to look convincing.

He followed Mira after a moment's hesitation until they reached the great hall, where Caleb was surprised to find that Lord Teyo was only a few years older than he was, dressed in armor that was slightly too big for him but with a look of steel in his eyes that Caleb had seen in everyone who saw war. Briefly, Caleb wondered what tragedy had befallen the previous ruler to lead Teyo to take his place at such a young age, but he decided against asking about it. He didn't want to remind the lord of any losses to dragons when he was one himself.

Despite his age, Teyo managed to convey a sense of regal severity. His armor didn't quite fit, his freckles were bright against sunburned skin, and his blonde hair didn't stay out of his eyes; but his gaze was steady, and something about him had Caleb biting back hot fire in his mouth in an instinctive response to peril. If Caleb wasn't careful, he'd end up with smoke slipping between his teeth, putting Lord Teyo on edge before Caleb even had the chance to talk to him.

In fact, the closer Caleb got to Teyo, the more each step felt like danger. He didn't know if it was magic or some instinct he didn't yet understand screaming at him to get out of there, but he found himself forcing his body to obey his commands to walk forward and then bow, taking one knee in deference to the lord. He hoped the submissive posture would lessen the suspicion he knew he was already under.

Mira curtseyed but didn't kneel, standing slightly behind Caleb as she addressed the lord. "This stranger came to our inn with nothing to his name and with powers I can't explain," she said. "He said that his powers were given to him by another man who was in our care at the time—and I'm inclined to believe him. The other man, Des, turned into a dragon when a pair of dragons attacked him outside our village."

Teyo nodded slowly. "Some of our watchmen reported a clash of dragons at our border," he said. "They are even now bringing the dragon in question to our prison." He didn't take his gaze off of Caleb, and Caleb could feel his face flushing with the heat contained behind his teeth. Caleb took each breath carefully, letting it out only

THE GODS' GIFT

when he felt he had enough control that it wouldn't come out in smoke, wishing *desperately* that he understood what about Teyo left him so uneasy. "And what of this one? He's a dragon too?"

"He says that he was born human and that Des—he calls him Alan—forced dragon-like powers upon him." Mira paused, and Caleb barely resisted the urge to look her way. "I have seen him breathe smoke, and I believe he can do more than he's shown me. But he also saved my life, so I'm inclined to listen to him, even if he isn't telling the whole truth."

Teyo's expression shifted, and his tone softened as he looked toward Mira. Caleb felt no less threatened by the lord's mere presence, but Teyo sounded much more like a young man and less like a leader as he repeated, "He saved your life?"

Curiosity won out against Caleb's desire to look deferent. He glanced toward Mira, smirking quietly to himself when he realized she had a light blush across her cheeks.

I'd love to see her overprotective father tell his own lord to stay away from his daughter, he thought, the mental image alone enough to relax him and lesson the pressure of claws at his fingertips.

Teyo turned his attention back to Caleb and pointed at him. "You," he said, and Caleb raised his gaze fully. "What brought you here? How did you find your maker, and why did you save Mira's life?"

Caleb cleared his throat, running his tongue over too-sharp teeth that he struggled not to bare. Speaking to the lord was an entirely new hurdle; he didn't know how long he could hide his growls or his smoke when his mouth was open.

"I've been searching for Alan for some time. Your village is far from the war and hasn't been touched by the dragons' attacks that have made the rest of this land uninhabitable," he explained. "Alan likes to experiment with dragon magic. He can't do that under constant threat of death. A haven like this is exactly where he'd be most likely to hide."

Teyo nodded but didn't give away in his expression or body language what he thought of Caleb's explanation thus far. "Go on."

Caleb took in a breath and let it out through his nose, controlling his movements. He wished he knew *why* Teyo felt like such a threat, but even as comfortable as he was in his dragon skin, he didn't yet understand all of his instincts. The fact that he had so much left to learn would have been more comforting—a reminder of the human he was born to be—if his lack of knowledge wasn't threatening his life. "I don't want to cause trouble to anyone who isn't involved in Alan's experiments," he said. "When I found him here, I was more than happy to drag him out to face my ally." He paused, choosing his next words carefully. "She's a dragon, but she wasn't born one. Alan poured dragon fire down her throat and forced her to change forms. Her name is Ziya, but her human name is Neva."

"And you trust this dragon?" Teyo asked, disbelief plainly written on his features. Apparently, the most unconvincing part of Caleb's story thus far was the idea that humans and dragons could trust one another and work together.

That wasn't exactly the best of signs for Caleb's hopes for an end to the dragon council's renewed declaration of war.

"She and I were both refugees and were conscripted into the army," Caleb explained, hoping that a common history would humanize Ziya and keep her out of the lord's concerns. "Alan had her in his clutches for much longer than he had me, and she has every right to kill him for what he put her through."

"And yet our traditions give us claim to him as well," Teyo said. He didn't sound like he was arguing, more like he was thinking out loud. "You cannot enact revenge on someone in my prison, and yet, our laws demand he stay there—or die as an enemy to humanity, if I judge him to be so."

Caleb nodded. "I don't know anything about your village; I'm sorry. I only came to right the wrongs that were done to me and my friend. I want answers from him about what he did to us. After that, I would not stop you from killing him if that's what you decided to do. You'd be ridding the world of a true evil." He shifted slightly, trying to alleviate the prickling sensation at his shoulder blades that told him his wings wanted to come out. No matter how well the conversation between him and Teyo had gone so far, it seemed his instincts refused to let him relax around the man. "Ziya and I both would want to see proof that he will never harm anyone else again, though. We let him escape justice once; we wouldn't be able to rest if we thought it had happened again."

"You and your friend are in no position to make such demands."

THE GODS' GIFT

"I know," Caleb said. "But I would ask anyway." The hall rang with silence as Teyo leaned on his hands, and Caleb didn't look away. He had been studied before, and he felt his cheeks flushing with the memory of his humiliation; but he kept thinking of Alan and of how badly he wanted an end to the doubts swirling in his waking thoughts and dreams. So, he kept his gaze steady and waited for Teyo to finish deliberating.

"And can your friend transform like Alan can?" Teyo asked, finally letting some of the expected suspicion creep into his questions. Caleb was honestly surprised it took him so long to come to questions like that.

Caleb tried not to show his teeth as he answered. "She can't. I can, to some extent, as Mira told you." He took a deep breath and held it, once more fighting back the urge to breathe fire. Now that Teyo's questions had become more probing, he felt even more on edge. "That's how I saved her. I can withstand dragon fire. When Alan saw me, he made threats against the village and inn that Mira couldn't ignore." He glanced Mira's way and saw that she was studying him as closely as Teyo was. That did nothing to help him stay in his human form, and he felt his fingernails itching. "If I hadn't gotten in between them, both Alan and Mira would be dead. He breathed fire, and she cast a powerful spell that I only survived because her father nursed me back to health."

Teyo glanced toward Mira, confirming Caleb's story. When Mira nodded, Teyo echoed her gesture, though he still regarded Caleb through thinly narrowed eyes. "I'm inclined to believe you, because you saved a dear friend. So, tell me what you want now, other than confirmation of Alan's fate once I decide it."

"I just want to talk to Alan," Caleb said. "That's all I want. I want him to answer my questions. I want to understand what he did to me. After that, you can do what you like with him—as long as you don't let him out to continue his cruel experiments." Caleb's eyes flashed with fire; he knew it had happened but couldn't stop it. "If he leaves this place, if he escapes, I can promise you the green dragon who fought with us will kill him as soon as he leaves your protection. He took her son from her."

Teyo leaned forward, resting his hands on his tented fingers. "And when you have your answers?"

"I'll never bother you again," Caleb swore. "I have family and friends I want to get back to."

Teyo's foot tapped on the stone floor close to the base of his seat. "What you say makes sense," he said slowly. "And yet. . . ." He stood up and took two deliberate steps toward Caleb. He changed nothing about his expression or his body language, but the proximity alone left Caleb almost shaking with nerves.

He couldn't stop himself any longer. Teyo hadn't even come to a stop before Caleb started to growl, a low sound that spilled out through pointed teeth as his lips pulled back to display not only those small fangs but the glow of fire behind them, with smoke in the air as he breathed a warning.

Every human in the hall drew a weapon or a staff—including Mira, who pointed Alan's staff his way with a whispered warning: "Don't be a fool."

Every human was ready to fight . . . except Teyo, who stopped where he was, his lips pursed. "You're not as human as you pretend to be," Teyo said. "I don't know what you are, but you're dragon enough that you can't hide your instincts." He took another step forward, and Caleb let out a rippling growl that moved through the stone around them.

Still, Caleb didn't move from his kneeling position, waiting to see what kind of test Teyo had in store. He had endured Alan's methods; Teyo was no different. As long as Caleb refused to yield, Teyo would have to tell him what he wanted from him.

Once more, Teyo stopped moving forward after Caleb's growl. He locked gazes with Caleb and then, slowly, reached for his sword. Caleb *still* couldn't stop growling, even knowing that the sound put him in imminent danger, but Teyo kept his gaze, unsheathing the sword to show Caleb its unusually white sheen and slight glow. "Do you know what this is?" he asked.

Caleb shook his head, not trusting himself to open his mouth to answer.

"This sword has been passed down through my family for generations. It was forged in dragon fire from the bones of a white dragon killed centuries ago when the war between humans and dragons was fought in every corner of our world." Teyo turned the sword in his hand a few times. "Because it came from a dragon, it has dragon power. It has a magic of its own. That's what you're feeling. Those nerves you've been showing since you walked in here—they come from this sword. You can sense it. The dragon you are can't help it." Teyo smirked. "My father said he could patrol the outskirts of our lands and find hidden dragons because they would growl when he passed with his sword drawn."

"I'm not a dragon," Caleb insisted, though his point was lost in the growl, the near-snarl that garbled his words.

Teyo took a step back at last. "I don't know what you are," he admitted. "And that is why I won't ask my guards to kill you where you stand for coming into my halls. But you're no human either." He gestured to his sides, and his guards made their way forward, some of them entering the room from entrances Caleb hadn't even seen, beyond the stone walls that, Caleb saw now, were cut in patterns that hid openings behind the throne. Within seconds, a dozen guards stood ready to apprehend Caleb should he make a run for it. "If you want so badly to talk to Des, I have no problem sending you to him. You can stay within earshot and eyesight of each other."

It was everything Caleb could do not to show his dragon form, though he could feel scales creeping down his arms and neck and wondered how much was hidden by his clothing and how much those around him could see. "I came here willingly," he said, his hands aching as his nails sharpened in preparation to become claws. "I'm no danger to you or your people."

"That remains to be seen," Teyo said. His expression softened slightly enough that Caleb only noticed it because he had his gaze set on the lord in front of him. "Truth be told, I'm curious to learn more about your story. But I can't do it while you lie to me in my own halls. So, you will remain with the other dragon until I can trust you. If you can manage to earn that much, I'll let you leave. You have my word."

Caleb thought about running. He did. He knew it would be a futile effort with so many people around him who knew how best to bring down a dragon, but he didn't think he could force himself to surrender, either. He couldn't bear the thought of captivity, even one with a promised end.

But if he changed, if he fought Teyo's men, they would either kill him or leave him to rot in chains. And that thought terrified him more than the idea of surrender did. So, he held his hands out to his sides and said, through his teeth, "There's no need for force. I'll go with you."

CHAPTER 12: CAPTIVE ONCE MORE

Alan's laughter echoed in Caleb's ears the second he walked into the prison on the opposite end of the village from Teyo's home. The prison itself, which had been carved out of the mountain the way Teyo's home had been, had been designed to hold people, not dragons. Caleb saw a few humans in cells big enough to be comfortable, unlike the one Alan had left Caleb in when he first chose him for his project. The men and women inside those cells could walk several feet in every direction, and they had cots and clothes that didn't look to be in tatters. Overall, this prison was a vast improvement over the last one Caleb had been in—not that he felt any better about his captivity because of the accommodations.

To hold Alan, the village magicians had apparently combined a few cells, carving out enough space for a dragon behind multiple locked doors. The guards wouldn't be able to see all of Alan at once; the doors had too much stone between them. But since Alan didn't have enough room to turn around, they didn't have to see all of him. They only had to see his mouth, claws, and tail—all visible through the five different barred doors.

Of course, doors and bars wouldn't stop a dragon for long, so the village guards had chained Alan to the wall, far enough away from the bars that he couldn't yank the doors out of the stone like Caleb had done when he'd freed Alan's prisoners what felt like forever ago. What's more, Caleb heard the guards posted in the prison greeting the "extra help," presumably more guards to watch Alan.

Once again, Caleb found himself thinking of Ziya and how she had insisted that killing Alan was the best way to stop him. Here was the evidence he needed to be convinced of her point of view: even those who specialized in stopping dragons seemed woefully underprepared.

Thankfully, the guards didn't take the same extreme measures with Caleb as they had with Alan. The guards that had accompanied him pushed him toward a cell that looked like any other. And that, finally, was an advantage he could exploit. He'd escaped from a place like this before—and with far harsher measures of containment.

Already, Caleb wanted to leave—not because the situation reminded him too much of his forced captivity under Alan but because Teyo had, in fact, arranged for Caleb to be held directly across from Alan, and Alan seemed to be amused by the situation.

"What's so funny?" Caleb growled, the demanded question barely audible over the sound of a guard opening his cell and scraping the metal door across the stone.

"It didn't take you long to find your way back to me, did it?" Alan said, still laughing. "What's the matter, Kaal? Wizards are harder to lie to than soldiers barely older than you are?"

Caleb couldn't help it; he snarled outright, baring his teeth at Alan as he hissed, "This is *temporary*." But the simple fact that he'd snarled had everyone in the prison on edge, and he found himself staring at the end of two swords as the guards closest to him took up defensive positions. Belatedly, he relaxed his expression and raised his hands, but the damage was done.

"Get inside. *Now,*" one of the guards barked, the tip of his sword pointed between Caleb's eyes.

"I'm going," Caleb promised, backing up several steps and nearly tripping over some loose rocks in the stone cell. He kept his hands raised, but the guards didn't relax until they backed him up nearly to the wall. Then, one of them held his sword at Caleb's eye level while the other fastened a shackle around his ankle.

The sound the shackle made as it closed seemed to echo too loudly in the small cave—or maybe Caleb had only imagined that it rang out so clearly. He didn't know if his dragon senses were so keen that the shackle was like a slammed door or if the panic rising in his throat and the tears springing to his eyes had more to do with it.

THE GODS' GIFT

He hated that he'd been reduced to tears, and he did his best to hide that fact, shaking his head and closing his eyes and trying to control his breathing that sounded more like hyperventilation than he was comfortable with. He fought the urge to claw through the chain of the shackle where it connected to the floor, knowing it was likely strong enough to resist a dragon's strength and knowing the guards could stop him even if he broke free. But all he could think about was the feeling of cold metal and the way the light cast shadows of bars against his skin.

"Hey, stop it," one of the guards said, his voice shaking enough to break Caleb out of his thoughts. When Caleb looked up, he saw that the guard had stepped back from Caleb, the hand that wasn't holding his sword on the door, though he hadn't shut it yet, as if he couldn't quite decide if he should leave Caleb be or react more aggressively.

All at once, Caleb realized that he had smoke hot enough to leave embers swirling in the air around him pouring out of his nose and mouth with every hyperventilated breath.

He closed his eyes and his mouth and clenched his hands in fists until he could feel hot blood on his palms. When he opened his eyes again, the guards were still at the door of his cell, but they had backed up and were watching him warily, ready to act if Caleb became a threat again but, for now, giving him space.

Caleb slowly, carefully, let out the breath he was holding, controlling every bit of air so that he couldn't produce any sparks or embers in the smoke. He couldn't stop his smoke, but he could lessen his perceived threat. When he gasped in another breath like a hiccough—because a single held breath couldn't quite make up for all of the hyperventilated panic previously—the guards tightened their holds on their swords but didn't act.

"I'm sorry," Caleb whispered. "I'm alright."

The guards glanced at each other but seemed to decide that they didn't want to fight if they didn't have to. So, they stepped back, closing the metal door with a scraping sound that reminded Caleb too much of the way the doors to Alan's cells had sounded when last he faced humiliation and captivity.

Caleb closed his eyes again, his whole frame shaking. He'd known he had been risking exactly this when he went to the village lord with Mira. He'd known he wouldn't be able to handle it. What he didn't know was why he still felt like he had to keep the peace, why he wanted so desperately to avoid a fight, why he was willing to risk everything instead of following Ziya's plan and simply killing Alan without searching for answers.

He should have listened to Ziya. He should have let her declare war. He should have left well enough alone.

And yet, he wouldn't have been able to live with himself if Alan died without telling him how he'd done what he had done. If Alan died without answering his questions, Caleb would forever wonder what was wrong with him that he was the only one like Alan. He'd forever second-guess his decisions. He'd forever fear that every mistake was bringing him one step closer to becoming the monster Alan was.

His thoughts turned around and around on themselves until he was shaking so badly that he had to sit down. He felt like he was at once reliving his captivity and his escape. He could hear Elena's shoes on the stone as she approached with his food. He could smell burnt flesh. He could smell saltwater and could hear crying.

At some point, he realized that he had pulled his knees up underneath him and had rested his forehead on top of his knees. Because he was only shackled at the ankle, he had enough freedom of movement that he could do whatever he wanted except leave, and yet what he had done in his panic was tuck into a small ball and *cry*.

He hadn't done that in a long time. He hadn't had the time. He hadn't had the luxury of safety to curl on himself and let his emotions drop around him. Even now, he wasn't entirely safe; Alan could see him from his own cell and could no doubt hear how badly he'd taken his latest captivity. But he was separated from Alan, and men trained in magic that could stop dragons stood between them. This was the closest he could get to privacy.

And besides that, he couldn't hold himself in anymore. That rush of panic had provoked something else in him, until he had no words, only the rushing of his heartbeat in his ears and a sensation in his throat that he couldn't swallow but needed to, desperately.

To his surprise, Alan didn't call out to him or try to take advantage of his obvious emotional vulnerability. Instead, he sat there, watching, until Caleb had found the point of emotional exhaustion that allowed him some minor control over his faculties. He had cried enough to feel that he'd let out some of what he'd been holding back but not so much that he felt empty or relieved, only enough that he could push it all down again without feeling the lump in his throat choking him.

And then, only then, did he hear Alan speak up, from across the jail. "It seems your freedom isn't treating you as well as you'd hoped it would without my guidance."

Caleb picked his head up, his eyes long dry, the tears now replaced with fiery indignation. "I wouldn't be in this position if not for you," he shot back. "And you know it."

"Oh?" Alan shook his head, moving the long chain with his neck. The sound of the metal shaking underneath his scales put Caleb's teeth on edge, and he closed his eyes to brace himself. He couldn't change. Not in front of the guards. "I didn't ask you to come looking, Kaal. You did that yourself."

"I came because Ziya reminded me what it feels like to have no power and to rely on others to help. You gave me power; that means I have an obligation to stop people like you from hurting anyone else."

Alan flashed a pointed smile at Caleb and let out a throaty chuckle that rumbled and echoed across the stones of the prison. "Ziya," he said, the simple word both a question and a statement, loaded with satisfaction and insinuation.

"No need to sound so surprised," Caleb said, even though he knew well enough that Alan sounded *pleased*, not surprised. He didn't want to deal with the implications of that, though, so he crafted his own narrative. "I know you're determined to dismiss her, but Ziya is more persuasive than you know."

"To you, perhaps," Alan chuckled.

Caleb rolled his eyes and then scooted back so he could lean against the wall next to the bars. He didn't want to stay in the middle of the cell with nothing but the chain and the floor. That was too familiar, and familiarity kept threatening to turn to blind panic. "We succeeded, you know," he said once he was slightly more comfortable than he had been before, despite the cold metal bars against his shoulder. "You won't be hurting anyone else from inside this cell. Being stuck here would be worth it for that alone."

Declaring his victory aloud, Caleb hoped, would make it true. He honestly didn't know if he believed the words falling from his tongue, if he believed that his life was a fair price to keep Alan locked up, especially when he knew Alan would outlive the guards and would likely try to talk his way out of his imprisonment if he couldn't escape outright in a moment of distraction or weakness in the guards' defenses. A lifetime of trying to stay in a prison cell along with Alan . . . what kind of fate was that? What kind of reward was that from the gods after all he'd been through?

Alan dropped his voice to a whisper only the two of them could hear with their dragon senses. "You don't believe that," he said. It wasn't a question. Alan always spoke as if his declarations were foregone conclusions.

"Of course I do," Caleb said, whispering back and trying to add conviction to his tone despite the drop in volume. It didn't work. "I have to stop you."

Alan readjusted himself, settling his massive wings against his shoulders and laying his head on the ground so he looked more comfortable. "And yet you and I both know you won't kill me. You don't have it in you."

"You'd be surprised," Caleb muttered darkly, looking down at his hands and clenching them in fists. No matter what his reasons had been, he had killed, and he could never take that back. Killing Alan, he kept telling himself, would be different. It would be *worth* staining his claws again.

Alan deserved to die.

"Yes, you've had to do things you never thought you would, right, Kaal?" Alan smiled, showing his pointed teeth. "I know you. You aren't a killer. Not truly. Not yet."

Caleb knew Alan was baiting him, and yet he rose to the bait anyway. He didn't like the implication that he could become any *more* like Alan than he already was. "What's that supposed to mean?"

"Lies only get you so far, Kaal," Alan said patiently, in the same annoying habit he'd had when Caleb was his prisoner: acting like Caleb was a wayward child and Alan was a longsuffering parent. "Humanity is not long for this world, and your course of action is to stand watch here until the day you die? Really?" Alan let out a puff of smoke as he snorted. "You said yourself I'd be surprised to

THE GODS' GIFT

see how much you've changed. You aren't a killer, but you certainly aren't still the child whose sword left marks on his leg."

"It's not your business," Caleb said and folded his arms over his knees.

Alan tilted his head lazily to the side, watching Caleb in silence as long as either of them could stand. Finally, he spoke up again. "You wouldn't surrender to chains again if it didn't suit you. And as much as you claim Ziya convinced you otherwise, you are no hero. You lie when it benefits you and run when you cannot lie your way out of a fight. You could have run from this village, Kaal. You didn't. What do you want?"

For some reason, Caleb could hear, ringing in his ears as if he'd only just spoken them, Alan's words when they'd first met, chiding him for his lies, insisting that they dispense with secrets. Under Alan's watchful gaze once more, Caleb felt just as naked as he had then, just as vulnerable. "I want to know why you and I are the only ones who can change," he said at last. Honesty had once earned him answers from Alan. To his frustration and humiliation, he found himself once again at Alan's mercy, trading his thoughts for what scraps Alan might toss him.

But this wasn't a time for pride. He'd come all this way for answers. If he had to play Alan's games a little longer, that was what he would do. He could manage that for a short time.

Alan didn't answer Caleb immediately, but Caleb held his gaze, unwilling to back down. Once, he had been a captive, and he had looked at the ground and tried to show obedience. Now, he and Alan were equals. Alan's only power was in the answers he held.

And Alan knew it.

With a slowly growing smile that showed more and more of his pointed teeth, Alan picked his head up from the floor and started to nod. "The truth is valuable, Kaal. It comes at a cost."

"You don't have much to bargain for," Caleb pointed out. "I don't have the power to get you out of that cell. I do, however, have my company and my own secrets." He smiled, showing his own pointed teeth in an almost aggressive move. "I'm sure you have questions too. I doubt you put all that work into finding rare humans to turn into white dragons without wanting to know how to duplicate that success."

132

"Your secrets for mine?" Alan's smile widened. "It's intriguing, I'll admit. But you only have a human child's years to talk about. The trade isn't even."

Caleb raised one eyebrow despite his best efforts to keep his expression neutral. Even though Alan hadn't agreed to anything, he had just alluded to living a life far longer than Caleb's—and in terms a dragon would have used. Caleb couldn't be completely sure of the truth yet, but hearing Alan speak that way, he had a feeling Alan had been born a dragon. Already, Alan had given him clues to the very answers he sought.

If Caleb could be clever enough to use his words as the weapons everyone kept telling him they were, he might extract even more answers that way, in clues and allusions without direct questions.

Alan shook out his wings, drawing the attention of the guards, who watched him warily and then settled back into their posts when they saw that Alan wasn't doing anything more than shifting his position. To Caleb, however, the message was clear: Alan was preening, gloating over the desperation he could see in Caleb's curiosity. But Alan didn't say anything further. Instead, he settled into easy silence, his head tilted Caleb's way as if to say, "Your move."

Caleb sighed heavily but forced himself to keep Alan's gaze. "What do you want if not my secrets?"

Alan didn't hesitate. "Heal me."

Whatever Caleb had been expecting, it wasn't that. "What?"

"A dragon cannot heal himself, only others," Alan explained impatiently. Normally, he would have relished the chance to lord his knowledge of dragons over Caleb's head, but he must truly have hated his vulnerability and couldn't be bothered to gloat now that he'd made his demands. "The injuries your allies dealt me led me to this cage, and I cannot escape this prison while I am still healing." He gave Caleb a significant look and moved just enough to rattle the chain attached to his neck. "I know you understand why I'd prefer to leave."

"I already told you I'm not letting you leave this place," Caleb insisted around the lump in his throat that grew at every rattle of the chain. Yes, he wanted answers, but he wouldn't crumble at Alan's first demand.

The second demand, he couldn't be so sure about.

THE GODS' GIFT

"I'm not asking you to aid my escape," Alan clarified. "Heal my wounds and then stand aside. That's all I ask. I don't need your *help* to deal with these humans."

Caleb let out a scoffing breath that hung in smoke and embers in front of his face. He wasn't sure if Alan realized that he had just confirmed, without a doubt, Caleb's suspicions. This time, Alan's revelation came not from his words but from his tone; Caleb had heard other dragons speaking the same way about humans, as if they were a nuisance, as if they weren't worthy of the life the gods had given them.

It made sense. The pride, the advanced magic, the way Alan threw human lives away so cavalierly. He must have been raised a dragon.

But that left Caleb with even *more* questions about his own transformation.

Caleb barely moved, watching Alan, thinking over his response and knowing each word was vital. Finally, slowly, he said, "I give you my word that I will not leave this village until your injuries have healed."

Alan barked out his laughter. "Clever and careful as always, aren't you, Kaal?" he said, soundingly annoyingly delighted. "But it's a good answer all the same. You've improved since last I saw you. There was a time when desperation would have blinded you to what you were promising."

"That's exactly why this is the only promise you'll get from me until you start answering my questions," Caleb said, his teeth bared once more. "I'll decide whether your answers are worth as much as you think they are. I already told you that my goal is to keep you from hurting anyone else. Healing you would go against everything I promised Ziya. I don't treat that lightly."

Alan's smile disappeared for only a moment, but it happened for a long enough time that Caleb knew he was bothered by the fact that Caleb, not Alan, was setting the terms of their agreement.

Good.

Caleb didn't like the way he still felt like Alan was in control even in this prison. If he could wrest some of that control back for himself, he would feel better prepared to deal with Alan's inevitable lies and half-truths.

But then, Alan's smile returned, and he let out a slow, even plume of smoke. "Then let the trade start now," he suggested. "Ask your questions and I shall ask mine."

Caleb nodded once, sharply. "Deal."

CHAPTER 13: ANSWERS

As difficult as it was to wait, Alan and Caleb both agreed that they would begin their interrogations after nightfall. Yes, they could easily have hidden their conversation from the guards as they had been doing up until that point, but the guards during the day shift had meals to bring and seemed to expect more rowdiness from their prisoners than they would at night. Once everyone but the guards had fallen asleep, the low rumble of Alan's responses could easily be mistaken for snores, and Caleb could talk quietly enough behind his knees that, propped up against the wall and sitting on his cot, he would simply look like he was dreaming.

Neither of them feared reprisals from the guards; they simply didn't want to be interrupted.

By the time Caleb could hear the sounds of nighttime creatures outside the cavernous prison, the other prisoners were asleep, and the guards had relaxed somewhat. And yet, Caleb was reluctant to speak first, even though he knew he could have. He and Alan were on equal footing; how many times did he have to remind himself of that fact before he believed it?

Perhaps his surroundings had left him without any confidence he might have had when he first saw Alan in the village, and the fact that Alan had more answers for Caleb than Caleb had stories for Alan also hung over his head. What's more, he had already promised to stay with Alan until he was healed; what else would Alan ask of him? What lines would he have to cross before he reached his limit?

He was so deeply lost in his concerns that he didn't speak up, so Alan filled the silence for him.

"Now then," Alan said, his tone prim and businesslike, "tell me how you first discovered your ability to change. I know it must have happened when you escaped, but *how*? Details, Kaal."

Caleb frowned and didn't immediately answer, already considering how Alan could use information like that against him. If Alan ever got the upper hand again, if Alan were ever able to establish himself in another base, he could too easily keep Caleb captive indefinitely.

But Caleb had agreed to the terms of the interrogation, and he had to have faith—if not in the gods than in the humans who hated dragons—that Alan wouldn't escape justice. So long as Alan remained a prisoner, Caleb was safe.

"You didn't make it easy for me," Caleb said at last, his head resting against the stone of the prison wall, his eyes closed. He wished he had spoken first. Now, sitting in a cell and letting Alan question him, he felt too much like the boy who had been forced to drink a daily potion, the boy who hadn't yet become a dragon. The soft cot underneath him was the only reminder he had of the difference in his situation, though even that was small comfort. "I had to seek out a softer, more vulnerable form in order to change, and your constant torment made my human form undesirable, to say the least."

Alan let out a hum that disguised a laugh well enough that the guards would have thought he was simply sighing in his sleep. "And you never were content to be human in the first place, were you?" he asked, sounding too delighted. Caleb could tell this was going to be a long night if Alan was *already* entertained with the stories Caleb had to trade. "I thought so. Liars cannot stand their lives and truths."

Caleb drummed his fingers against his side, the one that the guards couldn't see. "I lost everything to the war, Alan. This has nothing to do with how I survived after that."

"So you say."

But Caleb had no interest in playing Alan's mind games. He didn't want to second-guess himself more than he already was. He knew his lies had gotten him in trouble, yes, but he'd also managed to avoid being conscripted for long enough for Alan to find him, and he was learning to use his gift for shaping words to more benefit than simply misdirection and hiding. He reminded himself of

THE GODS' GIFT

Ziya and her baffling jealousy of his ability to shape a situation with words alone. She saw something good in what Alan saw as a flaw, and between the two of them, Caleb cared far more what Ziya thought.

So, Caleb let out a patient, controlled breath, kept his temper in check, and said, "Yes. And I stand by what I said."

"Well-spoken."

Caleb didn't thank Alan for the compliment; the words would have tasted bitter on his tongue anyway. Instead, he said, "You keep saying my words are weapons. You shouldn't be surprised I know how to use them."

"You were not this skilled with them when I saved you from the huddled masses at the mountainside."

"And my improvement has nothing to do with you," Caleb shot back coldly.

Despite their earlier attempts at privacy, Alan allowed a laugh to slip past his lips, drifting through the air and wrapping around Caleb like approval he didn't ask for. "No wonder the potion worked so well," Alan chuckled. "You are a dragon at heart, not a human."

Caleb had heard the same sentiment before, from Rikaa, but when Rikaa said it, he had spoken with affection and warmth. Alan had no warmth, only satisfaction, and Caleb couldn't help but growl—not bothering to hide it when he realized one of the guards was headed their way anyway, likely drawn there by Alan's laughter.

"You're not fooling anyone—either of you," the guard said, and Caleb opened his eyes to see that the man had his staff held neatly in front of him—pointed specifically at Alan, the dragon, though Caleb knew he wasn't safe either. "Go to sleep. Don't make my job unnecessarily complicated."

"Or what?" Alan asked, even though Caleb was shaking his head. Caleb knew better than to taunt anyone with power over him unless he had nothing to lose—like when he'd talked back to Alan. This guard could still take too much from them to make defying him worth the risks; Caleb was already actively keeping his body language submissive to avoid tighter chains or smaller rations.

But Alan was used to having power; he didn't know how to tread carefully, apparently.

As Caleb knew would happen, the guard reacted by walking toward Alan's cell, his staff glowing and raised, a spell on the tip of his tongue. "We have laws about how prisoners are treated here," the guard said. "But the laws don't apply to dragons. We've never let one live this long on our land."

Alan scoffed, the very tip of his tail flicking back and forth and betraying his irritation. "If you're going to threaten me, do it," he said in a rumbling growl. "Don't come here with words alone—and don't threaten what you don't intend to do. Your lord ordered me to be jailed here because he is curious. Don't cross him, little magician."

The guard's grip on the staff tightened, his face turning a deep amber. But as he opened his mouth for a spell, Caleb got to his feet to stop him with a sharp but quiet, "Don't give him the satisfaction."

The guard whirled to face Caleb, his face illuminated by the glow of his staff as well as by the warmth of his angry blush. "I thought you two were meant to be rivals—and yet you defend him?" The guard shook his head and continued before Caleb could answer, "Of course you do. You're a dragon too. You both should have been killed on sight."

"Believe me when I tell you I would never defend him," Caleb said in a hiss, his eyes flashing. "But I have dealt with him long enough to know that he likes to poke and prod at you until you lash out, and then, he revels in his superiority by calling you aggressive, reactive, and dangerous." He gestured with one hand toward Alan, who, as ever, looked annoyingly smug. "The moment you react in anger, he'll simply make sure that when Lord Teyo returns to satisfy his curiosity about us, you will have to explain why you allowed yourself to be goaded into torture when the lord himself hasn't decided whether we are to be treated as humans or dragons." He paused. "And he'll say you simply proved that humans are worse than dragons and are too quick to turn to their worst proclivities," he added, though that promise came from his experience with the dragon council, not with Alan. Still, if Alan had been born a dragon, Caleb felt safe in his assumption that Alan's view of humans would mirror that of the other dragons he'd met. Even Rikaa had thought of humans as warmongers until he met Caleb.

The guard looked between the two of them, a muscle working in his jaw, before he let out a disgusted noise and turned on his heel, leaving them alone as he muttered about dragons in colorful but vulgar terms.

THE GODS' GIFT

Alan was already chuckling before he even opened his mouth. "That tongue of yours—"

"I'm aware," Caleb said shortly. "Don't thank me."

"I wasn't going to."

"Good."

Alan chuckled once more, his tail swaying lightly even in the cramped space of the cell. "You are so unlike the boy I met, Kaal," he said, smiling more with every word. "You like the fire I gave you, don't you?"

Caleb curled his lip up and turned his back to Alan, sitting back down on his cot so he could get comfortable once more, ignoring as best he could the sound the chain on his ankle made as it followed the path he walked. "I keep finding myself in situations where fire is warranted, yes, but that's not all I am. You should have seen me with Lord Teyo. I'm still capable of being soft or meek. You haven't changed me as much as you think."

"Still a survivor," Alan mused, mostly to himself, and then lapsed into silence, leaving Caleb feeling distinctly like Alan had learned far more about Caleb than Caleb had meant to give him, especially since they were trading in information, and Caleb needed every piece of himself he could hold back to offer to Alan.

If Ziya could see me now, I wonder if she would still think I had a silver tongue. Alan is obviously much better at this than I am, he thought and then scratched idly at the wall with fingernails that were longer than usual. *I shouldn't have come.*

In the silence that permeated the rocks as Caleb and Alan pretended for the sake of the guards' pride that they were going to sleep, Caleb could hear the other prisoners dreaming. Some moved in their sleep, and others whimpered. Even here, war had left its mark. Caleb wondered how many of the people around him would have been imprisoned had they not been driven mad by the constant threat of dragon fire. Even in this village, this hidden paradise, trauma made its way into the corners and dark places and sank in its fangs, refusing to let go.

Even the guards were touched by the unsettling feeling of looming danger. He could hear their whispered conversations, and not all of them were about such warm topics as the guard whose daughter had taken her first steps that morning. As both Caleb and

Alan pretended to be asleep, the silence allowed Caleb to listen, too, as the guards talked about the last dragon attack and discussed whether they would be able to defend themselves against dragon fire both inside and outside the prison should another such attack occur.

Caleb let his gaze travel toward Alan, wondering if Alan had considered that possibility already. Alan didn't seem nearly as bothered by the bars and walls as Caleb was, and Caleb had a feeling his nonchalance was only partially because of his dragon pride.

I hope Teyo sentences him to death, Caleb thought and then immediately waved off the errant thought. Yes, letting Alan die at Teyo's hand would be preferable to committing the murder himself, but if Teyo found no humanity in Alan to redeem him, then what would be Caleb's fate?

Caleb frowned into his knees, so deep in thought that he jumped when Alan spoke again. "You still haven't told me how you changed," he said.

"Right," he said in a huff of smoke, stretching his fingers in front of himself as he tried to recover from startling. He examined his shorter fingernails with a smile caught near his sharp teeth, never fully formed but hiding there all the same. His thoughts had been on the fears of humans during war; that must have been familiar enough to return him to his original body. "The night before I escaped, I dreamed of my life before the war touched my village," he said. "That was what made me yearn for my human life again. No matter how miserable you made me, my memories were brighter."

"Dreams?" Alan's tail was still as he sat at rapt attention. "Interesting."

"It shouldn't be," Caleb said, frowning. "I couldn't have changed unless I wanted to be human. Isn't that part of why you went out of your way to make me miserable? Being a dragon kept me safer from starvation than I would have been as a human. It made the potions stop hurting. I *wanted* to stay in my scales. You can't tell me the only reason you made me suffer was to break me down. You never do anything for one reason."

Alan bared his teeth in what passed for a smile. "I missed our talks, Kaal. You reason so well."

"I've had a lot of practice in my life dealing with people who believe power is an excuse to hurt others, who think power is only power if you display it in comparison to the weakness of the less fortunate."

"As I said, you see the world as it is," Alan said, nodding his approval—which instantly left Caleb speechless, his cheeks bright red and his fire hot in his stomach. He hated when Alan treated him like his favorite toy. He hadn't asked for Alan's attention.

If Alan noticed Caleb's furious blush, he didn't say anything about it. Instead, he prompted him with, "And after your dream?"

"I woke up human," Caleb said softly, staring at the chain around his ankle. He wondered if he would be able to escape again when he could no longer shrink. He wondered if the chain would snap if he grew to be a dragon or if it would take his foot off instead. "I was too small for the chains you left me in, so when someone came with food, I slipped out through the open door."

"And changed again during your escape," Alan mused. "How did that happen?"

"I'll tell you that after you answer one of my questions." Caleb forced his gaze from his ankle, glaring through the bars. "That was the deal. You don't get two questions at a time."

Alan chuckled. "I was under the impression I was allowed to ask clarifying questions."

"And I think that asking about my first transformation into a human and my first transformation back into a dragon are two separate matters." Caleb kept his chin up. "You said yourself that I don't have nearly as much information to trade as you do. I need to guard every story."

Alan watched Caleb for a long time with his head tipped to the side and a smile showing his teeth. Then, slowly, he started to nod. "Ask your question, then. I'd suggest choosing your words carefully."

Caleb didn't need the warning. He had been thinking all day about what he wanted to ask—and how. Words were Alan's weapons as much as they were Caleb's, after all. So, now that it was his turn, Caleb took a deep breath, let it out in smoke, and spoke each word clearly. "I know you were born a dragon," he said, taking care not to phrase that statement like a question. If he didn't have to ask, he didn't use one of his valuable questions. When Alan didn't give Caleb any indication of whether his guess was right—expertly playing the same game—Caleb continued, "So I want to ask you how *you* first turned human. The potion you gave me works in the opposite direction. How did you find yourself in a different skin without a similar potion?"

"That," Alan said slowly, "will require far more explanation than your storytelling did."

"Then I guess you should have chosen your first question more carefully," Caleb said, allowing a smug smile to grace his features. He was painfully aware that he looked in that moment more like Alan than he was entirely comfortable with, but he actually relished in the opportunity to beat Alan in his own word games, to remind him that he was not infallible, that he was not all-knowing or almighty. Even a skinny little boy could beat him.

Well, not so skinny anymore. But he was still young, still human, and still able to take Alan's pride to task.

As Caleb had hoped, Alan huffed his annoyance. *I win that round*, Caleb thought grimly, though he had a feeling Alan would make him pay for his arrogance somehow.

Still, Alan had agreed to the terms, so despite hemming and hawing, he did, in fact, finally settle back down to answer Caleb's question. "In order you answer you, I will need to teach you the history dragons themselves have long forgotten, the history of white dragons."

Caleb tried not to look to eager, though his eyes shone as he sat up straighter. Before embarking on his hunt for Alan, he had been devouring every bit of knowledge he could get from Rikaa, trying to immerse himself in the new world he had been thrust into. Rikaa himself had admitted that he only knew about white dragons because he had seen one on the council when he was young; any history farther back than that was fast turning to myth among both humans and dragons. The dragons had spent so long fighting among themselves that they hadn't preserved the stories of those they killed; the white dragons were lost because of it.

Alan smiled and drew himself up proudly. "The first dragons were white dragons," he explained. "The gods created dragons without a color and sent them into a world of fire. Then, they filled the earth with creatures for us to eat and for us to care for. And they promised those first dragons that they would bestow gifts upon any dragons who asked for them." He shook out his wings, looking like

THE GODS' GIFT

a bird puffing himself up. "White dragons contained the potential for any of the changes you see in the other types of dragons. We hold all the other colors in our magic. Why do you think we are so powerful? We are the first dragons."

Caleb found himself leaning closer to the bars of his cell despite his earlier resolve not to show any interest. He hadn't been able to shake the feeling that the gods had given him something to do in this world. The fact that Alan had all but confirmed the gods' hands in white dragons' lives had him practically holding his breath, hanging on Alan's next words.

Alan smirked, obviously realizing the power his story held. "It's ironic, isn't it? An orphan of war, a lowly human, and you have all the power of the gods' greatest creations, their first beings."

The sneer in Alan's voice was enough to break the spell of his words, and Caleb leaned away from the bars again, letting out a noise of disgust. "Or maybe the gods gave me this power because you were squandering yours," he shot back, the words coming to him in a moment of anger. He wasn't sure he believed his own insult, but he liked the way it sounded and, in that instant, decided he would believe it until the gods or someone he trusted more than Alan proved him wrong.

Alan let out a growl that was so low the human guards wouldn't hear it, but Caleb could feel it in his teeth as it wrapped around him. The guards likely knew what was happening, but this time, they didn't come to investigate. Maybe they thought Alan was simply growling in his sleep, since it was a noiseless growl.

Still, Caleb waited until the guards seemed to relax again before he whispered his response. "You always get aggressive when I'm right."

Alan pulled back his lips in what would have been a snarl if they hadn't been trying to preserve their privacy. "No, I simply lose my patience when you insist on attributing my good work to anyone else." His eyes flashed with real fire in embers of smoke coming out of his nostrils. "The gods didn't give you anything, you lowly little boy. I did."

"If that were true, there would be more who can change forms like I can, wouldn't there?" When Alan bared his teeth, Caleb held up a hand. "But that's another question. You still haven't answered my first. You gave me a lesson in history, but I still don't know why you can change."

For a long time, Alan glared at Caleb, while Caleb held Alan's gaze, suddenly aware of how neatly he had reversed their dynamic. Now, *he* had the power to demand answers. Now, *he* was steadier on his feet than Alan was. He felt more in control than he had ever felt with Alan.

Finally, Alan let out a steady stream of white-hot smoke. "Yes," he said slowly. "The gods granted gifts to the white dragons—to their hatchlings," he clarified. "White dragons would ask the gods to bless each egg they laid. As the dragons went into the world to protect the gods' creations, they asked for help. They asked to blend into the sky. They asked to breathe underwater. They asked to be as red as fire so that other creatures would see them and know help had come." Alan's tail was starting to move again as he fell back into his story. "The dragon clans you now know took thousands and thousands of years to form. And as dragons staked out their territories, the gods stopped answering those pleas, refusing to give gifts to dragons who asked for power as the clans separated and began to turn on each other."

"But you were given a gift," Caleb said, suddenly wondering how old Alan was.

"Yes," Alan replied shortly. "My mother was a green dragon, but my father was one of the last white dragons. He knew the stories; he knew that the gods would hear him when he asked for help dealing with the newest creations the gods had asked us to tend despite their ungrateful nature and their violence."

"Humans," Caleb whispered.

"Exactly. I came into this world as you humans were killing dragons, stealing eggs, waging war. And the gods—" He drew himself up. "—the gods gave me what I needed to stop them. To destroy them."

Caleb blinked at him in disbelief. "That's not true. The gods wouldn't give you tools to kill the very creations they wanted you to protect!"

"Wouldn't they?" Alan sneered at Caleb. "What makes humans so special? Why do you think you can escape the wrath of the gods? *Your* people threatened to kill off the gods' chosen protectors, and you think the gods would leave us with no tools with which to defend ourselves?"

Caleb swallowed, but his mouth was dry. He'd heard stories of human atrocities, and he knew the dragons had suffered in their clashes with humans, but he hated to think that the gods would have *willingly* created Alan. If he believed that, then what did that mean the gods wanted *him* for?

Alan's eyes flashed as he continued his tale. "The first time I turned human was when human knights attacked my nest. They stole my nestmates to *sell* them before they could hatch, and they killed the rest. They took me home with them thinking they had rescued a human child from dragon clutches, and I burned them all to the ground." His chuckled, the sound as dark as the smoke curling around his words. "Kaal, the gods answered my father's plea for help by making me human."

Caleb clung to the edge of his cot, the thin fabric reminding him of the soft flesh of his human form. His heart raced as he thought of all he had told other dragons about Alan, as he thought of how devastating the war was now that humans had Alan's potions on either side of their conflict. He had once accused Alan of being short-sighted in his war efforts, of not seeing the impending doom of all humanity. Now, he realized that Alan's goal *was* such doom. "Even if that were true," he said softly, slowly, "even if the gods meant for you to defend yourself against humans, they didn't mean for you to *eliminate* humanity."

Alan snorted, and an ember landed on the metal bars, burning brightly before it fell, darkened, to the ground. "They turned their backs on dragons, stopped giving us gifts, and then made way for your kind to rule." He laughed once more, though it sounded hollow. "The gods also gave me the same silver tongue you have, Kaal. If they didn't want me to kill humans, they meant for me to *join* you, to step aside for your rule." He slammed his tail down hard enough to shake the walls of the prison. "And I refuse."

Caleb could hear the guards' footsteps. "Alan—"

"Why should you rule the earth with your wars and your magic and your swords when we were here first?" Alan demanded, no longer speaking at such a quiet level that the guards wouldn't hear their conversation. "Why shouldn't I take your greed and your anger and your hate and turn you against each other and show the gods what monsters you can be?"

"That's not—"

"As we speak, the council is executing your *extinction*, all because I reminded them who their true enemies are. All because I weakened your kind and your lands." Alan laughed, the sound more terrifying than the fire in his eyes. "You want to see the end of this war, Kaal? When I met you, you said you were a survivor. *This* is how you survive. You and the select few humans strong enough to *deserve* dragon power. When I'm through, only dragons will reign, humans will return to their cowering holes where they belong, and I will command my own clan of dragons." The guards were rushing toward Alan, but he paid them no heed. "And my clan will *never* let the humans gain the power they had before. They will never let the council forget their true enemy. And I will never be powerless again. I will be a *king* over dragons who owe me their very *lives.*" The guards pointed glowing staffs at him, but he drew himself up. "Is that answer enough for you, Kaal?"

Caleb winced as the guards sent ribbons of several different colors toward Alan, forcing him into sleep—and then whirled on Caleb. He held up both hands in a gesture of peace. "He's the one who—" He didn't get to say anything else before the guards turned their magic on him, and he slipped to the ground, unconscious.

CHAPTER 14: PURSUIT OF POWER

The first thing Caleb was aware of as he came back to consciousness was an intense feeling of anxiety that ran down his spine and filled his stomach with dread. It was the same feeling he'd had around Lord Teyo and his dragon bone sword, but this time, the feeling was much more intense, much more immediate.

He had been lying flat on his back and started to sit up, blinking sleep away from his eyes—but he stopped short after moving only a few inches. The tip of a sword was at his throat, and even that slight movement left him with a small but painful cut underneath his chin.

Alarmed, Caleb blinked and squinted, concentrating until his blurry vision cleared. He was dismayed but not surprised to see Teyo holding his dragon bone sword against Caleb's skin. He *was* surprised, however, by the change in location. He suspected that he was in Teyo's home, judging by the sparse but ornate decorations on a table at the other end of the room and by the cut stone that made up the walls around them. The couch he'd been reclining on was softer than any bed he'd ever slept in, too—which might have been why he hadn't yet transformed into a dragon. He was in danger, and his every dragon instinct rebelled against the sword under his chin; but he was comfortable, and that was barely enough to remind him of his humanity.

His lies to Teyo were so tenuous that he had been saved by one soft couch.

Once Teyo saw that Caleb was awake enough to take in his surroundings, he spoke up. "My guards tell me you and your friend were causing trouble last night."

Caleb started to shift his position, not to get more comfortable but to see if Teyo would back off at all. The sword at his throat was a threat, yes, but Teyo wasn't there to harm him—yet. He wanted answers. Caleb was curious to see how far Teyo's hospitality and curiosity extended past his suspicion and hatred of dragons.

Apparently, Teyo's patience was not enough to abide *movement*.

The moment Caleb shifted to put his weight on his hands so that he could have pushed himself up from the couch, Teyo hissed a warning through his teeth. "Make one move and I'll remove your head, dragon."

Caleb froze, suddenly keenly aware of every inch of his body. He didn't think he had grown any scales, and he knew he hadn't grown anything as obvious as a tail or wings, so the name "dragon" was Teyo's way of telling Caleb he didn't see him as human.

He saw him as an enemy.

Caleb carefully lowered himself back to the couch, and Teyo kept the sword at his throat the whole time. The longer the sword stayed underneath his chin, the itchier Caleb's palms became—until he realized that scales were breaking out and clenched his hands in fists to hide them. "I don't want any trouble," Caleb said, frustrated when his dragon accent slipped through and the words rang with a deep growl he simply couldn't stop. That dragon bone sword would ruin him if he wasn't careful.

"If that's true, then you shouldn't have any trouble telling me what you and Des were plotting during the night," Teyo said, his eyes narrowed. "My guards may not have heard everything you said, but they aren't as stupid as you seem to think they are."

"I never suggested they were," Caleb said. His nails felt sharp against the skin of his hands, and his fingers felt sticky as they merged together. If Teyo took his gaze off of Caleb's face, he would see the beginnings of claws. Caleb couldn't keep lying much longer.

"Then why conspire in secret when I offered you clemency on the condition that you proved you could be trusted?" Teyo demanded, leaning forward until the tip of his sword drew a drop of blood, and Caleb's arms burst into white scales despite his best attempts to keep his changes under control. "You claim Des is your enemy but plot with him in the dark. Why should I trust you at all? Why should I bother to keep you alive?"

Caleb couldn't swallow around the lump in his throat without driving his neck deeper into the sword. "I. . . ." He leaned back, deeper into the couch, swallowing when he had a slight reprieve, all too aware of how badly his shoulders hurt, how much his back itched. "You're right," he said at last, knowing he was caught and knowing if he didn't confess now that he would never see the light of day. "I've been hiding the full truth from you—out of fear that you will lock me up for the rest of my life the way Alan once threatened to do." His eyes were wide, pleading, the expression familiar to anyone who had seen him in the refugee camp. When he was smaller and scrawnier, he had won pity with exactly that expression. Now, Teyo barely blinked. "Please, don't punish me for what Alan did to me. I was born human, I swear—but I can become a dragon if I want to."

In the silence that followed Caleb's confession, Caleb could feel his scales meet his shoulders and could feel the beginnings of wing nubs forming where the scales ended. His arms and legs now had nothing human left about them—and the scales kept climbing. In a few more seconds, they would cover his neck, shielding him somewhat from Teyo's blade. If Teyo reacted in violence and anger, Caleb would complete his transformation—and face the consequences.

And yet, Teyo did nothing except meet Caleb's gaze, probably searching for any sign of deception. Seeing none, Teyo finally moved back enough that Caleb could shift position without meeting the end of a blade—and once that happened, Teyo saw how much Caleb had already transformed. His eyes narrowed, and his brows knit together. "I cannot trust someone who only tells me the truth when it is about to be revealed anyway."

"And it's impossible to tell the truth to someone who gives no pity, no sympathy, no room for nuance," Caleb said, his s's elongating as smoke spilled out of his mouth. "You see what color my scales are. I've spent all my time since meeting Alan being compared to him. If you think I'm like him too, I'll never be free again." Despite his best efforts, Caleb felt his voice break. A life of captivity would destroy him. He wasn't above begging for his freedom.

Once again, Teyo was silent, weighing out Caleb's words without looking away from him. "No dragon has ever been allowed to leave our village alive—not unless they escape in the heat of battle."

"And I'm not trying to break with tradition," Caleb swore, his neck itching as his skin started to fall away to scales. "I was born human. I told you the truth when I explained why I came here. Nothing I said was a lie except the extent of my ability to change." He gestured with one clawed hand and was instantly met with the point of the blade again. His shoulders felt like they were on fire. "Alan and I were arguing last night because I wanted answers from him. I already told you that was why I came. We kept our conversation private because I didn't want him to lie for the sake of your guards if they were listening in."

Teyo didn't move. "And did you get your answers?"

"Some," Caleb admitted. He didn't see a reason to keep those answers to himself, especially if Teyo ended up killing him. Someone needed to know the truth, or it would die with him and Alan there in the village prison. "I know he was born a dragon. I know he claims his ability to change as a gift from the gods. He thinks it gives him a mandate to destroy our kind any way he can—by changing us into dragons, stirring up wars, or provoking the dragon council. But I don't understand nearly enough." He didn't dare move other than to look down with his gaze alone to draw attention to his scaly appendages. "I don't know why I'm like this. I don't know if what he did to me is a curse or a blessing from the gods like he claims it to be." He let some of his frustration spill through in the growl already lacing his words, intensifying that growl until his words were only audible to Teyo. Anyone farther away from the two of them could hear the growl and nothing else. "Your men put us both to sleep before I could learn anything more than what I already knew: that he thinks he can play at being a god himself."

A few men on the outskirts of the room stepped forward, ready to protect their lord, but Teyo waved them off, still without taking his gaze from Caleb's face. "Why should I believe you and not him?" Teyo demanded. "If I drag him in here, won't he tell me that you're the enemy? That you are a dragon and he is a human?"

"Probably," Caleb admitted. "But your guards heard what he was talking about before they put him to sleep. He was boasting about his superiority. Alan can lie as well as I can, but the difference between us is that I only do it when my survival is at stake. He does it to get what he wants."

Teyo nearly smirked. "At least you admit now that you *have* been lying."

"To survive," Caleb reiterated. "The truth is easier to remember than a lie. I'd rather tell the truth if I can."

"I believe that much," Teyo said, finally lowering the sword, though he didn't sheath it. Still, despite his ready stance, Teyo finally moved his gaze from Caleb's face, frowning as he looked toward one of the windows. "The truth of the matter is that I no longer have the luxury of time. I must decide whether or not to trust you—and quickly. The fires of war are getting closer to my village every day, and I don't mean that in a poetic sense."

Caleb thought of the smoke and fire he had seen while he had been masquerading as a Junnin soldier and nodded. "I've been in the middle of all of that," he said. "I grew up watching the skies for dragons and running from soldiers. And I've never been able to escape it."

"Then you understand why I need to focus on protecting my people, not on your petty arguments with this wizard."

"Then don't worry about me," Caleb shot back. "I don't need your protection. I just need answers. All I wanted when I came here was to find Alan, interrogate him, and bring him to justice. I'm not asking you to get in the middle."

"That's not what I meant," Teyo said, sounding tired, though he seemed to realize he was showing his weariness and weakness and straightened up. "I haven't decided what to do with you yet. It would be easiest to kill you both and be done with it. You are both dragons, and you're on my land. I should do just that."

The only reason Caleb didn't transform fully in response to a threat like that was that he could see the hesitation in Teyo's expression and knew he had more to say. "But. . . ." he prompted when Teyo kept his silence long enough that Caleb's shoulder blades were starting to itch again.

"But I also can't ignore that you saved the life of a dear friend; and I can't ignore that, if your story is true, you didn't ask for this body. A good ruler avoids cruelty at all costs; I'm trying to do that."

Briefly, Caleb wondered how long Teyo had been ruling. He wasn't much older than Caleb, and despite the strength he projected, he slipped in moments like that one, moments that revealed he was the same as Caleb: a child who had grown up in a war faster than children were meant to do. "Tell me what you need from me," Caleb told him.

"A deadline," Teyo said frankly, so readily that Caleb knew he had been about to ask even if Caleb hadn't offered. "I can give you three more days, but after that, I don't want to be worrying about the dragons in my village. Three days to get your answers—and to give me a reason not to kill you both."

Three days? Caleb didn't argue, but he could feel his heart in his stomach. He'd barely gotten *one* question answered on the first night. Three nights . . . three questions . . . that wasn't nearly enough. "Then you have to tell your guards not to put us to sleep again," Caleb said. "I can't get answers if I'm unconscious."

"I can't make any promises for them when their job is to prevent criminals from causing further problems for my people."

"He was boasting about his power. You can at least tell them not to overreact to *words,*" Caleb pointed out. "If they don't know the difference between threats and actions, they are too reactive to guard anyone."

Teyo let out a huff that was almost a laugh. "Fair enough," he agreed and got to his feet, backing slowly away from Caleb, still unwilling to drop his defensive posture. "I'll speak to them. In the meantime, I would suggest you take a friendlier form. We only have one cell for a dragon, and we had to craft it out of others. If you want any deference at all, you'll want to avoid creating more problems for my men."

"I don't have as much control over my form as I'd like," Caleb admitted. "This—" He gestured with one scaled claw. "This is a reaction to danger. Something about this magic has taken over my instincts. When I need to protect myself, this happens—unless my human form is better suited for protection. I can stop the change if I concentrate hard enough, but. . . ." He trailed off. Yes, he knew he needed to tell Teyo the truth to win his trust and his freedom, and yet, he didn't want Teyo to have any more power over him than he already had. Admitting that Teyo's sword could induce a form

153

change could be dangerous. He didn't want someone else to be able to choose his form *for* him.

Teyo paused in his retreat, seeming to study Caleb anew. "How long ago were you changed?" he asked, his tone nearly gentle.

"I . . . don't know," Caleb said slowly, wondering what had changed between them. If he knew what he'd said that gained him an ounce of trust, he would do it again. Teyo's grip on his sword wasn't nearly as tight; his knuckles were no longer white. "It's been months since I escaped, but I have no idea how long I was in his grasp. The seasons changed, but I couldn't tell how much time passed when I wasn't always conscious—and when I was, I was in pain more often than not."

"You speak about it so easily," Teyo said.

"What did you expect?" Caleb asked, frowning. He couldn't understand what Teyo wanted from him, so he didn't know what answer he should give. "Did you want me to fall to pieces and beg for your protection when you already know I have dragon power in me? I doubt you would have believed that."

"That's not what I meant," Teyo said, matching the depth of Caleb's frown, though he hadn't made any more defensive moves either.

Caleb wished he could figure Teyo out, but he didn't have any prior experience with leaders. The closest thing he had was Alan, who styled himself the master of his creations but wasn't born to do anything but protect the world. Caleb had known captains in the army, too, but they had taken their orders from higher powers. But Teyo led a village; he led a group of humans who defended an entire way of life. He had a heaviness about him that Caleb couldn't understand, and it infected his every word.

And yet, he doubted other leaders were as thoughtful as Teyo. He doubted that the Junnin and Hayna nobility saw anything but their bloodlust; if they had Teyo's insight or care for their people, they would have tried to stop the war by now. They would have tried to salvage what they could of the world. Instead, they were likely dead by now, victims at last to the dragon fire the rest of their kingdoms had endured because of their choices.

Not that Teyo was much better. He definitely cared about his people, but he prioritized them over the rest of the world. Teyo's people had power that could have stopped dragons from burning the world down, but they hoarded their knowledge and magic.

"No one where I'm from knows about your village," Caleb said, giving voice to a thought that hadn't fully formed.

"We value our secrecy," Teyo said, his brows furrowing at the change in conversation.

"You turned your back on the rest of us." Caleb wasn't surprised when Teyo's eyes flashed, but with every word, he felt more confident. His shoulders hurt less as he squared them to Teyo's gaze. He always felt more like himself when he could stop cowering and could use his words as weapons, not as shadows to hide in. "You sit out here far away from everyone else and fight dragons on the border instead of stopping the war that's killing the rest of humanity."

"We can't—"

"You're just like the dragon council, but at least they were far enough away not to see the fires of war and the refugees like you do," Caleb said, his eyes flashing with fire stronger than Teyo's anger. He didn't know what possessed him to speak out like this when he had been so *careful* in his dealings with Teyo until that moment. He didn't know what made him think he was safe to speak his mind other than a single word of gentleness Teyo had spoken. And yet, Caleb could feel his scales retreating. He felt more in control. Maybe that was why he kept talking. "They decided a long time ago to let humans kill each other off. You're letting them win because you think your village's *spat* with the nearby dragons is anything like the war that's killing the rest of us."

"*How dare you*," Teyo bellowed—though he hadn't drawn his sword. He stalked forward, one finger pointed at Caleb in accusation. "How dare you compare us to those—those *monsters*? What gives you the right to pass judgement on the way my people have lived for generations? You think some white scales give you that kind of authority?"

"No, I think the life I lived before I got power gives me the right to tell those who have it the truth," Caleb shot back. "You asked for honesty, and here it is—I've met the dragon council. I pleaded with them for help, but they turned me away. And the moment Alan threatened *their* peace too, they declared war on humanity. They were just waiting for the excuse." When Teyo stared at him, his hand near his sword, his finger still pointed at Caleb, Caleb leaned back against the arm of the couch, softening his tone as he continued, "There will be nothing left. They'll come here too. All because the humans who knew how to stop dragons *wouldn't* and the dragons who promised the gods to protect us *refused.*"

Teyo was shaking with fury, but he still hadn't moved other than to work his jaw and glare at Caleb. And Caleb, for his part, held his gaze. He knew how to pick his fights carefully. Yes, he knew when to be invisible. But when he couldn't be invisible, he would rather make a difference, speak the truth he had seen when no one cared to pay attention to him.

When Teyo still hadn't responded, Caleb smiled grimly. "I'll keep trying to get the answers I came here for, but if *you* want answers, I'd suggest finding the tallest point in the village and watching the smoke on the horizon. That's the destruction of war getting steadily closer. That's humanity dying out. And when it comes here, all that will be left of our people will be a terrified few who managed to escape the flames but never the loss."

Teyo straightened up slightly and then let out a noise that sounded like he had tried to stop it in his throat. "I didn't bring you here to listen to you dictate to me."

"No, you didn't," Caleb agreed. "But you admitted yourself that you can see the war getting closer. The least I can do is tell you exactly what's in store." He raked his gaze over Teyo, searching for understanding. "You're as young as I am. You can't possibly know what's out there. Please, before it gets here, ask your own questions. You have enough refugees here to find answers."

For a long time, the two of them stood like statues, taking each other's measure with their gazes alone. Then, Teyo tsked and waved his guards forward. "My men will take you back to our prison," he said as the guards approached Caleb from every side. "In three days' time, you will either have your answers or I will make my decision." With that, Teyo turned on his heel and stalked out the door, leaving Caleb, as promised, with guards that would escort him back to the prison.

And yet, even with how bone-deep Caleb's terror was when he faced the prospect of further imprisonment, he actually felt more relaxed when Teyo left the room. Part of that, yes, was the simple fact that the sword had left with Teyo, but Caleb also felt satisfied knowing he had at least attempted to influence a leader of men, someone who actually had the status to *change* things.

The gods gave me a silver tongue and white scales. I know how to use one of those gifts, Caleb thought to himself, still smiling even as the guards approached.

The guards looked understandably wary of Caleb's pointed smile and the scales running up and down his arms and legs. The trousers Mira had given him had split in some places, especially above his ankles as his claws came out, so they could see exactly *what* he was. Even if Teyo had promised not to kill him yet, the guards clearly didn't think much of their lord's decision and seemed hesitant to approach.

Caleb purposefully stretched his smile wider so the guards could see how sharp his teeth were, forcing them to reckon with the changes they could see. "I don't bite," he said, smiling wider when he saw them take a slight step back.

And then, all at once, he realized what he was doing. Intimidation. Flaunting his power. Reveling in someone else's fear because it gave him a sense of control in an uncontrolled situation. This was *exactly* what he hated soldiers for doing. Exactly what *Alan* did.

Caleb lost his smile entirely and nearly lost track of his stomach as well, suddenly dizzy in a way that had nothing to do with the fact that he was unsteady on his feet when the guards pulled him upright. He could walk on two scaly legs when his spine wasn't yet bent with wings and a tail, but it was an awkward proposition made more difficult when his mind was elsewhere and the guards on either side of him were eager to get rid of him and kept up a brisk pace.

His head was swimming, and he couldn't hear what the guards were saying over the sound of his own heartbeat. Not that he believed they were saying anything more than threats and insults. Still, he couldn't concentrate on even something that trivial when his body felt rigid. He could feel the scales retreating from his shoulders. His skin was softening. For the first time in a long time, he didn't *want* the scales. He didn't *want* the power Alan had given him. He didn't *want* to be a dragon, not if dragon power made him anything like Alan.

All this time insisting I was nothing like him, and now. . . .

THE GODS' GIFT

Caleb bared his teeth before he could even finish the thought. No, he wouldn't allow himself to fall into the trap of becoming the thing he hated. He would be more vigilant, more aware. He wouldn't let power drive him into pride and domineering. He couldn't.

He had to retain his humanity. If he couldn't do that, then what was the point?

CHAPTER 15: COMPARISONS

Caleb was still so shaken by his brush with Alan's style of imperious pride that he forgot to be upset about going back to his cell. Once the shackle was closed around his ankle, however, the same feelings that had consumed him the last time he was chained down overcame him. Combined with the guilt he was already carrying, he nearly choked on the weight of it all, and he simply put his head in his hands, ignoring the guards as they left.

He was aware, somewhere in the back of his mind, that Alan said something to him, but he was so lost in the crushing sensation of panic, guilt, and self-hatred that he didn't hear the words properly. Even if he'd heard Alan, though, he would have done his best to ignore him. The last thing he needed was for Alan to worm his way back into his ear with comparisons. Caleb was already doing a good enough job likening himself to Alan without help.

He would have been content to sit like that until he naturally came out of his thoughts, until he could feel the ground beneath his feet and could remember his own worth, but Teyo's deadline floated back into the forefront of his mind after half an hour. And while Caleb could feel sorry for himself any time he liked, he couldn't make up for lost time if the allotted three days passed and Caleb had no answers to show for it.

He clenched his hands in fists hard enough that his palms bore the imprints of his fingers long after he released the tension in his hands. He took in a breath, held it, and forced his shoulders down. He cracked his neck. And then, at last, he picked his head up and looked toward Alan, not at all surprised to see that, despite his silence, Alan was still watching his every move.

THE GODS' GIFT

When Alan saw Caleb meet his gaze, he smiled. "I take it your dalliance with the lord didn't go well?" he said pleasantly.

Caleb nearly replied with a caustic remark, but he paused before he formed the thought. Alan genuinely didn't *know* what Teyo had planned. He didn't have the same information Caleb did. For once, Caleb had a strong advantage. He could manipulate the situation to his liking.

And yes, he had promised himself that he wouldn't become Alan. But when dealing with Alan himself, he was willing to lie and manipulate. He only had three days, after all.

He told himself that he would stop making compromises like that, but he didn't actually believe it. He believed in the gods and was trying to be a good person, a good dragon, but old habits were hard to break, especially habits that had kept him alive and sane through a war that threatened to kill every last member of his kind. He told himself, too, that ending the war would drive out the *need* for compromises, but in the meantime, he would simply have to endure his discomfort. Just a bit longer.

When Alan waited expectantly for an answer, Caleb let out a derisive noise and let his head drop to rest on the tops of his knees. "For some reason, he doesn't believe me when I tell him that I'm not a dragon."

Alan's smile widened. "Imagine that."

Caleb pulled his lips back into a snarl. "It isn't funny," he said, allowing some of his anger and fear because of the situation to enter his tone; his emotions fit his lie and made it easier to believe. "I didn't *ask* to spend my entire life locked away like some animal!" Caleb worked hard not to react in anything like triumph when he saw Alan pick his head up in obvious interest. He couldn't give away his game now. So, he kept his lip curled back and let smoke out of his mouth as Alan replied:

"I told you humans aren't worth protecting."

"I wouldn't be here if not for you," Caleb shot back. "I'll be stuck here the rest of my life, and if Ziya tries to come. . . ." He trailed off and looked away. He knew what so many people and dragons thought about him and Ziya. He knew, too, that Alan had been interested in their fast friendship. If Alan thought he would one day rule over a new race of dragons, he likely saw potential in manipulating an entire family of dragons, particularly one started by two dragons Alan had made himself. And Caleb didn't mind playing into that fantasy—as long as Ziya wasn't there.

"Maybe we should reconsider our arrangement," Alan said, his tone disinterested, but Caleb knew he couldn't have been as careless about his proposal as he sounded. "I doubt these humans will give Ziya the same consideration they give us. She cannot change."

Caleb knew Alan was right, and he *was*, in fact, worried about what Ziya might do over the next three days if she decided he was taking too long and needed rescuing. So he was only partially lying when he said, "I'd rather find a way to help her myself, even here."

"And how do you intend to do that?" Alan pointed out. "You are stuck. Humiliated."

"Don't remind me," Caleb said sharply. When Alan smiled, as he always had when Caleb would let some aggression show, Caleb looked away and shook his head, taking a deep, obvious, calming breath. "Tell you what," he said slowly. "*Maybe* I'll think about something new. But I still have questions. I can't trust you."

"Then we start where we were last night," Alan said, his teeth reflecting some of the sunlight that had filtered in through the long tunnel that led outside.

"Try not to scare the guards again. They'll kill us both if you're not careful, and I've already suffered too much for *your* crimes."

"I'll do as I wish," Alan said—which was about what Caleb had expected him to say. Still, Alan didn't raise his voice or draw attention to their conversation as he said, "I think I'll start the questions again. You never did tell me the rest of your escape."

Caleb smirked to himself. Maybe he had only succeeded in changing the dynamic of their relationship *slightly,* but at the moment, Alan didn't know about the deadline Teyo had set. He didn't know the war with the council was getting closer. He didn't know that Caleb had a possible way out of the prison that didn't involve a deal with Alan. And as long as Alan believed he held a position of power over Caleb, he would probably be more willing to give Caleb answers. He liked to gloat. He liked to make Caleb figure out the truth. He liked to test Caleb's intelligence. And all of that was better than holding information hostage if he thought Caleb held more power than he did.

THE GODS' GIFT

So, Caleb gladly told Alan more about his escape, about how he had changed back into a dragon out of desperation and fear, about how he'd heard Ziya calling out for help and had followed her lead. But when Alan pressed him for details of what happened after he left the cave, Caleb shook his head.

"I fell into the side of a mountain and was buried in the snow. Your men didn't find me because I blended in. If you want to know how I came to find other dragons, that's a new question."

Instead of arguing against splitting the questions, Alan nodded his approval. Caleb had been right to believe Alan was more comfortable thinking he had power; Alan didn't seem to quibble over every scrap of information when he thought he had time to cajole Caleb into subservience again.

"Alright," Alan said. "And your question?"

Caleb didn't hesitate. "You say you're a white dragon, but you and I are so different. You even tried to study my fangs when you held me captive. So, why didn't you recognize me as another white dragon? Are all white dragons different from each other?"

"That's two questions, Kaal," Alan chuckled, though before Caleb could clarify which one he wanted answered, Alan went on. "Still, I'll answer you, because the answer to both is the same."

"Lucky me," Caleb said.

Alan laughed again, a few embers floating past his eyes. He might have been relaxed, acting like he had the upper hand, but those embers told Caleb that Alan hated his captivity; his fire was too hot in his belly to contain it all. Whether that fire was because he thought he was too good to be held captive by humans or whether he had his own history with confinement, Caleb couldn't be sure. But Alan wasn't at the top of his game.

Caleb, on the other hand, had hope for the first time in a while. Teyo could have struck Caleb down when he criticized his rule. He could have ordered his men to kill the troublemaking dragons in his prison. He could have run Caleb through with his dragon bone sword as soon as he saw how much Caleb had transformed into Kaal. Instead, he had given Caleb a deadline.

Teyo might not have said as much out loud, but Caleb had a feeling that the lord didn't feel right about keeping Caleb captive. Something had changed when Caleb told him the truth. Caleb didn't know what, but he wasn't going to question his luck—especially when he didn't have good luck too often.

And so, Caleb had hope for freedom, while Alan had angered too many people in the village to find allies there. *Caleb* was Alan's best hope for freedom while he was still weak from his last battle. Yes, every day that passed made him stronger as his wounds healed on their own, but he couldn't fight off a village full of wizards in his current state.

Alan shifted his wings so he could get more comfortable, drawing Caleb's attention. "I don't know the true answer to why you look so different," he admitted, and Caleb tried not to smile. Alan so rarely admitted to weakness or ignorance; that admission alone was a promise of honesty Caleb couldn't have gotten otherwise. Or, at least, it was as close to honesty as Alan could get. "That's why I wanted to study your teeth. You don't seem to have some of the advantages I do, like the venom I used on your friends."

Caleb pulled his lips back in a growl low enough that the guards couldn't hear it but could probably feel it. He still hadn't forgiven Alan for how badly he'd hurt Ziya, Rikaa, and Aonai. How he'd hurt his *family*.

Alan chuckled. "Aggression. You're becoming more dragon-like with every day."

"Thank you."

Alan's smile widened even more. "So, you can also see that dragons are so much better than the mud-crawling—"

"I like being a dragon. I didn't say I hated humans," Caleb said, cutting Alan off before he could get going. He wouldn't have been surprised if Alan's previous outburst had been calculated not just to upset Caleb but to draw the guards' attention and ire. Yes, Alan had a temper and was prone to shouting, but Caleb didn't think he was prone to speeches. Last time Alan had soliloquized the foibles of humanity, their interrogation had been interrupted just as Caleb learned *exactly* what no other dragon could tell him. Caleb wouldn't have been surprised if Alan interrupted his own answers to make Caleb come crawling back for more such knowledge. And Caleb wasn't going to let Alan pull the same trick twice. If he had to, he would interrupt every arrogant speech.

Alan let out a derisive sound. "You hate being human."

THE GODS' GIFT

"Yes." Caleb didn't see any advantage in hiding that truth. "But the life I lived before was miserable. If I'd been born before you egged the kingdoms into burning down every last bit of life, I don't know that I'd be a dragon nearly as often or as well as I am now." When Alan sneered and opened his mouth to form a retort, Caleb held up a hand. "You're not answering my question, though. You and I are different. Why?"

"That's not quite the question you asked, Kaal."

"It's the essence of the two questions you promised to answer."

Alan bared his teeth, but rather than responding with another outburst, he chuckled and shook his head, settling his shoulders and his head so that he was resting on the floor again. "I think," he said, slowly, "that you, Kaal, are as the white dragons of old once were."

Caleb's eyebrows shot up, and he found himself leaning forward. "Oh?"

Alan nodded, though he looked annoyed instead of pleased with Caleb's obvious interest, embers flashing once more in the smoke that came out of his mouth as he continued, "Not every white dragon who asked the gods for a change then changed colors. Some asked for help in war as the world grew more dangerous with each new creature the gods placed on the earth." His tail was still except for the very tip, which kept twitching, giving away his irritation in addition to the glow in his mouth. "I inherited traits from both sides of my family. My mother's sharpness. My father's venom. But before those gifts, at the very start, the first dragons, the ones who contained all the colors at once, were not made for war. They were made for the gods' delight."

"So your potion made an ancient creature out of me." Caleb leaned back until his back hit the wall and then reached up to run his hand through his hair, his eyes wide. "Wow."

Alan straightened up, trying to seize his pride back. "Yes, you should be awed," he agreed. "I did what only the gods could do."

"You're no god," Caleb shot back, ignoring the warning growl Alan gave him. "I'll bet you didn't mean to create anything like me. You were so surprised when I developed the way I did."

"Don't presume to know *anything*—"

Caleb snarled at Alan in response to his angry outburst. The guards headed toward them with magic staffs in hand, ready to break up the fight, but Alan looked both surprised and pleased and started to laugh, leaving the guards standing at the ready, their brows furrowed as they tried to decide if they were needed.

"It's nice to have power, isn't it, Kaal?" Alan said, still laughing. "It's nice to be able to intimidate others into silence."

All at once, Caleb couldn't keep hold of the glare he'd meant to give Alan. His lips parted, and his eyes widened. He hated that he had so obviously shown Alan how badly his words pierced him, but he couldn't help it. The pain of realizing that his good intentions were not enough to stand against the temptation of abusing his dragon power—it was all too fresh. He couldn't hide how much Alan's truth hurt him, because he still hadn't come to terms with it himself.

As Caleb leaned against the wall with both of his hands in his hair, the guards stood between their two cells, turning to look at each dragon captive in turn. Alan didn't say anything and didn't try to provoke their anger, but he did let out a soft laugh when the guards finally could find no reason for their presence and returned to their posts and their patrols.

"Careful, Kaal," Alan said. "You'll lose yourself."

Caleb finally regained his glare, but it didn't have the same power that it had held before. "Like you? You gave up on the gods and embraced the authority you could find with humans. I'll bet you hardly recognize yourself lately."

Alan pulled his lips back, his eyes flashing and his claws extended to their full length. If Caleb hadn't spent as much time with dragons as he had, he wouldn't have known how angry Alan was, because his tone was perfectly calm as he replied, "I embrace power, Kaal. You run from it."

"No, I try to use it correctly."

"You wield power like a child," Alan replied. "You revere it and tell yourself lies so that you feel more comfortable with it, but you use what I gave you like a toddler holding a sword. You know it's dangerous, but you can't help imagining you are a hero the second you pick it up."

"I'm no hero," Caleb said, his eyes narrowed. "And I never said I was."

"All your actions and insistences on honor to the contrary."

THE GODS' GIFT

Caleb let his hands drop away from his hair and let out a mirthless laugh. "I would have been perfectly happy staying with the friends I've made as a dragon and starting a new life. I wouldn't have come after you if Ziya hadn't—" All at once, he cut himself off, realizing that he was revealing more than he meant to when information was all he had to trade. "I'm no hero," he said, his face flushed red and his stomach hot with fire.

Alan smirked. "Go on. What were you about to say?"

"Is that a question?" Caleb shot back.

"If you like."

Caleb didn't like how *amused* Alan sounded, but he wasn't going to break their agreement either, not when he still had more to ask. So, Caleb answered, "Ziya convinced me to seek you out." When Alan picked his head up, showing his interest, Caleb swallowed and continued, "She reminded me that we both grew up hating the soldiers who turned their backs on the suffering their friends and families were going through. *Ziya* is the hero. She's the one who believes power means nothing unless it's used to save the weak." He glared down at the ground, bitterness creeping into his tone. "I hide. I always have. Ziya's the hero. I'm just the one the gods blessed with the ability to change."

Alan was quiet for a long enough period of time that curiosity got the better of Caleb, and he looked up to see Alan watching him with exactly the same intensity that had once made Caleb believe Alan could see right through him. When Alan saw that he had Caleb's attention again, he said, "You think too much of yourself."

"Really?" Caleb chuckled dryly. "I told you I'm a coward and praised Ziya instead. What more do you think I should do to debase myself?"

"No, it's not that," Alan said. "You think too much of yourself when you say the gods blessed you. They had nothing to do with your power. I gave it to you." He spoke lazily, his tone almost bored, as if the topic of conversation was no more important to him than the details of Caleb's escape, but his tail twitched at the very end; he was angry over being considered *after* the gods.

"*You* think to much of yourself," Caleb shot back, his eyes flashing. Until he'd become a dragon, he had believed the gods didn't care about their creations, but evoerything he'd learned since then told him they still cared about the fate of the earth. Even Alan's story corroborated that belief; they had once given gifts to dragons so they could bless the earth on their behalf. Hearing Alan take credit for *their* generosity had Caleb's blood boiling.

He could actually feel scales breaking out over his neck and face, and he had to take a deep breath to calm back down. Teyo might have kept his reaction composed when he saw Caleb's scales, but Caleb didn't trust the guards to do the same—especially not when they still had their staffs out despite returning to their posts.

"I had no idea you thought so much of the gods," Alan said. "They let this world drown in war and destruction, and you think they care about *you*?"

"Yes." Caleb held his head high, power in his gaze.

Alan snorted black smoke that filled the space between their cells. "We'll see who is right."

"We will," Caleb said. He refused to back down, sure that, in this one thing, he knew better than Alan did. Everything he had learned from Rikaa about the love the gods had for the world had felt right in a way he couldn't explain. He had learned to trust his instincts and feelings since becoming a dragon, especially when those feelings reached all the way down to his bones. He was right about this.

He *was*.

But as Alan kept laughing, Caleb decided not to start a fight that would use up precious time. So, knowing he was right, he set aside that argument and asked, "What do you plan to do now that the dragon council has declared war? Will you keep hunting down humans to turn into dragons?"

Alan seemed taken aback by Caleb's question—maybe he thought Caleb was still too angry and defensive because of their previous topic of conversation to approach something entirely new—but recovered quickly enough. He even looked thoughtful, his head tipped to the side as he formed his response. "I may," he said.

Caleb blinked and raised both eyebrows. That wasn't the response he'd expected. He had anticipated something more . . . forceful. Planned. It sounded to him like Alan didn't know what his next step was, and that didn't sound like Alan at all. "You *may*?" he repeated, his nose wrinkled.

THE GODS' GIFT

Alan shrugged, moving his wings with the motion. "I'd like to see the humans die. I want to see the end of what I began. I doubt the council will kill every last one of you. I would have to see what remained of your kind before I decided whether or not to bother." He sneered, his lip curled back. "I'd hate to waste my life's work on the undeserving *dregs*."

Caleb growled, showing his own teeth in the process. "You self-absorbed, pompous—"

"Careful, little Kaal," Alan said, the laughter in his voice as biting as a growl would have been. "You keep drawing attention. I thought you liked to hide."

Caleb narrowed his eyes but then looked toward the nervous-looking guards and sighed. *Gotta keep my temper. I don't have time for childish outbursts. I haven't been a child in so long that there's no excuse.*

He took in his breath and let it out through his teeth to keep any embers from escaping. He could feel the heat of his breath and knew he was close to fire. "Fine," he bit out around his teeth. "Ask your next question, then."

CHAPTER 16: THE WAR COMES TO CALL

Caleb fell asleep on edge of his cot after an exhausting night of questions. His throat was sore from talking, especially after Alan had asked about the council's reaction to his pleas. If he'd had any faith in the council, he might have held back in his descriptions and indictment of them, especially given the nature of Alan's questions about their makeup. He could tell Alan was trying to learn the strength of the dragons he'd left behind, likely to set himself up for more power in his preferred form. Alan thought that, after the war's end, he could be the head of his own clan of human-made dragons and hold a seat on the council itself as a representative of not only that clan but the white dragons of old. If Caleb had held any love for the council, he would have held back.

But Caleb *wanted* Alan and the council to meet. He *wanted* the council to see the true source of the war. And so, if Alan's ambitions brought him to the council, far be it from Caleb to stop them from clashing. If everything went well, the council would destroy Alan for endangering dragons, provoking war, and perverting dragon magic; and Alan's crimes would prompt the dragons to shift the focus of their blame.

He knew he was holding onto a dwindling hope. The more the council burned of the human lands, the more they would gain confidence in their success. Humanity had driven itself to weakness on its own; the dragons could too easily wipe them out. Even if they believed Alan was the mastermind behind the creation of human-made dragons and the effort to kidnap dragons from the council's shores, they might never turn their gaze away from destruction now that they'd tasted it.

Still, Caleb gave Alan the answers he wanted about the council; he kept his details about Rikaa and his family sparse, however. Alan wanted to know about the dragons who had discovered him, and Caleb crafted Alan a narrative that he thought would fit Alan's belief in human-dragon relations. He talked about how Rikaa had taken him to the council in the hopes that someone else could teach him. He made it sound like Rikaa had wanted to get rid of the responsibility of a lost little human.

He couldn't say how much Alan believed him. He knew he'd already shown that he cared for Rikaa and his family, and he knew that, in turn, Rikaa's family had shown their protectiveness when they came to rescue him at the mouth of Alan's cave. But Caleb did his best to make them sound like allies, maybe even friends—not family.

And for Caleb's part, he wanted to know more about how Alan came to live among the humans, how he had decided to shed his scales and fire to fight wars in a much more delicate skin.

The answers weren't encouraging.

Alan seemed to think humans were no more than beasts, the way Caleb had once considered dragons. Alan thought very few of them were intelligent enough to deserve the life the gods had given them, and so, he believed he would find power more easily with "stupid" humans than with dragons, especially after the dragon council was formed and the clans retreated to their separate homes.

Alan had worked with both the Junnin and the Hayna, teaching wizards on both sides the basics of his approach to creating dragons, though the human wizards could only produce mindless beasts. The human-made dragons who kept their minds all came from Alan's guidance. He wasn't terribly bothered by that, especially since those beasts were then used to kill more humans.

And yet, while Alan liked to *talk* about how he wanted all the humans dead, Caleb noticed something else in all his stories that he didn't think Alan was fully aware of. Alan was fascinated by the process he had perfected over the centuries. He was fascinated by the types of humans he met and couldn't help his curiosity when faced with powerful personalities. He seemed genuinely delighted by the dragons he'd made that could have stood toe to toe with naturally-born dragons, given enough time to flourish outside of humanity's internal wars.

Alan said he hated humans, but he loved the *idea* of them. He loved their potential. He loved thinking of new ways to use and exploit them.

Caleb didn't like the way Alan regarded humans as objects of study—but he also didn't think Alan was prepared for what his plan would reap. After all that time living as a human, Alan's bluster told Caleb more than his words did. Alan had wanted humans to die for all this time, but he thought like a human himself. He was devious. He was curious. He wanted to push the limits of what was possible.

Caleb thought of the night he and Ziya had escaped, of the way Alan had fallen to his knees, clinging to his staff, after dragon fire had killed everyone else in the cave. At the time, Caleb had assumed Alan was weak because he hadn't wanted to be killed by fire and had been forced to use all his magic to keep himself safe. Now, having experienced fire in his human form without suffering any damage, Caleb knew that what Alan feared was not fire but exposure. He hadn't wanted anyone to see his dragon form, because he didn't want to give up the power he had in the army. Alan spoke of his future as a king of human-made dragons, but he was already drunk on the authority he found in his own human form.

Humanity had changed Alan. Maybe not for the better, but it *had* changed him.

And again, Caleb was struck by a comparison that bothered him, because he, too, had been changed by his immersion into another culture. He had only spent a few months among dragons, but he had been told often that he reasoned like a dragon, that he understood the world like a dragon. If Alan was the dragon who became a human, Caleb was the human who became a dragon.

He wondered if the gods meant him to be that way, if he was supposed to be like Alan to balance out the damage Alan had done.

After Alan and Caleb had talked themselves to exhaustion, that night, Caleb had dreamed that he was trapped in a dragon egg, surrounded by a white and silver-speckled surface as hard as a dragon's scale. He was human, and he couldn't break through. He kept pounding on the eggshell, shouting for help, but he didn't even make

THE GODS' GIFT

a dent. His hands were bloody and bruised, but the eggshell simply sparkled with flecks of red, immovable and sharp.

He didn't know if the dream meant anything or if it was simply the result of an overworked mind trying to make sense of a man he suspected had left everything about dragonkind behind except their pride and their hatred of humanity. Either way, he woke up sweaty and panting—and flushed when he realized Alan was watching him from across the prison hall.

"Bad dream?" Alan asked pleasantly when he saw Caleb's gaze on him.

"It's not your business," Caleb said, reaching up to flatten his matted hair and straighten his sweaty tunic. When Alan chuckled, Caleb huffed and got to his feet, walking a circle as wide as his shackled ankle would allow him to walk. He stretched and paced, but he couldn't find much to do to distract him believably from Alan's attention. "What do you want, Alan?"

"I already told you what I wanted," he said. "Your conversation is only balm for my curiosity and boredom, not my physical injuries."

Caleb kept his expression neutral as he replied, "And yet our talks are all you're going to get while I'm still behind bars."

Alan bared his teeth and laughed. "What on earth makes you think the two of us together couldn't escape this place?" he asked, speaking at a low whisper. He might have been full of a dragon's pride, but he was no fool. A threat like that would get them both attacked by the guards, and without Caleb's promise of cooperation, Alan wasn't going to draw down that kind of trouble.

Yet.

Caleb turned toward Alan with his whole body, his teeth pulled back before he'd even considered what to say in his response. He saw Alan's smile and let loose a deep snarl. "I'm not risking anything for you," he said through the snarl, well-aware of the guards' attention.

"No, you don't risk anything for anyone, do you?" Alan replied, also speaking in a snarl.

The two of them glared at each other, refusing to break eye contact no matter how close the guards came to their cells. But they didn't get the chance to test the limits of their contest of wills. Their silence was broken by a sound from outside the prison: one that both of them knew only too well.

Caleb's face drained of blood, and he ran to the bars of his cell, straining to see what was going on even though he couldn't see farther than the entrance of the prison, even with his enhanced dragon senses. He could only listen in panicked helplessness as a dragon roared toward the village, screaming fire in its wake that Caleb could smell before it hit the trees outside the village.

He heard villagers shouting spells and heard others screaming as they ran for cover. From the sound of things, more than one dragon had come to deal with this enclave of wizards. In fact, Caleb wouldn't have been surprised if the council had brought as many dragons as they'd brought to deal with Alan's base. They knew the danger posed by these people and their magic and would react accordingly.

Caleb could smell smoke drifting through the entrance to the cave and let out a frustrated snarl. He couldn't sit there and let another village burn to the ground around him. He'd seen too much destruction and too much death—all of it so *needless*—that he couldn't stand aside.

He wasn't aware that he'd made the decision to change until he felt his claws break through his fingers and gasped, clutching his hand to his chest. The changes still hurt, and when he hadn't been prepared for them, they caught him off his guard in the worst way.

He was dripping blood on the stone floor as the battle raged outside the cave, but he still hadn't fully changed. Once he had realized what he was doing, he had tried to hold it in, tried to remain human a little longer, tried not to give the villagers one more dragon to be afraid.

His hearing had fuzzed out once the screaming had started, but all at once, it rushed back in, and he heard someone calling his name. He blinked a few times and looked across the hall to see that Alan had shifted forms as well—though he had gone the opposite way. Now, he was a human, smirking as he stepped out of the chains that were made for a much bigger creature.

Suddenly, Caleb regretted telling Alan the details of his escape.

"You cannot hope to stand against dragons when they are on a quest for vengeance, Kaal," Alan said. His grin was wide and sharp as he reached the bars of his cell, allowing himself to transform enough to form claws that he used to yank the bars toward him. It took him several tries before they budged, but, at last, he had enough space to walk through the bent metal.

Caleb couldn't let Alan escape—he *couldn't*—but he was still shackled at the ankle. He kept growling, but Alan simply laughed and went to the next cell over, ignoring the way the prisoner inside shrank away from him.

Caleb could feel his mouth going dry as Alan yanked on the bars to the next cell. He had to *do* something.

He closed his eyes, let out a low growl, and allowed the changes to overtake his body. He could feel his spine lengthening and screamed in agony as a tail burst from the base of his spine. He fell to his knees as wings sprouted from his shoulders and snarled when the shackle at his ankle bit into his skin and then his scales until, finally, it snapped under the pressure of Caleb's quickly-expanding leg.

That was lucky. He hadn't known for sure that the shackle would come off.

The cell was too small to contain his full dragon form, and he panicked as he felt the bars of the cell pressing against his side. *This was a mistake. I'm going to get crushed,* he realized, his eyes wide—until he heard the creak of metal and felt the bars give under the weight of his body and the stress of his sudden expansion.

He fell sideways into the hallway as the last of his scales covered his face and his ears lengthened into horns. He let out a terrible gasp that sounded like a snarl and then shook his head, trying to ignore the way every part of his body felt like it was on fire.

He heard a terrible scream that brought him back to the present reality and stumbled forward. He wasn't nearly as graceful when he changed forms as Alan was—but then again, he didn't have nearly the same amount of practice Alan did. Still, he managed to get his feet underneath him faster than he had before and rushed to the other cell.

He wasn't surprised to find that Alan had killed the cell's inhabitant or that he was stealing the dead man's clothes, but he found himself growling all the same. "He did nothing to you," he snarled.

Alan turned toward Kaal and looked him over with a critical eye. "You're getting faster. I remember the last time you shifted forms. The pain will dull eventually too, you know."

Kaal snarled. "I don't care what you think."

"No, you've made that perfectly clear," Alan agreed as he pulled on the dead man's tunic. He tutted at the stain on the collar and wiped ineffectually at some of the sticky red blood. Alan had always been meticulous about his appearance and surroundings when he'd had control of the Hayna base. Kaal couldn't help but wonder if that penchant for cleanliness was a white dragon trait. Alan's scales would show even the slightest smudge of dirt, after all.

Kaal, on the other hand, didn't care whether he was dirty or not. He'd been dirty most of his life. Even before the war had taken his family and his home from him, he had worked outside. He had worked with animals. He was used to stains and blood and dirt and the vestiges of barn life.

He found himself fixated on Alan's need for cleanliness in a desperate attempt not to look at the murdered man in the cell. He was tired of seeing death, but more than that, he couldn't stand the image of a man lying in the remains of his captivity. It was too familiar.

He looked away from the body and forced himself to swallow down the memory of the young man he'd killed. He had plenty of experience ignoring unwanted memories. The sound of dragon wings. The whimpering sound his mother made every time she moved after she heard her son had died in battle. The sound of spiders crawling in his cell scratching the dirt with their legs so loudly he thought he might lose his mind.

He could push all of that aside, crush it down to deal with later. That was how he survived.

All he needed was something to replace the thought he was trying to ignore.

So, he focused his loathing and rage not on himself but on Alan. He snarled, letting the sound ripple around him. The guards of the prison were too busy rushing toward the dragons outside to care about the dragons inside, though a few did pause when they heard Kaal's snarl—louder than any one he'd used before. It was a declaration of war—but not against them.

But Alan simply laughed. "Really?" He strode out of the cell, standing directly in Kaal's path, his eyes flashing with power that spilled out into the growl in his words. "After everything that has happened, after all you've learned, after all I've told you, you still think it's a good idea to fight me?"

Kaal narrowed his eyes. "I told you many times that I won't let you hurt anyone else."

"You've done wonderfully so far," Alan replied, gesturing with one hand toward the dead prisoner.

Kaal snarled in response.

Alan stood his ground. "You forget, little Caleb, that I chose you after I saw you refuse to fight. I saw that you were a survivor, capable of change. But I also saw that you have honor in your heart. You won't strike a man who is no immediate threat to you. I'm just standing here, Caleb. Are you going to murder me in cold blood? Are you that much like me?"

"I'm *nothing* like you," Kaal snarled, his claws flaring out with each word.

"No, of course not." Alan hadn't moved, still looking exactly as Kaal remembered him from his time in captivity. Even then, he had a way of making Kaal feel inferior, making him feel like his every move was expected and exactly what Alan wanted out of him. "You promised to heal me, Kaal. How can you keep your word if you turn to murder instead?"

Kaal bared his teeth. "That's not what I promised," he replied.

"No, you were careful with your words, weren't you?" Alan said thoughtfully. "When the war is over and there is nothing left of your people but a few scurrying pests to be exterminated at our whim, I can find a use for that tongue of yours. You seem to engender trust. That's a good tool to have."

Kaal didn't know why he just kept standing there, letting Alan battle him verbally, when he could have attacked while Alan had the physical disadvantage. It would have been too easy to sink his claws into his weak human flesh or to bite him in half before he could transform. So why didn't he? Why was he *still* afraid to get too close to Alan?

All he knew was that each time he tried to urge his body forward, each time he thought of closing his teeth around Alan, he could hear his own screams, could feel the ice-cold pain of Alan's spells running through his body as he whimpered at the entrance to Alan's base in front of his newfound family of dragons. Each time he thought of sinking his claws into flesh, he could hear the sickening sound that came with that exact motion, the sound that had ended a young man's pleas to die.

So, he stood there, snarling, until Alan chuckled and turned his back on Kaal. "You still don't know what you want, do you?" Alan said without looking over his shoulder. "You want so badly to be the hero you think Ziya is, but everything you are holds you back. You can never be anything but a shadow, nothing but lies at the end of the day."

Do it, Kaal urged himself, digging into the dirt beneath his claws for purchase, trying to give his body every reason to respond to his mind's pleas. *If you don't do it now, he'll step outside and turn into a dragon. He'll help the council destroy this place. And it will be your fault for hesitating. Your fault for letting him get away. After everything you did to get here, you're going to let him live—and your voluntary captivity will have meant absolutely nothing.*

He felt the pit of his stomach drop as he finally—*finally*—found something stronger than his fear, louder than the memories that kept screaming in his mind. The idea of enduring chains for all that time only to return to Ziya empty-handed was too much to bear.

His snarl preceded him like the point of a sword as he pounced, his claws flared out to their full extent, his teeth flashing. He led his attack with his mouth, intending to bite Alan in half if he could, both because his head was closer to Alan and because he was still reluctant to use his claws to end a human life. He was sure he would be haunted by a bite as well, but he wasn't yet.

Alan leapt out of the way of Kaal's teeth at the last second, but Caleb managed to snag part of his tunic, and he came away with a large swath of fabric in his mouth, hanging around one of his fangs like drool. Kaal tried to slash at Alan with his claws, but he'd been reluctant to use them in the first place, and he no longer had the element of surprise; Alan easily avoided them by ducking behind the bars of the cell he'd murdered a man in, letting Kaal bash into the metal instead of his body.

Alan's eyebrows were high on his forehead as he spun to face Kaal fully. Then, he let out a delighted laugh. "What's this?" he said, already gaining height, his fingers lengthening into claws. "I thought you were smarter than this."

177

THE GODS' GIFT

Kaal bared his teeth. By that point, his growl was constant; he couldn't do a thing to stop it. "No, you thought you'd cowed me."

"True." Alan laughed again. "Shall we take this outside, then?" he asked politely, as if this were a simple duel, as if they had the time for pleasantries when the dragon council was out there burning down the last safe haven for humanity. "I doubt there's room in here for two dragons—and I do mean that literally."

Kaal narrowed his eyes but found himself moving toward the exit all the same. He'd lost the element of surprise, and now, Alan had the advantage in close quarters. Alan moved with a grace that Kaal hadn't yet earned in his new body, no matter how good he was getting at living as a dragon. As much as he hated to acquiesce to any of Alan's requests, this was actually a reasonable one: they would be crushed together if Kaal didn't move. And considering Alan's venom, Kaal didn't want to be trapped in a small space to fight.

They were nearly to the exit when Alan pounced, using his temporarily smaller body to get underneath Kaal's neck and to draw his claws down where Kaal's neck met his shoulder. If Kaal hadn't been in motion toward the exit, he would have been caught with his back against the wall and with a grievous wound hampering his ability to avoid another blow.

He stumbled out into the open air, gasping and reeling from the bad hit. And as he watched, Alan grew, becoming a white dragon with fire already spilling out of his mouth.

ZIYA

CHAPTER 17: IN THE FLAMES

The sun was starting to set, and Ziya found herself once more turning her attention toward the village with a hum of displeasure. Now that she and Lioia knew where Alan was, they had nothing to do but wait, and Ziya didn't know how much more her patience could take. Lioia wasn't much help; she was dealing with her frustrated desires by flying circles around the village until she needed a break. Ziya, meanwhile, had chosen to stay on her perch and watch the village for any sign that Caleb needed her help. He was outnumbered in there. And she couldn't stand the idea that he might be in trouble and she couldn't see it.

She had done this once before, waiting outside of a cavernous base while Caleb infiltrated it. It wasn't any easier the second time.

"He should be done by now," she muttered—and to her surprise, the recently-returned Lioia moved so that she was standing shoulder to shoulder with Ziya, looking down on the village.

"He trusts too easily," Lioia said. "These humans have long killed and hunted the dragons in this area. They will not forgive him if they know the truth."

"That's what worries me," Ziya said, speaking softly. She took a deep breath, held it, and let it out slowly enough that the smoke was thick and black from being held in her mouth for so long. "But I trust him."

"This isn't a question of trusting *him*," Lioia said, shaking her head in disbelief. "He could be a dragon warrior of legend, and these humans would still be a threat. They have had generations to perfect their arts. My mother once said that they could find dragons and kill them simply by taking a leisurely stroll with their swords and their magic."

"That doesn't ease my mind at all."

"I wasn't trying to ease your mind, Ziya. This morning, you worried instead of trusting him. Now, you see a second sunset and try to ease your worry with the false hope of trust."

Ziya watched the village as, one by one, the houses started to light lanterns. Faint, glowing fires flickered in their windows, making the houses below look like twinkling stars when viewed from as far away as Ziya and Lioia were. Whatever the humans had done with Alan, they'd hidden him away where no one would be bothered by him, where no one would remember he existed.

If he was even still alive.

Honestly, Ziya wouldn't weep if Alan had been executed. He had done nothing to deserve sympathy in his sorry life, and the sooner the world was rid of him, the better. She had only agreed not to kill him on sight because Caleb wanted answers, and she didn't want him to be haunted by Alan for the rest of his life. He didn't deserve a life like hers.

But if they'd killed Caleb as well as Alan. . . . Well, she might even have said that the price wasn't worth the reward.

She was surprised by the desperate tone of her thoughts. Until recently, her only thought had been revenge—first on Kaal and then on Alan. And somehow, in the short time she had known Caleb, she was prepared to exchange revenge for his safety.

He had that way about him, though. She didn't understand it, and she didn't think he did either. But the light he had in him attracted others to him. Attracted loyalty. Even hers.

Once more, she took a deep breath, held it, and let it out. She used to do that all the time before she was a dragon. Her mother used to tell her that anything that could still make her angry after she'd held her breath, calmed down, and refocused was actually *worth* being upset about. Everything else was nothing but the heat of the moment and wasn't worth the energy she would spend on it.

So, when she still felt the heaviness of dread weighing her down as she watched the villagers go about their lives, she nodded and turned toward Lioia. "I think," she said slowly, "it's time to go get him. And if they've killed him—"

THE GODS' GIFT

"If they killed him, we will respond in kind," Lioia said, her eyes flashing with fire. "If they killed him, I will get my husband and gather the other dragons in this area who have clashed with these humans before, and we will rain down fire for their cruelty."

Ziya almost laughed to herself. *Kaal, you have no idea the effect you have on the dragons and people around you,* she thought. But instead of laughing, she met Lioia's gaze with her own fire. "I can't lose him, Lioia." She didn't agree to raze a village, even though she knew how; she had been trained by a human army bent on destruction. She didn't agree to cruelty. She only wanted Caleb back, safe and sound.

"Then I will let you lead the way," Lioia swore.

Ziya nodded her gratitude and got to her feet, stretching her wings and limbs. If she had been human, she would have needed to shake feeling back into her arms and legs after sitting still for so long, but she didn't need to do that in a dragon body. Still, the urge was there from years of habit. She wasn't used to a body that could go days and days without moving by *choice*. Yes, she had once been confined and captive, but her stillness had been an imposition, not a state of being.

Thankfully, Lioia didn't comment on Ziya's strange human habit, letting her prepare in her own way while Lioia watched the village below.

"We cannot rush in with fire until we know where Kaal is," Ziya said once she had shaken out the nonexistent tingles in her legs.

"I know," Lioia promised. "He means too much to you."

Ziya didn't confirm or deny Lioia's claim but gestured with one claw toward the village. "Maybe we can earn an audience if we announce ourselves instead of attacking."

"I doubt they will be so understanding," Lioia scoffed.

"Maybe not. But Kaal was going to talk to their leader. Maybe he will be willing to listen now that he knows our story. You know for yourself how persuasive Kaal can be," Ziya reasoned, her desire to save Caleb warring with her desire to preserve human lives. The dragon council had already killed so many of her people; she couldn't sanction wanton destruction no matter how badly she wanted Caleb safe and no matter how much revenge had been woven into her soul. "There are children there. We shouldn't be so devastating in our attack that they can't flee."

Lioia let out a throaty sound. "You keep changing your mind. Are you a warrior or not?"

"I am," Ziya insisted, her claws pushed deep into the dusty dirt of the mountainside. "But that doesn't mean I kill innocents."

Lioia let out a huff of smoke through her nose, but before the two of them could get into yet another argument, a new sound split the horizon, and both Ziya and Lioia looked toward the south.

Ziya knew instantly what that sound meant. She'd heard it all too many times before, and even as a dragon, she still could feel her blood running cold. She took an unconscious step backward, shaking her head, and let out a low growl that could be felt but not heard by anyone but another dragon.

Lioia frowned, but when she saw the way her companion shrank back from the sound of dragon wings and the call of dragons about to go to war, she turned her full attention Ziya's way. "Do you know those dragons?" she asked. "Are they like you?"

Ziya tried not to take another step back, but she couldn't help herself. "I don't know," she admitted. She swallowed and shook her head, purposefully flaring her wings out in an attempt to remind herself of the power she now had to fight back.

"Then why. . . ." Lioia frowned. "You were not this scared of me when we met."

"No, but you weren't on your way to destroy a town." Ziya glared at the horizon. She could see the outline of dragon wings now, along with the haze of smoke from villages farther out from their position, far enough away to be unseen, far enough away that the people who had died in those fires might not have even known there was another village they could escape to, but not far enough away that their loss didn't touch the horizon. "I have heard that exact sound so many times. I know what happens next."

Lioia hesitated, looking between Ziya and the approaching dragons. And then, with surprising gentleness, she leaned forward and nudged Ziya with the end of her snout. "I will not let them hurt you," she said.

Ziya blinked but didn't back away. She hadn't expected Lioia to comfort her after all the time Lioia had spent defending dragons and degrading humans. Ziya didn't have the same persuasive power Caleb did; she didn't expect anyone to care about her.

THE GODS' GIFT

Maybe she just needs to keep me safe because she knows Caleb won't help her get to Alan if I'm hurt, she thought and decided that was the easier explanation to believe than the idea that Lioia was starting to see Ziya as anything more than a temporarily-allied future enemy.

Ziya waited for Lioia to pick her head up to her eye level again and met her gaze, steeling herself for a fight. As much as she hated to admit it, Lioia's gentle touch and warm assurances had actually helped her to calm down, and she wanted to press her advantage while she still could, try to convince Lioia further to her cause. It was what Caleb would have done. "They're likely council members here to kill the last of the humans," Ziya explained. "They declared war; they want to kill us all."

"In that case, I will not stop them," Lioia said, and while Ziya could appreciate the honestly, she also couldn't help but growl at her. After all their arguments about what dragons did and did not stand for, about whether dragons had earned respect or admiration, Lioia still sided with those trying to murder an entire species for the sins of its leaders and the actions of an interloper.

"So much for your promises," Ziya said through her teeth.

Lioia bared her teeth and growled right back. "I gave a promise to you, not those killers. I hold no love for humans. You already know that."

"Then why give me a promise at all?"

"I will not allow the council to kill a young dragon who has already had too many reasons to fear dragons in her short lifetime." Lioia made an angry, sharp movement with her tail and head together. "If you choose to fight them, I will not aid you. But I will heal you if you are so foolish."

"You know I will go anyway."

"I know you are so kind you would forgo revenge to save the innocents in a village full of those that would sooner kill you than listen to you. I don't trust you not to injure yourself in the name of your strange human pride."

Ziya's tail stilled behind her. Since becoming a dragon, she'd never considered herself to be kind. She was vindictive, quick to anger, full of a fire that she couldn't stop and didn't want to stop. She still reacted without thinking sometimes, purely because she had spent so long suppressing her anger and fear that it felt like it was spilling beyond the borders of her body, beyond her control. The last word she would use to describe herself was "kind."

Perhaps she *seemed* kind to Lioia, who thought nothing of punishing her and Kaal for being human until she had formed her own attachment that made such anger inconvenient for her. Or perhaps Lioia had seen Kaal's extreme kindness and hope and belief in the best of nearly everyone he met and thought that Ziya must have felt the same way because she was so devoted to their friendship.

No, Ziya couldn't imagine herself to be kind. Asking for the lives of innocents to be spared was the least anyone could have done. She only meant to keep herself from becoming as evil as the soldiers, dragons, and wizards who had turned the human lands into a desolate landscape unfit for life. She was *decent*, yes, but not *kind*. She couldn't be kind. She'd given that up in the same instant she'd agreed to drag Kaal back to Alan for him.

So, she didn't have a good response for Lioia other than to gape at her, even as the members of the dragon council drew ever closer. She could hear the villagers below their perch rushing to meet the coming attack, but she couldn't look away from Lioia's penetrating gaze. "Kind?" she repeated—which was not at all what she meant to say, but she was still so shocked she couldn't ignore her description.

Lioia drew her head back and then leaned forward, studying Ziya closer. "You think too little of yourself," she said at last. "I don't know who to blame, but I assure you, if Alan has anything to do with your inability to see your strengths—"

"I'm no kinder than any other human—except the ones who chose to join the army and the ones who lead the war," she amended. "But ask any human who lacks the power to end the war on their own, and they'll tell you the same thing. We have all seen too much death; we don't want any more people to die unnecessarily, especially innocents."

Lioia hummed but turned her attention away from Ziya. And Ziya thought their conversation had ended until Lioia said, "You make a good argument." She looked toward the approaching dragons but didn't make a move to stop the council either, seemingly lost in thought.

I'm so tired of dragons agreeing with me and Kaal and then doing nothing about it, Ziya thought, her anger getting the better of her as she let out a frustrated snarl and then pushed herself forward, already running quickly enough that she'd be able to take to the skies in a few more steps. "Sit here if you like," she snapped at Lioia as she passed. "But you can see with your own eyes that your council came to murder us all. Stay here and let humanity die if you like. I can't hide like a coward." With that, she took to the skies, leaving Lioia snarling behind her.

Ziya knew she couldn't feasibly stand against the entirety of the dragon council as they rained their wrath on one of the last strongholds of human power, especially a stronghold that she knew actually posed a direct threat to dragons. She and Kaal had seen how mercilessly the council burned down villages that *didn't* have the same history of dragon-slaying. For this village, she knew the dragons were likely saving their hottest fires.

So, instead of rushing directly into the path of the approaching dragons, Ziya flew toward the village. Yes, she knew that she was taking a huge risk of being shot down, but she didn't get close enough to see any wizards or archers. She flew a wide arc around the village, looking for any sign of where the humans were seeking refuge or what path they would take to flee.

To her growing concern, she didn't see a line of refugees like she'd thought she would. The villagers probably thought they didn't need to flee their homes. They assumed they could stand against this attack the same way they'd withstood other attacks since their founding. And while that was a fair assumption in the best of times, Ziya didn't think they fully understood the council's motives. This wasn't a battle in a war. This was an attempted genocide.

She saw some humans scurrying to defensive positions and lost her temper. "Run!" she roared at them, drawing their attention—and was immediately forced to retreat to stay out of reach of their spells and arrows. Thankfully, she'd circled the village with Lioia before and had a good idea of how close was too close, so she wasn't hurt—but she was furious and desperate. All that time she'd spent accusing the dragons of being prideful, and here was the last vestige of human civilization refusing to even *consider* the idea that they could be wiped out like the other humans had been.

Ziya snorted smoke, circling the edges of the village on the other side of the valley from the direction the council was taking—

and then realized that the people below her might have thought she was there to corral them. She huffed again and changed course, drifting toward the council members without outright engaging them.

And still, no one fled the village.

She narrowed her eyes but couldn't do anything more without endangering herself. And she still didn't see Caleb.

At last, the dragon council members announced their arrival with plumes of fire—but this time, the wizards who defended the village met the dragons with more force than Ziya had ever seen waged against dragons. She had seen human-made dragons pitted against each other and had seen a few wizards stand against a handful of dragons at most, but with a dozen different naturally-born dragons attacking a relatively small haven, she hadn't expected the battle to be so evenly matched.

Despite the desperation of the situation, she found herself hanging back, watching with wide eyes as the humans erected spells of ice-cold winds that blew out fire as quickly as the dragons could breathe it out. She saw familiar ribbons rushing toward the dragons, burrowing under their scales. The dragons' fire hadn't yet penetrated the homes in the village, and already, a dragon had fallen from the sky, succumbing to the sleeping spell in those ribbons.

Ziya was so shocked she didn't know what to do. She'd been prepared to defend these people with everything she had. It hadn't occurred to her that there *was* a place left in the world that wouldn't fall to the evils she had been subjected to.

"Do you really have so little faith in your people that you thought they would die so easily?"

Ziya turned to see Lioia gliding toward her. Had she been human, she would have wrinkled her nose, but she couldn't manage that movement to illustrate her disgust—with herself, with the situation, and with Lioia for continuing to stand to the side of a war while passing judgement on its survivors. "The sound of dragon fire has always meant death in my experience," Ziya hissed, mangling the words so badly that she was barely understood, because each word carried a growl on the wind. She was still stressed, still scared—no matter how well the humans were fighting back.

"And now you see why I had such a hard time believing your tale," Lioia said, jerking her head toward the battle. All around the village, the story was the same: as soon as the dragons approached, the humans met them with freezing spells, with icy winds, with spells that could sneak under scales, with wind strong enough to send fully-grown dragons into a tailspin.

And yet, with so many dragons attacking at once, the wizards could only hold the line for so long. A blue dragon managed to penetrate the magical defenses and came screaming into the village, spewing fire in a long line down the center of town as she passed through and then climbed higher into the air to avoid the archers on the ground who couldn't do the same kind of magic the outer defenders could do.

Ziya swallowed hard, her ears ringing with a too-familiar sound, her sensitive nose and mouth full of smoke and the taste and scent of burning homes. She could hear screaming and then, finally, saw that the villagers did have a path out of danger. Several humans were rushing out of the line of houses toward the cliffside, where Ziya could see openings big enough to hide people but not big enough to hide dragons.

She hoped that the outcroppings and caves were deeper than they looked from the sky, or they'd all be burned to a crisp the second the dragons realized where they were hiding.

"Well?" Lioia broke into Ziya's thoughts, flying closer than Ziya was entirely comfortable with. "What will you do? You can see these humans don't need your help."

Ziya didn't have an answer for Lioia. Not for a long time. Ever since she'd become a dragon, her life had been defined by the next fight, the next enemy. She had long ago accepted that she was a weapon and had decided to use herself as such a weapon in a war of her *choosing*. She couldn't fathom seeing suffering and not stepping in. Not anymore.

But even if this village didn't need her help, she couldn't leave, either. If not for the villagers than for Caleb. "Find Kaal," she said at last.

"I don't know why I asked," Lioia said dryly, though Ziya caught her smiling and gave her a playful growl she hadn't realized she was capable of until it burst from her. Maybe she was finally starting to relax—or at least to panic less upon hearing dragons going to war.

"Can you find Kaal the way you taught me to look for Alan?" Ziya asked as she and Lioia found a spot to land and to reevaluate their plans. They could see the evacuation from their vantage point, which made a few wizards and archers nervous, but Ziya and Lioia didn't attack those fleeing the battle—and, in return, the fleeing humans didn't attack them.

Lioia watched the humans warily before giving her answer. She obviously didn't trust the small truce, but then, she had probably never been this close to the village without attacking them and perpetuating the hurts of the war. "There are too many dragons," she said. "I wouldn't be able to distinguish his power from any other dragon's—if I found it at all. I didn't find Alan, remember?"

Ziya let out a growl from the back of her throat. "They could be anywhere in that village!" she snarled. She wasn't angry at *Lioia*, but she couldn't keep her temper in check, either. She hated feeling helpless. She had spent far too long unable to make a difference, and now, she found herself unable to help either the refugees or Caleb.

What was the point of all her power if she couldn't use it?

Lioia scratched the ground a few times before a thought seemed to occur to her, and she stilled. "There is an old spell, one forged in fire," she said slowly. "We could search for him in the flames."

"What are you talking about?"

"I have not seen it done before," Lioia admitted. "I don't know that I can do it, either. I remember my grandfather telling tales of humans who learned magic from dragons, and that was one of the tricks we taught them in the old days." Ziya could feel the shift in the air as Lioia gathered her power, her magic, to search herself for the ability to do this spell. "Dragons are tied together by fire. At one time, humans who won our favor could call out to their dragon friends through those flames. You're human. Perhaps you could do the same."

Ziya stared at her. "I can barely access the dragon magic I have because of my new body," she said incredulously. "What makes you think I can do *that*?"

"I told you I wasn't sure." Lioia shrugged up her wings, watching as another dragon broke through the village defenses to leave a line of fire in her wake. When Ziya turned to see the destruction, she realized it was the same blue dragon as before—and nearly swallowed her long tongue because of the strength of her gasp when she recognized Drui, the member of the dragon council who had visited her while she was captive.

Of course she came herself. She wanted to see humanity fall with her own eyes, Ziya thought, letting out a snarl that she couldn't stop, one that pulled her lips all the way back from her teeth and left her with her wings slicked back and her claws pushed out, completely prepared to spring into battle.

Lioia instinctively moved away from Ziya and flared out her own claws. "It's not *my* fault you—"

Ziya snarled again but swallowed it before it could become quite the same declaration of war as the one before it. "Not you," she managed to say, her voice so low that her words would have been lost in the air for anyone much farther away than Lioia. "That blue dragon. I know her."

"Ah." Lioia turned to see the blue dragon make another pass and then nodded slowly. "Drui. When I took my hatchling to see the council and announce her name, I got the distinct feeling she wanted more power. She hated letting Aonai speak for the council in even minor matters."

"You have no idea," Ziya said, though her snarl had softened significantly at the mention of Aonai. She hadn't heard any news of him since he had volunteered to speak to the council and to plead the case of the human-made dragons. Ziya had tried to tell him that he was wasting his time and putting himself in harm's way, but he believed too much in dragonkind not to give them a chance. Now, she had to wonder if he was wasting away in the same ring of fire he'd once seen her in. "Not long after you were there, Aonai left the council because Drui nearly killed me."

Lioia's tail went totally still. "What?"

"The council kept me captive but didn't feed me. I was already nearly starving, and I was bleeding badly after they tore me down to keep me there." Ziya didn't look at Lioia; she didn't want to see the pity she knew was there. "Aonai saved my life when he brought me a fish to eat without telling the others he was going to see me. He lost his place on the council because he disagreed with their treatment of me and because he didn't agree with this war."

"I had no idea," Lioia said, a new rage in her voice that Ziya hadn't heard at any time other than when she talked about how Alan had taken her son and about how the humans in Ytona had killed dragons. For the first time, one of Ziya's stories had stirred Lioia's vengeful heart—and Ziya, cynically, couldn't help but wonder if it was because Aonai was a green dragon. Dragons, after all, might have formed a council to unite their clans, but they were not as united or as civilized as they liked to think they were.

"The last time I saw Aonai, he had elected to go to the council to speak to them on our behalf," Ziya told Lioia. She gestured toward the chaos below them with her claws instead of her tail. "I didn't expect them to listen, but seeing this war raging on, I wonder whether he's alright. Kaal and I were going to go back to Rikaa and then approach the council when we were done with Alan— to save Aonai if need be. I don't want him hurt for my sake."

Lioia was quiet for a long time, but Ziya could see fire in her gaze—and something else, something Ziya couldn't identify. She wished she could read the small clues in dragon body language that she would have understood if she'd been born in the body she currently had. So, because of her ignorance, she wasn't expecting Lioia to say, "I think that's the first time I have heard you speak so well of a true dragon."

"I've talked about Aonai before," Ziya said, frowning.

"Yes, but I've never heard so much *concern* before." A smile flirted with Lioia's mouth until it won out and spread all the way to her eyes. "When you rescue him from the council, let me come with you. You're right to place your trust in him. Aonai is a good dragon. He deserves better than to be discarded by those who want power."

Ziya had met many people like Lioia as she went from place to place looking for refuge from the war, people whose loyalty only extended to those they knew personally, to those they could trust from experience. She didn't blame most of those people for their views, especially in a time of war. She had seen men steal from each other in the dead of night, women fighting over food. Trust was a luxury in these times.

THE GODS' GIFT

Lioia lived in a place where the war between dragons and humans was far from over. She had seen loss and violence. Perhaps she, too, could only bring herself to trust a select few.

Now you're thinking like Caleb, she thought. *He'd find a way to explain anyone's actions away to garner sympathy. Next thing you know, you'll be talking about the gods' directive to the dragons and trying to save the world one dragon at a time.*

She shook her head, choosing for the time being not to respond to Lioia's overture. She turned toward the battle, watching as a black dragon broke through the humans' defenses but didn't get close enough to the ground to ring the village with fire as he clearly planned to do. The moment he got past the wizards, an archer fired an arrow directly into the dragon's open mouth, in the second between when he opened his mouth and when he would have spewed fire. The arrow gleamed in the air; it must have been made entirely of metal, like a small spear. That made sense; wooden arrows would do nothing against dragons who could burn the shafts.

The black dragon let out a strangled sound as the arrow embedded in his throat, and he veered to the side, shaking his head hard. He spewed fire several times as he tried to get the arrow out, but it was stuck too deeply. Ziya couldn't see him after he stumbled into the trees, trying desperately to find relief, but she knew he wouldn't be able to remove the arrow on his own. At best, he could enlist another dragon's help by asking that dragon to remove the arrow with a claw or with the tip of his tail, but even that would be dangerous, delicate work.

The archer had known exactly how to take down a dragon, and Ziya couldn't help but feel proud of the humans around her. These were dragon killers. They had no reason for fear.

"I don't see Kaal anywhere," Lioia said, reminding Ziya of their true mission—and of the dragons who were, in fact, terrified of the humans who lived in that village. Every war had two sides.

Ziya pulled her gaze away from the injured dragon and back to the village, searching for a white dragon or a cloaked boy (though one would be much easier to spot than the other). "Right," she said softly. Had she been human, she would have bitten her lip, a nervous habit she'd picked up from her father. "Tell me about this spell. I don't think I will be able to find Kaal in this crowd of humans, especially with all this smoke. It's worth trying something else, even if it doesn't work."

"As I understand it," Lioia said slowly, "it's like the spell I showed you before, but you can use fire itself to direct your search." Her tail moved behind her, and she seemed to measure each word precisely. "In the old stories, a human would build a fire and then reach into it, protected by magic. He would then call out to the fires within dragons. Bolstered by the dragon fire of their friends, the human could search any flames in any place until he found who he was looking for."

"That doesn't tell me what to do." Ziya huffed. "That's a nice story, but I don't know how to reach into fire; I can barely heal!"

"I can't tell you anything more than that," Lioia replied, drawing herself up in response to Ziya's obvious frustration. "It's nothing but a story to me; I have no experience to draw from. And I am a dragon; you were born a human. In all the stories, I only heard of humans using this magic; I don't know if I can do it for you!"

Beyond their position, a dragon snarled in pain, and another screamed as it released fire on the village below. Ziya sighed, knowing her options were limited. "Right." Ziya let out a long breath, trying to will herself to calm down. She thought of Kaal, alone in enemy territory listening to the sound that had always preceded loss in their lives. She *did* want to find him. She *was* willing to try anything to do so. She just didn't have much faith in Lioia's plan.

"Let's try it anyway. The worst that'll happen is that it doesn't work," she decided. "I just need some fire to reach into." Ziya blew fire onto the craggy plants that managed to live on the rocky side of the mountain and watches as the flames licked the thorny branches. The fire didn't look any different to her now that she was a dragon, and she didn't feel a connection to it other than the knowledge that it had come from inside her. But she closed her eyes, put her claw in the fire, and tried all the same.

Please, she thought as she reached out with the same *something* she'd found inside herself when she first healed Aonai. *If . . . if you gods care about this world, help me find him. He can do so much more than I can to stop this before it gets any worse.*

She wasn't sure why she thought that would do any good, but, well, Caleb had talked about the gods so often that she believed, at this point, that they had a plan for him. After all, if anyone was chosen by the gods, it was Kaal. She didn't believe that they cared about anyone but the ones that had earned their favor; she barely believed they cared enough to favor Kaal in the first place. But . . . she was trying unknown magic in the middle of a battle. She could try a little faith, she supposed.

With her eyes still closed, she finished her silent plea and concentrated, trying to learn how to use a sense she wasn't sure she had. She didn't know what muscles to flex, what thoughts to think—she just knew she had to try. She tried concentrating on Kaal, on the image of him as a white dragon standing on the precipice of Alan's base with her. She tried thinking of Caleb, the boy who turned bright pink every time he changed back into a human no matter how delicately she defended his modesty.

And then, she tried to clear her mind of any thoughts at all, hoping that the magic of the fire would fill her thoughts instead.

That was what finally did the trick. As soon as she was able to find calm—in a quiet lull of the battle as both sides regrouped—an image came rushing into her mind of a fire close to an opening in a cave. She couldn't see anything more than that, so she called out: "Kaal!"

"Ziya?" Kaal sounded both bewildered and hurt, but he was alive, and that was more than enough to leave her giddy, almost breathless with relief—especially when his response seemed to strengthen the spell and gave her the ability to see more than fire. She could see, as if she were standing in the flames of what she now saw was a fallen tree, a large cave that had apparently once housed humans; Ziya could see several men running away from the dragons at the cave entrance. Both Kaal and Alan were in dragon form, circling each other warily. Both were heavily injured; they must have been fighting. One of Kaal's legs was so badly hurt that he couldn't walk on it and kept it close to his center. The only reason Alan hadn't pressed his advantage was that Kaal had apparently managed to strike a blow of his own; Alan's scales were torn and red in a long line down his neck into his belly. What's more, Alan's wing was still badly torn after the last time he had clashed with one of his dragon creations.

Ziya was too worried to revel in the damage she'd done.

"I'm coming," she promised, looking around once more to see if she could identify Kaal's location. The mountains were dotted with caves. She needed something she could use as a landmark. . . .

There. As she looked, a dragon attacked, and the trees near Kaal's position caught fire. Ziya yanked her claw out of the burning brush, breaking the connection with the fire, and blinked heavily, trying to readjust to seeing the world with her own eyes, looking desperately for the new fire before it blended in with the rest of the battle's destruction.

"Where did that dragon breathe his fire just now?" she demanded of Lioia, who was frozen as she watched Ziya—either shocked that the spell had worked or startled by Ziya's sudden return to the present moment.

Lioia's eyes were wide. "What do you—"

Ziya let out a frustrated growl and searched the village below with her gaze, looking for burning trees near the mountains. Unfortunately, the scene she'd witnessed could have taken place nearly anywhere; the village was surrounded by both mountains and trees, and fires were popping up everywhere. But when she saw the flash of magic near the southernmost edge of the village, she nodded to herself. The wizards might have been pushing back the dragon she had seen attacking.

"Come on," she said, already unfolding her wings in preparation for flight. "I saw him." She didn't wait to see if Lioia would follow her, not now, not when she knew Kaal was actively battling Alan as they spoke.

Kaal couldn't defeat Alan on his own. Ziya had known that from the start. But now, she had a way to get to him before he died trying.

CHAPTER 18: HEAL ME

Ziya flew as fast as she could, determined to reach Kaal before he lost his battle with Alan or before he was discovered by the dragon council. She took some comfort in knowing Alan was still nursing his wounds from not only the fight with Aonai and Rikaa but the one with Lioia and Ziya. Had Alan had his full strength, Kaal would already have been either dead or so badly injured that he would have had no choice but to do whatever Alan asked of him if he wanted to be healed.

Ziya knew she was on the right track when she heard not the sound of dragons snarling and spewing fire—but, particularly, the sound of an injured, *young* dragon. The high-pitched whine couldn't have come from any of the council members; they were all well past adolescence.

Ziya had to wonder why she hadn't thought to listen for a whine like that in the first place. But then again, she'd been hoping Kaal was okay, not expecting him to be injured already. And besides, if he was whining, the villagers knew he was a dragon. And she hadn't known he was Kaal instead of Caleb. And she'd been beside herself with fear and worry, so she couldn't have been expected to think clearly. She'd been reacting, not strategizing. She'd have to work on that.

Once Lioia, hot on Ziya's heel, so to speak, heard the whine, she seemed somehow to go faster than she had been flying before, even though she and Ziya both had been pushing themselves to get to Kaal as quickly as they could. But Ziya had seen what effect a whine like that could have on mothers in particular. Lioia was a mother of *hatchlings*. She couldn't possibly ignore Kaal's cry.

Ziya wondered how the parents on the dragon council could ignore it themselves. Were they so caught up in their lust for the destruction of all humanity that they could turn against their instincts for anything but war? If so, she would never listen to a single member of the council talk to her about the gods' plans for dragons. They had no right to claim the gods' favor when their actions only made them the beasts of human legend.

When Ziya and Lioia reached Kaal, Ziya was relieved to see that the battle hadn't shifted too badly against Kaal in the time since she had seen him in the fire. Both Alan and Kaal had more marks on them than they'd had before, but they were still evenly matched—because they were unevenly injured.

Alan, who seemed to wince with every movement, let out a snarl when he saw Lioia and Ziya, his claws flared out and his teeth bared when the two of them landed. "What are you doing with them?" he demanded of Lioia—surprising Ziya, who was absolutely certain he would do as he usually did and would criticize her or make her question her loyalty to Kaal.

Lioia looked surprised to be addressed, too, and she paused, frowning between the two white dragons before her. Then, she bared her teeth at Alan and said something in the dragon language that Ziya didn't understand but that had Alan squaring up with her despite his injuries. It sounded like a challenge or a threat—understandably so, considering Alan had kidnapped her son. Lioia might have hated humans, but she wouldn't side with a dragon who would do *that*. She had her limits.

With Lioia and Alan keeping each other in their sights, Ziya edged toward Kaal, who was still whimpering and holding his leg close to his body. He'd been watching Alan until that moment, ready to continue the fight, but once Ziya got close enough that she could have reached out to touch him with her wings, he finally looked her way, his eyes wide and full of hurt.

"How did you find us?" he asked, the whine lacing every word.

Ziya let her shoulders drop as she approached him, raking her gaze over every missing scale. He looked terrible. She should have gotten there faster. "Didn't you hear me tell you—"

"No, no," he said, making an irritated sound in the back of his throat. "How did you do that spell? The only one I've ever seen do

197

that was *Alan*." His tone wasn't accusatory, but he was staring at her more warily than she'd expected from him.

She was surprised by how much that *stung*. Kaal had always been forgiving and understanding, and she had come to rely on his kindness. He didn't blame her for allowing Alan to twist her mind so badly that she was willing to let Kaal take her punishment in her place. He kept assuring her that she wasn't a bad person (or dragon) for being manipulated. And any time she tried to put voice to the nagging thought in the back of her mind that she was exactly as bad as she thought she was, he wouldn't listen to her.

So now, seeing the suspicion in his eyes, she could feel her fire warm in her belly. Had she still been human, her eyes might have been wet with tears, too. "I didn't learn it from *him*," she said, spitting the last word out with exactly as much disgust as the idea merited. "Lioia taught it to me."

Kaal didn't bother to hide his surprise as he picked his head up higher and his tail went still. "Lioia?" he repeated.

"I wouldn't use *his* methods to look for you unless I had to," she said. "You should know that."

Kaal was quiet for a longer time than she felt was necessary. "I know," he said at last. "I'm sorry." He seemed to be trying to make himself smaller without actually changing form, submissive in a way that didn't make Ziya feel any better now that he wasn't suspicious of her. She didn't want him to be *afraid* of her, either!

So, Ziya swallowed her anger and tried to give him the same understanding he'd given her. "You're hurt," she said gently. "Let me heal you."

"Later," he said, holding his leg closer to his center. "We need to get out of here. The council won't let us live if they find us."

"And the humans?" Ziya asked. "Will they attack us if they win the day and drive out the council?"

Kaal paused. "I don't know," he admitted frankly. "I think Lord Teyo and I understand each other, but in the heat of a battle like this. . . ."

"Then let's not take risks," Ziya said. "Let's just deal with Alan and go."

Ziya had a feeling Alan was eavesdropping on their conversation, but he and Lioia had also been growling at each other, so she wasn't sure he was listening until he cut in. "Deal with me?" he repeated, a laugh rumbling through the sharp rocks that made up the reddish-brown caves. "Do you think you're capable, little Ziya?"

"You can hardly hold yourself upright," she snarled, losing all traces of the warmth she had been trying to give Kaal as she rounded on Alan, her eyes flashing. "You stole my life out from under me. And you stole Lioia's son." She looked briefly toward Kaal. "You tell me, Kaal. Can you think of one reason to keep him alive?" She didn't ask him directly if he'd gotten all the answers he wanted, but she hoped he understood the implication.

Even if he hadn't understood, he didn't argue with her. "No," he said in a low growl. "I can't."

Despite her driving desire to kill Alan, to make him pay for every hurt he'd inflicted on her and everyone else, Ziya nearly stopped to ask Kaal if he was alright, since he had never been so calm when the topic of Alan's death came up. He'd understood it as a necessity, but now, he seemed . . . hardened to the idea. Prepared in a way that left Ziya wishing he wasn't.

I shouldn't have left him alone with Alan. With that thought, she turned toward Alan, her head dipped low and her wings pressed nearly flat on her back. She let out a snarl that echoed the valley and then rushed Alan, more than ready to rid the world of a man willing to take the innocence of children and then twist them into whatever he needed them to be.

She hadn't expected him to avoid fighting with her altogether by shrinking to human size as she pounced. Instead of tearing him apart, she missed him entirely, sailing over his head into the wall of the cliff with an embarrassing crash.

Thankfully, she wasn't the only one trying to finish Alan. Lioia saw Alan transform and immediately blew a huge plume of fire, lighting the trees south of the cave in a long line until the fire reached an outcropping of rock and stopped. Several branches fell, and that sound coupled with the sharp cracks of a fire in full blaze masked all other sounds until the smoke had cleared enough for even dragons to be able to see.

Ziya peered eagerly through the smoke, but before she could make out anything but the vague shapes of trees, Kaal sprang past her, galloping on three legs toward the fire. "That won't work," he called over his shoulder. "Even as a human, he won't burn. I'd know. I'm the same way."

Neither Ziya nor Lioia had the time or the inclination to question Kaal. They rushed after him, keeping pace as they crashed through the trees in search of a man who knew too well how to disappear and how to operate in the shadows. All the smoke and fire only served to give him more hiding places.

Kaal let out a snarl of sheer frustration that Ziya couldn't help but echo. This was the closest they'd ever come to getting rid of Alan for good. When else were they going to find him injured and subject to a group of humans who actually knew how to hurt him? If he escaped now, if he were able to nurse his injuries and to establish himself with dragons or humans elsewhere, he would be much more powerful and much harder to stop. They had to find him *now*, while he was weak.

As the three of them stood there in the smoke, trying to find any sign of their quarry, Ziya felt a sudden, overwhelming sense of dread. If she had believed more in the gods, she might have said they were trying to warn her; but even if she did believe in them, she didn't believe they were interested in her personally. So, she reasoned, there must have been some other explanation for the feeling. Some spell or some instinct—that last one was more likely, since she still didn't understand all the instincts and powers of a dragon.

She looked toward Kaal and was surprised to see that he was nearly smiling. The expression wasn't complete, but one half of his mouth was pulled back past his teeth, and he had his head cocked to the side as he listened, waiting.

And then, a growl rang out to the east of their position, and Kaal broke into a laugh as he bounded in that direction. "Alan's this way," he called out.

"How do you know?" Ziya asked, though she followed him all the same. She trusted him, especially since he'd spent all that time alone with Alan and likely had answers that they didn't. But that didn't mean she would follow him without question—especially when following him meant rushing *toward* the sense of impending doom.

"Lord Teyo's there," Kaal replied without any further explanation and without slowing down.

Ziya growled—not just out of the frustration of not knowing what was going on but because that ominous feeling kept getting more oppressive. Every instinct in her body told her that she needed to stop, if not turn back. But Kaal kept going, so she did too.

He wasn't supposed to be the braver one.

Sure enough, somehow, Kaal had been right. When Ziya, Lioia, and Kaal rushed into a smoke-filled path of fallen and burned trees, they found Alan, still in human form, practically stumbling away from a young human around Kaal's age. This must have been the lord of the village; he was well-dressed and well-groomed and had come with a pair of guards who lay on the ground near Alan. Although the guards were badly burned and likely dead, the young man was holding his own, in large part thanks to the sword in his hands that seemed to Ziya to be too bright-white to be natural. In fact, just looking at the sword made her nervous. She didn't know why. She'd seen swords before.

Maybe she was scared because *Alan* looked nervous. And Alan never looked nervous, scared, or even slightly ruffled. He had a thing about appearances. He didn't even like to get blood on him when he subjected his human-made dragons to unspeakable torture. To see him with his hair falling in his face, to see him *stumbling* . . . Ziya didn't understand it at first. His back and shoulders were bloody, so she thought at first that he was stumbling because of his injuries. But, no, his gaze was fixed on the young lord. He was *scared*.

As she watched, Alan breathed fire at the young man—*Teyo*, she remembered Kaal saying—but Teyo held up his sword, cleaving the fire so that it parted around him without burning him. In the next motion, Teyo swung his sword in a sharp but graceful arc. The only thing that kept him from taking Alan's head off was the fact that Alan managed to get his arm between the sword and his neck—and his arm was covered in white scales. And yet, somehow, the sword went *through* the scales, cutting deeply enough that Teyo met bone.

As Alan howled, Teyo yanked his sword back, readjusting his stance so he could thrust forward. Once more, Alan narrowly escaped being stabbed, but this time, he only did so by practically falling backward, catching himself on a downed tree so that he didn't end up on his backside.

THE GODS' GIFT

But, true to form, Alan didn't cower for long. When he saw Teyo preparing for another swing, he let out a roar loud enough to shake the burning leaves from the trees and then breathed out a stream of fire so large that Teyo couldn't escape all of it. Instantly, Teyo started to scream in agony, nearly dropping his sword. While Teyo stripped off his still-burning shirt, Alan started to grow, taking advantage of Teyo's distraction to return to his dragon size and presumably finish off his opponent.

The other three dragons burst into action at the same time, finally able to get between Teyo and Alan instead of watching a too-close combat. Ziya and Lioia both rushed toward Alan, hoping to get to him before he could finish transforming. Lioia could move so much faster than Ziya could, especially in a forest, so she reached Alan first. And to Ziya's shock, Lioia knocked Alan away from Teyo before she pounced on him. Ziya could see Kaal putting his body between Teyo and Alan, too, but that was to be expected. Lioia had now acted in the best interests of *two* humans, Mira and Teyo. Ziya wondered if Lioia even realized what she was doing.

Lioia sank her claws into Alan, aiming for the arm Teyo had cut into—now an injured leg—and bellowed a triumphant roar when Alan let out a scream that became a dragon's roar to match hers. He retaliated before she could remove her claws by biting down on her leg, and she snarled in pain, stumbling back, obviously reeling.

Ziya winced. She could remember being bitten by Alan and knew what agony that was. Even if Ziya and Kaal had told Lioia what Alan was capable of, nothing could quite prepare someone for the icy poison seeping through dragon veins.

Ziya wasn't about to let Alan get the upper hand, though, so when she realized Lioia was no longer capable of finishing the fight, she rushed to put herself between Alan and Lioia, the way Kaal had used his body as a shield for Teyo. Alan's claws dug into Ziya's side as the blow he'd meant for Lioia instead crashed into her, but he had been aiming beyond her body and therefore caught more of his leg than his claws on Ziya. She got hurt, yes, but it wasn't as bad as it would have been for Lioia. And she'd managed to get underneath his neck while she was at it.

Before he could react, she bit him, clamping her teeth down on scales that were too hard to be normal. But she'd learned her lesson after the last time they fought. She didn't *just* bite him. No. She used one foot of claws to dig into his scales below her mouth, digging in until she felt some scales give—and then, she bit down on the newly-revealed flesh.

Alan howled in anger and agony but couldn't bite Ziya in return, not when her head was underneath his chin. She'd chosen her placement well—thanks to *his* training. If she'd had time to think about anything but making sure Alan didn't walk away from that fight, she might even have enjoyed the poetic justice of becoming the weapon Alan wanted her to be just to kill him. It was what she'd dreamed about all that time in his clutches.

She didn't get to enjoy her victory, though, because even though she could taste warm copper as blood flowed freely across her teeth and tongue from his wound, Alan wasn't dead yet—and he had sharper claws than she did. He slashed at her, sinking his claws into her neck near her shoulder, digging in until Ziya *had* to let go or risk suffering a fatal wound.

As she jerked away from his claws, she tore herself open even more than before, and her vision swam as she tripped over her own feet. She had enough wherewithal to get herself several steps farther from Alan than she would have done if she'd collapsed then and there, but her vision went white with each step.

No, she thought, her teeth flashing, though she couldn't let out the growl she wanted to when her neck was so badly damaged that the sound had nowhere to go. Instead, a strange, wet sound came out. *No,* she thought again. *I can't die before him. He can't kill me first. I can't die worried that he'll get away.*

For some reason, that thought alone was enough to keep her conscious through sheer force of will, though her vision was blurry. She watched Alan stumbling as well, closed her eyes, and then took far too long to open them again. When she did, she nearly flinched away when she saw white scales in front of her—but she didn't have the energy to do more than let out a soft sound of fear.

"It's me," Kaal whispered, and Ziya nearly cried in relief—except dragons couldn't cry. She could only let out a soft whimper as Kaal began to heal her.

His warm breath washed over her like the comforting embrace of the ocean, and she closed her eyes, drinking in the reassurance that came with his healing. Kaal was the best healer in the world—Alan not included, since he didn't care much for others and would only heal another human or dragon if he thought it would benefit them. But Kaal . . . Ziya trusted her life in his hands. Or claws. Whatever the case might be.

She felt much less dizzy after only a minute, so she opened her eyes, reminding herself that she couldn't surrender to the peace of healing while Alan was still alive. To her relief, Alan hadn't escaped; she'd done more damage than she'd thought she had, apparently. He was trying to stumble away, trying to take advantage of the fact that all three of the dragons who had come after him were injured or distracted, but he kept tripping over his own feet. He looked weak, and his head kept drooping.

"I'll heal you more when I have the energy," Kaal promised Ziya, gasping in a breath as he stepped back from her. He still had his bad leg tucked up underneath him, and the other injuries littering his body must have been weighing him down. How he had any energy to share with her was a mystery to her, not that she was ungrateful.

"Get Alan," Ziya croaked out. If Kaal only had so much strength left, that was where she wanted him to spend it. She could heal later.

Kaal grinned in a manner Ziya had never seen him do before, a disturbing, nearly predatory look that made him look more like the kind of dragon she had always feared than he had ever looked before. "Watch," he said, gesturing with the tip of his tail and then lifting the tail entirely, giving space for a human to run underneath him, drawing his sword as he ran.

Once again, Ziya felt an overwhelming sense of panic wash over her, but this time, she could identify its source. The moment she saw the unnaturally white blade, she could feel her entire body recoiling. That sword had to be magic; there was no other explanation for why she couldn't stop growling or trying to get distance. Even Kaal, who seemed to be on good terms with Teyo, couldn't help but growl as his newest ally ran past him. That sword couldn't be good for any of them.

As Ziya watched, Teyo rushed toward a stumbling Alan. Alan breathed fire at Teyo, but Kaal was also in motion and flung his wings out, blocking Teyo from the fire. Alan let out a sound of pure anger and tore a huge, gaping hole in Kaal's wings for his interference, and Kaal screamed out a roar that rang in Ziya's ears. She'd heard a sound just like that when Alan had been torturing Caleb to taunt her and the others who had come to break up his base: a roar combined with a whine, caked in fear and pain.

But Teyo didn't stop. Kaal had bought him exactly as much time as he needed to get close enough to Alan to drive his too-white blade into Alan's heart, cutting through his scales like they were nothing and leaving a long line down his belly. He might have cut Alan open entirely if not for Alan's claws and wings as Alan thrashed, trying desperately to stop Teyo from killing him outright.

One of Alan's feet bashed into Teyo, tearing a large gash through Teyo's skin from shoulder to hip and sending him flying into a tree. Teyo hit it hard and lay still, ending his assault—but Alan was still so badly injured that no one there could possibly believe he'd survive.

Alan looked down at himself, at the scales and blood beneath him, and took in a sharp, ragged breath that turned into an angry snarl. He looked back up, and his gaze found Kaal. All at once, he pulled his lips back from his teeth, showing off fangs dripping in poison as he hissed out a single command: "Heal me."

Ziya nearly laughed, but then, she saw the look on Kaal's face, and the laugh died in her throat. She'd thought the command was Alan's desperate way of trying to exert control over them, but to see Kaal's expression, she would have thought not a day had passed since Alan had been giving Kaal orders. Kaal was rooted to the spot, his mouth slightly open, as if he were actually *considering* listening to Alan's ridiculous request.

"You can't be serious," she hissed when she saw Kaal hesitate.

Alan ignored Ziya, his gaze squarely fixed on Kaal. "You swore you would heal me," he told Kaal, his voice as commanding as possible when he was literally dying before their eyes. "Are you going to let everyone here know you can't keep your word? I thought you wanted to live up to Ziya's *heroics*." He spit the last word out with all the vitriol he could, flinging blood and venom and spittle into the air. When Kaal still hadn't reacted in any way, Alan snarled again. "Answer me!"

THE GODS' GIFT

"No." Kaal hadn't moved, and his answer came out as nothing more than a whisper, but it still echoed in the burning trees with a dragon's power.

The forest rang with stunned silence broken only by Lioia's sounds of pain—she was still poisoned—and Ziya's heavy breathing—she was still hurt. And then, Alan let out a growl that was somehow powerful and deep enough to rumble through every inch of Ziya's body despite how badly he was hurt.

"What?" Alan snarled, trying and failing to get to his feet, to attack Kaal and make him pay for his insolence. He wasn't used to being denied, especially not by his former prisoners. "You *owe* me, you ungrateful *child*."

"No," Kaal said. He'd finally started to move again, but only to stand in front of Teyo's unmoving form so that Alan couldn't lash out at Teyo while he lost his temper. "I owe you *nothing*. I told you I was here to stop you. You knew that. I won't save you."

"What happened to your honor?" Alan demanded, his smoke a sickly gray color that smelled putrid, another sign of his impending end. "You held it with such *jealousy*. When I met you, you wouldn't kill an unarmed man; you wouldn't stoop to debasing methods while you were begging for scraps from the army. And now you can't keep one promise?"

The same terrifying smile Ziya had seen before spread over Kaal's mouth and made Ziya's blood run cold. She couldn't see any trace of the boy she knew. "You said yourself that I have lived this long by lying," he said. His sharp smile lost some of its strength, and she heard a resignation and despair in his voice that nearly broke her heart. Whatever had transpired during his time with Alan, it had broken him in a way nothing had until that moment.

She could have cried—if she'd been able to. Kaal had been her source of hope, but now, he'd lost his own faith.

Alan, on the other hand, was furious, breathing out smoke that got lost in the winds of so many fires around them. "Listen to me," he insisted, but Kaal snarled loudly enough to quiet him.

"No," Kaal said. "No, you listen to *me*. You will die here, Alan, and no one will mourn you. And you will never harm another creature again. If I lose my honor, if I must break a promise for that to happen, then so be it."

Alan was beyond words as he spewed fire and invectives, but the flames lost their strength and became sparks, and still, not one of the dragons offered him any aide.

He died angry, but not alone.

CHAPTER 19: THE GODS' MISTAKE

By the time Alan died, the dragon council had retreated. Neither side had won the battle; the humans were fleeing and their homes were in flames, but several dragons had fallen in battle, and the dragons did not have enough remaining in their number to continue their attack with any hope of success. So, the dragons gathered up their wounded and flew in strange formations of three, with one injured dragon spreading its wings across the backs of two less-injured dragons. Their flights were awkward and crooked, but they could at least get out of range of the archers and wizards faster that way. What they did after they rounded the mountaintops, Ziya didn't know.

Ziya doubted the dragon council would stay away for long. This village represented everything they believed humanity to be. It was full of people who knew how to hurt dragons and who actively hated them. Their leader had a sword with such strong magic that even a human-made dragon knew, instinctively, to fear it. The council wouldn't be able to leave this village alone.

And yet, the reprieve would grant both sides time to build up their defenses as well as their strategies of attack. The next battle, Ziya knew, would be worse. That was how war worked—a constant escalation until nothing remained but ashes and death.

And survivors.

Ziya looked away from Alan toward Kaal, who was rooted to the spot, staring at Alan's unmoving form, his chest heaving and his eyes wide. Ziya knew she couldn't possibly guess what he was thinking, but she knew panic when she saw it. He'd looked nearly the same way when the dragon council had declared war.

She was still sore and hurt from her fight with Alan, and she could see as she got closer to Kaal that some of his injuries were also starting to weep. But he didn't seem to feel his pain at all, watching Alan as if he expected to see the rise and fall of his chest despite all odds. Not that Ziya blamed him for that fear. Alan had always seemed more powerful than he was. But Ziya doubted even he could overcome death.

Carefully, she got close enough to Kaal to nudge him with her shoulder, finally drawing his attention away from Alan. When he looked her way, she moved even closer, nudging him just underneath where his jaw met his neck, nuzzling into him gently to reassure him that the fight was over—even temporarily. "Are you alright?" she asked in a whisper low enough that not even Lioia could have listened in.

Kaal made a noncommittal noise and then turned toward her. "You're hurt," he said, as if he'd only noticed that fact that second, despite his earlier attempt to heal her.

Ziya let out all her breath in a whoosh of hot air. She'd seen so many other people do exactly this after a hard battle or after a loss. He was in too much shock to think clearly. And if she didn't break him out of it, he'd lose himself to this state, wallowing in whatever had broken him, whatever had made him look like the vengeful dragon she'd seen when he faced Alan at the end.

"You're hurt too," she said, gesturing with the tip of her tail toward his torn wing and then to the rest of him. His white scales were covered in dirt, leaves, ash, and blood. She knew she didn't look much better, but her dark scales could hide more than his could. No one looking at him could think he was alright.

Kaal looked down at his wing, grimaced, and then looked quickly away again. "Looks like I won't be flying anytime soon," he said dully.

"I'd heal you, but—"

"It's alright," Kaal said quickly. "All of us were hurt. We can deal with it later." His gaze drifted toward Alan's still form again as the conversation lulled. "I. . . ." He let the thought die unspoken and looked away.

THE GODS' GIFT

"I know he made you promise you'd heal him," Ziya said, "but no one could blame you for refusing."

Kaal's shoulders led the way as his body sank, careful of his bad leg but otherwise simply falling to the ground where he was. "He didn't make me do anything," he said without looking at anything in particular. "I asked him to tell me the truth, and that was part of our deal."

Ziya frowned and sat down beside him as close as she dared. "What did you learn?" she asked quietly.

Kaal rested his head on his good leg, staring forward, unseeing. "I learned the history of the dragons," he said softly. "I learned that dragons had no color at first. They all had white, unadorned scales. The gods gave them their colors as they chose their callings. Black for the deep sea. Blue for the sky. Each new egg contained a deeper color and new changes to better protect the world as their families saw fit."

"That's beautiful," Ziya said, trying to draw a smile from him. She knew he loved to learn as much as he could about the world the dragons inhabited, and it sounded to her like he'd gotten his wish. Not even Rikaa knew old stories like that; if he had, he would have shared them with Kaal by then, especially knowing how desperately Kaal wanted to understand his newfound history.

Kaal nearly smiled, but it wasn't the bright warmth she was used to; he came close to that smile and then backed away from it, still staring into the smoke beyond them as the forest continued to burn long after the dragons had retreated. "Alan is likely the last white dragon," he said. "Or one of the last. He came from a white and a green dragon who asked the gods for aid in waging war with humans." Ziya understood at that moment why he was still staring toward the burning forest. "The gods stopped granting requests as the dragons asked for tools of war against each other and against humans, but not until after some white dragons like Alan had venom and other gifts." He pulled back his lips to reveal his teeth, which looked nothing like Alan's fangs. "Alan may have white scales, but apparently, I look more like the dragons the gods first created. A white dragon. No purpose, no home." He let out a mirthless laugh. "Alan was right. I survive by lying, by being whoever I need to be. No wonder his spell made me a white dragon."

210

Ziya shook her head, disagreeing without the words she needed to convince him of how wrong he was. "No," she said—eloquently.

Kaal glanced up at her and gave her a tired smile. "It's alright. I know who I am," he said in a bare whisper.

"No, you don't," Ziya said, finding her voice at last after the shock of hearing Kaal so callously defining himself. He couldn't have understood how much strength she drew from him, so to hear him talk so negatively of himself . . . she couldn't stand for it. "We all told lies to survive, Kaal. That's not all that you are."

"Alright, Ziya," Kaal said, though his tone told her he didn't believe her and was only trying to placate her.

Her eyes flashed, but rather than arguing with someone so despondent, she decided to draw him back into conversation. She couldn't lose him to Alan's manipulations, and so, she needed to know what Alan had said so she could undo the damage he'd wrought. "Did he tell you how he can change like you can?"

Kaal nodded. "That's the gift the gods gave him. His parents wanted a child who could stand against the humans. The gods gave them one who could stand *with* humans." He made an irritated noise from the back of his throat. "Alan took that gift and used it to infiltrate our world. He stirred up trouble, stoked anger and wars, and learned how to give those in power more weapons, all in an attempt to provoke humans into destroying each other and weakening their own defenses so that dragons could regain their rule of the earth."

Ziya blinked at Kaal a few times. "I thought the gods asked dragons to *defend* this world," she said. "I . . . I don't understand. Why give a dragon the ability to destroy us from within?"

"I don't think they meant for him to use their gifts the way he has," he said. He glanced toward the sky. "But I can't know what the gods wanted. None of us can. We can only try to do what they asked us to do and keep the world they created safe." He snorted a black puff of smoke. "Even from those who got undeserved gifts."

Ziya nodded softly, though she didn't take her gaze off of Kaal. She couldn't place what in his body language told her how hurt he was—not physically, not like the way he held his leg, but the kind of hurt that lingered in dreams and in thoughts that surfaced whenever loneliness met silence. But she could see his pain all the same and nudged him with her snout again. "Then they chose you to make amends for their mistake with Alan," she decided. She might not have believed in the gods as deeply or as sympathetically as Kaal did, but she wasn't about to let him lose his faith and his hope because of Alan.

Kaal turned her way, his mouth slightly open with surprise, since she never talked about the gods like he did, like they actually cared what happened in their world. "Ziya, didn't you hear what he said?" he asked, choking on his words as if he might break down sobbing. Ziya wondered what that would look like when dragons couldn't cry. "I'm nothing but a silver tongue. Teyo's the hero who killed Alan. You're the one who rallied the dragons to rescue their own without massacring innocents. All I can do is talk my way into the good graces of whoever I think will keep me alive."

"I heard what he said, and he lied," Ziya insisted, fire in her eyes and in her mouth so that her words came out with sparks. "He lied because he saw the dragon you became without him, and he knew you didn't need him. He lied and told you that you were nothing so you would agree to heal him in the first place. He lied. You *know* he lies. And yet you still think you're like him." Ziya drew herself up to her full height. "You're not what he says you are, but you are so *gullible*."

Kaal drew himself up to match her, though Ziya didn't think he was aware he'd done so. "You're not listening," he started to say, but Ziya cut him off with a growl.

"I'm not listening because you're using *his* words," she snapped. "Use your head, would you? You're the one who believes in the gods. You're the one who thinks they actually care what happens to us. You're the one who believes in the mandate they gave dragons. Do you really think they would have allowed Alan to *stumble* upon a way to replicate *their* gift to him? Do you honestly think Alan had anything to do with your ability to change your shape?" With each word, she picked up speed and volume until she could have been heard almost anywhere in the village. "What kind of faith do you have that you think Alan is anywhere near as good as they are?"

As her words echoed the trees around them, Kaal stood in shocked silence, his mouth open for a long time before he remembered himself and closed it again. "I thought you didn't believe the gods cared about us," he said quietly.

"No, but you do," Ziya said without losing any of the heat in her tone, though she did speak more quietly now that she could see Kaal thinking for himself. "And you had me nearly convinced you were right, too. Your hope and your empathy and your ability to see the good in everyone, even the gods—that's why I was willing to follow you, Kaal. That's why dragons and humans alike listen when you speak. I know I tease you about your silver tongue, but that isn't your gift. Your gift is your heart. Your words are just tools, Kaal. That's all. Just tools." By the time she'd finished, she was practically whispering—and had moved much closer to him, too. "Don't let Alan's lies define you, or he'll never truly die. You know that."

Kaal stared at her in silence that stretched out for so long that Ziya heard Teyo start to stir before Kaal had moved a muscle. And even then, Kaal didn't stop staring—not until Teyo let out a soft moan. Then, at last, Kaal looked away from Ziya and toward his new ally—and Ziya tried not to think too hard about how relieved she was to see some warmth returning to his silver eyes, replacing his cold fury.

"I can heal you once I have time to recover," Kaal said, offering his tail to Teyo as leverage to stand, though Teyo refused it and pulled himself up using the remains of a tree.

Teyo frowned as he looked around the forest, taking in the damage he could see—and likely imagining all that he couldn't. This was his home, and it had been ravaged by dragons. Ziya didn't begrudge him the moment he took to glare around at the smoke and fire before he fixed his angry gaze on the three badly hurt dragons in front of him. As soon as he did, he put his hand on his sword, ready to draw it if need be. "What happened after he hit me?" he demanded, his tone ringing with authority but also fear.

"Alan pleaded for us to spare him," Ziya said before Kaal could respond. She didn't want Kaal in his vulnerable state to say something he might regret in front of someone who had the power to end his life. Normally, she would have let Kaal do the talking, since he always knew how to phrase his stories in a way that would draw the most sympathy from those who heard him speak. But now, as he doubted his own gifts, she would take that burden from him the way she had been prepared to take the burden of killing Alan from him. "He didn't deserve our pity."

THE GODS' GIFT

Teyo looked toward Kaal for confirmation, and Kaal simply nodded once. When Kaal didn't add anything more, though, Teyo frowned deeper, taking a step closer to Kaal and looking now not at Alan and the forests on fire but at Kaal and his damaged wing— and then at Ziya and Lioia. Every single one of the dragons in that forest was badly injured. Even though Teyo was limping and tired and likely needed medicine of his own, he had no reason to fear the dragons around him but great reason to pity them—if he was capable of pity for the creatures that harangued his village.

"You won't get anywhere on that wing," Teyo said.

Kaal shrugged, though the motion jostled his wing and elicited a hiss and high-pitched whine that he made an obvious effort to swallow. "I'll heal," he said. He tipped his head, studying Teyo closely, and Ziya took a step back, not wanting to interfere with whatever understanding the two of them had. "Do you intend to lock me up again?" he asked with a quiver in his voice that told Ziya Kaal was on the brink of losing everything that gave him the light she *needed* to see in him to stay sane herself. Another captivity on the heels of everything Alan had said and done to him would destroy him; she just knew it.

Teyo seemed to understand the weight of the question, too, because he met Kaal's gaze for a long time, being careful with his reply. "Not today," he decided at last. "You showed me you could fight alongside me. I owe you some consideration."

Kaal dipped his head in a silent show of gratitude. "Maybe we could work together again."

"Maybe." Teyo continued to regard Kaal with a mixture of caution and curiosity. "I can't let you stay in my village, however."

"We can stay in the forests," Kaal promised. "Lioia knows her way in the trees and can take us somewhere safe."

"Good." Teyo fell silent once more, resting his hand on his hilt—but not to draw it. Instead, he was absently playing his fingers against the bright gold. Ziya didn't blame him for his nervous energy; she wouldn't have been comfortable being outnumbered by dragons either.

Kaal glanced toward Alan, his tail moving as he thought over his words. At least he was *thinking* now. "I know I have no right to request anything of you," he started to say to Teyo.

"No, but I will hear you anyway," Teyo said, finally removing his hand from his sword to fold his arms across his chest and draw himself up. What little remained of his clothes was torn and mangled and burned, and he looked like he was trying to keep himself steady enough to meet a dragon's eye.

All four of the living beings there were barely putting aside the pain the battle had put them through to continue this conversation, and Ziya knew that wouldn't last much longer. Eventually, they would have to let their hurt and their emotions wash over them, or they would never fully recover. A hurt deferred only festered.

"The whole of Niyala has been destroyed by the dragon council," Kaal explained. "The lands have burned. The people have all run away or died. By the time we stop the council, there will be nothing left but your stronghold, a few survivors, and ashes." He pointed with his tail toward Alan. "Please, have your people collect his scales. Save them for when this is over. As evil as he was, his scales still have healing power." Kaal took a deep breath and let it out, the barest wisps of smoke trailing out of his nostrils. "I think we can reclaim the burned land and the dried riverbeds if we plant the scales across the land."

Ziya stared at Kaal, starting to smile for the first time since Alan had died. She could hardly believe him sometimes. Here she'd thought he was caught up in his hurt and in the lies Alan had told him, and yet he was *still* finding a way to be the dragon the gods wanted other dragons to be. He was *still* looking for ways to protect and heal the earth, to undo the damage of war, and to give life back to the earth's inhabitants.

She didn't know why she was surprised.

KAAL

CHAPTER 20: WHO'S THE HERO?

After Lioia led the way back to her home, Lioia's husband immediately took her under his wing and urged her toward the spot where he had been recovering from his own battle not long ago. He looked stronger than the last time Kaal and Ziya had seen him—one of his hatchlings was hanging off of his side with sharp claws until he gently nipped at him to get him to let go so he could talk to the three older dragons.

"What happened?" Oad asked once he got Lioia settled. He sat down beside her with his legs tucked into him, nudging her nose with his. Although she wasn't as visibly injured as Kaal and Ziya were, she was still taking stuttered breaths, wincing through the pain of Alan's venom.

"We killed the one who took your son," Ziya said before Kaal could begin to explain. She usually liked to hang back and let him deal with dragons, but ever since Alan had died, she had gained a strange new confidence. He was glad to see it; he hoped it meant that all the awful things Alan had done to her would fade with his death so that Ziya could live in some semblance of peace.

"Good." Oad nuzzled Lioia again, and she whined. "But what happened to Lioia?"

"Alan is a white dragon," Kaal told him, seeing no reason to lie to him—and besides, he was too tired to censor his words. "And he has venom."

Oad moved away from Kaal, his lips pulled back from his teeth in a display of defensiveness. "And you?"

"I don't," Kaal said in a sigh. "I'm not the same as he was." He looked toward Ziya, and she nodded encouragingly. She had refused to hear him say a word of comparison between him and Alan, and he supposed, for her sake, he should try to pretend he hadn't believed every word Alan had said to him during their shared captivity. So, he swallowed, returned Ziya's nod, and continued, "I am more like the dragons of old. He had parents from different clans and inherited traits that the clans had asked of the gods; I'm a blank slate, like the gods' first dragons." He shrugged, but the motion jostled his hurt wing, and he ended up wincing badly.

Although Oad had been wary of Kaal, he moved forward on instinct when Kaal whined. As a parent, he couldn't ignore a young dragon in that much distress. "If you can give me an oath that you will not harm me or my family, you can stay with us until you get your strength back," Oad said. He paused and visibly softened his stance when he heard his wife moan in pain. "You healed me before. Let me return the favor."

"Thank you," Ziya said, once again speaking up for the two of them. Kaal turned her way, frowning, but she simply replied with a blissful smile, as if this were completely normal behavior for her.

Kaal wasn't sure what Ziya was up to, but he wouldn't question her in front of Lioia and Oad. So, he held his tongue and followed Lioia's little ones to a spot where he and Ziya could curl up and regain their strength. He thanked them for their hospitality several times before they were finally left to themselves, and once that happened, he wanted nothing more than to go to sleep.

He'd thought Ziya would be of the same mind, but instead, she moved closer to him until they were sharing the same space, her wings against his side, arranging herself so that neither of them knocked into each other's injuries. And when she answered his surprised look with a serene smile, Kaal couldn't take any more and blurted out, "What are you doing?"

"I won't let you stay alone in your thoughts until I believe you are past all that Alan made you think of yourself," Ziya said in a tone that brooked no argument.

Kaal stared at her. "Ziya, we already talked about this."

"Yes, we did. While you were still in shock. We can talk again when we get away from this place. I guarantee Rikaa will take my side." Ziya smiled, flashing her sharp teeth at him. "I know you don't want to speak about what Alan said to you, and I don't blame you. If you need something else to occupy your mind, we should make plans. Alan may be dead, but we're not done, you and I. Aonai went to the council, and I don't see any sign that they listened to him. If he's in trouble—"

"Ziya, I can't fly," Kaal interrupted her. Before she could respond, he continued, "I know you're a hero, Ziya. I admire that about you. But I'm not. I need to rest. I want to go *home*." He let his gaze drop and moved away from her, unwilling to see the betrayal he knew he'd find in her gaze. "I won't stop you from rescuing Aonai. You're right; he's in trouble. But I'll slow you down if I come too."

Ziya let out a hot huff of smoke as she reached for him with one clawed foot but stopped short of actually touching him, letting her claws fall back down in leaves that crackled underneath her touch. "You're still listening to him," she said. "He's gone, and you still believe what he told you."

"No, Ziya," Kaal said wearily. "I've known since you escaped who the hero is between us. All I want is a family among the dragons. You want *justice*." He finally raised his gaze to hers, his fire hotter in his belly than he'd expected it to be. Her eyes were a sharp green color that he'd never noticed before. They had looked black, but now that the two of them were so close, he could see the truth, and he didn't know why he was so caught up in that small detail instead of in his shame. "I tried to keep up with you, but you're so much better at this than I am. All I can do is talk my way out of trouble. You seek it out and rescue anyone in your path while you're at it."

Ziya stared at him openly. "Kaal. . . ." She shook her head. "You don't give yourself enough credit."

"You keep saying that," Kaal said. He looked down at himself and at his badly damaged wing. "If I could fly, maybe I'd go with you to find Aonai. I wouldn't want you to be by yourself, and if you think we should go there first, I'll support you." He didn't raise his gaze to look at her, but he could see her green eyes in his mind. "But I don't want you to be caught because of me. Not again. Not after what it did to you last time."

At the allusion to her earlier captivity, Ziya finally stopped arguing, her eyes bright and her head held high. She let out a rough snort and then turned her head away from him so that he couldn't see her expression. He knew he'd hurt her by bringing up those old wounds, but he wanted to tell the truth. He was tired of lies, and he didn't *want* to be the silver-tongued liar he knew he was when he faced Ziya. He wanted to be better. For her.

"Rest, Kaal," Ziya said at last without looking his way or moving any closer to him. "Heal. We can talk again in the morning."

Kaal opened his mouth and then closed it again, thinking better of the argument he'd been trying to form. He usually trusted himself and his words, but ever since his captivity with Alan, he couldn't seem to say the right thing around Ziya. Yet another way he'd failed to become the dragon he wanted to be. Outside of Rikaa's influence, he seemed to fall back into the same patterns he'd had as a human. Survival. Lies. Everything that had made Alan take notice of him in the first place.

Kaal frowned and settled in to sleep. His body was screaming for rest and overtook his anxious mind, though his mind rebelled and kept working even though he'd fallen asleep. His dreams were filled with all that Alan had told him, every secret that the dragons had lost because of their wars and their divisions. He dreamed of fangs that hurt his mouth as they dripped venom onto his tongue. He dreamed of wizards attacking him while he flew. He dreamed of the cavern in which Alan had trapped him, the one he had been chained in. And there, his dreams stayed. He stayed chained down. He stayed with Alan and Elena. He was their pet forever. He never changed.

"Kaal."

He wasn't awake enough to realize he was awake, but he could hear someone calling his name all the same. He was too tired to understand what was happening, and he started to drift back to sleep.

"Kaal."

That time, he realized Ziya was calling him—at the same time he felt a snout underneath his jaw, nudging him awake. He let out a soft sound and pulled away, blinking several times until he saw Ziya watching him carefully. "Sorry," he muttered, though he was shaking from head to tail. "Bad dream."

"It's alright. I get them too," Ziya said. She didn't move away from him. "I'm sorry," she said after a long bout of silence.

THE GODS' GIFT

He frowned. "Why?"

"I shouldn't have let you go with Alan," she said. "I should have killed him."

"I told you I wanted to know—"

"I know," she interrupted him. "And I'm glad you got your answers. I am. But I don't know that the cost was worth the answers." She let out a long sigh and nudged him with her snout. "You managed to become a better person while you were running around in your dragon skin away from his influence. But as soon as Alan got you alone, he turned you into *me*—doubting yourself and your own humanity and believing every lie he told you."

"That's different," Kaal argued. "You were his prisoner. I—"

"He still had power over you because he knew you wanted answers," she pointed out. "You know how he was. Any power he could exercise, he would." She drew herself up, her wings scraping against his because of how close they were sitting. "I miss the Kaal I met when I escaped."

"I'm sorry," he said, letting his shoulders fall and his head dip down in a perfect picture of contrition. "I'm sorry that I can't live up to—"

"You can; you just don't think you can," Ziya said. "And I'm not going to let you throw yourself away." She held his gaze steadily, her tail moving behind her. "So, no, I won't let you give up. But I *will* stay with you through all your nightmares if you'll promise to stay with me through mine. I still get them too."

"I don't blame you," he said softly, because he couldn't understand how she wanted him to respond to anything else she'd said.

"And I don't blame *you*." She watched him, waiting, but he didn't know what she wanted, so he didn't move. When he couldn't respond the way she wanted him to, she sighed and resettled so that her head was on her front legs and she wasn't practically tucked into his side anymore. "You should try to get some rest. We need to heal each other so we can leave as soon as we can."

"Right. Aonai—"

"It's not just Aonai I'm worried about," she told him. "You need to get back to your family. And I need to get back to my mother." She let her tail go still. "I think we should leave this place while we are still weak and then do the rest of our healing with allies."

He understood instantly and nodded. "It's hard to relax while our hosts watch us for any sign of betrayal."

"Exactly." Ziya made a sharp gesture with her foot that would have been clearer with a human hand. "Lioia and I came to an understanding while you were gone, but I don't trust her."

Kaal rested his head on the ground, exhaustion pulling his shoulders down too. "Then we'll leave as soon as we can. I promise."

"Good." Ziya moved away from him so she could get comfortable enough to rest as well. He thought she might go to sleep, too, but then, she spoke up again: "I liked what you told Teyo about burying Alan's scales. You said you're not a hero, but you're already thinking of how to save humanity from dying."

"I only did what I wished I could have done when I was human," Kaal said quickly, unwilling to take the title Ziya kept trying to shove at him, convinced that she thought so highly of him because she thought she owed him her allegiance. He didn't like the dynamic of their relationship; he knew Alan had pitted them against each other and, therefore, had stained the way they looked at one another, perhaps irreparably. "Didn't you ever daydream about how much better the world would be if everyone stopped fighting and all the dragon scales people hoarded were used to replace all the land we lost?"

"I didn't take you for a daydreamer, Kaal," Ziya said, her smile soft enough to catch his attention where it creased the scales around her mouth.

"When I was younger," Kaal said with a wistful sigh. "Tris and I used to talk about the end of the war all the time. Even after he died, I could still hear his voice in my dreams talking about the gardens we could plant when all was said and done."

"He'd be proud of you," Ziya said.

Kaal felt his stomach twist, and he looked away. "No," he said quietly. "No, he wouldn't."

"There you go again," Ziya said, shuffling closer and nudging his shoulder with hers. "Trust me when I tell you that you can't let Alan get in your head. I spent far too long believing him when he told me I was a weapon, and I'm not going to let him take your humanity too. I'm just barely starting to believe I can get mine back; don't take that hope away from me."

THE GODS' GIFT

Kaal swiveled his head back to look at her, surprised by the fear he heard in her voice. "You never lost yours, Ziya. You're the one who made sure the dragons didn't kill innocents," he said, moving closer to her without thinking about it, as if his presence would be enough to quiet the doubts ringing in her mind.

"I won't have this argument with you because you're still in shock, but eventually, you're going to have to accept the fact that I ran into you only because I agreed to drag you back to Alan to be tortured—and I was *excited* about it. Gleeful. I wanted you to suffer, Kaal," Ziya replied, her words steel but her voice wavering. "Whatever picture you have in your mind of my heroism, you're going to be disabused of it sooner or later, and I'd rather it was sooner. I don't like the version of me in your head; she doesn't exist."

Kaal fell silent and stared out into the darkness between the trees. He couldn't answer her, because he recognized too many of his own arguments in what she said. So, he simply moved away from her and sat down heavily. She didn't speak up again either; they had reached an impasse.

But now, he couldn't go back to sleep. His mind was too busy. And without Ziya's conversation, he found himself drowning in memories of what Alan had wanted to make of him, so he quickly looked around for something else to draw his attention.

With his dragon senses, he could see movement out in the leaves near their position but didn't know what brave creatures had made their homes so close to a dragon nest. Maybe those creatures were small enough that the dragons didn't need to hunt them for food. Maybe those creatures were fast enough to avoid big dragons lunging for them. Maybe they were using the dragon nest as their own form of safety against predators.

Funny how the dragons are actually protecting those creatures, he thought. *I wish they'd do the same for humans, like the gods asked them to.*

At the thought of the gods, Kaal felt his gaze drifting toward Ziya. Her eyes were closed, but she wasn't relaxed enough to be asleep. And so, rather than let her go to sleep still angry at him, he ventured a quiet, "Did you mean what you said before? About the gods?"

Ziya peeked one eye open. "What?"

"I thought you didn't believe in them—or at least that you

224

didn't think they cared about what happened to us. But you said you thought they had plans for me," Kaal explained and then felt his fire rush in his belly as he blushed. He sounded self-conceited. He didn't mean to ask about himself; he meant to ask what had changed her mind about the gods. He'd found faith because of Rikaa and because of his stories that *felt* right. Ziya . . . he didn't know what had changed her, and he couldn't help feeling curious.

"Ah." Ziya nodded slowly, obviously choosing her words. "I think," she said, pausing again to order her thoughts. "I think that if the gods really were involved in our lives, if they really did care about the earth, then they would stop their chosen protectors from killing humans entirely. Maybe they don't stop wars, maybe they let their creations reap the consequences of their own actions, but they don't want the earth wiped clean of an entire species either." She paused again, her tail moving the earth around her. "I don't know that they would get involved themselves, but they could certainly empower others to act. If what Alan told you is true about the gods gifting dragons with different colors and talents so that they could protect the world, then why would you be any different?" She smiled tightly. "You think I'm a hero, Kaal, but all I know how to do is fight. You think ahead. You think of others. You find healing and family and allies everywhere you go. If anyone is chosen by the gods—if I can find faith in anyone—it's you."

Kaal stared at her for a long time. "I. . . ." No, he couldn't find words yet. He shook his head, scratching at the ground. "All I want to do is go home," he said softly.

"Then let's go home," Ziya replied just as softly. "The council is still licking its wounds. We have time. And we can't rescue Aonai while we are still so hurt. There's nothing wrong with retreating and regrouping."

Kaal nearly chuckled. "You sound like such a seasoned soldier."

"I heard enough about strategy to last me a lifetime," Ziya replied, almost smiling as well. "I was supposed to go into the war and fight, remember?"

"I remember. That's why you're so suited to daring rescues and heroic plans."

"And you're so good at picking up the pieces and turning them into peace," she replied. She moved forward and nudged his head underneath his chin in a soft, comforting gesture. "If you don't believe you're a hero, at least believe me when I tell you that I rely on you."

Kaal smiled and rested his head on top of hers. He closed his eyes and let himself relax as he listened to the soft sound of her body. Dragon bodies were always moving, even when they were still. The fire inside their bellies and throat made a soft rush of sound that Kaal could normally only hear if all other sounds were silenced, but he could hear it underneath his chin with Ziya so close to him. He listened to the churning sound of fire and tried to push all thoughts of Alan out of his mind. Ziya was trying so hard to cheer him up; the least he could do would be to listen to her.

She's so much like Tris, he thought—and that thought finally brought a genuine smile to his lips. *He couldn't stand to hear me talk poorly of myself either.*

Finally, he let out a long sigh that washed warmth and healing over Ziya even though he hadn't been thinking about healing. He'd been thinking about how much he appreciated her, though, and he'd been thinking about how much he wanted to support her and give her his strength so she could be the hero he knew she was meant to be. "You say I'm chosen by the gods, but I think you are too," he said, opening his eyes to see her standing there in shock—not just from his statement but from the healing he'd given her. He stopped, too, and then smiled delightedly when he saw that she held herself less like a hurt dragon and more like a tired one, relaxing her wings and allowing her legs to drift farther from her center. "Maybe I'm supposed to keep your path clear."

"Funny," Ziya hissed. "I keep thinking the same thing about you."

Kaal smiled and settled back down. "Well then," he said, "at least we agree on one thing. The gods mean for us to help each other. And so we will."

CHAPTER 21: AN OFFER OF HEALING AND SONG

O h, I'm sorry. I didn't mean to interrupt."

Kaal startled awake when he heard the new voice breaking through his dreams of captivity and fear, blinking several times until he was awake enough to realize Oad had come to check on him and Ziya. Oad had averted his gaze, turning his body slightly away from the two adolescent dragons, and Kaal felt his fire heat up in his belly even though he and Ziya hadn't been doing anything untoward. Sometime in the night, they had moved closer to each other in their sleep, but that appearance alone was enough to fuel more rumors. Everyone that saw them together tried to put a name to their relationship, but neither Kaal nor Ziya could define how they felt if asked. They needed each other; they didn't have time to consider more than that.

Kaal got quickly to his feet and then swayed slightly. He was tired and hurt and, he realized as his stomach growled on top of everything else, hungry. And the sound of his stomach elicited a tired smile out of Ziya as she, too, got to her feet.

When Kaal's stomach grumbled, Oad took that as his cue to meet his gaze again. "I need to go hunting," he explained. "Will you stay with Lioia and our hatchlings? I will bring back enough for you to eat too, but Lioia is in no state to watch them alone."

"Yes. Of course. Thank you for thinking of us," Kaal agreed. He stretched out his legs and then winced when he unfurled his damaged wing. He had seen dragons with scars on their wings and knew he would one day be able to fly again, but he wasn't looking forward to seeing how long he would be grounded and in pain. And he wasn't entirely sure where his injury would manifest itself if he were to become human, so he didn't want to try changing form, either. He was stuck and hurting, so he was more than happy to have a task to keep his mind off of those facts.

"Thank you," Oad said, not bothering to check that they were following him before he bounded off.

Ziya let out a great yawn, stretched her limbs and wings, and tipped her head at Kaal. "How are you feeling?" she asked.

"Comparatively?" Kaal asked, and Ziya chuckled. "I'm alright," he said. "I want to go home, as you know, but I'm alright." He started forward, following Oad's path toward the sound of hatchlings growling and playing. As long as he kept moving, he wouldn't think of how sore he was. "And you?"

"Alright," she replied, a rote response, and followed him.

"I'm sorry we're stuck here," Kaal said as they walked through the dense trees. "I know you and Lioia don't exactly see eye-to-eye."

Ziya flicked a fallen branch as she passed it by. "We can tolerate each other," she said carefully. "She thinks I'm too young to listen to, and I think she's too proud to adapt to this moment in history."

"We *are* young."

"Old enough to fight," Ziya pointed out. "Old enough to be conscripted."

"And yet compared to the centuries of a dragon. . . ."

Ziya chuckled and shook her head. "Alan admitted to you that he was born a dragon and that he hated humans so much that he did everything in his power to encourage wars and to subdue, control, and destroy us—and you still see them as mythical beings. How do you do that?"

"I met Rikaa," Kaal said simply. That was all the explanation he would ever need, and he hoped that, now that she had met Rikaa, she would see what he saw. Rikaa and his family—and dragons like Aonai—stood for what dragons were supposed to stand for. They wanted to help the earth. They had saved Caleb and so many other humans from Alan's clutches. He would rather think of dragons like Rikaa as the norm than dragons like Alan and Drui.

Even Lioia was a better dragon than Alan was. Yes, she made no secret of her disdain for humanity, but she was still capable of working with Kaal and Ziya and even capable of empathy when she heard their stories. She might not have liked them, but she could tolerate them, and that was a far cry from what others did.

Ziya let out a soft sound that sounded more like a rumbling murmur than a laugh. "You love him, don't you?" she said. Before Kaal could respond, she continued, "It's not a bad thing. I'm glad your dragon family suits you. But I think you're letting them blind you to what dragons are capable of."

"No, I'm letting them tell me what dragons are capable of and demanding that the rest of dragonkind live up to that potential."

This time, Ziya's laugh was more genuine and came from the depths of her belly. Kaal could feel his own stomach leap at the sound. She was so serious all the time, so hurt, that hearing her laugh and knowing *he* had made her laugh brought a smile to his face and warmth to his heart. He wasn't ready to admit that Rikaa was right about his assessment of Kaal's feelings toward her, but he could admit that he cared about her—deeply—and wanted her to be happy. Hearing her laugh when she rarely had occasion to do so was healing in its own right.

Kaal kept grinning at her as the two of them made their way to where Lioia was curled up underneath a canopy of entwined branches. All three of her hatchlings were playing around her, offering little nudges with their snouts and sounds of concern. To Kaal's relief, Lioia looked better than she had the night before; the night's sleep had done her some good. But she was still obviously not her usual self.

Kaal watched the hatchlings and their concern and then made up his mind, knowing his decision before he made it, the same way he'd known on the day he and Ziya had been plucked out of their group of refugees that he would carry a little girl up the mountain. These hatchlings needed their mother to be alright; Alan couldn't be allowed to hurt this family any more than he already had.

So, Kaal made his way forward and sat down facing Lioia. "How are you?" he asked gently.

She picked her head up to look at him, sighed, and then laid her head back down. "Tired and sore," she admitted. "I hope never to fight another white dragon. His bite is worse than anything I've ever endured."

THE GODS' GIFT

"Yeah, it's bad," Kaal agreed, though he didn't have the same personal experience Ziya did.

Lioia gave him a tired smile. "And you?" she asked. "How are you? I might not have had the strength to enter your argument with Ziya after Alan died, but I heard what you said." She reached out to rest a clawed foot on his leg. "You can't possibly believe that you are anything like Alan. You healed my husband. You managed to bridge an alliance between the humans in that village and yourself and Ziya. No other dragon has managed to do that."

"I wouldn't call it an alliance," Kaal said, unwilling to take praise he hadn't earned when he still felt like both Lioia and Ziya were willfully blind to what he was. "We have an understanding. I doubt Teyo would hesitate to kill me if he thought for a second it would be in the interests of his people."

"Then he will never kill you." Lioia's breath swirled a few leaves in front of her nose. "You go out of your way to avoid making enemies, and Ziya trips over herself in her attempts to protect humans who don't need her protection. Between the two of you, that village has nothing to fear."

"You sound disappointed."

"I have spent my life in the shadow of Ytona expecting to either attack or be attacked at any time. You and Ziya talk so much about the war you've faced in your youth; this is mine. Did you expect me to be any less affected by my war than you are by yours?" Lioia pointed out, drawing herself up as best she could when she was still in such a weakened state.

"No, of course not," Kaal said quickly. He waited for Lioia to relax her stance before he said, softly, "Actually, I came to see if I could heal you."

Lioia frowned, her body completely still. "You should save your strength for yourself. You of all people should know that magic takes something from you in exchange for what it gives you, and that includes healing magic."

Kaal nodded, thinking of what Alan had told him what seemed like a lifetime ago. Alan had explained why Caleb had been so exhausted and hungry every time he drank Alan's potion; the potion stole Caleb's strength and gave it to the dragon growing inside of him. It made sense that healing worked the same way, though he hadn't experienced the same level of exhaustion when he healed as he had when he'd taken the potion. Perhaps gods-given magic like healing required less sacrifice.

"Your offer was kind, though," Lioia said. She looked past him to Ziya, who hung back, away from the two of them. Although Ziya had been outspoken in Kaal's defense in the immediate aftermath of Alan's death, she seemed to be falling back into their usual pattern in which he would do the talking and she would watch, listen, and plan.

Funnily enough, Kaal took that as a sign of trust. If she trusted him enough to fall back into silence, then she trusted him not to be self-destructive.

He knew he hadn't been thinking clearly after Alan died, and he knew Ziya had stopped him from losing the trust of their allies when he'd been so lost in hating himself that he couldn't see the ramifications of his own words. That in itself was unlike him. He was usually so careful, so precise, so aware of what and who he needed to be for survival. For some reason, Alan's death had thrown all that into chaos, and he wasn't ready to think of what that meant to him, what it said about him that he was so affected by a loss he should have celebrated.

"You should concentrate on healing her if you have the strength," Lioia continued, breaking Kaal out of his thoughts of self-doubt. He looked toward her, but her gaze was on Ziya, her expression soft and nearly teasing. "She was also hurt, and you care about her far more than you care about me."

"You're hurt worse than I am," Ziya argued. "Don't let your pride get in your own way."

Once more, Lioia smiled softly at Ziya, and Kaal found himself looking between the two of them. He was glad to see, of course, that they had worked out their differences, but the last time he'd seen them—before they had faced Alan together—they could barely stand each other. And he somehow doubted that their new camaraderie was due entirely to the inevitable bonds that formed after such a traumatic event as Alan's final battle. He wished he could have seen those divisions being healed; he might then have had a pattern he could follow in approaching other dragons like Lioia.

Ziya liked to say that Kaal was the diplomat between them, but here, Kaal could see evidence of the exact opposite. He somehow doubted that Ziya would listen if he were to point that out to her, though.

Kaal tipped his head toward Lioia. "Your hatchlings deserve your strength," he said, trying a different argument. "And I was the one who hesitated to kill Alan when I had the chance."

"Ziya told me you waited because you wanted to know more about yourself," Lioia said. "I don't blame you. What I heard of his lies would have shaken me had I been subjected to them as you have." She paused and looked toward her hatchlings, who were playing quietly nearby. They kept her within their line of sight and stopped whenever she got too quiet. And Kaal could see the instant Lioia made her decision, because her shoulders dropped. "Alright. I will accept your help."

Kaal smiled, moving slightly closer to her, closing his eyes to draw from the power deep within himself that allowed him to heal, and then breathed that power over Lioia. He was getting better at using magic as a dragon and hoped that it would one day come as naturally to him as it did to those that had been born dragons.

When he opened his eyes again, Lioia smiled at him and moved so that she could touch the end of her snout to his. "Thank you," she whispered.

"You're welcome," Kaal said, feeling more tired than he had expected to feel. Healing didn't usually require too much of him— but then again, he had never tried to heal when he was so badly injured that he was still nursing an unusable wing. And yet he knew he might be asked to do something similar in the future; he had the most advanced healing power of any other dragon. His allies had the right to ask for his help.

Once Lioia's hatchlings realized that their mother was feeling much better, they pounced on her, pulling on her tail and cajoling her into games with them. Kaal nearly laughed when he saw Lioia turn from a prickly ally into a playful mother in an instant, melting her hard edges in favor of her children until she had run off into the trees, growling playfully and nipping at their heels.

He was glad to have played some part in giving those hatchlings back a mother who so obviously adored them, even if he still carried the weight of guilt on his shoulders for the fact that she had been injured in the first place.

"You know," Ziya said, breaking into his thoughts once Lioia and her hatchlings were far from them, "I could try to heal that wing for you."

Kaal wasn't sure how much good Ziya would be able to do him when the damage was so substantial, but he wasn't about to trivialize her power, either. He knew that she'd been able to keep Aonai from death when they'd escaped the council; she was a force to be reckoned with. And besides, her pride was itself another force he needed to avoid. She might have teased the dragons for their pride, but she could be just as guilty of refusing to see any truth but her own as any other dragon could be.

So, he simply said, "Alright."

Ziya moved closer to him, and Kaal tried not to stare too obviously. She still moved like she was injured, and he noticed that she was stiff and slow. And yet he couldn't tell her not to try healing him until she was better healed herself; he had just helped Lioia despite his deep hurts. And he didn't want to be a hypocrite in addition to his many, many other faults.

As she settled in close to him, he was struck by the same realization he'd had when he first saw her in Alan's caves: she was, truly, the most elegant dragon he had ever seen. She always looked like the night sky to him, but under the cover of the trees, he could have sworn she carried light and stars in her scales the way the trickled-down sunlight played off of them. Now that she was comfortable in her own skin, she moved more like a dragon, too—even more so now than she had before he left with Teyo. He wondered if she had learned anything from Lioia, if that was the reason the two of them got along better lately.

He jerked out of his thoughts when Ziya leaned forward to blow her soft breath over him, and all at once, he remembered what they were supposed to be doing.

I'm tired, he thought, closing his eyes. *She's going to ask why I'm distracted, and what am I supposed to tell her? That I like her scales? Ridiculous.*

"Are you alright?" Ziya asked, nudging him with her snout. "Does your wing feel any better?"

Kaal looked over his shoulder at the tattered wing and nodded. Although he still couldn't use his wing, he could see webbing starting to form in between the sections that had been torn apart as his wings pulled themselves back together, aided by Ziya's healing. He would have scars, but he would be able to fly again eventually.

"It's better," he said, turning back to Ziya, surprised to find that she had started walking a path around him. "What are you doing?"

"Looking for myself," she replied, completing one more circle before she stopped, her tail moving behind her and disturbing some of the plants and animals nearby—though she didn't seem to care. Instead, she was lost in thought until, finally, she spoke up again: "I wonder if I could heal that entirely if you were human."

Kaal sat up straighter. "I don't even have wings as a human, Ziya. How do you expect me to—"

"I could heal you better as a human when we rescued the dragons Alan captured, remember?" Ziya interrupted him. "It's worth trying, isn't it?"

"I don't want you to tax yourself."

"I thought you said you wanted to go home. Even if I can't heal your wings, I can at least carry you when you're human. We could leave sooner with you on my back than we could if we wait for you to fully heal."

Kaal narrowed, not at all pleased to hear her throwing his own words back in his face. But he did want to find Rikaa again. He wanted to feel safe again. He wanted someone who would listen to all Alan had told him without judgement.

Still, he didn't know what would happen if he changed. His wings came from within his back and his shoulders. If he changed back into a human, would he even be able to walk? Would his back be too badly hurt to move? What would a shredded wing look like inside him?

Ziya watched him with her head cocked to one side before she suggested, gently, "If it's terrible, you'll change back, won't you? You told me you change when you're in danger."

He didn't actually have an argument for her. So, he sighed and let his shoulders and damaged wings drop. "You think of everything, don't you?"

She looked pleased with herself. "I'm learning."

He couldn't help but smile at her understated smirk. It wasn't a smile, but he liked to see it all the same. "Alright," he said. "But let's go somewhere else. I don't want to scare the hatchlings."

"Agreed." With that, she let him lead the way, following the path that they'd taken to get to Lioia until they were back where they'd started.

Even though he'd agreed to let Ziya try to heal him, Kaal could taste the metallic tang of fear in his mouth. He didn't want Ziya hurt on his behalf. And now that his own healing had left him feeling drained, he wanted to spare Ziya the same outcome. "Do you have the energy for another healing so soon? Do you want to eat first?"

"I don't need as much energy to heal a human as I do to heal a dragon," Ziya pointed out. "I'll be alright. If I need to take a break, I promise I'll let you know."

Kaal nodded curtly, though he couldn't quite relax enough to think about changing back into his human form. Ziya was right; he used his dragon form to protect himself. Now, standing in front of Ziya as she asked him for vulnerability, he found he couldn't do that.

He trusted her. He *did*. But he was too afraid of pain to slip into it willingly in front of another being. He had spent too long being watched while he was in agony; he couldn't make himself do so again.

When the two of them had been standing there, staring at each other, for what felt like an eternity, Ziya took a deep breath and let it out. "I . . . I'm not much of a singer," she said slowly, her tail moving at the very tip and showing her discomfort, "or I'd try singing like my mother did."

Kaal felt his fire heating up in the pit of his stomach as he remembered Dahlia's warm lullaby and the way it had allowed him to remember a time before the war, the way he'd felt safe in those memories. And, with his fire burning ever hotter, he thought of how he had spent days with Rikaa trading songs over the sound of rushing wind.

He knew he could sing, and he knew doing so would likely remind him of home. But for some reason, the thought of singing to Ziya left him warm and hesitating.

"It was just a thought," Ziya said, looking as embarrassed as he felt—though neither of them was able to articulate anything beyond that simple statement, and they were left in silence.

235

CHAPTER 22: A SHEPHERD'S SONG

After a hearty breakfast, Kaal tried not to look too much like he was trying to run away from Lioia's family's hospitality in favor of spending time with Ziya. He really did want his wing healed, and he really did want to get back to Rikaa, but he also chafed under the look Oad kept giving the two of them. It bothered him more than similar looks had in the past. He couldn't say why.

Maybe because Rikaa's teasing always stopped at just that—teasing. And even Dahlia, who was not as subtle as she thought she was, made it clear that her intentions were to keep her daughter's heart safe and to coax her into remembering the laughter the two of them used to share before the war. Oad, on the other hand, wasn't teasing. He genuinely thought Ziya and Kaal were at least considering becoming mates or were already there. And the evidence was in his favor, given how neatly they defended each other and how completely they relied on each other.

Ziya seemed unbothered by Oad's attention. But then again, she'd told him when they were first reunited that she still wasn't prepared to think of anything but alliances yet. Friendship, family—those would come to her later, when she had time to rediscover who she was away from the desperation of war. So, she might have been flustered by teasing and implications, but she knew her own limitations. She wasn't interested.

Kaal shook his head. He had more important things to do than to get lost in his own tumultuous emotions this soon after Alan had died. Besides, what if, once the adrenaline died down and he was able to think, he realized that he only felt so attached to Ziya because of how desperately he *needed* her? No, he wasn't going to be able to sort out his tangled feelings until he could breathe—and that couldn't happen in the forest so close to the village and so far from his new family.

Since Ziya apparently wasn't wrestling with any of those conflicting feelings, however, she had no problem excusing herself and Kaal for another attempted healing once their stomachs were full, leaving Kaal to thank Oad profusely for the meal and to endure Oad's knowing looks once more.

He could have sworn he heard Oad say something to Lioia about courtship, but Oad had said it in the dragon language, and Kaal only caught that single word because he'd heard Rikaa use it so often in teasing.

And so, with his fire scorching hot in his belly, Kaal followed Ziya back to privacy, absolutely certain that, had he been human, his entire face would have been red, right down to the tips of his ears.

"Are you alright?" Ziya asked once they were out of earshot of the other dragons. "You hardly said a word the whole time we were eating, and you're the one who always knows what to say."

"Tired," Kaal lied smoothly, though he felt himself getting even warmer the second he lied. He didn't want to lie to her, but he hadn't hesitated to protect himself, either. How was he supposed to convince himself—or anyone else, for that matter—that Alan had been wrong when he couldn't even stop telling lies to the closest friend he had?

Then again, what would her reaction have been if she heard the truth?

Maybe lying was justified in this one instance.

"So," Ziya said, breaking into his thoughts. "Do you think you can change on your own now that you've eaten?"

Kaal took a beat too long to answer, because his mind was still on other things. And then, he had to swallow down the fire in his throat. He was sure the second he opened his mouth, Ziya would see how flustered he was, and he didn't want to have to explain himself. He was a mess. He wanted to go home. He wanted to forget everything Alan had told him. He wanted to get away from Ziya for a while and figure out if she was his anchor or something else. He wanted to curl up into a small ball, sleep on some heated rocks, and wake up with the war over and with Rikaa and his family playing hunting games. Life had felt so much simpler during the short time he'd been alone with Rikaa's family, away from Alan's games and wars that determined the literal survival of an entire race.

He realized Ziya was still watching him, swallowed, and shook his head. "I'm not sure," he admitted. "There's so much. . . ."

Ziya smiled kindly. "That's alright," she said. He thought it might have been his imagination—maybe he was looking too hard for something that wasn't there because his own fire was so hot in his belly—but he could have sworn he saw fire in the back of her throat when she opened her mouth to speak again. "I . . . I wouldn't bring it up if I had any better ideas, I promise, but last time, with my mother. . . ."

Kaal scrunched his shoulders and wings together, unconsciously trying to be smaller when he remembered their previous conversation. The shepherd's lullaby *had* worked. And Ziya wasn't wrong to ask him to at least *try* using it.

"I won't judge your singing, if that's what you're worried about," Ziya offered, shifting from one foot to the other in a motion that looked odd on a dragon.

"Actually, ah, I liked singing. As a human," Kaal admitted. "My brother couldn't carry a tune, but I could. He used to make up silly dances to go with my songs when we were bored watching the animals and trying to pass the time."

Ziya smiled, settling into a more comfortable position. "I wish I could have met your brother. You light up whenever you talk about Tristan."

"He was my hero," Kaal said. He tried to relax to sit with her, but he couldn't quite manage it. Not yet, anyway. "He raised me. Taught me everything I know."

Ziya's smile widened, and she leaned forward as if she could absorb more of his story by proximity. "Then I guess the world has him to thank for turning you into a hero."

Kaal felt his fire burning hotter than ever. "I thought I told you that you're the hero."

"I think we agreed to disagree," Ziya said.

Kaal looked away—not because he disagreed with her or because he was embarrassed by the compliment but because the look on Ziya's face made his stomach twist in knots. He still didn't trust that he wasn't seeing her in a new light purely because of his recent brush with captivity. He wished for Rikaa's gentle clarity more than anything else in that moment, but he would have to settle for his own swirling thoughts until he could get airborne.

Ziya cleared her throat—a sound that, again, didn't sound natural to a dragon. She had kept her human habits and traits, while he had done everything he could to do things the way true dragons did. She should have been the one the gods blessed with humanity; she wanted it more than he did.

"I can't carry you home, Kaal. We have to think of something," she pointed out. He thought he heard some exasperation in her voice, even if she didn't express her frustration in words, and he didn't blame her. She could have been well on her way to reuniting with her mother and then rallying a force to rescue Aonai, who had done so much to help her that he knew she felt indebted to him. Instead, she was stuck waiting for him to get over himself long enough to transform.

He sighed. Knowing he wasn't being fair to Ziya was actually a better motivator than anything else he'd tried. "I . . . I know a few songs," he said slowly.

Ziya nodded encouragingly. "Go ahead. I'd give you privacy, but if you're right and you transform into a gravely injured human, I need to be here to heal you as soon as you change."

"Right." Kaal didn't argue, though he did appreciate the respectful nature of her offer, despite its limitations. The longer she was away from Alan, the more he could see the human she used to be peeking out, and she was uncommonly kind, even if she didn't think she was. Yes, she had a sharp tongue, but he had only ever seen her use it when she felt she was on the side of justice or when she was defending those who couldn't defend themselves.

He let his chest rise and fall a few times as he tried to clear his thoughts and to reach for the few memories of home he still had. The few good ones, anyway. With his eyes closed, he could almost remember the sensation of grass on his bare back or the sun shining on him after a hard day's work. He could almost hear Tris laughing as

THE GODS' GIFT

he chased the last of the goats into the barn. He could almost smell his mother's tea.

Almost was close enough to settle the feeling in the pit of his stomach. Almost was enough to remind him that he used to love singing for other people. Almost was enough to let him remember a time when he hadn't cared what other people thought—as long as Tris loved him.

Finally, a song came to his mind, one that he used to sing with Tris even though his brother was a *horrible* singer.

> *You take a coal to the fire*
> *And I'll shovel dirt on your flames*
> *You bring your pail to the water*
> *And I'll dump it out once again*
> *You put the nail in the fence post*
> *And I'll run the sheep into it*
> *You close the barn door behind me*
> *And I'll leave it open a bit*
> *You're stuck with a shadow behind you*
> *That's what little brothers will do*

By the time he finished singing the first verse, he could already feel himself shrinking. He wasn't surprised. Whenever he thought of Tris, whenever he was able to reach for that bond, he always wanted to be human. He wanted to hide in his older brother's shadow. He wanted to go back to tending to animals and caring about nothing but making his brother laugh.

That was what being human meant to him—when he didn't think of his humanity as what forced him into being a refugee.

The second verse should have been Tris's to sing, but he wasn't there. Still, Kaal could almost hear his brother's off-tune singing. Tris would always come in on the wrong note, but he made up for it with silly dances until he got tired of Caleb laughing at his singing and tickled his little brother into a different kind of laughter.

Kaal could feel himself changing, but as his scales softened into skin, his smile at remembering Tris fell away instantly, giving way to a grimace and then a gasp of pain. His entire back felt like someone had driven a sword into it, and the second the scales fell away from his spine, he felt like he was *still* being stabbed. He'd been concerned about exactly this, about transforming and opening up

240

a wound that was worse to a human than to a dragon—and he'd been right to worry.

He screwed his eyes tightly shut and tried to hold onto the image of his brother singing and dancing. He could hear Ziya gasp and locked his jaw tighter to keep from screaming. His back was soaked in blood, and he could have sworn he could feel his heartbeat out of his ribs—though he doubted the injury was that bad, or he'd be dead.

He could feel Ziya's warm breath wash over him, and fire seemed to settle into his shoulder blades. He was exhausted, and he could feel his grip on consciousness slipping away, but he clung to the image of his brother in his mind, trying to stay human as long as he could.

And then, he couldn't hang onto his humanity any longer, and he let out a sigh of pure relief despite the pain of his transformation as he felt his scales returning, running over his back and arms until he felt protected. Armored. Safe.

He kept his eyes closed, reveling in the feeling of being a dragon again. He could feel his chest heaving and was still tingling from the hurts he'd endured in changing forms and exposing his human side to grievous harm, but he no longer felt exposed or raw.

As he took deep, cleansing breaths, he felt a dragon's snout underneath his chin and winced instinctively. Ziya immediately drew back, but then, in a soft rumble, she asked, "Are you alright?"

"Gi- give me a minute," Kaal ground out, still trying to get his heaving chest back under control. He kept his eyes shut and held his breath as long as he could, then let it out again, slowly. "That hurt," he said, though he didn't stutter this time. His shoulder and wing still felt like someone had torn them open freshly, but otherwise, the regular transformation aches were fading.

"It looked like it," Ziya said, speaking at barely over a whisper. "Your back . . . it looked like someone had torn a hole out of it where your wings sprout."

"Felt like it too." Kaal groaned, stretching almost like a cat, with his back bowed down and his legs pressed out, his wings flat against his back to complete the picture. Once he felt less sore, he finally looked over his shoulder at his wing—and was pleasantly surprised to see how much webbing had grown to connect the slashes together. "But, hey, you were right. It looks like you could heal me even when I didn't have wings to heal."

"Oh good," Ziya said, obviously relieved. She sounded tired, too; Kaal wondered how much of herself she had poured into her healing attempt. Still, she made her way around him so she could better see his wings. "Those . . . those almost look usable," she said cautiously.

Kaal looked over his shoulder again at the tattered wing. He could still see holes in it, but they were much smaller than before. As he considered the situation, he thought of watching birds fly while molting. It stood to reason that dragons could fly while their wings were healing—once the healing reached a certain point, obviously. "Maybe," he said slowly.

"If you need to stay longer, we can," Ziya promised quickly. "I don't want you to hurt your wing because I'm in a hurry—and I'm not," she added, once again speaking too quickly for him to interrupt her. "Take your time."

"I'd rather not linger," Kaal said. He nodded to himself and then beat his wings experimentally—but he immediately let out a hiss of pain and displeasure and pulled his wing back into him.

"What happened?" Ziya asked, her mouth hanging partly open, showing off her long teeth.

"Sore," he hissed. He closed his eyes and tried again, spreading his wings out more slowly this time. He didn't try to fly, but he did beat his wings through the air a few times to see what would happen.

Once again, he hissed and gasped as his still-healing wing screamed at his muscles for daring to move. He felt like he was putting pressure on a bruise; the pain wasn't nearly as bad as the initial sharpness of the injury, but moving it reminded his body of what it had been through. He didn't need to beat his wings more than twice before he knew it was a pointless exercise, and he quickly tucked his wings back into his sides, gasping heavily.

"What was that for?" Ziya asked, circling him a few times as she looked for further injury, probably checking to make sure he hadn't torn open the wing she'd spent so much time and energy on healing. "You *just* said you were sore!"

"I wanted to see how much air I could catch beneath my wings," he explained in a hoarse, tense voice, struggling not to show

how much he'd hurt himself, since Ziya was already upset with him. He didn't want her even more worried than she already was. He took each breath carefully and kept his mouth shut as much as possible, hiding his fire from her despite the smoke in his nostrils.

"You couldn't wait?" Ziya shook her head. "You can be so stupid sometimes, you know that?"

Kaal gave her a grimace of a smile. "Only sometimes?" he asked, trying to calm her down by teasing, since everything else he'd done so far seemed to have her on edge.

She blinked at him and then huffed out her breath, shaking her head. "Boys," she muttered like a curse, curling up to rest her head on her front legs.

ZIYA

CHAPTER 23:
PREOCCUPATION

W hat are you doing?"

Ziya paused just as she would have turned around to continue her pacing, only then realizing what she'd been doing. She could see matted dirt and upended brush in her wake and could see the way the forest floor was starting to succumb to the pattern she'd walked into it, bowing in as she deepened the line with each heavy footfall. The grass was nearly gone, and the dirt looked more like a road than the loose pebbles and debris that befitted a forest.

Ziya flared her claws out and dug them into the earth to relieve the need to keep moving. The simple feeling of her claws in the dirt soothed her somewhat, but it didn't seem big enough for the nervous energy traveling down her very spine.

But she could feel Lioia's gaze on her and felt her belly expand with fire in a blush. "Sorry," she said.

"That doesn't answer my question," Lioia pointed out, edging toward Ziya now that she was no longer moving around in such an un-dragonlike way.

"I can't say the word with a dragon tongue," Ziya admitted. "I can try . . . it's called 'pacing'. . . ." She couldn't pronounce the word right at all; it sounded almost like "hazy" in her mouth, and she shook her head, letting out a growl of frustration.

She trailed off, deeply embarrassed—not at being caught doing something so human but at the underlying reason for her nerves. She couldn't stop worrying over Kaal's fate and over the distinct change that had come over him since his time with Alan. And she'd thought that she was alone, that she had the privacy to let her anxiety show while he slept off all the healing and trauma his body had been through. Now, she had to explain the very concept she didn't want to admit to: she cared so much about him that she couldn't stand *still*.

She worked her mouth around a few times, trying out a few explanations in her head until she found one that suited her. "When humans get agitated or angry or worried or any negative emotion that seems too strong to ignore, we don't have claws to sharpen on the ground or tails to move. Our bodies are small and compact and wiry, and all that emotion has to come out somehow."

"So, you walk your own path several times over," Lioia said, her head tipped nearly completely sideways to illustrate her pure confusion. "If you must move, do so with intent."

"That's the way dragons move," Ziya said. "You must be aware of each motion. Humans are smaller."

"You use your size to excuse your lack of self-control?" Lioia let out a sound from the back of her throat. "Laziness."

"No." Ziya growled without meaning to. Lioia had proven herself an ally, but she still seemed to go out of her way to find ways to complain about humans and to criticize everything about Ziya, from her lack of knowledge to her nervous habits. "But we show our emotions through motion, not fire or growls."

Lioia blew a tuft of gray smoke. Ziya was getting better at learning to read dragon expressions, but she couldn't quite place the strange light in Lioia's gaze. "And what emotion," Lioia said softly, a smile tugging her lips back from her teeth, "has caused you to move so energetically?"

Ziya threw her head back—and the motion only *added* to her frustration because it felt unnatural on her long neck and made her shoulders and back sit strangely in relation to her head. She lowered her head and let out a huff of smoke. "I don't like waiting," she said at last, deciding on the safest explanation instead of venturing into the strange waters of her tangled feelings.

She wouldn't describe her feelings as romantic, though frustratingly, that was the conclusion so many wrongly jumped to. No, the longer she considered Caleb and their relationship to one another, the more convinced she was that he occupied a space in her heart that was too complicated to name. Yes, she cared about him as a friend. An ally. A boy. And yes, he was handsome—in his own way. He had grown into his height and seemed to get taller each time he transformed into a human. His shoulders were broad, but his muscles were wiry. Even as a human, he looked like a white dragon, all tension and power ready to spring. His eyes were silver in his dragon form and human form, and they seemed to hold a depth that Ziya understood without prying. And when he smiled, when he spoke about the future as if they would actually see one without war in their own lifetimes, a light shone in his eyes that, she could swear, left shadows where his beetle-black hair met his forehead.

Even now, when his dragon form meant she would always regard him with trepidation, when his scales and teeth reminded her sharply of everything she had been through, when his growls still elicited the drop in her stomach that came from fear and not excitement, she saw his silver eyes and found, strangely, some comfort.

But, no, she wouldn't say she was attracted to Kaal. Caleb, perhaps. But Kaal was a strange creature, one who felt more like a dragon sometimes than even other dragons. Even though she had only known Rikaa for a short time, she found him to be much like her father, ready with a quick word of comfort and gentle teasing. Lioia, despite her flaws, was like the women Neva and her mother had met as they traveled from place to place looking for a home, the ones who reacted to the war by finding every small thing they could possibly complain about. But Kaal was a powerful force. He was a mystery. He was sharp fangs and bright scales and a belief in something greater than him. He seemed so far away from her, and she didn't want to close the gap.

So, if she wasn't attracted to Kaal, what answer could she give Lioia that Lioia would believe? She cared deeply about him all the same. She wanted him safe. She wanted him near her. She took comfort from his presence and from his health. When he was hurt, she felt like she was losing one of the few good things left to her in her life. Was there a name for that feeling other than love?

As Lioia held her gaze, Ziya could see Lioia stripping away everything about Ziya's feelings for Kaal until they were nothing but romance, and she bristled at that gross oversimplification. At that assumption. At that insolence. As if Ziya could feel nothing but youthful infatuation because Caleb was a boy and Ziya was a girl and they both cared for each other.

As if Ziya was capable of acting on such feelings in the first place. She was a dragon in form but a human in her heart. She doubted she would ever feel comfortable with romantic love in her new body. Loyalty and adoration and affection, she could give. Romance, she could not. And she didn't want to. Not when she had so many other paths to take.

"You're worried," Lioia said, and Ziya let out an impatient huff.

"For good reason," she said. "I'd worry over anyone who had been stuck with Alan that long. No dragon should endure Alan's tortures, but Kaal has done so twice. Of course I'm worried."

"I see," Lioia said simply. Then, spreading her wings, she darted up through a small opening in the trees that Ziya wouldn't have noticed had Lioia not shown her it was there. "I wonder if my hatchlings will be anything like you when they reach adolescence," Lioia said, looking over her shoulder with a sharp smile. "Thank you for the practice."

"Excuse me?" Ziya flared out her own wings, rushing to fly when Lioia responded to her indignation by taking to the skies. Ziya took several stumbling steps before her wings caught the air; she felt like such a newborn dragon, uncomfortable in her own body.

When Ziya caught up to Lioia, Lioia was laughing easily as she glided on the wind. She let Ziya see her laughter only long enough for Ziya to snort in frustration and leave sparks and smoke in the air before Lioia beat her wings in two sharp bursts and changed direction.

"What are you doing?" Ziya asked under her breath. She didn't expect an answer, though she didn't care if Lioia overheard her. She and Lioia didn't have a relationship that lent itself to playfulness, so she doubted Lioia meant to start a game in the skies. But that was almost what it felt like: a game of tag played in the clouds.

Finally, Ziya caught up to Lioia, frustrated still by the laughter that, if not audible, was still present in Lioia's eyes as she said, "You're getting better all the time. Soon enough, you will fly like a real dragon."

"I didn't ask you to teach me anything," Ziya said. "Why do you insist on treating me like a child?"

THE GODS' GIFT

"As long as you insist on acting like one, I will treat you like one," Lioia replied.

"It's not my fault I'm still learning how to use my new body," Ziya started to say, but Lioia cut her off sharply with a sound almost like a playful snarl, if snarls could be playful. Ziya hadn't heard a sound like it before, but it didn't scare her, somehow.

"That's not what I meant," Lioia said. "You treat yourself like a child and don't allow the breadth of your emotions to wash over you." She let herself glide closer to Ziya. "No one is as preoccupied as you are without reason."

Ziya rolled her eyes. "I'd rather learn to fly with you than listen to yet another dragon tell me how I do and do not feel about Kaal."

"Okay," Lioia said in a tone that was far too amused for Ziya's tastes. "You should know how to control your body anyway. As strange as you are, as much as I hate your kind, I don't think the world would do well without you in it."

"Careful," Ziya said. "That almost sounds like you like me."

"I said nothing so drastic."

"Right." Ziya shook her head. She knew she would never convince Lioia to trust humans, just like she also knew she would never be able to explain why she cared so much about Kaal without a romance being thrust upon her long before she was ready to consider a future for herself. "Show me what you think I should know," she said instead of arguing fruitlessly.

To Lioia's credit, she was actually a good teacher. Apparently, she had learned from her first attempts to lead Ziya into the life of a dragon and no longer assumed Ziya knew anything about her techniques or beliefs. This time, Lioia waited until they were gliding next to each other and then explained the finer details of flying, the things no human trainer would ever have been able to tell her. Things like the way she could take turns sharply when she led with the tip of her wing, not with her shoulder. Like the way she could feel her way through the air and ride updrafts that she never would have noticed on her own.

By the time Lioia and Ziya found a spot to rest their wings at the edge of a canyon, they were both tired but smiling. Even though neither of them trusted the other, something about the open air made conflict difficult unless they were specifically seeking it out.

So, Ziya couldn't help but smile as she settled down next to Lioia, her chest still heaving from the complicated maneuvers and sharp turns. "Thanks," she said.

Lioia swung her head around to look at Ziya. "Did . . . did you just thank me?"

"I won't do it again if you're going to react that way every time," Ziya said.

"No, no." Lioia tried to school her smile but couldn't. "There's the Ziya I know. I thought that gratitude meant you might have grown up in the sky, but I was mistaken."

Ziya made a face at Lioia, letting her long, pink tongue hang out of her mouth. "You keep treating me like a child."

"You are one," Lioia said, shaking her head. "What are you doing with your mouth?"

"It's something human children do."

"As I said."

"I did something childish on purpose, Lioia."

Lioia shrugged, moving her wings as she settled down beside her. "You really are getting better at flying," she said instead of provoking another fight. And she seemed *sincere* in her compliment.

Something had changed between them since Lioia had seen Ziya's terror in the face of a dragon attack. Ziya didn't know what to make of the shift, but she was glad for it all the same. Constantly confronting Lioia, constantly fighting to be recognized and listened to, was exhausting, and Ziya needed all of her energy for Kaal.

"My last trainer was a human who treated me like a beast of burden," Ziya admitted.

"They only know how to get you in the air. That isn't flight." Lioia sniffed.

Ziya chuckled and rested her head on her front legs. "You sound like Kaal," she said softly. "He also talks about being a dragon like he's writing poetry. And he's enamored with the power and grace that dragons exude."

"As he should be," Lioia said, her eyes aglow with the familiar dragon pride that Ziya had come to hate.

Ziya huffed, and smoke spilled from her nose. "No," she said. Lioia turned to glare at her, but Ziya held her gaze. "I don't see dragons the way Kaal does. You have to *earn my* respect. Otherwise, you're like the soldiers under Alan's command who think their uniforms give them power when they've only earned fear."

Lioia snorted sparks. "Your past clouds your judgement."

"No," Ziya said. "I judge everyone by their actions. The only dragons who have ever earned my respect are Aonai and Rikaa's family. They're the only ones who saw the damage Alan and his spells did and tried to help instead of blaming those he hurt for his actions."

Lioia narrowed her eyes but didn't immediately respond, turning her gaze back toward the forest, toward her home. And then, after some time, she spoke again:

"You humans are lucky," she said. Ziya scoffed, but she continued, "You are. Generations have passed for you since your kind declared open war on ours. Yes, this particular settlement continues to wage war, but you're right. Most humans have forgotten our conflict." She sighed but didn't turn toward Ziya or raise her gaze. "Generations haven't passed for us. Too many dragons still live who remember that war. They bear those scars. They remember those they lost." At last, she turned toward Ziya. "Could you forgive the army that took you captive?"

"Not the ones who were involved, but—"

"Don't lie," Lioia said sharply. "Not to me, not to yourself. Tell me truly: do you honestly think that if you saw a human in the armor of those soldiers who took everything from you that you would not react in hate and anger?"

"I'm not lying," Ziya shot back just as sharply. "When I fought soldiers, when I rescued Kaal, I *insisted* that any soldiers who wanted to leave be allowed to go. I know all too well how many of those soldiers are not there by choice. I know what it means to be innocent. Do you?"

Lioia's mouth hung open for a few long seconds before she looked away. "You humans and your words," she said. It wasn't exactly a refutation of Ziya's argument, but Lioia didn't try to talk down to her or say anything, really, after that. So, Ziya considered that Lioia's way of conceding without conceding.

Dragons and their pride, she thought and snorted out smoke.

Still, she was pleased with herself. Lioia tolerated Ziya and Kaal because they had dragon forms, but she had no love whatsoever for any true humans. And while Ziya knew she would never change

Lioia's mind, she was pleased with her success in getting Lioia to stop acting so superior.

Kaal wasn't even here with his silver tongue to help, she thought, grinning. *And yet Kaal would know what to say to bring back the peace.* Ziya watched a few embers float out of her mouth into the canyon air. She desperately missed the Kaal that she knew before he had fallen prey to Alan's manipulations. She trusted that dragon, and she didn't fully understand *why.*

Maybe she simply trusted his kindness. From the moment he had arrived in the refugee camp where they met, she had noticed that. He never complained. He kept to himself. But he also made quiet space for scared kids who needed a corner to cry. And he had helped that little girl up the mountain. And he had cared only about what his own pain would do to those who loved him when Alan had tortured him in front of the other dragons. A heart like Kaal's was rare, especially in war. She would have been a fool not to trust him.

You can't rely on Kaal to interact with the dragon world for you, she told herself. *You have to adapt, or you won't survive. It doesn't matter how right you are if you drive away all your allies. And Kaal is allowed to have his own life, his own moments of weakness. He won't always be there for you.*

She sighed and let her shoulders drop along with her wings. "Lioia," she said, too quietly at first. She tried again: "Lioia."

A soft almost-growl drifted on the wind until it reached Ziya. "Is something wrong?"

"No, I just. . . . I'm sorry," she said, hating the taste of the words but knowing they were necessary. And still hating them.

Lioia swung her head around fast, the very end of her tail moving. "What?"

Had she been human, Ziya would have gritted her teeth. As it was, she barely stowed her growl. "You have to understand: all the dragons I've met since Alan changed me have blamed *me* for what he did. They've called humans nothing but pests. Creatures unworthy of compassion. The council locked me up on sight and nearly starved me to death simply because they decided after meeting Kaal that human-made dragons were a threat. When I hear dragons talking about being the guardians of this world and being worthy of respect and admiration, I think of all the hatred I endured and lash out. I'm sorry I keep reacting in anger."

THE GODS' GIFT

Lioia blinked a few times. "Why the sudden change?"

"What do you mean?"

"You insist on being right and being heard. Why say you're sorry?"

Ziya let out a long, smoky sigh. "I don't want to spend the rest of my life as a dragon who can't get along with other dragons. I'm still learning. I'm not like Kaal; I can't just jump into a new life with both—or, sorry, all four feet. If he'd been here, he could have told you all I did without getting angry, but he wasn't. I'm trying to learn how to talk to dragons without blaming them for all that I have lost." She shrugged her wings up. "It's hard. And I'm sorry I'm still so new at this."

Lioia opened her mouth a few times and then closed it again until she finally seemed to find her response. "You're young," she said—which was not what Ziya had wanted or expected to hear.

"You said as much," Ziya said, scrunching down, already regretting trying to be the more mature dragon. Her first instincts had been right; Kaal was *so much better* at talking to dragons than she was. She should have waited for him to come back to himself and ignored Lioia in the meantime so she didn't make anything worse.

"Yes, but I don't mean it as an insult," Lioia said. When Ziya snorted, Lioia grimaced. "Not this time. I am sorry you thought I was belittling you."

"You were," Ziya pointed out, not about to let Lioia get away with a half-apology.

Lioia made a noncommittal noise in the back of her throat. "Yes, well, I meant to say that you are young and allowed to make mistakes. Considering how little time you've had to acquaint yourself with other dragons—and the time you have been given has been plagued by war—I don't blame you for your anger."

"Alright." Ziya wasn't thrilled with Lioia's response, but she wasn't going to start a fight either. "Thanks, I think. I'll try to be a better dragon, I guess."

"You'll get there," Lioia promised. "You have a dragon's heart and fire. Maybe that's why you didn't lose your mind when you became one. I know not every human comes out of the spell with their mind intact. You and Kaal both seem to be dragons at heart—in different ways."

"Huh." Ziya snorted a perfect circle of smoke. "I never thought about that. Everyone always says Kaal is the natural dragon."

"He is," Lioia clarified. "But you have a dragon's conviction."

Ziya didn't know what else to say, so she simply whispered: "Thanks," knowing Lioia meant the assessment as a compliment.

KAAL

CHAPTER 24: ABOVE THE TREES

For three days, Kaal shared stories about Tris, turned into Caleb for as long as he could, and then rested his wings as they got stronger and stronger. All the while, Ziya did her best to hide her exhaustion and even busied herself with Lioia and her family—but Kaal wasn't fooled. He knew how much healing could weigh on any dragon; he didn't think Ziya was an exception, no matter how exceptional she was.

So when, on the third day, Kaal transformed into Caleb and didn't immediately feel like he was falling to pieces, he held up a hand. "Wait," he called out to Ziya, still panting from the transformation but feeling better than he had felt as Caleb in a long time. Yes, he still felt like every inch of his body was on fire, but that was relatively normal. His shoulder didn't feel like a gaping wound this time. And he could even find the wherewithal to be aware of dew-kissed grass on his fingertips instead of being completely overwhelmed by pain. "Give me a minute."

Ziya, thankfully, waited for him to get his breath before she pressed him for an explanation. He could feel her presence, but other than the shadow she cast, she didn't impose on him until he sat up from his hands and knees and even tried to find some modesty behind some bushes. "What do you need?" she asked, coming gradually closer.

He nearly smiled at the way she phrased the question. He had no right to ask any more of her than she had already given him, and yet, she offered herself freely. The gods had blessed him when they put her in his path. "If you try to heal me again, will you be too tired to fly?" he asked.

Ziya stood up taller, obviously realizing why he was asking her a question like that. "Do you think you can make it?"

"I think if you can heal me one more time, my shoulder won't tear open again," he said, proving his point by stretching his back and arms a few times, showing off a range of movement that he hadn't had in days. "And in that case, if you're comfortable with it, I can ride on your back. You'll just have to fly slowly so I don't hurt myself holding on too tightly. That way, we don't have to wait for me to heal fully."

"I don't mind flying slowly," Ziya promised. "I'm ready to get out of here as much as you are. Oad is getting more and more obnoxious the longer we stay."

Caleb cleared his throat in a puff of smoke. "You noticed that too, huh?"

"Hard not to." Ziya looked toward the pathway that would have led them toward the other dragons. "He's worse than Rikaa, you know. At least Rikaa is only teasing."

Caleb smiled into his chest. He didn't think that she realized how *affectionate* she sounded when she spoke about Rikaa. "I miss him too."

Ziya paused but didn't look his way, still preserving his modesty. "I didn't think I would miss any of them," she admitted. "You managed to get all the luck, didn't you? You stumbled into the best dragons the world has ever seen and turned them into your family. The gods truly must be smiling on you, Kaal."

Caleb couldn't help but grin. "You sound more and more like you believe in the gods."

"How can I not when I'm spending all my time with you?" Ziya asked, gesturing to Caleb with one clawed leg and then catching herself. She gestured with her tail, the movement more dragon-like than her initial human instincts, though she seemed more subdued. She always looked embarrassed when she caught herself showing her discomfort in her new body.

"Let's hope the gods care as much as you think they do, then. I've already played my part in killing Alan; for all we know, they stopped interfering the second Alan was dead."

"I don't know," she said. "I think if they only wanted a human-made dragon to end Alan, they would have chosen me. You don't have the same heart for revenge and violence that I do."

"And you only have the heart for it because of what Alan did to you. I still don't think you're as heartless as you think you are."

Ziya snorted. "Did you want me to heal you or not?"

"Right," he said, recognizing the end of their discussion for what it was. Ziya didn't want to receive compliments any more than he wanted to hear that he wasn't a liar. So instead of butting heads, they would focus on what they could control, on healing and leaving. He closed his eyes as Ziya breathed her healing power over him, stretching out his muscles as his shoulder healed just that much more. When he pulled his arms back, he could feel his back stretch without opening up the wound again. That was good enough for flying.

"Thanks," he said, turning to face her—and then blushing when he realized she still wasn't looking directly at him. "Do you still have any extra clothes?"

Ziya shook her head without looking his way. "I can go look," she offered.

"Thanks," he said, throwing his hands up over his head to protect himself against the rush of wind as Ziya unfurled her wings and took off. She looked more graceful than usual; he supposed that was thanks to the time she was spending with Lioia while he recovered his strength. Even while she waited for him, she found ways to strengthen herself for the battles ahead.

He made a mental note to do something nice for Ziya when they had more time to themselves. After all she'd done for him, after all her support, the least he could do would be to find a fitting thanks.

Not that he knew what to get her. She didn't like her dragon form, and even if she did, Caleb wasn't versed enough in dragon culture to know what an appropriate gift would be. Maybe he could *do* something for her instead. Find her a place to live with her mother when the war was over. Give her one of his scales to heal the land so her mother wouldn't have to eke out a living on whatever was left in the ashes.

Yes, that was a good idea. He wouldn't mind parting with a scale for Ziya.

He was nodding to himself when he heard the sound of wings and hid behind the nearest tree trunk as Ziya landed. She was getting better at navigating between the trees, but then, he remembered how nimble she had been when they had been rushing through Alan's tunnels searching for an escape route; she had always been effortlessly graceful.

He realized he was staring as Ziya came toward him and quickly averted his gaze. *Of all the times to get your head stuck in romance*, he berated himself. *You get rid of one evil dragon and think it's okay to relax? You know better than that. The council is still out there, and humans still want to kill dragons. This isn't over by a long shot.*

"Kaal!" Ziya called out, pulling Caleb out of his thoughts. "I couldn't get too close to the village, but I stole a few cloaks and blankets that washed down the mountain."

Caleb peeked around the tree and waved to catch her attention. "Are they still wet?"

"Damp," Ziya admitted, grimacing slightly. "I'm sorry. I tried to air them out as I flew, but I'm not very good at flying unbalanced like that, and I didn't want anyone to spot me."

"It's okay," he promised quickly. "I can probably dry them out; I'll just smell like smoke for a while." He held his hand out, and Ziya edged closer to drop the long fabrics in front of him.

Working quickly, he laid out two cloaks and then blew breath as hot as he dared to make it without reaching for fire. He thought he saw an ember in the air, but thankfully, it didn't catch the fabric of the cloaks. Instead, smoke settled into the clothes—not that he was concerned. Even if he and Ziya were separated, no one would think twice about a human who smelled like smoke.

He tore one of the cloaks in half and tucked and tied it together for a makeshift kilt, then draped the other cloak around his shoulders, clasping it underneath his chin. It was slightly too small for him, and he had to tear the neck so that he could breathe in it, but it would have to do.

Once he was dressed, he blew smoke over the other piece of clothing Ziya had brought—a long cape that had once belonged to a wizard, judging by the insignia on the clasp—so that, when it was packed away, it wouldn't stay damp and invite living creatures to make their homes in it. He might have been part dragon, but that didn't mean he wasn't bothered by fleas or ticks or any other sort of infestation. He hated to think how badly he would itch if skin irritations from bugs like that were to also appear on his scales.

He stepped out of the trees with a bundle of fabric in hand to attach to Ziya's leg once more. Once he was close to her, without thinking, he reached out to touch her shoulder, running his hand over her smooth scales. "Thank you," he said softly. "I don't know what I'd do without you."

"The feeling is entirely mutual," she promised, though he could feel the heat from her center coming off of her in waves.

He ran his hand down her neck as he walked toward her face and then rested it against the horns near the top of her head. He couldn't bring himself to scratch there, even though he knew it would have felt good, because Elena had done that as a way of reminding him that he was an animal, showing her dominance over him. But he thought about it, because it might have been a kind gesture under different circumstances.

He let his hand fall away and met her gaze. "Let's go," he said. "We can thank Lioia before we leave, but—"

"But quickly," Ziya finished for him. "I miss our families too."

He nodded, smiling, and waited for her to lower herself so he could climb onto her back, adjusting himself so that he could balance without tearing open his freshly-healed wounds. "Go slowly," he warned. He knew he'd already told her once, but the warning bore repeating. "I'm still one bad turn away from opening my shoulder again."

"I'll be careful," Ziya promised, making a show out of slowing down when they walked through the trees so that he could duck overhanging branches. Even though they had walked the forest paths of Lioia's home many times, they were still visitors in the trees. They still needed to be careful, to avoid the creatures that lived in the leaves as well as stray vines that wouldn't stop a dragon but would ensnare a human.

Still, Caleb couldn't help but grin as he clung onto Ziya's scales. She was actually easier to ride than Rikaa was, even though she looked sleeker and slenderer. Because she was smaller, he wasn't completely dwarfed by her neck and shoulders, and he could even fit his leg into the joint of one of her shoulders without getting crushed.

"Would you look at that," Lioia said, announcing her presence long before they spotted her. "You found your old body after all."

Caleb smiled toward the sound of her voice until she stepped out of the shadows of the dense trees, still cloaked in shade but visible to those with dragon's eyes. "My wings aren't ready for flight, so we decided this was a better arrangement," he explained.

"You look like you did when I first met you," Lioia said, shaking her head. She didn't do nearly as much sneering and snarling about him riding a dragon as she had when they first met, but he could still see that she was bothered by him using Ziya as a means of transportation. And that was her right; Caleb himself wasn't entirely comfortable with the concept. But Ziya was okay with it, and that was what mattered. She was the one doing the flying, after all.

"You might see more dragon riders in the future," Caleb said, speaking to her discomfort even though she hadn't voiced it. "There are other human-made dragons, and they're probably okay with humans riding them as long as they're friends or family."

"Or if they've lost their mind and are still being used as beasts of burden," Ziya muttered under her breath.

Caleb let his shoulders drop. "Yeah. If the dragon council wasn't waging war against humanity, they could be figuring out what to do with those mindless dragons."

"I'm sure you'll come up with an answer," Ziya said, her tone light enough that it could have been mistaken for teasing.

"You really do have too much faith in me."

"You're the one that taught me to have faith in the first place," she shot back.

He didn't have a good response for that, so he simply smiled and leaned forward to pat the scales along her neck. "The feeling's mutual."

Lioia smiled as she watched the two of them and then caught their attention with a quiet puff of smoke. "You should get going before the day passes you by. If you stay here too long, my hatchlings will want to pepper you with questions about your new body, and you'll never leave before sundown."

Caleb didn't bother to hide his crooked smile. "Careful," he said. "It almost sounds like you and your family are starting to have a better opinion of humans."

The Gods' Gift

"We have decided to make a few exceptions," Lioia said, her smile disappearing entirely. "I still think you give your people too much credit. You are yourself a product of their worst inclinations."

"And you saw the council try to destroy an entire species off the face of the earth," Caleb said. "But I won't keep having this argument with you. I can't change the way you feel, and I don't blame you for holding a grudge against people that have wronged you in a war."

Lioia huffed, though one corner of her mouth had turned up against her will. "Ziya's right to praise your skill with words. You keep almost convincing me to take your side—until I remember that your side is the side of the humans."

Caleb smirked. "I'd like to think that my side is the side of exceptions."

Lioia laughed at that. "We'll see." She straightened up when she heard a sound neither Caleb nor Ziya could hear, but then again, mothers were always better in tune with the sounds of their children than anyone else could be. "You'd better leave. It sounds like their father has made them excitable again this morning," she said in a tone ringing with affection.

Caleb chuckled. He loved seeing families like Lioia's and Rikaa's, because they reminded him of how similar humans and dragons were. Watching Rikaa's grandsons and Lioia's hatchlings playing together, he always ended up thinking of how Tris would lead the local kids in roughhousing as often as possible, trying to inject joy into a world that was fast turning into a wasteland.

Tris, I think you would have liked dragons if you'd met true dragons and not the ones Alan and the humans he taught turned into weapons, he thought to himself.

"Until we meet again," Ziya said, drawing Caleb back out of his thoughts as she unfurled her wings, took a few running steps, and took to the skies.

For just a moment, Caleb felt a jolt of jealousy run through him. Ziya was better at taking to the skies than he was—much better, even, than she had been before she spent all that time alone with Lioia. She had the advantage of staying in one body and, therefore, of not having to deal with the soreness and the unfamiliarity of new limbs every time she changed. She could learn how to master one body, one form, without regressing into old habits.

And then, they took to the skies, and Caleb forgot all about his worries over human-made dragons, over what the gods wanted from him, over what Ziya thought of him, over what he thought of himself. As soon as Ziya broke through the trees with Caleb on her back, Caleb closed his eyes and nearly laughed with relief. He'd spent so long locked away in a prison and then hidden underneath a thick canopy of trees that he'd nearly forgotten what direct sunlight felt like.

Even though Ziya had done an excellent job of healing him, Caleb felt better still for being in the light. He leaned heavily against Ziya's neck, closing his eyes and drinking in the warmth of the sun. He even went so far as to adjust his cloak so that it fell to one side, exposing his shoulder. Immediately, his wound stung less. The sunlight wasn't as effective as a dragon's healing, but it was a balm of its own kind all the same.

And so, basking in warmth and the feeling that sunlight always elicited in his body, Caleb fell asleep on Ziya's back.

Chapter 25: Home At Last

Caleb felt stronger and stronger with every day spent above the smoke and ash and trees. The sun made his wounds hurt less, and the silence of a long trip with someone he trusted helped him gather his thoughts better—so that he felt less like he was reacting to everything as it happened and more like he could plan ahead.

He appreciated, too, that Ziya didn't mind flying in silence. Rikaa didn't like being treated as a beast of burden—understandably so—and had always preferred traveling while singing and sharing stories. Ziya, on the other hand, kept her own silence. Caleb had a feeling that she was thinking through everything that had happened in her own way and would likely tell him what she thought when she felt she had better words to put to her feelings. She was never one to shy away from speaking her mind, even if she preferred to leave the talking to Caleb when diplomacy was needed.

Still, so much had happened since they last saw their families that neither of them had words to give each other. And that was fine. Silence was preferable after so long spent in confusion and anger and hurt. They would have their fill of love and warmth and friendship when they got home.

For his part, Caleb kept thinking about what Ziya had said about the gods' intentions for him. Yes, Alan was dead, but the council still raged, and the world was still burning. If he was supposed to be chosen by the gods to help the world, why did he feel so impotent? He could convince a dragon or two that he and others like him were worth sparing, but only because his story was a sympathetic one. He couldn't convince two entire species to stop hating each other. If Ziya was right and his purpose was more than to bring justice to Alan, then he had far more to do than he could comprehend. He couldn't relax; he couldn't be *done*. He would have to push himself even harder for even longer—and he didn't think he could.

The gods should have given the power to change forms to Ziya. She could see her path clearly. But since they had chosen him instead, Caleb found himself trying to live up to their trust—now that he had some distance from Alan and some time to think, to consider his strengths.

He was good at lying and coming up with a new person to be, someone who suited the situation. Perhaps he could use that skill to mold himself into the dragon the gods wanted him to be. He could pretend to be as heroic at Ziya, at least until the war was over. Pretending was as good as anything else, as long as the end result was the same. No one needed to know he wasn't really all Ziya thought he was.

As for Ziya, she seemed to think that his newfound lack of self-deprecation was an improvement; she even remarked on his progress that night. They had stopped to look for food, though he hadn't had much success and was starting to remember how much he hated being hungry after several nights of nothing. The dragon council had burned much of the land between Rikaa's home and Teyo's village; there was nothing left but ash and the remnants of trees that crumbled under the slightest wingbeat from Ziya. And so, in an attempt to distract Caleb from his loudly growling stomach, Ziya said, "You seem . . . happier."

"I like being in the sunlight," Caleb admitted, wrapping his cloak around his arms and shoulders—not because he was cold but because he was self-conscious about his stomach growling and wanted an excuse to hunch over and muffle the sound. "White dragons were born in the fires of volcanoes; we always do better when we're warm."

"Then I'll have to build you a bonfire the next time you talk so poorly of yourself," Ziya decided, laughter hidden in her words. When he glanced up at her, she smiled. "I'm only trying to help."

"And I appreciate it," Caleb said, almost automatically.

THE GODS' GIFT

Ziya smiled and settled in close to the fire he was trying to build. Most of the trees and plant life had been burned until nothing was left, so he'd only been able to find wood to burn by changing the form of his hand into claws and hacking through trees to get to the dead wood beneath the charred bark. Even that wouldn't be enough to last him through the night, so he hadn't started burning the wood until he had needed the warmth and light.

Caleb sat down near the flimsy fire and frowned at it. The dragons had destroyed the earth they swore to protect, and what did they have to show for it? So long as a few humans survived, humanity itself would spring back to life in a relatively short amount of time in the lifespan of a dragon. But in the meantime, everything else living would suffer.

He wished he could help.

The thought had barely crossed his mind when the setting sun reflected light off of a scale on his right hand, the one that still had claws and some scales so that he could use it to gather wood. He frowned and held his hand up to the light to examine it better, an idea forming in the back of his mind.

I wonder. . . .

Before he could think too deeply about what he was about to do—and before he could talk himself out of it—he clenched his left hand in a fist tight enough to start shaking with exertion and then closed his eyes, wishing for both hands to become claws. He gasped in shock and pain when claws erupted through the ends of his fingers, but he'd expected the hurt and was prepared to stifle it. Yes, Ziya looked toward him in an unasked question, but he didn't pay her any heed. He was too focused on his thoughts.

Carefully, tenderly, he took one claw and scratched it against the surface of one of his scales. It didn't hurt *too* badly. He took a deep breath, held it, and pushed his claw past the surface of the scale until he found where the scale connected to his rough skin underneath his armor. He could feel more scales creeping up his arms as his eyes watered from the sharp pain of his claw drawing blood, but he dug in harder all the same—and yanked.

"*Augh.*" He couldn't stop himself from letting out a cry of surprise and pain. Yes, he'd known that pulling out one of his own scales would hurt, and he'd thought he'd prepared himself. He'd thought that after feeling his body switch back and forth from a dragon form to a human one that he would have been used to that sensation. But as it turned out, forcibly removing a scale hurt much, *much* worse than his transformations did.

"Are you alright? What's wrong?" Ziya asked, immediately getting to her feet in a rush of legs and wings. She was usually graceful, but when startled, he could see the evidence that she still wasn't entirely comfortable in her new body.

"Fine," he said through his teeth, though tears were leaking down his cheeks, and he had started to unconsciously rock himself back and forth in an effort to alleviate the pain. "I'm fine. Really."

Ziya let out a scoffing sound that told him she didn't believe him. "You're not."

"I am." He took in a breath that whistled through his teeth, winced, and knew he had to explain himself or risk going a few rounds of questions with Ziya. "I pulled a scale out."

"How?" Ziya leaned close enough to him that her breath threatened his fire. "I have to work hard to scratch up your scales; what did you do to *lose* one?"

"It was just a thought," he defended himself, already sure that he'd get an earful. "There's nothing left of this land after the dragons came through—"

"So you thought you'd fix their mistakes by hurting yourself?" Ziya asked incredulously. "Kaal, you can't do things like that!"

"I just want to see what one scale can do," Caleb explained. "We could go back to Teyo and tell him and Mira how far apart they need to plant Alan's scales. . . ." He trailed off, knowing that he wasn't explaining himself properly. So, instead of getting into an argument, he simply knelt down in the dirt and carefully dug out a patch of earth so he could plant his scale.

And then, he waited.

He didn't know how long the magic of a dragon's scale would take to start working, but he didn't expect immediate results. If that were the case, all battlefields would also be places of spontaneous growth and greenery in addition to fire and smoke. Granted, he'd never been close enough to a battle to see what one looked like, but he imagined that instant dragon magic falling from the sky would end up in tales passed from soldier to soldier.

THE GODS' GIFT

When several minutes passed with no sign of magic, Caleb let out a sigh and leaned against Ziya, rubbing the spot on his arm where he had taken his scale. A warm trickle of blood ran down his skin and between his fingers, but the wound itself no longer pained him too badly. It had gone from a sharp pain to a dull ache quickly enough that Caleb was tempted to do it again.

But, no, he fought back that thought. Alan's body would be more than enough to give humanity a place to start again, and the earth could heal itself over time. He couldn't give in to thinking that he was so beyond saving that his only use was his scales. If he let himself dwell on that thought, he didn't think he would be able to escape it.

"Maybe we'll see some green in the morning," Ziya said, settling herself back down again so that her head was close to his body. He reached out without thinking and automatically rested his hand on top of her head, and when she pushed against his body, he leaned on her, starting to relax with each breath he could feel on his skin. He wondered, too, if she was healing him without meaning to; if she wanted him to be alright, she could stave off starvation with her power. He had done an accidental healing before; he knew they were possible.

Whatever the case, he felt better leaning on Ziya—so much so that he ended up falling asleep with his head and hand on top of her head, breathing nearly in time with her at first, though obviously, when she moved away from him to curl up on her own, that was no longer the case.

He woke up the next morning with a slight crick in his neck, but he felt refreshed all the same—despite how long he had gone without food. He smiled sleepily—and then blushed when he realized what he had done. He hadn't *meant* to fall asleep, and he hadn't meant to make her feel as awkward as he was sure she felt.

He shook his head. *Rikaa is going to be beside himself when he realizes he was right.*

To distract himself from his bright blush, he tried to find some small animal for a meal. He listened for movement beyond them in the forest but couldn't hear anything, not even the soft, padding footsteps of a field mouse. No breakfast, then. With a sigh, he crouched down to check that his fire had burned completely out and would not threaten the already-burned lands with a stray spark—and then paused when he saw that a small patch of green had started to spread right where he'd planted his scale.

It wasn't much. The patch of grass and dandelions only extended about the length of his hand in any direction. But it was lush and green and nothing like the dark, dead earth that surrounded him and Ziya.

Look at that. Something good out of all this.

He gently ran his hand over the small patch of grass, reveling in the feeling of something so soft and *alive* against the constant embers and drifts of charred leaves that choked the air everywhere else. He had made this. He had brought this little patch of ground to life. He had *revived* the earth.

"Now there's a smile I haven't seen in a long time," Ziya rumbled sleepily, startling Caleb out of his thoughts until he was brightly blushing all over again.

"I didn't hear you wake up," Caleb said, wiping his hand on his leg self-consciously, as if the stain of grass would give away his moment of contemplation, as if he'd done something amiss.

"I didn't want to tear you from your thoughts," Ziya told him. "I haven't seen you look like yourself until this morning. What changed?"

Caleb glanced down at the grass and knew that he wouldn't have to say anything to explain himself once she saw it too. But he opened his mouth all the same. "It's nice," he said, slowly, "to actually see a positive outcome after all we've been through."

Ziya smiled, scooting as close as she dared to the patch of green. "If we can stop the council, the land can breathe, and this green will spread."

Caleb let his shoulders fall. "If," he repeated softly. He'd been in such a good mood waking up to see tangible results from the pain of losing a scale, but hearing her remind him of all he had left to do, he felt suddenly small. How was he supposed to stop a war that had been going on since before he was born, since before Rikaa was born? The dragons and humans had been at each other's throats for so long that this confrontation seemed the natural end of their rivalry.

How was he supposed to stop all that?

THE GODS' GIFT

Ziya made it seem so simple. It was their duty to end the war, their destiny, their creed. For someone who didn't believe in the gods, she was so much more assured of what they wanted than he was.

"Let's see if we can find you something to eat," Ziya suggested after Caleb had apparently been quiet for too long for her tastes.

"Yes, let's," he agreed softly, climbing onto her back and clinging to her neck as they once more took to the skies. Even though he had been on several dragon rides by that time, he would never get used to the dropping feeling in the pit of his stomach or the way the wind screamed in his ears and slapped his face. Humans weren't meant to fly, but it was exhilarating when they did.

As they flew over the lands near Rikaa's mountain home, Caleb leaned over Ziya's side, searching the ground more and more. He had spent much of the trip allowing the sun to heal him and basking in the heat far from the stifling, choking winds of a burning world—but now, he held on as tightly as he dared and watched the too-brown ground pass below them.

Before the dragon council came to war, the mountains had been one of the few green places left in Niyala. Yes, the trees were evergreen and bore no edible fruit, and yes, the humans had driven out most of the wildlife fit for eating—so, the mountains weren't easy to live on. But there was a reason the army set most of its bases into mountainsides—and not just because the caves they found were large enough to house dragons. Even humans who gave their hearts to warfare craved the green color of life.

Now, even the patches of green that had survived the human wars were nothing. The mountains were bare. The air stunk with death and ash.

The council is killing the earth along with its enemies, Caleb thought, frowning the more he saw of the path of destruction. He and Ziya had seen much of it while they had been searching for Alan, but they had been ahead of the council, watching the fires burn behind them in the thick fog of active-burning smoke. Seeing the barren landscape left behind was somehow worse than watching the bright orange of dragon fire lighting up the sky. There was no fight to join. There was only death and loss.

Caleb swallowed hard and righted himself, leaning into Ziya until he could feel her breath underneath his right ear. The sound was comforting, calming, and he leaned into her scales until he felt less like crying, until he felt less like the world was doomed because he wasn't up to the task Ziya thought the gods had appointed them.

He heard the beat of dragon wings and opened his eyes again, his entire body tense, prepared for a fight, convinced by that point that the gods would give him no rest. But as soon as he saw the outline of the dragon making his way toward them, he relaxed. Even as far away as he was, he recognized Rikaa. They had spent enough time with each other that their silhouettes were familiar.

He could feel Ziya tense underneath him, though, and he reached out to rub her neck. "It's Rikaa," he told her.

"Are you sure?"

"I know him when I see him."

Ziya let out a soft chuckle that Caleb felt before he heard. "You're such a dragon, Kaal."

"I can never tell whether you think that's a good thing or not."

"Neither can I."

He laughed and held onto her tighter as Rikaa flew toward them. Soon enough, Rikaa flew parallel to Ziya, obviously looking the two of them over for injury before he even attempted speech. And then, the first thing he asked was, "Are you alright? Were you successful?"

"Yes," Caleb replied, though his response was lost on the wind. He nodded to convey what he meant, but Ziya was already answering for the two of them.

"Kaal hurt his wing, so I'm carrying him," she said, and Caleb let out a disbelieving scoff. He couldn't believe the first thing on her mind was disclosing his welfare to Rikaa. "He was locked up in a human prison with Alan, too."

"Now, wait a minute," Caleb said, but again, no one seemed to be paying him any attention. This time, he wasn't entirely convinced that their ignorance was a product of his voice being lost in the wind. This time, he thought they were conspiring against him.

And not that long ago, Ziya barely trusted Rikaa, Caleb thought and decided that he did, in fact, like this predicament better. Even if Ziya and Rikaa were united in worrying over him, at least they were on the same side.

"And Alan?" Rikaa asked.

THE GODS' GIFT

"Dead," Ziya said. She didn't elaborate, but the look on Rikaa's face told Caleb that Ziya's simple explanation wouldn't be enough.

"The head of a human village killed him with a dragon-bone sword," Caleb said, loud enough to be heard but not quite shouting.

Rikaa was quiet for some time, giving away nothing of what he thought of their report, before he responded, "You both need rest. Follow me—but, please, be careful. Some of Alan's human-made dragons are trying to nest in this area, and they have no minds of their own. They only have a territorial instinct and a penchant for violence trained into them."

Caleb could feel Ziya grimacing as badly as he did. "I'm sorry," he started to say, but Rikaa cut him off.

"We must relocate soon anyway. The council left nothing in its wake, and even dragons who don't need to eat every day must find homes filled with more life than this."

Caleb narrowed his eyes and looked back down at the charred ground, a growl churning in his stomach that he never fully vocalized. The council had to be stopped; they would take dragons down with them if they continued on their paths.

He just hoped he was good enough to stand up for the earth in the gods' place.

ZIYA

CHAPTER 26: CRY

Iuan's home had changed so much since the last time Ziya had been a visitor there.

For one thing, in the time Ziya and Kaal had been gone on their quest to find Alan, several humans had found permanent lodging with Iuan's family. Ziya could see makeshift beds scrounged from what was left of army cots after the council's fires, and she could see patterns of circular stones in the corners of the caves, firepits where the humans could cook what food they could find in the bare landscape.

A few human-made dragons had made their home there, too, and they stayed close to the humans, even allowing some of the younger humans to climb all over them. They obviously felt safer and more comfortable with humans, but Ziya saw that Iuan's sons were part of the group as well; she was relieved to see how well the two species were intermingling.

If only things could be that easy across the land, she thought.

Once Ziya was far enough into Iuan's cavernous home that Caleb no longer needed to ride on her back, she stopped and let him slide down. Although she fully intended to join the humans and human-made dragons—and especially to find her mom—she didn't immediately make good on her plans. Instead, she placed her tail strategically in front of Caleb and then looked toward Rikaa, who was a few paces behind her.

"Talk to him," she told Rikaa, and she heard Caleb scoff beside her. "He listens to you."

Rikaa stopped, concern written across his body language in a way that, Ziya was proud to say, she could actually identify. He was perfectly still, so that he could listen to every word Caleb might offer in his own defense. "And what would you have me say?" Rikaa asked.

Caleb waved one hand, obviously trying to play off Ziya's concerns. "She saw me in the immediate aftermath of too much time with Alan. That's all."

"Alan convinced him that he is too much like Alan, and he's been questioning himself ever since," Ziya said, not about to let Caleb sabotage himself with lies.

Caleb turned her way with his whole body. "Really?"

Ziya held his gaze. "You saw for yourself your capacity for healing. Your scales aren't the only good thing about you, Kaal. And if you won't believe me when I tell you you're a hero, maybe you will listen to the one dragon I know has your absolute trust."

Rikaa looked between the two of them and then stepped past Ziya, leaning into her space so that he could reach Caleb and bump him with the end of his snout. "I think," he said softly, "I should like to hear what happened to you."

"Oooh, us too!" One of Iuan's sons called out, prompting both of his brothers to break away from their playing. Before Rikaa could tell them he would have preferred a private conversation, all three were tumbling over each other to hear tales of adventure.

And Caleb positively latched onto the ready-made escape from Rikaa's interrogation. As Ziya watched, everything about Caleb changed, and he actually looked like the child he was as he wrapped his arms around the snouts of each of Rikaa's grandchildren in turn and then climbed onto the rocks of a dragon's bed so he could be better seen.

"Which do you want to hear about first? The magic sword or the huge battle between dragons and humans?" he asked, puffed up like a peacock in a way that she imagined his older brother had done, based on the stories he'd told her about Tris.

Ziya sighed, shook her head, and shared a glance with Rikaa. In that glance, she could see his promise that he would look after Caleb when the distraction of storytelling wore off. And then, knowing Caleb was safe, she finally started to relax and to turn her attention away from taking care of Caleb.

Now, she could attend to herself. And at that moment, all she wanted to do was find her mother.

THE GODS' GIFT

She approached the humans tucked away at the back of the cave and saw her mother come out of a small crack in the walls, chatting easily with a young girl who must have once been assigned to work in the army kitchens. Ziya wasn't surprised to find her mother already taking little girls under her wing.

"Dahlia!" Ziya called out, using her mother's first name simply because it was easier to say.

Instantly, Dahlia's head came up, and she gasped in delight and relief, rushing past the other humans toward Ziya so fast that her hair came up off her shoulders. Before Dahlia could reach Ziya, Ziya dropped her entire body close to the ground until she all but collapsed in front of her mom—except for her head and neck, which she used to nose toward Dahlia, grasping for a hug that she wouldn't ever be able to get—not the way she used to get them, anyway. Not the all-encompassing experience that left her wrapped in her mother's arms and feeling safer there than anywhere else.

Still, Dahlia did her best. She could obviously see that her daughter was hurt and needed comfort, though Ziya didn't think Dahlia could hear the high-pitched whine Ziya could feel escaping her. It wasn't *quite* like the whine young dragons used when they were physically hurt, but it was similar enough that Ziya produced it on instinct, alerting all other dragons in the cave to how hurt she was in *other* ways.

And yet, as soon as Dahlia started to run her hands over Ziya's head, walking along her snout and trailing her hand up to her eyes, Ziya felt better. Her mother was there. She was safe.

She'd *needed* this.

All at once, in the safety of her mother's embrace (or as close to an embrace as they were capable of under the circumstances), Ziya felt her breath catch in her throat. And then, the sound coming from her belly shifted its tone so that even the humans could hear it. Dahlia stopped what she was doing to listen as Ziya let out a soft, mournful sound, like a hum that carried with it all the fear and anger and hurt and confusion she'd been carrying around for so long.

It was, Ziya realized, the closest thing dragons had to crying.

"Oh, my darling," Dahlia murmured, continuing to run her hands over Ziya's snout as she tried to reassure her daughter. "You're alright. I'm here."

Ziya closed her eyes and leaned deeper into Dahlia's touch, yearning to disappear into her embrace. But she couldn't speak; she couldn't do anything but hum her sadness. There was too much to express at once. Where would she even begin to tell her about all she'd been through while she was gone? She had seen the ashes and destruction the dragon council left in their wake as they murdered an entire species. She had seen the closest friend she had reduced to a mess of self-doubt and fear because of Alan's mere words. She had tried to carry him and the hopes of the very gods themselves until he could get home to his family, and she still wasn't convinced she had done enough.

"What did he do?" Dahlia asked, fire dripping from her words despite the fact that she wasn't a dragon.

Ziya glanced up at her, finally opening her eyes to see the way her mother's eyebrows were drawn together, the way her chin was pointed up, the way her stance had widened as if she were preparing to go to war that very second, just waiting for Ziya to tell her where to go. And seeing her mother so prepared to defend her, she finally smiled.

"That's alright," Dahlia said, laying her head down on Ziya's and then kissing one of her scales so lightly Ziya couldn't even feel her touch. "You don't have to tell me, but at least tell me he paid—or I'll make him pay myself."

Ziya smiled, showing her teeth. "He's dead, Mom," she whispered. "Alan is dead."

Dahlia stared at her daughter for some time, absently rubbing her scales, until, at last, she nodded sharply. "Good."

"He convinced Kaal the two of them are the same," Ziya said, trying to impress upon her mother why she was still upset—not because of Alan's loss but because of what had happened since—but Dahlia instantly waved off the notion.

"That poor boy is too young to know any better. And he's used to dealing only with evil. He'll be alright, given enough time. Look at him with his family."

Ziya followed Dahlia's gaze to see Caleb answering eager questions from Rikaa's grandchildren as they demanded details of his trials and tribulations. She could hear him describing the sword Teyo had carried and couldn't help but laugh when she realized that the young dragons were hanging onto every single word of Caleb's' story, even gasping in delighted horror as Caleb told them how Teyo had threatened him with that sword.

When Ziya had been caught up in watching Caleb's storytelling for too long, Dahlia cleared her throat to get her attention. Then, as Ziya turned her way, Dahlia smiled triumphantly.

"What?" Ziya asked.

"You don't realize how much you care for him," Dahlia said, nodding toward Caleb and his adoptive family.

Ziya was already shaking her head before Dahlia could finish her statement. "You're wrong."

"You don't see what I—"

"No, that's not what I meant." Ziya sighed and turned her gaze back to Caleb. She was so *relieved* to see him happy that her relief and happiness for him nearly drowned out the regret lingering in the back of her mind over the fact that she couldn't give him that same happiness. She was a good partner for him in their fight, but what he *needed* was family, and she didn't want that. She couldn't settle down long enough to consider it. She didn't want to hide away in domestic bliss until she knew the dragon council wouldn't come for the last of their people. And even then, even when he fulfilled the gods' mandate, she had more work to do. She wouldn't be able to rest until she knew Alan's victims would be alright—especially those who had lost their bodies to scales.

Caleb might have been chosen by the gods, but he would retreat from heroism to live in peace the second he could. Ziya couldn't stay still that long. As long as she had a goal, she could distract herself from her own scales, her own reminders of what she had been through. She was a tempest; he was the eye.

"I care for him so much it hurts," she said in a whisper torn from her throat. "And I'm not right for him."

Dahlia let her shoulders drop and kissed one of Ziya's scales. "Oh, my sweet girl," she said in a heartbroken tone, "you can't tell me you're upset with him for believing Alan's lies when you're still doing the same thing."

Ziya frowned. "It's different—"

"It's not at all," Dahlia said, cutting her off before she could finish her sentence, let alone her argument. "You let Alan convince you that you're nothing but a weapon, nothing but his pawn. And you believe him even more sincerely than Caleb does." Dahlia gestured to Caleb and his enraptured audience. "At least he's *trying*."

Ziya felt her breath catch in smoke. "That's . . . that's not fair. I'm trying too."

"Try harder," Dahlia said gently.

Ziya still couldn't quite fill her lungs, and she felt her fire burn hotter in her mouth that she was entirely comfortable with around her mother. So, she swallowed hard and started to stand. "I . . . I have to go talk to Rikaa and Iuan. If Aonai still isn't back, we need to rescue him. And . . . and there's a human village that has managed to withstand the dragon council. If we can gather more humans there, we can give them a safe place to hide. Once you're out of harm's way, we can confront the council and free Aonai—"

"You can do that later," Dahlia said, putting both hands on Ziya's snout. Ziya couldn't stand up without bringing her mother with her or shaking her off, and so, she settled back down. "The war will still be out there waiting for you in the morning. You can take a day to rest. Or isn't that what you came here to do for Caleb? Give him a chance to recover?" Dahlia raised a single eyebrow. "What makes you think you can take care of him but not yourself?"

"He's still dealing with a torn wing," Ziya argued, knowing her words held no weight but saying them anyway, like a child caught misbehaving. "He healed me. I'm fine."

"Physically, *maybe*, but you're exhausted, emotional, and likely sore after such a long journey. Not to mention hungry," Dahlia said, listing all of Ziya's ailments on her fingers. "You may be so much bigger than me now, Neva, but you're still my little girl. I'm still your mother, and I'm telling you to take a break—or so help me, I will make you stand in a corner of the cave and think about how very far you've strayed from what your father taught you."

Any further argument Ziya might have made instantly dried up at the mention of her father. He had always been an optimist, and he'd tried to make his wife and daughter laugh at every opportunity. Ziya and Dahlia hadn't seen him since he was called away to war, and they had given him up for dead long ago—but Ziya had always tried to remember what his laugh sounded like and what his beard felt like when he kissed her cheek.

THE GODS' GIFT

He'd always said that Neva and Dahlia were his whole world, and he wouldn't let them say a word about themselves that wasn't positive. If he'd been there, he would have refused to even *hear* Ziya talk poorly of herself and would have pointed out every good thing that she'd ever done, including any good she had done as a dragon. He likely would have pointed out that she had saved plenty of humans simply by forcing the dragons she worked with to recognize that some people weren't going along with the war willingly. He would have pointed out all the support she'd given Kaal and praised the friendship she was starting to share with him and Aonai as well.

Ziya nearly smiled and then caught herself—but not before Dahlia saw the expression and let out a triumphant "ha!"

Ziya shook her head. "Alright," she said. "You're right. Dad would find a way to convince me I'm a hero, despite everything I know."

"And you are a hero," Dahlia said, smiling warmly. "You've been hurt, and you've made some mistakes, but that doesn't change the truth." She brushed her hand over the scales near Ziya's eyes. "You're already making plans for more rescues and talking about the grander problems facing the world. If you weren't a hero, wouldn't you let others deal with the dragon council? After all, you've gotten your revenge. Alan is dead. You're safe under the protection of these dragons—dragons who, I might add, would never push you into conflict if you told them that you wanted to stay out of the rest of the war. So, why are you already planning ways to save what's left of humanity?" Dahlia kept trailing her hand down Ziya's face until she was directly in front of her again. "That sounds like a hero's quest to me."

Ziya shook her head lightly, but even though she felt like she had barely moved, she brought Dahlia moving with her. "I have to live in this world too. I don't want to see everyone dead."

Dahlia sighed. "I know," she said. She looked like she wanted to say more, but instead, she stepped back, straightened her dress, and gestured with her head to the side to indicate Caleb and the hatchlings. "Go. I'm sure the other dragons will mount a rescue for Aonai as soon as the two of you have recovered." She paused and then couldn't help but give Ziya one last push. "They wouldn't want to leave without their heroes."

282

Ziya chuffed and left smoke in her wake. "Love you too," she said, obediently following her mother's pointing finger to Caleb, if for no other reason than that she knew her mother would continue to insist on her relaxation if she didn't at least pretend to go along with Dahlia's advice.

Caleb smiled when he saw her coming and gestured for her to join the storytelling, looking as much like a dragon as he ever had (despite his human form). Surrounded by dragons who loved him, he had a glint of life in his eyes that only came out when he talked about his family—Tris and Rikaa alike. "Come join us, Ziya," he called out. "I was just telling everybody about our fight with Alan. Don't worry; I made sure they knew all about your amazing magical prowess that led you to rescue me from certain death. They know you're the *real* reason we're all here."

Ziya shook her head, a smile escaping her despite her best intentions. "You're exaggerating," she said, unwilling to completely contradict him in front of the little ones.

"I am not," he insisted. Then, with his head tipped to the side, he amended his statement. "I didn't give you *all* the credit. Teyo killed Alan; he did the hard part."

"With the dragon bone sword?" one of the hatchlings asked excitedly. Ziya still couldn't remember which of Iuan's sons was which, but then, she hadn't spent nearly enough time with them to learn how to distinguish them.

Caleb grinned and nodded, and the boys appropriately oohed and ahhed. Even Ziya found herself caught up in their enthusiasm as they bounded around Caleb, demanding more details of the fight. She'd been there, and she still enjoyed listening to Caleb get more and more dramatic, emphasizing the scary parts without making them too scary, playing up the roles of the dragons they liked and making Alan sound even more melodramatic than he actually was— which was itself an impressive feat.

Ziya settled in, unable to hide her smile, wondering what Caleb's brother would think if he could have seen Caleb now. He was kind and funny and knew what to say to young dragons to make them laugh. Watching him with Rikaa's grandchildren, she knew that her mother was right: Caleb would be just fine. He had his family to watch out for him.

THE GODS' GIFT

So now, all they had to do was stop the council, and they could both go back to living their lives. Him with his family and her with her mother. They just had to somehow negotiate a peace between dragons and humans and prevent either side from completely annihilating the other.

I hope the gods are paying attention, she thought as one of the boys jumped on his brother and started an impromptu wrestling match right there in the middle of the cave, *because we are going to need plenty of help.*

ABOUT THE AUTHOR

Shelby Hailstone Law was raised in Georgia by an amazing family that instilled in her a love of books and learning from a young age. By the time she went out to Brigham Young University in Utah to get her degree in political science (with a minor in editing), she was obsessed with words and their capacity to become art. In fact, during college, she made her first forays into publishing, working with Wild Child Publishing to produce her first novel, *Lady Thief,* which she republished herself a few years later. She also wrote her second novel, *Birthright Unknown,* in college and published it shortly after her graduation.

Just before graduation, she met her sweetheart, Matthew Law. They were married in May 2013 and moved to Georgia a little over two years later, as soon as Matt had graduated. After the move, Shelby started to publish again, starting with the *Halfsie* series, which just finished in 2021. *Scaleshifter* came out in 2019, and you can bet there will be more beyond that, too!

Now, they live in Acworth, Georgia, where Shelby works from home as a freelance writer and mom and Matt works as an IT professional. They hope to fill their home with stories and music to instill in their own children that same love of stories and far-away places. She wrote about the hardship of infertility and the struggle to find a new normal in *We Still Don't Have a Miracle Baby: When "Someday" Feels Like a Four-Latter Word,* which came out in fall 2018. She and her husband then began fostering a little girl in 2019 and adopted her in summer 2020, and she gave birth to their baby boy in 2020. So, she might need a new book to update that story!

Shelby also writes with her best friend and shares a pseudonym with her: C. C. Robbie. Their series is called *Magixtinction.*

Scaleshifter will return in:

SCALESHIFTER:
THE DRAGON
BONES

Printed in Great Britain
by Amazon

77979956R00171